Snapshots

Snapshots

20th Century Mother–Daughter Fiction

edited by

JOYCE CAROL OATES

and

JANET BERLINER

DAVID R. GODINE
Publisher · Boston

First published in 2000 by

DAVID R. GODINE, Publisher
Post Office Box 450
Jaffrey, New Hampshire 03452
www.godine.com

Due to limitations of space, permissions
acknowledgments appear on page 239.

LIBRARY OF CONGRESS CATALOGUING IN PUBLICATION DATA

Snapshots : 20th century mother-daughter fiction/
edited by Joyce Carol Oates and Janet Berliner.— 1st ed.
    p. cm.
ISBN: 1–56792–114–0 (hardcover : alk. paper)
ISBN: 1–56792–172–8 (softcover : alk. paper)
    1. Mothers and daughters—Fiction. 2. Short stories, American—
women authors. 3. English fiction—Women Authors. 4. Short stories,
English 5. Women—Fiction. I. Oates, Joyce Carol, 1938– II. Berliner, Janet.

PS648.M59 S63 2000
813'.01083520431 — dc21   00–057669

Design and typesetting by Carl W. Scarbrough

First Edition 2000

This book was printed on acid-free paper.
Printed and bound in the United States of America

 *Contents*

 *Foreword*

A woman is her mother.
That's the main thing.
— Anne Sexton

BUT IS IT SO?

Most days I think, no. Certainly a woman isn't her mother. Or, if resembling her mother, she isn't totally her mother; she is her father as well, and any number of ancestors known and unknown. A woman is the sum of all her influences — genetic, environmental, personal, and impersonal. I know this; I believe this. Yet, so strangely, Anne Sexton's flat, dogmatic lines sometimes resound in my imagination — whether as curse or blessing, as explanation or mystery, I can't say. (The lines are from a terse, rather terrifying poem, "Housewife," from the much acclaimed collection of 1962, *All My Pretty Ones.* The book established Anne Sexton as a new and disturbingly talented poet, an innovator in what would be called "confessional" poetry, a poetry in which women poets would excel.)

This gathering of mother-daughter, or daughter-mother, stories speaks to the daughter in all of us, for, if women, we have all been daughters. And while we may not all be mothers, we have surely played "mother" roles and have imagined ourselves, for better or worse, as mothers. Reading such powerful stories as Edna O'Brien's "A Rose in the Heart of New York," Ursula K. Le Guin's "Solitude," and Margaret Atwood's "Significant Moments in the Life of My Mother" jolts us into realizing the extraordinary range and depth of what the term *mother* can mean. Perhaps no word in our language has accrued so many stereotypical associations as *mother* (though it may be outdone by the term *God*), and yet — how mysterious mothers are! In our collection, it seems to be mothers who, for obvious reasons, exert the most influence, whether benign or malevolent. A subtly disquieting story like Lorrie Moore's "How to Talk to Your

Mother (Notes)" would seem to be making the point that, finally, you don't know how to talk to your mother because you don't have a clue who your mother is. Between the stunning cessation of her (mental) life and the utterly bewildering beginning of your own life (your birth), you live together yet inhabit separate worlds. Even the more relaxed, less unsettling of these stories — Margaret Atwood's buoyantly written "Significant Moments in the Life of My Mother" and Jane Shapiro's witty "Mousetrap" as well as Jamaica Kincaid's defiant monologue "Girl" — make the point that Mother is an object of continuous, frustrating speculation.

Though sharing a common subject matter, these stories scarcely repeat one another in voice, tone, atmosphere, or "meaning." There is a highly interior poetic voice in Martha Soukup's gently fantastic "Up Above Diamond City"; there is an American-vernacular idiom of ease and humor in Alice Walker's "Everyday Use," Gloria Naylor's "Kiswana Browne," and Katherine Dunn's "The Allies." A tauter, more ironic tone is appropriate for the cautionary tale, "Cleaning Up," by Mary Gordon, while a more fabulist note is struck in Lois Gould's "La Lloradora" and in Isabel Allende's "Wicked Girl."

Janet Berliner's tautly poetic "Everything Old Is New Again" springs from the mysterious juncture of the interior and the exterior — the world of memory and the world of present-time. This is our only story in which the very balance of the generations is considered, as a woman at the midpoint of her life reaches out to forgive (her eighty-year-old mother) and to be forgiven (by her estranged daughter). The arrival of a battered doll (herself?) out of her turbulent past triggers a crisis of emotion that resolves itself into the realization to which we all, if we're lucky, one day come: Everything old is new again, if we will it to be so.

Like all of the stories we've included, this one is ardently written and often achingly sincere; like the others it is meant, above all, to engage and entertain you.

If it does — if they do — we have done our job.

— Joyce Carol Oates

🍃 Introduction

The best and most enduring works
of literature have one thing in
common, their universality.
— Dr. Samuel Draper

SOME YEARS AGO, when I was working with David Copperfield on the anthology *Tales of the Impossible*, I asked Joyce Carol Oates if she would write an original story for that volume. She graciously sent me not one but two stories. One of those, "The Hand-Puppet," appeared in the Copperfield volume. The other, a novelette called "Death Mother," was the seed from which this volume grew.

Joyce says of this story: "There are religions like Hinduism that honor the paradox of the amoral mother (Nature) who both nurtures and destroys, gives the precious gift of life and snatches it away again; but our more individual-centered, action-oriented tradition favors resistance. In a dream I saw the malevolent figure of the mother who tells us the worst things about ourselves and urges us to defeat, not triumph; I felt her chilly fingers clasping my wrist; I woke with a shudder, and was determined to write, not a parable of defeat, but one of a difficult victory."

I am always impressed by Joyce's work, but there was something in this story that particularly affected me — not the least because it is about a mother and a daughter, and I am both of those. This dual identity is the universal bond that links me to other women.

With that in mind, I reread Gloria Naylor's "Kiswana Browne," from her best-selling *The Women of Brewster Place*. The story was as I remembered it. Wry, earthy, and timely, it relates with remarkable accuracy the dilemma of this decade's so-called independent, single, urban woman.

I began to understand the road I was traveling and asked Joyce if she would collaborate on a gathering of stories about mothers and daughters. To my delight, she said yes. Thus began a lengthy and fascinating correspondence, which included commentary and discussions about the stories under consideration. In this introduction, I have tried to recreate some of these discussions by interspersing Joyce's comments with my own.

About "Kiswana Browne," for instance, she wrote:

"This wise, funny tale pits a mother's strong personality against her daughter's less defined personality, and subtly presents, as if for our judgment, the daughter's ambivalence toward her mother. One of its epiphanies is: 'Black isn't beautiful and it isn't ugly — black is! It's not kinky hair and it's not straight hair — it just is.'" Later, she added "This is one of only a few stories in our anthology that can be called 'political'—though its politics is thoroughly steeped in intimacy."

Next, synchronicity took over. I received a call from my youngest daughter, then a graduate student at Brown. She had fallen in love with Isabel Allende's *Eva Luna* and wanted to talk about the book. I pulled it down from my shelf and "Wicked Girl" jumped out at me.

Constructed in inimitable Allende fashion, this coming-of-age story once again surprised me with its loops and twists. As for Joyce, what she found "most delightful" about "Wicked Girl" was "the sharply observed, intimate details of a life remote from our own, yet immediately recognizable. Here is a revelation of the 'insupportable longing' of sexual infatuation — and its eventual denouement."

In full gear now, I reread Ursula Le Guin's futuristic "Solitude" and Edna O'Brien's "A Rose in the Heart of New York," and juxtaposed them against two stories that Joyce suggested, Jamaica Kincaid's "Girl" and "Consuelo's Letter" by Julia Alvarez.

The settings could not have been more dissimilar — Outer Space, New York City, the American South, and Cuba — and the stories ran the gamut from sad to funny, from thought provoking to visceral. But dissimilar or not, they were bonded by more than the common theme of mother-daughter relationships.

Seeking a definition of that bond, I asked Joyce to comment.

"Ursula K. Le Guin is one of our best philosophical writers," Joyce wrote to me. "Her imagination is both poetic and conceptual."

Philosophical? Of course. Early in her off-world mother-daughter story, Le Guin writes, "There is no magic in things, only in minds," and toward the end she goes on to say, "Being aware is the hardest work a soul can do, I think." The story and the statement dance around something about which I have often wondered: Is a soul, if such a thing exists, everyone's birthright, or are we supposed to create our souls by the way we live and think?

I thought again about the O'Brien story. When I first read it, my mother was dying. Her mind was as sharp as ever, so I convinced myself that she wasn't yet ready to die and did everything I could to try to keep her alive. Was that an act of selfishness on my part, born of the fear of facing my own mortality? I don't know that there's an answer, but I suspect we all ask the question — though never more eloquently than Ms. O'Brien does in "A Rose in the Heart of New York."

Joyce agreed. "This is one of the most poetic and subtle stories in our collection," she wrote, "a lyric, beautiful and heart-rending Irish story which evokes a sense of the fabulous and mythical." And of the philosophical, I thought, as she went on to talk about "Girl" and "Consuelo's Letter." "'Girl' is a perfect miniature narrative, a daughter's monologue deft and compelling and economically structured as a sonnet," she said. "As for 'Consuelo's Letter,' it shares with several other stories in this anthology an honoring of the invisible community of women extending sympathy and aid to one another."

I have lived in the West Indies. A piece of my heart will always be in the islands. I swear I have met Consuelo and Ruth; if I have not done so, then I have met their counterparts. I have given them mangoes from my trees in exchange for figs from theirs. I have given them pens and paper and books, and they — like the old woman in the story — have passed on their philosophies and given me kindness. As for the Kincaid, some writers construct an opus around a small thought. Here, Kincaid speaks volumes in a mere seven hundred words.

By now it seemed as if every good female writer, every sensitive female writer, had penned at least one superior mother-daughter story. To avoid a volume of encyclopaedic size, we had to narrow our choices. After much debate, we selected another cluster of stories: Margaret Atwood's "Significant Moments in the Life of My Mother" from her collection, *Bluebeard's Egg*; "The Allies," a story by Katherine Dunn; "La Lloradora," excerpted from Lois Gould's *La Presidenta*. To those, we added Bette Greene's "An Ordinary Woman" and "How to Talk to Your Mother (Notes)" from Lorrie Moore's first collection, *Self-Help*. "Mousetrap" by Jane Shapiro and Alice Walker's "Everyday Use" completed our reprint list.

I have long admired Ms. Atwood's work, so I was particularly gratified when she agreed to send us a contribution for this anthology, then dismayed when "Significant Moments in the Life of My Mother" arrived in the mail. I loved the piece, but I had distinctly asked for fiction, and this, surely, was nonfiction. After delaying as long as I could, I wrote a letter restating that this was a collection of fiction and sadly declining the essay.

Fortunately I was wrong. The story's apparent truth was simply further testimony to the author's storytelling skills.

Amused by my error, Joyce sent me the following note:

"Margaret Atwood is one of those writers whose prose is so irresistibly engaging, we are always tempted to believe anything it tells us; her mother-portraits, like her father-portraits, are so vivid and lifelike, we invariably think the author is writing autobiography. Perhaps this is the highest compliment a fiction writer can receive?"

Joyce called Katherine Dunn's "The Allies" "a touching double portrait of an artistically talented, emotionally volatile mother and her sharply observant adolescent daughter, set against a very American background of UFO's and 'savior' aliens." If that sounds simplistic, think again, remembering that it was Dunn who wrote the wonderfully skewed, award-winning novel *Geek Love*.

The stories by Lois Gould and Bette Greene were especially personal choices for me. I had, decades ago, read Gould's novel *La Presidenta*. Though I did not know the author personally, I wrote to her care of her publisher to tell her how much I loved the book. She signed a copy and wrote me a charming note. The book, oft-reread, and the note, yellowed with the years, have resided on my desk-shelf ever since. Like a pulp fiction detective, I tracked her down to ask if I could excerpt from her book for this volume. Joyce called the excerpt "a lush, unpredictable, wonderfully imaginative adventure reminiscent of the magic realism of Latin American literature," in which "the legend of Eva Perón is explored from an intimate perspective." For my part, I hope that once you have read the excerpt you will make it your business to find the novel and read that, too.

As for Bette Greene, the author's first novel, *Summer of My German Soldier*, had a profound effect on my own writing life because it convinced me that it was possible to entertain readers while conveying a serious message. It's rather like giving someone chicken soup: first it should taste good; then, with luck, it should be curative. Her story "An

Ordinary Woman" is about single parenting, addiction, tough love, and survival, yet it paints a portrait of a mother who, as Joyce puts it, "is both ordinary and not-so-ordinary."

When Joyce sent me "How to Talk to Your Mother (Notes)," she called it "a story that brilliantly combines the author's quirky, sharp-edged talent for humor, pathos, heartbreak and the perfectly chosen image. Beginning with the mother's powerfully noted absence, the story moves swiftly backward in time to a moment of unspeakable mystery: the narrator's birth."

Joyce was right. This wonderful piece of writing is a movie run in reverse, a chronology beginning in 1982, when the protagonist is forty-three, and ending in 1939, with her as a newborn. It says that while you can readily search for your roots, understanding them is only really possible after you've learned to understand yourself.

By way of introduction to "Mousetrap" by Jane Shapiro, Joyce wrote: "Jane Shapiro often writes, with similar humor and sagacity, about the inevitable conflict between generations. Her characters are all gifted with their creator's droll, sometimes sardonic but always perceptive sensibility. In 'Mousetrap' we meet the quintessential Jane Shapiro mother: sharp-tongued, very funny, and very sad." To that may I add that the story will remain timely for as long as critical daughters have aging mothers who yearn to shout, "Look at me. Really look at me. You may find this hard to be believe, but I used to be a person, just like you."

In "Everyday Use," Alice Walker asks whether we can define ourselves or whether we are ultimately defined by the eye of the beholder. Of this story, Joyce wrote: "This is a deservedly famous story of two very different sisters who perceive the world of their birth in opposing terms. Wonderfully 'symbolic,' yet utterly domestic and matter-of-fact, 'Everyday Use' will provoke you to wonder: What does it mean to memorialize the past? How can we best express our love for our heritage? Through isolating it, as art; or using it, as life?"

These stories completed our reprint selections, but the book itself remained incomplete. It needed something entirely fresh, something new. I therefore contacted two more writers and asked if they would each consider writing original stories. One of them, was Mary Gordon, who sent me "Cleaning Up."

No matter what the theme, a new Mary Gordon story is an event.

Here, she puts her unique touch on a tale of revenge that Joyce accurately describes as "both gracefully executed and viscerally hard-hitting, an austere and unexpectedly elegiac story of a lost girlhood." In the story, a poor but proud single mother loses her mind and is institutionalized. Her daughter is taken in by one of the town's upper-crust families. They feed her and clothe her, but never quite accept her as an equal. Feeling eternally patronized, she plots to avenge herself and her mother. Does she?

I was still asking myself that question and thinking about lost girlhoods when Martha Soukup's "Up Above Diamond City" arrived. I sent it on to Joyce at once.

"This is a delicately fantastic story of the imagination's powers," Joyce wrote back. "Out of the tension between a mother and her daughter there arises, as if by magic, a dream-world 'Diamond City' as a place where time moves swiftly — and where one can take refuge. We come away with a sense of mystery and of the joy in mystery."

I could not agree more.

Martha and I were once part of the same writers' workshop. Her voice captivates me. Her stories haunt me. Knowing that she rarely agrees to write a commissioned story, I nevertheless twisted her arm for this anthology. I am deeply glad that I did, for how else could the child protagonist of this story have shown me Diamond City. Now I can go there whenever I please.

While there are doubtless other wonderful stories out there and tales as yet unwritten that rightfully belong in this collection, that story — and the one I still wanted to write — completed the book. For me, it presents Motherhood in microcosm and affirms the truth that, while we do not all like being daughters or like our mothers, women are inextricably bonded by something that neither ethnicity nor age nor stage of life can remove. Thus those of us who call ourselves writers inevitably turn to exploring, in words, the mother-daughter relationship.

I hope that you enjoy the stories Joyce and I have seen fit to include, and that the pleasure derived from them leads to new insights. That was — and is — certainly true for me.

— *Janet Berliner*

Snapshots

❧ Wicked Girl

ISABEL ALLENDE

AT THE AGE of eleven, Elena Mejías was still a scrawny whelp of a girl with the dull skin of solitary children, a mouth revealing gaps still unfilled by second teeth, mouse-colored hair, and a prominent skeleton, much too large for the rest of her, that threatened to poke through at the elbows and knees. Nothing about her betrayed her torrid dreams, nor presaged the sensuous creature she would become. Among the nondescript furnishings and faded draperies of her mother's boardinghouse, she went completely unnoticed. She was like a melancholy little waif playing among the dusty geraniums and enormous ferns in the patio, trooping back and forth between the kitchen range and dining-room tables to serve the evening meal. On the rare occasion some boarder took notice of her, it was only to ask her to spray for cockroaches or to fill the water-tank in the bathroom when the creaking pump failed to draw water to the second floor. Her mother, exhausted by heat and the grind of running her boarding-house, had no energy for tenderness or time to devote to her daughter, so she failed to notice when Elena began to change into a different creature. She had always been a quiet, shy child absorbed in mysterious games, talking to herself in corners and sucking her thumb. She emerged from the house only to go to school or the market; she seemed uninterested in the noisy children of her own age playing in the street.

The transformation of Elena Mejías coincided with the arrival of Juan José Bernal, the Nightingale, as he liked to call himself and as a poster he tacked to the wall of his room loudly proclaimed. Most of the boarders were students or employees in some obscure division of city government. Real ladies and gentlemen, Elena's mother always said, for she prided herself on not taking just anyone under her roof, only respectable persons with a visible means of support, good manners, and enough money to pay a month's room and board in advance, who were also disposed to live by the regulations of her boardinghouse — more fitting for a seminary than a hotel. A widow has to think of her reputation and be able to command respect; I don't want my home turned into a haven for bums and perverts, her mother frequently repeated, so no one, especially Elena, would ever forget. One of the girl's responsibilities was to spy on the guests and keep her mother informed of any suspicious behavior. Eternal stealth exaggerated the ethereal air of the child who moved in an aura of silence, vanishing in the shadows of a room only to appear suddenly as if returning from another dimension. Mother and daughter shared the many chores of the boardinghouse, each immersed in her silent routine, feeling no need to communicate with the other. In truth, they spoke very little, and when they did, during the brief freedom of the hour of the siesta, it was about the clients. Sometimes Elena tried to embellish the gray lives of those transitory men and women who passed through the house leaving no trace of a memory by attributing to them some extraordinary event, coloring their lives through the gift of some clandestine love affair or tragedy, but her mother had an infallible instinct for detecting her fantasies. She also knew when her daughter was hiding something from her. She had an unassailable practical sense and a clear notion of everything that went on under her roof. She knew exactly what each lodger was doing at any hour of the night or day, how much sugar was left in the pantry, who was being called when the telephone rang, and where the last person had left the scissors. She had once been a cheerful, even pretty, young woman; her frumpy dresses barely restrained the impatience of a still-young body, but all the years spent scratching out a living had slowly drained away her spirit and zest for life. When Juan José Bernal came to inquire about a room, however, all that changed for her, and for Elena as well. The mother, seduced by the Nightingale's pretentious manner of speaking and the hint of fame represented by the poster, ignored her own rules and accepted him as a guest, despite the fact he did not in any way fit her image of the ideal boarder. Bernal told her that he sang at night and therefore needed to rest during the day; that he was between engagements and thus could not pay the month in advance; and that he was extremely fussy about his food and hygiene — he was a vegetarian, and he needed to shower twice a day. Amazed, Elena watched, without comment or question, as her mother wrote the name of the new guest in her book and then showed him to his room, struggling with his heavy suitcase while he bore the guitar case and the cardboard tube containing his treasured poster. Camouflaged against the wall, Elena followed them up the stairs, noting the new guest's intense appraisal of the cotton skirt clinging to her mother's sweaty buttocks. As she went into the room Elena flipped the switch, and the great blades of the ceiling fan began to turn with the screech of rusted metal.

Bernal's arrival signaled an immediate change in the household routine. There was more work now, because Bernal slept until the other guests had left for their various employments; he tied up the bath for hours on end; he consumed an astounding quantity of rabbit food, which had to be prepared especially for him; he was constantly on the telephone; and he made liberal use of the iron for touching up his dress shirts without any charge for this unusual privilege. Elena came home at siesta, when the sun was blazing and the day languishing beneath a terrible white glare, but even at that hour Juan José Bernal would still be fast asleep. As her mother had ordered, Elena would remove her shoes to keep from disturbing the artificial quiet of the house. She was aware that her mother was changing day by day. She could see the signs from the very beginning, long before the residents began to whisper behind her mother's back. First it was the fragrance that clung to her mother and lingered in the rooms as she passed through. Elena knew every corner of the house, and her long training in spying led her to the perfume bottle behind the packets of rice and tins of conserves on the pantry shelf. Next she noticed the dark pencil outlining her mother's eyelids, the touch of red on her lips, the new underclothes, the immediate smile when finally Bernal came down in the evening, his hair still wet from the bath, and sat in the kitchen to wolf down strange dishes fit for a fakir. Her mother would sit across from him and listen while he recounted episodes from his life as an artist, punctuating every adventure with a deep laugh.

For several weeks, Elena hated that man who was claiming all the space in the house and all her mother's attention. She was repelled by the brilliantine-slick hair, the polished nails, the excessive zeal with a toothpick, the pedantry, the brazen assumption they all would serve him. She wondered what her mother could see in the man: he was nothing but a small-time adventurer, a bar entertainer whom no one had ever heard of, why, he might be an out-and-out scoundrel, as *señorita* Sofía, one of their oldest boarders, had suggested in whispers. But then one warm Sunday evening when there was nothing to do and time seemed to have stopped within the walls of the house, Juan José Bernal appeared in the patio with his guitar; he installed himself on a bench beneath the fig tree and began to strum a few chords. The sound drew all the guests, who peered out one by one, at first with a certain timidity — unsure of the reason for this unusual occurrence — and then with increasing enthusiasm; they hauled out the dining room chairs and set them in a circle around the Nightingale. The man had an ordinary voice, but he had a good ear, and sang with a certain charm. He knew all the stock boleros and rural ballads of the popular repertoire, and a few songs from the Revolution sprinkled with blasphemies and four-letter words that made the ladies blush. For the first time that Elena could remember, there was a festive air in the house. When it grew dark, they lighted two kerosene lamps and hung them in the trees, and brought beer and the bottle of rum reserved for treating colds. Elena was trembling as she filled the glasses; she felt the heartrending words of the songs and the lament of the guitar in every fiber of her body, like a fever. Her mother was tapping her toe to the rhythm. Suddenly she stood up, took Elena's hands, and the two began to dance, immediately followed by all the others, including *señorita* Sofía, all fluttering and nervous giggles. For an endless moment Elena danced, moving to the cadence of Bernal's voice, held tight against her mother's body, breathing in the new flowery scent, blissfully happy. Then she felt her mother gently pushing her away, pulling back to dance alone. With her eyes closed and her head tipped back, her mother swayed like a sheet drying in the breeze. Elena stepped from the floor, and all the dancers returned to their seats, leaving the mistress of the boardinghouse alone in the center of the patio, lost in her dance.

After that night, Elena saw Bernal through new eyes. She forgot that she had detested his brilliantine, his toothpicks, and his arrogance, and whenever she saw him or heard his voice she remembered the songs he had sung the night of that impromptu fiesta and again felt the flush on her skin and the confusion in her heart, a fever she did not know how to put into words. She watched him when he was not looking, and little by little noticed things she had not at first appreciated, his shoulders, his strong, muscular neck, the sensual curve of his heavy lips, his perfect teeth, the elegance of his long, fine hands. She was filled with an insupportable longing to be close enough to him to bury her face against his dark-skinned chest, to hear the resonance of the air in his lungs and the beating of his heart, to smell his scent, a scent she knew would be sharp and penetrating, like good leather or tobacco. She imagined herself playing with his hair, examining the muscles of his back and legs, discovering the shape of his foot, dissolving into smoke and filtering down his throat to inhabit his entire body. But if he happened to look up and meet her eyes, Elena, trembling, would run and hide in the farthest and densest corner of the patio. Bernal had taken possession of her thoughts; she could not bear how time stopped when she was away from him. In school, she moved as if in a nightmare, blind and deaf to anything except her inner thoughts, where there was room only for him. What was he doing at that moment? Perhaps he was sleeping face down on the bed with the shutters closed, the room in darkness, the warm air stirred by the blades of the fan, a trail of sweat marking his spine, his face sunk in the pillow. At the first sound of the bell marking the end of the day, she ran home, praying he was not yet awake and she would be able to wash and put on a clean dress and sit down to wait for him in the kitchen, pretending to do homework so her mother would not burden her with household chores. Later, when she heard him leaving his bath, whistling, she was tormented by impatience and fear, sure that she would die of pleasure if he touched her, even spoke to her, dying for him to do just that but at the same time ready to fade into the furniture, because although she could not live without him, neither could she endure his burning presence. Stealthily, she followed him everywhere, waited on him hand and foot, tried to divine his wishes and offer whatever he needed before he asked, but always moving like a wraith, not wanting to reveal her existence.

Elena could not sleep at night because he was not in the house. She would get up from her hammock and roam the first floor like a ghost, working up courage finally to tiptoe into Bernal's room. She would close the door behind her and open the shutter a crack to let in the reflection from the street to light the ceremonies she invented to enable her to claim the bits of the man's soul left behind in his belongings. She stood staring at herself in the oval of a mirror as black and shiny as a pool of dark mud, because he had looked at himself there and the vestiges of their two images could blend together in an embrace. She walked toward the glass, eyes staring, seeing herself through his eyes, kissing her own lips with a cold hard kiss that she imagined warm as Bernal's lips. She felt the surface of the mirror against her breast and the tiny grapes of her nipples hardened, generating a dull pain that flowed downward to an exact point between her legs. She sought that pain, again and again. She took a shirt and boots from Bernal's clothespress and put them on. She walked a few steps around the room, very careful not to make any noise. Still in his clothes, she burrowed through his drawers, combed her hair with his comb, sucked his toothbrush, licked his shaving cream, caressed his dirty clothes. Then, without knowing why, she took off her nightdress, his boots and shirt, and lay naked on Bernal's bed, greedily inhaling his scent, invoking his warmth to wrap herself in. She touched every inch of her body, beginning with the strange shape of her skull, the translucent cartilage of her ears, the sockets of her eyes, the opening of her mouth, and continued down her body, sketching all the bones, folds, angles, and curves of the insignificant whole of herself, wishing she were as immense and heavy as a whale. She imagined her body filling with a sweet, sticky liquid like honey, swelling, expanding to the size of a mammoth doll, until she overflowed the bed and the room, until her tumescence filled the entire house. Exhausted, she would doze for a few minutes, weeping.

Then one Saturday morning, watching from her window, Elena saw Bernal walk up to where her mother was bent over the trough scrubbing clothes. He laid his hand on her waist and she did not move, as if the weight of that hand were part of her body. Even from a distance, Elena could see his gesture of possession, her mother's attitude of surrender, their intimacy, the current that joined them in a formidable secret. Elena broke out in a sweat, she could not breathe, her heart was a frightened bird in her rib cage, her hands and feet tingled, her blood rushed until she thought it would burst her fingers. That was when she began to spy on her mother.

One after another, she discovered the clues she sought; at first it was only a glance, an overly long greeting, a complicitous smile, the suspicion that beneath the table their legs were touching and that they were inventing pretexts to be alone. Finally, one night as she was returning from Bernal's room after performing her lover's ritual, she heard a sound like the whisper of an underground stream coming from her mother's room, and she realized that all that time, every night while she believed Bernal was out singing for a living, the man had been just across the hall, and while she was kissing his memory in the mirror and breathing in the trace of his presence in the sheets, he had been with her mother. With the skill learned from many years of making herself invisible, she glided into the room and saw them locked in their pleasure. The fringed lampshade glowed with a warm light that exposed the lovers on the bed. Her mother was transformed into a round, rosy, moaning, opulent siren, an undulating sea anemone, all tentacles and suckers, all mouth and hands and legs and orifices, rolling and turning and cleaving to the large body of Bernal, who by contrast seemed rigid and clumsy, moving spasmodically like a piece of wood tossed by inexplicable high winds. Until that moment the girl had never seen a man naked, and she was taken aback by the essential differences. His masculinity seemed brutal to her, and it was a long time before she could overcome her terror and force herself to look. Soon, however, she was conquered by fascination and watched with absolute attention to learn from her mother the formula she had used to snatch Bernal from her, a formula more powerful than all Elena's love, all her prayers, her dreams, her silent summons, all her magic ceremonies contrived to draw him to her. She was sure that her mother's caresses and sighs held the key to the secret, and if she could learn them, Juan José Bernal would sleep with her in the hammock hung every night from two large hooks in the room of the cupboards.

Elena spent the following days in a haze. She lost interest in everything around her, even Bernal himself, whom she stored in a spare compartment of her mind, and she submersed herself in a fanciful reality that completely replaced the world of the living. She continued to follow her routines by force of habit, but her heart was not in anything she did. When her mother noticed her lack of appetite, she attributed it to oncoming puberty — though Elena still looked too young — and she found time to sit alone with her and explain to her the joke of having been born a woman. Elena listened in sullen silence to the peroration about biblical curses and menstrual flow, convinced that none of that would ever happen to her.

On Wednesday Elena felt hungry for the first time in almost a week. She went into the pantry with a can opener and a spoon and devoured the contents of three cans of green peas, then peeled the red wax from a Dutch cheese and ate it as she would an apple. Immediately after, she ran to the patio, doubled over, and vomited a vile green soup over the geraniums. The pain in her belly and the bitter taste in her mouth restored her sense of reality. That night she slept tranquilly, rolled up in her hammock, sucking her thumb as she had in her cradle. Thursday morning she woke happy; she helped her mother prepare coffee for the boarders and ate breakfast with her in the kitchen. Once at school, however, she complained of terrible pains in her stomach, and she writhed so and asked so often to go to the bathroom that by midmorning her teacher gave her permission to go home.

Elena made a long detour, consciously avoiding familiar streets, and approached the house from the back wall, which overlooked a ravine. She managed to scale the wall and jump into the patio with less difficulty than she had expected. She had calculated that at that hour her mother would be in the market and, as it was the day for fresh fish, it would be a while before she returned. The house was empty except for Juan José Bernal and *señorita* Sofía, who had been home from work a week because of an attack of arthritis.

Elena hid her books and shoes under some bushes and slipped into the house. She climbed the stairway, hugging the wall and holding her breath, until she heard the radio thundering from the room of *señorita* Sofía and felt more calm. The door to Bernal's room opened with a push. It was dark inside, and for a moment, having just come from the brilliant daylight outside, she could see nothing. She knew the room from memory, however; she had measured that space many times and knew where each object was, the precise place the floor squeaked, how many steps it was from the door to the bed. She waited, nevertheless, until her eyes adjusted to the darkness and she could see the outlines of the furniture. A few moments more and she could see the man on the bed. He was not sleeping face down, as she had imagined so often, but lying on his back on top of the sheets, wearing only his undershorts; one arm was out flung and the other across his chest, and a lock of hair had fallen over his eyes. Instantly, all the fear and impatience that had accumulated for days disappeared, leaving Elena cleansed, with the calm of one who knows what she has to do. It seemed to her she had lived that moment many times; she told herself she had nothing to fear, this was a ceremony only slightly different from those that had gone before. Slowly, she stripped off her school uniform down to the cotton panties she dared not remove. She walked to the bed. She could see Bernal better now. Gingerly, she sat on the edge of the bed near his hand, concentrating on not adding even one wrinkle to the sheets. She leaned forward slowly, until her face was only a few centimeters from his and she could sense the warmth of his breath and the sweet scent of his body; then with infinite care she lay down beside him, extending each leg so cautiously he did not even stir. She waited, listening to the silence, until she resolved to rest her hand on his belly in an almost imperceptible caress. With that touch a suffocating wave flooded her body; she feared the sound of her heart was echoing through the house and would surely wake Bernal. It was several minutes before she recovered, and when she realized he had not moved, she relaxed, and let her arm fall limp — its weight, in any case, so slight it did not alter his sleep. Recalling her mother's movements, as her fingers crept beneath the elastic waist of his undershorts, Elena sought Bernal's lips and kissed him as she had so often kissed the mirror. Still asleep, Bernal moaned; he wrapped one arm around the girl's waist while his free hand took hers to guide her and his mouth opened to return her kiss, as he whispered his lover's name. Elena heard him name her mother, but rather than drawing back, she pressed even more closely to him. Bernal took her by the waist and pulled her atop him, settling her on his body as he began the first movements of love. Then, sensing the extreme fragility of that birdlike skeleton on his chest, a spark of awareness flashed through the cottony fog of sleep, and he opened his eyes. Elena felt his body tense, felt herself seized by the ribs and thrown aside so violently she fell to the floor, but she sprang to her feet and ran back to the bed to embrace him again. Bernal slapped her full in the face and leapt from the bed, terrorized by who knows what ancient prohibitions and nightmares.

"Wicked, *wicked* girl!" he screamed.

The door opened, and *señorita* Sofía was standing in the threshold.

❊ ❊ ❊

Elena spent the next seven years with the nuns, three more attending college in the capital, and then began working in a bank. In the meantime, her mother married her lover and the two of them continued to run the boardinghouse until they had saved enough money to retire to a small house in the country, where they grew carnations and chrysanthemums to sell in the city. The Nightingale hung the poster proclaiming his artistry in a gilt frame, but he never sang in a nightclub again, and no one missed him. He never accompanied his wife when she visited his stepdaughter, and he never asked about her — not wanting to stir up doubts in his own mind — but he thought of her constantly. The child's image had stayed with him, intact, untouched by the years; she was still the passionate girl he had rejected. If truth were known, as the years went by, the memory of those light bones, that childish hand on his belly, that baby tongue in his mouth, grew to be an obsession. When he embraced the heavy body of his wife, he had to concentrate on those visions, meticulously invoking Elena's image to awaken the always more diffuse impulse of pleasure. Now in his middle years, he went to stores that sold children's clothing and bought cotton underpants and pleasured himself, stroking them and stroking himself. Then he would be ashamed of such salacious moments and he would burn the panties or bury them in a deep hole in the patio in a vain attempt to put them out of his mind. He began to loiter around schools and parks where he could stand at a distance and watch the prepubescent girls who for an all-too-brief moment bore him to the abyss of that unforgettable Thursday.

Elena was twenty-six when she visited her mother for the first time, bringing her boyfriend, an army captain who for years had been begging her to marry him. The two young people — he, not wanting to seem arrogant, in civilian clothes, she laden with presents — arrived on one of those cool November afternoons. Bernal had awaited that visit like a jittery teenager. He stared at himself in the mirror at every opportunity, scrutinizing his image, wondering whether Elena would see any change, or whether in her mind the Nightingale had remained immune to the ravages of time. He had prepared for the meeting, practicing every word and imagining every possible answer. The only possibility he failed to consider was that in the place of the smoldering child who had consigned him to a life of torment he would find an insipid and quite shy young woman. Bernal felt betrayed.

As it grew dark, after the euphoria of the arrival had worn off and mother and daughter had exchanged all their latest news, they carried chairs to the patio to enjoy the cool of evening. The air was heavy with the perfume of carnations. Bernal suggested a glass of wine, and Elena followed him into the house to bring glasses. For a few moments, they were alone, face to face in the narrow kitchen. Bernal, who had waited so long for this opportunity, held Elena by the arm while he told her how it had all been a terrible mistake, how he had been half asleep that morning and had no idea what he was doing, how he had never meant to throw her to the floor or call her what he did, and would she please take pity on him and forgive him, and maybe then he could come to his senses, because for what seemed a lifetime he had been consumed by a constant burning desire for her that fired his blood and poisoned his mind. She stared at him, speechless, not knowing what to answer. What wicked girl was he talking about? She had left her childhood far behind, and the pain of that first rejected love was locked in some sealed compartment of memory. She did not remember any particular Thursday in her past.

Consuelo's Letter

JULIA ALVAREZ

THE OLD WOMAN CONSUELO, what a dream she had last night! She tossed and turned this way and that as if the dream were a large fish she was trying to haul in — without success. Finally she gave a great roll to one side and her little granddaughter Wendy let out a yelp that woke Consuelo up. *¡Dios santo!* She ran her hand over her face, wiping off sleep, and maybe it was in doing so that she lost a part of the dream that all the next day she was trying to recall.

In the dream Consuelo was counseling her daughter Ruth about her predicament. Consuelo had not seen her daughter since five years ago, when Ruth had come by the village with the surprise of a baby she had given birth to in the capital. Along with the infant, the daughter had brought an envelope of money. She counted out over two thousand pesos to leave with the grandmother. The rest was for a plan that Ruth would not tell the old woman about. "You'll just worry, Mamá," she had said, and then, throwing her arms around the old woman, she added, "Ay, Mamá, our lives are going to be so much better, you'll see."

And everything that had actually happened was also so in the dream. Ruth had made it to Puerto Rico on a rowboat, then on to Nueva York where she worked at a restaurant at night and at a private home as a maid during the day. Every month, Ruth sent home money along with a letter someone in the village read to Consuelo. Every few months the Codetel man came running through town. "International call!" Consuelo would be out of breath by the time she arrived at the telephone trailer to hear her daughter's small voice trapped in the wires. "How are you, Mamá? And my baby Wendy?" Consuelo would curse herself later, for she would fall into that mute bashfulness she always suffered in the presence of important people and their machines. Words to her

14

were like the fine china at the big houses she had worked in, something she felt better if the mistress was handling.

Then, just as with her own Ruth, the dream Ruth had gotten married. It was not a true marriage, she had explained in a letter, but one of convenience in order to get her residency. Consuelo prayed every night to el Gran Poder de Dios and la Virgencita to turn this mock marriage into a true one for her daughter's sake. He is a good man, the daughter had admitted. A Puerto Rican who wants to help a woman of a neighbor island. Hmmm. Then the letter that occasioned the dream had arrived. Even though she could not read the words, Consuelo studied the dark angry marks that were so different from the smoother roll of her daughter's usual handwriting. The man — it turned out — would not give Ruth a divorce. He was saying he was in love with her. If she tried to leave him, he was going to turn her in to the immigration police. What should she do? ¡Ay, Mamá, aconséjame! It was the first time Consuelo's daughter had asked for her advice.

How she wished she could sit her daughter down and tell her what to do. Use your head, she would say. Here is a good man who says he loves you, m'ija, why even hesitate? You can have a fine life! It is within your grasp! Next time her daughter called, Consuelo would have her advice all prepared. For days as she washed or swept or cooked, Consuelo practiced saying the words, the little granddaughter looking up surprised to hear the taciturn old woman speaking to herself.

Then the shock of last night's dream! It was as if her daughter were by her side listening. But what Consuelo was saying was not what she had planned to say — that much she remembered. Her daughter was nodding her head, for Consuelo was speaking wonderful words that flowed out of her mouth as if language were a stream filled with silver fish flashing in the water. Everything she said was so wise that Consuelo wept in her own dream to hear herself speak such true words.

But the devil take her for forgetting what it was that she was saying! When she had run her hand over her face, she had wiped the words away. All morning, she tried to recall what it was she had said to her daughter in the dream ... and once or twice ... as she swept out the house ... as she braided the child's hair into its three pigtails ... as she pounded the coffee beans and the green smell of the mountains wafted up to her, why there it was, the tail of it, quick! grab it! But no, it inched just out of her reach.

And then, she could almost hear it, a far-off voice. She crossed the yard to María's house after it. Almost a year ago, María's youngest boy had drowned in Don Mundín's swimming pool. María had stopped working in the big house, and even after the period of mourning, she continued to dress in black and to hold on to her grief as if it were the boy himself she was clutching to her side.

"I have had such a dream," Consuelo began. María had placed a cane chair under the samán tree for the old woman. She sat by, cleaning the noon rice in a hollow board on her lap. The child accustomed only to the company of the old woman, hid her face in her grandmother's lap when María's boys beckoned to her to come look at the leaping lizard they had caught. "In the dream I was speaking to my Ruth. But this one woke me, and I cleared my face before remembering, and there went the words." The old woman made the same gesture as María, flinging the rice chaff out beyond the shade of the samán tree.

"My Ruth has written for my advice," Consuelo went on. Among her own people and out of the sight and presence of the rich and their machines, the old woman found it much easier to speak her mind. "In the dream, the words came to me. But I have forgotten what it was I said to her."

María combed her fingers through the pile of rice as if the lost words could be found there. "You must go down to the river early in the morning," she began. With her long, sad face and her sure words, she was like the priest when he came up the mountain once a month to preach to the campesinos how to live their lives

"You must wash your face three times, making a sign of the cross after each washing."

The old woman was listening carefully, her hands folded as if she were praying. The child at her side looked up at the old woman and then folded her small hands.

"And the words will come to you, and then immediately you must go to the Codetel and call your daughter — "

Just the thought of speaking into that black funnel stopped the words in Consuelo's throat. She took a deep breath and made the sign of the cross and the words blurted out. "I do not have a number for my daughter. She is always the one who calls."

María stood up and shook out her skirt. She called the child to her side and asked again how old the child was and whether she was going to school to learn her letters. The child shook her head and held up five fingers but then thought better of it and help up another five. Consuelo watched the playful conversation. A tender look had come on the grieving woman's face. It was as if she had forgotten the dream altogether.

María sat back down. The interlude with the child seemed to have put a new thought in her head. "You have gotten letters; there is an address on the envelopes, no?"

"I do not know," Consuelo shrugged. "There are marks on the envelopes."

"You must bring me the letters," María concluded. "And if there is an address, then a letter must be written with the words of advice that will come to you by the river tomorrow."

"Who shall write this letter?" Consuelo worried. She knew María could read letters, but Consuelo had never seen her write them. And once written, how would the letter be sent to the daughter?

"My hand is not good." María confessed, "but there is Paquita." Consuelo could see the same caution on María's face that she herself was feeling. The letter writer in town, Paquita Montenegro, always broadcast your business as if you were paying her, not just to write your letter, but to tell everyone about it. Consuelo did not want the whole village to know that Ruth had paid a man to marry her and was now wanting to divorce him. There was already enough talk about how Consuelo's good-looking daughter had come by the money to end up in Nueva York.

"I am thinking now," María said, interrupting the old woman's thoughts. "A woman has come to the big house. Don Mundín's relation. She is from there. She will help you write this letter and then she will see to it that your daughter receives it."

At these words, Consuelo could feel her old bones lock with fright. Before she would talk about her daughter's problem to a stranger, she would rather pay Paquita the forty pesos to write the letter and blab its contents to everyone. Again she found it hard to get the words out. "Ay, but to bother the lady ... what if ... I could not...." Her voice died away.

But now María seemed more determined than ever. "What do you mean? They bother us enough when they want." Consuelo could see the face of the boy surfacing in the mother's face — before it was washed away by a look of terrible anger. "Sergio will take you tomorrow after the words come to you in the river." The younger woman grabbed the old woman's hand. "It will go well. You will see."

Consuelo did not know if it was the fierceness in María's eyes, but the look struck deep inside her, flushing out the words that she had spoken in the dream! Right then and there, she knew exactly what it was she must say in the letter this stranger would write to her daughter.

Just as Sergio had reported on their walk over to the big house, Don Mundín's relation was so easy. She was standing at the door, waiting for them — as if they were important guests she had been expecting. She was not the usual run of rich ladies, calling your name until they wore it down to nothing but the sound of an order. All her life, Consuelo had worked for many such fine ladies who kept everything under lock and key as if their homes were warehouses in which to store valuable things.

But this lady addressed her as Doña Consuelo and asked to be called Yo. "It's my baby name and it stuck," she explained. And what a little lady she was — you could fit two or three of her inside Ruth and still have room for little Wendy. She was dressed in pants and a jersey shirt, all in white like someone about to make her first communion. She spoke easily and gaily, words just sputtering from her lips. "So, Doña Consuelo, Sergio says you need help with a letter?"

Consuelo prepared to say something.

"What a pretty little girl!" The lady crouched down, crooning until the child was beside herself with fear and excitement. Before Consuelo knew it, the child's pockets were full of Don Mundín's mints and the lady had promised that before they left, she would take the child out to see the swimming pool shaped like a kidney bean. No one seemed to have informed the lady that only last summer in that pool, María and Sergio had lost their boy, no bigger than this little girl.

"We do not want...," Consuelo began. "We ask pardon for the molestation." Her heart was beating so loud she could not hear herself thinking.

"No bother at all. Come in and sit down. Not on that old bench."

And the lady pulled Consuelo by the hand just as little Wendy did when she wanted the old woman to come attend to something. Consuelo felt her heart slowing to a calmer rhythm.

Soon, they were settled in the soft chairs of the living room, drinking Coca-Colas from fancy fluted glasses. Every time Consuelo took a sip of the syrupy liquid, the ice tinkled against the glass in a way that made her feel distracted. She kept reminding the child to hold her glass with both hands as she herself was doing

But the lady did not seem fazed by all the breakable things around her. She propped her glass on the arm of the couch, and went on speaking, waving her hand within inches of the vase beside her. Consuelo pulled the packet of letters from the sack and waited for a pause in which she could insert her request. But the lady spoke on, a whole stream of words whose sense Consuelo could not always follow. How beautiful the mountains were, how she had come for a month to see if she couldn't get some writing done, how she had noticed that so many families in the village were headed by single mothers —

"The child is my granddaughter," Consuelo informed her. She did not want the lady to get the wrong idea that in her old age Consuelo had been going behind the palms with a man.

"Ay, I didn't mean that!" The lady laughed, slapping the air with her hand. Her eye fell on the packet of letters in the old woman's lap. "But let's get to your letter. Sergio told me about your daughter..." And off she was again, telling Consuelo all about Ruth going to Puerto Rico in a rowboat, about Ruth living in New York, working hard at two jobs. It did spare Consuelo the trouble of having to tell the story from the very start.

A silence followed the lady's coming to the end of what she knew. Now it was Consuelo's turn. She began haltingly. Each time she stopped, at a loss for words, the lady's eager look reassured her. Consuelo told how Ruth had married a Puerto Rican man, how she had done so for her residency, how the man had fallen in love. As she spoke, the lady kept nodding as if she knew exactly what it was that Consuelo's Ruth had been going through.

"But now she has written for my advice." Consuelo patted the packet of letters on her lap. "And in my dream it came what I should say to her."

"How wonderful!" the lady exclaimed, so that Consuelo felt momentarily baffled as to what exactly the lady felt was so extraordinary. "I mean that your dreams tell you things," the lady added. "I've tried, but I can never make sense of them. Like before I got divorced, I asked my dreams if I should leave my husband. So I dreamed a little dog bites my leg. Now what's that supposed to mean?"

Consuelo could not say for sure. But she urged the lady to visit María, who would know what to make of the little dog.

The lady waved the suggestion away. "I've got two therapist sisters who are full of theories about the little dog." She laughed, and her eyes had a faraway look as if she could see all the way home to the two sisters giving the little dog a bone.

Consuelo eased the topmost letter from the packet in her lap and watched as the lady read through this last letter Ruth had written. She seemed to have no trouble with the writing — Ruth had a pretty hand — but as her eyes descended on the page, she began shaking her head. "Oh my God!" she finally said, and looked up at Consuelo. "I don't believe this!"

"We must write to my daughter," Consuelo agreed.

"We sure should!" the lady said, pulling over the coffee table so that it was right in front of her. On it lay a tablet of clean paper and a pretty silver pen that gleamed like a piece of jewelry. The lady looked over at Consuelo. "How do you want to start?"

Consuelo had never written a letter, so she could not say. She glanced back at the woman for help

"My dear daughter Ruth," the lady suggested, and at Consuelo's nod, she wrote out the words quickly as if it took no effort at all. The child came forward on the couch to look at the lady's hand dancing across the paper. The lady smiled and offered the child some sheets as well as a colored pencil. "You want to draw?" she asked. The child nodded shyly. She knelt on the floor in front of the table and looked down at the clean sheet of paper the lady had placed before her. Finally, the child picked up her colored pencil, but she did not make a mark.

"Okay, so far we've got, *My dear daughter Ruth,*" the lady said. "What else?"

"*My dear daughter Ruth,*" Consuelo repeated. And the ring and skip of those words were like a rhyme the child often said to herself skipping in a ray of sunshine. "*I have received your letter and in my dream came these words which this good lady is helping me to write down here with all due respect to el Gran Poder de Dio. and gratitude to la Virgencita without whose aid nothing can be done."* It was just as it had been in her dream: the words came tumbling from her tongue.

But the lady was looking at her, perplexed. "It's kind of hard … you haven't really…" Now she was the one at a loss for words. "It's not a sentence," she said at last and then she must have seen that Consuelo had no idea what she meant because she added, "Let's say one thing at a time, okay?"

Consuelo nodded. "You're the one who knows," she said politely. It was a phrase she had been taught to say when asked by the rich for an opinion.

"No, no, it's your letter." The lady smiled sadly. She looked down at the paper as if it would tell her what to do. "Never mind, it's fine," the lady said, and she marked a whole half page in her quicksilver hand and turned the paper over. "Okay, let 'em come!" She whooped as if she were urging lazy cows across the evening pasture.

"My daughter, you must think of your future and the future of your child for as you yourself know marriage is a holy vow — " Consuelo stopped briefly to catch her breath, and for a moment, she could not go on. She had begun to wonder if these indeed were the words she had spoken in her dream or had she confused them with what she herself had wanted to say to her daughter?

"And so my daughter, honor this man, and he will stop beating you if you do not provoke him for as the good priest has taught us we women are subject to the wisdom and judgment of our fathers and of our husbands if they are good enough to stay with us."

The lady lay the pen on top of the paper and folded her arms. She looked over at Consuelo and shook her head. Her face had the stony gravity of María's face. "I'm sorry. I can't write that."

Consuelo's hand flew to her mouth. Maybe she had misspoken? Maybe this young woman, skinny as a nun at Lent, maybe she could tell that Consuelo was not speaking the correct words. For a second time, the words of her dream seemed to have fled her memory. "My daughter will make another foolish choice," Consuelo pleaded. She indicated the child with her chin in order to present proof of Ruth's errors without giving the child the evil eye by saying so. The little granddaughter, who had been studying her blank sheet for a while, bore down on her pencil and made a mark.

The lady bit her lips as if to keep back the words that were always so ready on her tongue. But a few slipped out, full of emotion. "How can you advise your daughter to stay with a man who beats her?"

"The man would not beat her if she did as she was told. She should think of her future. I have always advised her to think of her future." Again, Consuelo felt the words she was speaking were not the wonderful words of the dream that had drawn agreement even from the stubborn Ruth. In a much smaller voice, she concluded, "She has always been too willful."

"Good for her!" The lady gave a sharp nod. "She needs a strong will. Look at all she's done. Risked her life at sea ... supported herself on two jobs ... sent money home every month." She was counting out the reasons on her fingers like the shopkeeper counting out the money you owed him.

Consuelo found herself nodding. This woman had an eye that could see the finest points like the eyes of the child, who could thread a needle in the evening light.

"If I were you, I definitely would not advise her to stay with a man who abuses her," the lady was saying, "but, I mean, you write what you want."

But Consuelo did not know how to write. The brute of a man who had been her father had beat her good and hard whenever he found her wasting time like the child now bent over her sheet of paper. "You have reason," she said to the lady. "Let us say so to my Ruth."

She had meant for the lady's words to be added to the ones that had already been written. But the lady crumpled the sheet in her hand, and commenced a new letter. The child retrieved the crushed letter, unfolded it and ironed it out with the flat of her small hand.

"*My dear Ruth,*" the lady began, "*I have thought long and hard about what you have written to me.* Does that sound all right?" The lady looked up.

"*Sí, señora.*" Consuelo sat back in the soft chair. This indeed was a better start.

"*You have proven yourself a strong and resourceful woman and I am very proud of you.*"

"I am very proud of her," Consuelo agreed. Her eyes were filling with tears at the true sound of these words of praise for her daughter.

"*You entered upon a clear agreement with this man, and now he*" *refuses to honor it. How can you trust him if he so badly abuses your trust?"*

"That is so," Consuelo said, nodding deeply. She thought of Ruth's father, stealing into the servants' quarters in the middle of the night, reeking of rum, helping himself to what he wanted. The next morning, Consuelo was up at dawn preparing the silver tray so it would be ready when the mistress rang the bell in her bedroom.

"A man who strikes a woman does not deserve to be with her," the lady wrote.

"A man who lifts a hand," Consuelo echoed. *"Ay, my poor Ruth ... you should not suffer so...."* Again Consuelo felt the words knotting in her throat, but this time, it was not from bashfulness, but from the strength of her emotion.

"And so, Ruth, you must find a way to get help. There are agencies in the city that you can call. Do not lose heart. Do not let yourself get trapped in a situation where you are not free to speak your own mind."

And as the lady spoke and wrote these words, Consuelo could feel her dream rising to the surface of her memory. And it seemed to her that these were the very words she had spoken that Ruth had been so moved to hear. "Yes," she kept urging the lady. "Yes, that is so."

As the lady was addressing the envelope, the child held up the sheet she had filled with little crosses, copying the lady's hand. Consuelo felt a flush of tender pride to see that the child was so apt. And the lady was pleased as well. "You wrote your mami, too!" she congratulated, and she folded the child's letter in the envelope along with Consuelo's letter.

Significant Moments in the Life of My Mother

MARGARET ATWOOD

WHEN MY MOTHER was very small, someone gave her a basket of baby chicks for Easter. They all died.

"I didn't know you weren't supposed to pick them up," says my mother. "Poor little things. I laid them out in a row on a board, with their little legs sticking out straight as pokers, and wept over them. I'd loved them to death."

Possibly this story is meant by my mother to illustrate her own stupidity, and also her sentimentality. We are to understand she wouldn't do such a thing now.

Possibly it's commentary on the nature of love; though, knowing my mother, this is unlikely.

My mother's father was a country doctor. In the days before cars he drove a team of horses and a buggy around his territory, and in the days before snow ploughs he drove a team and a sleigh, through blizzards and rainstorms and in the middle of the night, to arrive at houses lit with oil lamps where water would be boiling on the wood range and flannel sheets warming on the plate rack, to deliver babies who would subsequently be named after him. His office was in the house, and as a child my mother would witness people arriving at the office door, which was reached through the front porch, clutching parts of themselves — thumbs, fingers, toes, ears, noses — which had accidentally been cut off, pressing these severed parts to the raw stumps of their bodies as if they could be stuck there like dough, in the mostly vain hope that my grandfather would be able to sew them back on, heal the gashes made in them by axes, saws, knives, and fate.

My mother and her younger sister would loiter near the closed office door until shooed away. From behind it would come groans, muffled screams, cries for help. For my mother, hospitals have never been glamorous places, and illness offers no respite or holiday. "Never get sick," she says, and means it. She hardly ever does.

Once, though, she almost died. It was when her appendix burst. My grandfather had to do the operation. He said later that he shouldn't have been the person to do it: his hands were shaking too much. This is one of the few admissions of weakness on his part that my mother has ever reported. Mostly he is portrayed as severe and in charge of things. "We all respected him, though," she says. "He was widely respected." (This is a word that has slipped a little in the scale since my mother's youth. It used to outrank *love*.)

It was someone else who told me the story of my grandfather's muskrat farm: how he and one of my mother's uncles fenced in the swamp at the back of their property and invested my mother's maiden aunt's savings in muskrats. The idea was that these muskrats would multiply and eventually be made into muskrat coats, but an adjoining apple farmer washed his spraying equipment upstream, and the muskrats were all killed by the poison, as dead as doornails. This was during the Depression, and it was no joke.

When they were young — this can cover almost anything these days, but I put it at seven or eight — my mother and her sister had a tree house, where they spent some of their time playing dolls' tea parties and so forth. One day they found a box of sweet little bottles outside my grandfather's dispensary. The bottles were being thrown out, and my mother (who has always hated waste) appropriated them for use in their dolls' house. The bottles were full of yellow liquid, which they left in because it looked so pretty. It turned out that these were urine samples.

"We got Hail Columbia for that," says my mother. "But what did we know?"

My mother's family lived in a large white house near an apple orchard, in Nova Scotia. There was a barn and a carriage house; in the kitchen there was a pantry. My mother can remember the days before commercial bakeries, when flour came in barrels and all the bread was made at home. She can remember the first radio broadcast she ever heard, which was a singing commercial about socks.

In this house there were many rooms. Although I have been there, although I have seen the house with my own eyes, I still don't know how many parts of it were closed off, or so it seemed; there were back staircases. Passages led elsewhere. Five children lived in it, two parents, a hired man and a hired girl, whose names and faces kept changing. The structure of the house was hierarchical, with my grandfather at the top, but its secret life — the life of pie crusts, clean sheets, the box of rags in the linen closet, the loaves in the oven — was female. The house, and all the objects in it, crackled with static electricity; undertows washed through it, the air was heavy with things that were known but not spoken. Like a hollow log, a drum, a church, it amplified, so that conversations whispered in it sixty years ago can be half heard even today.

In this house you had to stay at the table until you had eaten everything on your plate. "'Think of the starving Armenians,' mother used to say," says my mother. "I didn't see how eating my bread crusts was going to help them out one jot."

It was in this house that I first saw a stalk of oats in a vase, each oat wrapped in the precious silver paper which had been carefully saved from a chocolate box. I thought it was the most wonderful thing I had ever seen, and began saving silver paper myself. But I never got around to wrapping the oats, and in any case I didn't know how. Like many other art forms of vanished civilizations, the techniques for this one have been lost and cannot quite be duplicated.

"We had oranges at Christmas," says my mother. "They came all the way from Florida; they were very expensive. That was the big treat: to find an orange in the toe of your stocking. It's funny to remember how good they tasted, now."

When she was sixteen, my mother had hair so long she could sit on it. Women were bobbing their hair by then; it was getting to be the twenties. My mother's hair was giving her headaches, she says, but my grandfather, who was very strict, forbade her to cut it. She waited until one Saturday when she knew he had an appointment with the dentist.

"In those days there was no freezing," says my mother. "The drill was worked with a foot pedal, and it went *grind, grind, grind*. The dentist himself had brown teeth: he chewed tobacco, and he would spit the tobacco juice into a spittoon while he was working on your teeth."

Here my mother, who is a good mimic, imitates the sounds of the drill and the tobacco juice: "*Rrrrr! Rrrrr! Rrrrr! Phtt! Rrrrr! Rrrrr! Phtt!* It was always sheer agony. It was a heaven-sent salvation when gas came in."

My mother went into the dentist's office, where my grandfather was sitting in the chair, white with pain. She asked him if she could have her hair cut. He said she could do anything in tarnation as long as she would get out of there and stop pestering him.

"So I went out straight away and had it all chopped off," says my mother jauntily. "He was furious afterwards, but what could he do? He'd given his word."

My own hair reposes in a cardboard box in a steamer trunk in my mother's cellar, where I picture it becoming duller and more brittle with each passing year, and possibly moth-eaten; by now it will look like the faded wreaths of hair in Victorian funeral jewellery. Or it may have developed a dry mildew; inside its tissue-paper wrappings it glows faintly, in the darkness of the trunk. I suspect my mother has forgotten it's in there. It was cut off, much to my relief, when I was twelve and my sister was born. Before that it was in long curls: "Otherwise," says my mother, "it would have been just one big snarl." My mother combed it by winding it around her index finger every morning, but when she was in the hospital my father couldn't cope. "He couldn't get it around his stubby fingers," says my mother. My father looks down at his fingers. They are indeed broad compared with my mother's long elegant ones, which she calls boney. He smiles a pussycat smile.

So it was that my hair was sheared off. I sat in the chair in my first beauty parlour and watched it falling, like handfuls of cobwebs, down over my shoulders. From within it my head began to emerge, smaller, denser, my face more angular. I aged five years in fifteen minutes. I knew I could go home now and try out lipstick.

"Your father was upset about it," says my mother, with an air of collusion. She doesn't say this when my father is present. We smile, over the odd reactions of men to hair.

I used to think that my mother, in her earlier days, led a life of sustained hilarity and hair-raising adventure. (That was before I realized that she never put in the long stretches of uneventful time that must have made up much of her life: the stories were just the punctuation.)

Horses ran away with her, men offered to, she was continually falling out of trees or off the ridgepoles of barns, or nearly being swept out to sea in riptides; or, in a more minor vein, suffering acute embarrassment in trying circumstances.

Churches were especially dangerous. "There was a guest preacher one Sunday," she says. "Of course we had to go to church every Sunday. There he was, in full career, preaching hellfire and damnation" — she pounds an invisible pulpit — "and his full set of false teeth shot out of his mouth — *phoop!* — just like that. Well, he didn't miss a stride. He stuck his hand up and caught them and popped them back in his mouth, and he kept right on, condemning us all to eternal torment. The pew was shaking! The tears were rolling down our faces, and the worst of it was, we were in the front pew, he was looking right at us. But of course we couldn't laugh out loud; father would have given us Hail Columbia."

Other people's parlours were booby-trapped for her; so were any and all formal social occasions. Zippers sprang apart on her clothes in strategic places, hats were unreliable. The shortage of real elastic during the war demanded constant alertness: underpants then had buttons, and were more taboo and therefore more significant than they are now. "There you would be," she says, "right on the street, and before you knew it they'd be down around your galoshes. The way to do was to step out of them with one foot, then trek them up with your other foot and whip them into your purse. I got quite good at it."

This particular story is told only to a few, but other stories are for general consumption. When she tells them, my mother's face turns to rubber. She takes all the parts, adds the sound effects, waves her hands around in the air. Her eyes gleam, sometimes a little wickedly, for although my mother is sweet and old and a lady, she avoids being a sweet old lady. When people are in danger of mistaking her for one, she flings in something from left field; she refuses to be taken for granted.

But my mother cannot be duped into telling stories when she doesn't want to. If you prompt her, she becomes self-conscious and clams up. Or she will laugh and go out into the kitchen, and shortly after that you will hear the whir of the Mixmaster. Long ago I gave up attempting to make her do tricks at parties. In gatherings of unknown people, she merely listens intently, her head tilted a little, smiling a smile of glazed politeness. The secret is to wait and see what she will say afterwards.

At the age of seventeen, my mother went to the Normal School in Truro. This name — "Normal School" — once held a certain magic for me. I thought it had something to do with learning to be normal, which possibly it did, because really it was where you used to go to learn how to be a schoolteacher. Subsequently my mother taught in a one-room schoolhouse not far from her home. She rode her horse to and from the schoolhouse every day, and saved up the money she earned and sent herself to university with it. My grandfather wouldn't see her: he said she was too frivolous-minded. She liked ice-skating and dancing too much for his taste.

At Normal School my mother boarded with a family that contained several sons in more or less the same age group as the girl boarders. They all ate around a huge dining-room table (which I pictured as being of dark wood, with heavy carved legs, but covered always with a white linen tablecloth), with the mother and father presiding, one at each end. I saw them both as large and pink and beaming.

"The boys were great jokers," says my mother. "They were always up to something." This was desirable in boys: to be great jokers, to be always up to something. My mother adds a key sentence: "We had a lot of fun."

Having fun has always been high on my mother's agenda. She has as much fun as possible, but what she means by this phrase cannot be understood without making an adjustment, an allowance for the great gulf across which this phrase must travel before it reaches us. It comes from another world, which, like the stars that originally sent out the light we see hesitating in the sky above us these nights, may be or is already gone. It is possible to reconstruct the facts of this world — the furniture, the clothing, the ornaments on the mantel-piece, the jugs and basins and even the chamber pots in the bedrooms, but not the emotions, not with the same exactness. So much that is now known and felt must be excluded.

This was a world in which guileless flirtation was possible, because there were many things that were simply not done by nice girls, and more girls were nice then. To fall from niceness was to fall not only from grace: sexual acts, by girls at any rate, had financial consequences. Life was more joyful and innocent then, and at the same time permeated with guilt and terror, or at least the occasions for them, on the most daily level. It was like the Japanese haiku: a limited form, rigid in its perimeters, within which an astonishing freedom was possible.

There are photographs of my mother at this time, taken with three or four other girls, linked arm in arm or with their arms thrown jestingly around each other's necks. Behind them, beyond the sea or the hills or whatever is in the background, is a world already hurtling towards ruin, unknown to them: the theory of relativity has been discovered, acid is accumulating at the roots of trees, the bullfrogs are doomed. But they smile with something that from this distance you could almost call gallantry, their right legs thrust forward in parody of a chorus line.

One of the great amusements for the girl boarders and the sons of the family was amateur theatre. Young people — they were called "young people" — frequently performed in plays, which were put on in the church basement. My mother was a regular actor. (I have a stack of the scripts somewhere about the house, yellowing little booklets with my mother's parts checked in pencil. They are all comedies, and all impenetrable.) "There was no television then," says my mother. "You made your own fun."

For one of these plays a cat was required, and my mother and one of the sons borrowed the family cat. They put it into a canvas bag and drove to the rehearsal (there were cars by then), with my mother holding the cat on her lap. The cat, which must have been frightened, wet itself copiously, through the canvas bag and all over my mother's skirt. At the same time it made the most astonishingly bad smell.

"I was ready to sink through the floorboards," says my mother. "But what could I do? All I could do was sit there. In those days things like that" — she means cat pee, or pee of any sort — "were not mentioned." She means in mixed company.

I think of my mother driven through the night, skirts dripping, overcome with shame, the young man beside her staring straight ahead, pretending not to notice anything. They both feel that this act of unmentionable urination has been done, not by the cat, but by my mother. And so they continue, in a straight line that takes them over the Atlantic and past the curvature of the earth, out through the moon's orbit and into the dark reaches beyond.

Meanwhile, back on earth, my mother says: "I had to throw the skirt out. It was a good skirt, too, but nothing could get rid of the smell."

"I only heard your father swear once," says my mother. My mother herself never swears. When she comes to a place in a story in which swearing is called for, she says "dad-ratted" or "blankety-blank."

"It was when he mashed his thumb, when he was sinking the well, for the pump." This story, I know, takes place before I was born, up north, where there is nothing underneath the trees and their sheddings but sand and bedrock. The well was for a hand pump, which in turn was for the first of the many cabins and houses my parents built together. But since I witnessed later wells being sunk and later hand pumps being installed, I know how it's done. There's a pipe with a point at one end. You pound it into the ground with a sledge hammer, and as it goes down you screw other lengths of pipe onto it, until you hit drinkable water. To keep from ruining the thread on the top end, you hold a block of wood between the sledge hammer and the pipe. Better, you get someone else to hold it for you. This is how my father mashed his thumb: he was doing both the holding and the hammering himself.

"It swelled up like a radish," says my mother. "He had to make a hole in the nail, with his toad-sticker, to ease the pressure. The blood spurted out like pips from a lemon. Later on the whole nail turned purple and black and dropped off. Luckily he grew another one. They say you only get two chances. When he did it though, he turned the air blue for yards around. I didn't even know he knew those words. I don't know where he picked them up." She speaks as if these words are a minor contagious disease, like chicken pox.

Here my father looks modestly down at his plate. For him, there are two worlds: one containing ladies, in which you do not use certain expressions, and another one — consisting of logging camps and other haunts of his youth, and of gatherings of acceptable sorts of men — in which you do. To let the men's world slip over verbally into the ladies' would reveal you as a mannerless boor, but to carry the ladies' world over into the men's brands you a prig and maybe even a pansy. This is the word for it. All of this is well understood between them.

This story illustrates several things: that my father is no pansy, for one; and that my mother behaved properly by being suitably shocked. But my mother's eyes shine with delight while she tells this story. Secretly, she thinks it funny that my father got caught out, even if only once. The thumbnail that fell off is, in any significant way, long forgotten.

There are some stories that my mother does not tell when there are men present: never at dinner, never at parties. She tells them to women only, usually in the kitchen, when they or we are helping with the dishes or shelling peas, or taking the tops and tails off the string beans, or husking corn. She tells them in a lowered voice, without moving her hands around in the air, and they contain no sound effects. These are stories of romantic betrayals, unwanted pregnancies, illnesses of various horrible kinds, marital infidelities, mental breakdowns, tragic suicides, unpleasant lingering deaths. They are not rich in detail or embroidered with incident: they are stark and factual. The women, their own hands moving among the dirty dishes or the husks of vegetables, nod solemnly.

Some of these stories, it is understood, are not to be passed on to my father, because they would upset him. It is well known that women can deal with this sort of thing better than men can. Men are not to be told anything they might find too painful; the secret depths of human nature, the sordid physicalities, might overwhelm or damage them. For instance, men often faint at the sight of their own blood, to which they are not accustomed. For this reason you should never stand behind one in the line at the Red Cross donor clinic. Men, for some mysterious reason, find life more difficult than women do. (My mother believes this, despite the female bodies, trapped, diseased, disappearing, or abandoned, that litter her stories.) Men must be allowed to play in the sandbox of their choice, as happily as they can, without disturbance; otherwise they get cranky and won't eat their dinners. There are all kinds of things that men are simply not equipped to understand, so why expect it of them? Not everyone shares this belief about men; nevertheless, it has its uses.

"She dug up the shrubs from around the house," says my mother. This story is about a shattered marriage: serious business. My mother's eyes widen. The other women lean forward. "All she left him were the shower curtains." There is a collective sigh, an expelling of breath. My father enters the kitchen, wondering when the tea will be ready, and the women close ranks, turning to him their deceptive blankly smiling faces. Soon afterwards, my mother emerges from the kitchen, carrying the teapot, and sets it down on the table in its ritual place.

"I remember the time we almost died," says my mother. Many of her stories begin this way. When she is in a certain mood, we are to understand that our lives have been preserved only by a series of amazing coincidences and strokes of luck; otherwise the entire family, individually or collectively, would be dead as doornails. These stories, in addition to producing adrenalin, serve to reinforce our sense of gratitude. There is the time we almost went over a waterfall, in a canoe, in a fog; the time we almost got caught in a forest fire; the time my father almost got squashed, before my mother's very eyes, by a ridgepole he was lifting into place; the time my brother almost got struck by a bolt of lightning, which went by him so close it knocked him down. "You could hear it sizzle," says my mother.

This is the story of the hay wagon. "Your father was driving," says my mother, "at the speed he usually goes." We read between the lines: *too fast.* "You kids were in the back." I can remember this day, so I can remember how old I was, how old my brother was. We were old enough to think it was funny to annoy my father by singing popular songs of a type he disliked, such as "Mockingbird Hill"; or perhaps we were imitating bagpipe music by holding our noses and humming, while hitting our Adam's apples with the edges of our hands. When we became too irritating my father would say, "Pipe down." We weren't old enough to know that his irritation could be real; we thought it was part of the game.

"We were going down a steep hill," my mother continues, "when a hay wagon pulled out right across the road, at the bottom. Your father put on the brakes, but nothing happened. The brakes were gone! I thought our last moment had come." Luckily the hay wagon continued across the road; and we shot past it, missing it by at least a foot. "My heart was in my mouth," says my mother.

I didn't know until afterwards what had really happened. I was in the backseat, making bagpipe music, oblivious. The scenery was the same as it always was on car trips: my parents' heads, seen from behind, sticking up above the front seat. My father had his hat on, the one he wore to keep things from falling off the trees into his hair. My mother's hand was placed lightly on the back of his neck.

"You had such an acute sense of smell when you were younger," says my mother.

Now we are on more dangerous ground: my mother's childhood is one thing, my own quite another. This is the moment at which I start rattling the silverware, or ask for another cup of tea. "You used to march into houses that were strange to you, and you would say in, a loud voice, 'What's that funny smell?'" If there are guests present, they shift a little away from me, conscious of their own emanations, trying not to look at my nose.

"I used to be so embarrassed," says my mother absentmindedly. Then she shifts gears. "You were such an easy child. You used to get up at six in the morning and play by yourself in the play room, singing away..." There is a pause. A distant voice, mine, high and silvery, drifts over the space between us. "You used to talk a blue streak. Chatter, chatter, chatter, from morning to night." My mother sighs imperceptibly, as if wondering why I have become so silent, and gets up to poke the fire.

Hoping to change the subject, I ask whether or not the crocuses have come up yet, but she is not to be diverted. "I never had to spank you," she says. "A harsh word, and you would be completely reduced." She looks at me sideways; she isn't sure what I have turned into, or how. "There were just one or two times. Once, when I had to go out and I left your father in charge." (This may be the real point of the story: the inability of men to second-guess small children.) "I came back along the street, and there were you and your brother, throwing mud balls at an old man out of the upstairs window."

We both know whose idea this was. For my mother, the proper construction to be put on this event is that my brother was a hell-raiser and I was his shadow, "easily influenced," as my mother puts it. "You were just putty in his hands."

"Of course, I had to punish both of you equally," she says. Of course, I smile a forgiving smile. The real truth is that I was sneakier than my brother and got caught less often. No front-line charges into enemy machine gun nests for me, if they could be at all avoided. My own solitary acts of wickedness were devious and well concealed; it was only in partnership with my brother that I would throw caution to the winds.

"He could wind you around his little finger," says my mother. "Your father made each of you a toy box and the rule was" — my mother is good at the devising of rules — "the rule was that neither of you could take the toys out of the other's toy box without permission. Otherwise he would have got all your toys away from you. But he got them anyway, mind you. He used to talk you into playing house, and he would pretend to be the baby. Then he would pretend to cry, and when you asked what he wanted, he'd demand whatever it was out of your toy box that he wanted to play with at the moment. You always gave it to him."

I don't remember this, though I do remember staging World War Two on the living-room floor, with armies of stuffed bears and rabbits; but surely some primal patterns were laid down. Have these early toy-box experiences — and "toy box" itself, as a concept, reeks with implications — have they made me suspicious of men who wish to be mothered, yet susceptible to them at the same time? Have I been conditioned to believe that if I am not solicitous, if I am not forthcoming, if I am not a never-ending cornucopia of entertaining delights, they will take their collections of milk-bottle tops and their mangy one-eared teddy bears and go away into the woods by themselves to play snipers? Probably. What my mother thinks was merely cute may have been lethal.

But this is not her only story about my suckiness and gullibility. She follows up with the *coup de grâce*, the tale of the bunny-rabbit cookies.

"It was in Ottawa. I was invited to a government tea," says my mother, and this fact alone should signal an element of horror: my mother hated official functions, to which however she was obliged to go because she was the wife of a civil servant. "I had to drag you kids along; we couldn't afford a lot of babysitters in those days." The hostess had made a whole plateful of decorated cookies for whatever children might be present, and my mother proceeds to describe these: wonderful cookies shaped like bunny rabbits, with faces and clothes of coloured icing, little skirts for the little girl bunny rabbits, little pants for the little boy bunny rabbits.

"You chose one," says my mother. "You went off to a corner with it, by yourself. Mrs. X noticed you and went over. 'Aren't you going to eat your cookie?' she said. 'Oh, no,' you said. 'I'll just sit here and talk to it.' And there you sat, as happy as a clam. But someone had made the mistake of leaving the plate near your brother. When they looked again, there wasn't a single cookie left. He'd eaten every one. He was very sick that night, I can tell you."

Some of my mother's stories defy analysis. What is the moral of this one? That I was a simp is clear enough, but on the other hand it was my brother who got the stomachache. Is it better to eat your food, in a straightforward materialistic way and as much of it as possible, or go off into the corner and talk to it? This used to be a favourite of my mother's before I was married, when I would bring what my father referred to as "swains" home for dinner. Along with dessert, out would come the bunny-rabbit cookie story, and I would cringe and twiddle my spoon while my mother forged blithely on with it. What were the swains supposed to make of it? Were my kindliness and essential femininity being trotted out for their inspection? Were they being told in a roundabout way that I was harmless, that they could expect to be talked to by me, but not devoured? Or was she, in some way, warning them off? Because there is something faintly crazed about my behaviour, some tinge of the kind of person who might be expected to leap up suddenly from the dinner table and shout, "Don't eat that! It's alive!

There is, however, a difference between symbolism and anecdote. Listening to my mother, I sometimes remember this.

"In my next incarnation," my mother said once, "I'm going to be an archaeologist and go around digging things up." We were sitting on the bed that had once been my brother's, then mine, then my sister's; we were sorting out things from one of the trunks, deciding what could now be given away or thrown out. My mother believes that what you save from the past is mostly a matter of choice.

At that time something wasn't right in the family; someone wasn't happy. My mother was angry: her good cheer was not paying off.

This statement of hers startled me. It was the first time I'd ever heard my mother say that she might have wanted to be something other than what she was. I must have been thirty-five at the time, but it was still shocking and slightly offensive to me to learn that my mother might not have been totally contented fulfilling the role in which fate had cast her: that of being my mother. What thumb-suckers we all are, I thought, when it comes to mothers.

Shortly after this I became a mother myself, and this moment altered me.

While she was combing my next-to-impossible hair, winding it around her long index finger, yanking out the snarls, my mother used to read me stories. Most of them are still in the house somewhere, but one has vanished. It may have been a library book. It was about a little girl who was so poor she had only one potato left for her supper, and while she was roasting it the potato got up and ran away. There was the usual chase, but I can't remember the ending: a significant lapse.

"That story was one of your favourites," says my mother. She is probably still under the impression that I identified with the little girl, with her hunger and her sense of loss; whereas in reality I identified with the potato.

Early influences are important. It took that one a while to come out; probably until after I went to university and started wearing black stockings and pulling my hair back into a bun and having pretensions. Gloom set in. Our next-door neighbour, who was interested in wardrobes, tackled my mother. "'If she would only *do* something about herself,'" my mother quotes, "'she could be *quite attractive*.'"

"You always kept yourself busy," my mother says charitably, referring to this time. "You always had something cooking. Some project or other."

It is part of my mother's mythology that I am as cheerful and productive as she is, though she admits that these qualities may be occasionally and temporarily concealed. I wasn't allowed much angst around the house. I had to indulge it in the cellar, where my mother wouldn't come upon me brooding and suggest I should go out for a walk, to improve my circulation. This was her answer to any sign, however slight, of creeping despondency. There wasn't a lot that a brisk sprint through dead leaves, howling winds, or sleet couldn't cure.

It was, I knew, the *zeitgeist* that was afflicting me, and against it such ample remedies were powerless. Like smog I wafted through her days, dankness spreading out from around me. I read modern poetry and histories of Nazi atrocities, and took to drinking coffee. Off in the distance, my mother vacuumed around my feet while I sat in chairs, studying, with car rugs tucked around me, for suddenly I was always cold.

My mother has few stories to tell about these times. What I remember from them is the odd look I would sometimes catch in her eyes. It struck me, for the first time in my life, that my mother might be afraid of me. I could not even reassure her, because I was only dimly aware of the nature of her distress, but there must have been something going on in me that was beyond her: at any time I might open my mouth and out would come a language she had never heard before. I had become a visitant from outer space, a time-traveller come back from the future, bearing news of a great disaster.

◟ *The Allies*

KATHERINE DUNN

THE RADIO purred from the top of the refrigerator and Mrs. Reddle paused, listening, with her smallest sable-hair brush an inch from the canvas. Her eyes went soft, turning to the gray sky outside the window.

"Another Unidentified Flying Object reported near the coast," said the radio. "And in Texas, an insurance salesman and a hitchhiker report that they were taken aboard a huge spherical vessel which stopped their car in the desert south of Burkburnett. More on these and other stories after this..."

Mrs. Reddle's eyes shifted back to the canvas. Her brush moved forward delicately, laying a sliver of light on the face beneath her hand. The rough, two-by-four easel stood in the windowed bay of the kitchen where anyone else would put a table and chairs. The Reddles' table was in the middle of the kitchen with a discreetly rosy bowl in the center of its brown cloth. The bay was jammed with working rubble — boxes of magazine clippings and old photographs, a stained bench holding bottles, jars, cans stuffed with brushes, and rags smeared thick with pigments.

Mrs. Reddle sat with her left side to the daylight. The windows looked down the yellow grass knoll and across the highway to the service station. Her husband was leaning over a windshield, his massive arm swabbing at the glass, the grease on the belly of his overall threatening the finish of the car's hood. His laugh drifted in faintly, causing Mrs. Reddle's mouth to press in on itself as she bent to the paint.

"Further sightings reported..." said the radio. "A squadron of white lights moving in patterns in the sky above this small coastal town..."

Mrs. Reddle lifted the last stroke of the paint until it melted smoothly into the surrounding shadow and then fell back in her chair with a sly tilt at the corners of her mouth. She slid the brush into the turpentine can and squinted at the canvas through her eyelashes. The smells of turpentine and linseed oil and her own lean flesh drifted around her.

The bell on the pavement of the gas station rang. Her son stood on the bell cord in the shadow of the canopy. His child arms moved in wide circles describing something to his father. A truck passed on the road, blocking the view, but her husband's laugh mingled with the engine noise and the rush of air. Further down the highway a familiar, squat figure toiled up the hill.

Edie Reddle heard her father's laugh rattling through the traffic and knew her mother was in a decent mood. Edie thought of the laugh as phony but it was the only laugh her father had. On the days when her father laughed, or waved at her as she climbed the hill, Edie went straight in through the kitchen door to talk with her mother.

If her father moved heavily around the cars at the gas pumps or stared sullenly at her from the office window, she went around the house to the front door and directly up to her bedroom to listen until she could tell which direction the anger was moving.

Her mother was either happy or furious, with no mediocre moods for transition or warning. Edie might set off for the high school in the morning, leaving her mother whistling merrily in the kitchen. But she could arrive home the same afternoon to grim, ripping accusations, screams of fury, breaking glass, flailing blows, a toxic mayhem that went on muttering and clanging into the night while she lay rigid, listening in the dark for the inexplicable escalation that could hurl a shrieking monster into her bedroom. Usually Edie's father or her younger brother was the target of the anger, but no one was safe until it passed, and the storm in the house froze them all.

It had to do, Edie figured, with what her mother thought about during the day. Whether she remembered something you'd done years ago or was imagining what you might be doing out of her sight. But it might also be triggered by something on the radio, or a phrase overheard in the supermarket, a chance comment by a clerk or passerby that twisted in her mother's mind and grew fangs.

But today she heard the laugh clearly and could see the swift flash of her father's heavy body working across the road so Edie stepped up to the kitchen door and opened it.

Turpentine. A soothing oil seeping through the pungency. The brown kitchen with its cunning light was warm and neat. A faint hint of roasting meat softened the paint smells. As long as her mother was actually painting she was fine. Once she put her brushes down anything could happen. Edie took a full breath and put her books on the table.

"Further reports on the UFO sightings at Seaside on the news at 4:30. This is Radio AUZ, The Voice of Gold."

"Mama?" Edie fumbled with her coat buttons.

"Come here, dear."

The wilderness of the alcove ended precisely where it bordered the kitchen. No spot of paint or dropped rag, not even a leg of the chair she sat on was allowed to protrude into the clean kitchen. Only the smell went everywhere, gently.

Mrs. Reddle, with a fist full of brushes on her knee, sat watching, waiting. Edie did not look at her. Looked only at the canvas. She waited a minute and then started the smile in her chest and let it flow up to her eyes first and then down to her mouth. She turned the smile on her mother. Mrs. Reddle smiled back hesitantly, her eyes anxious, her fist spreading the brushes into the denim of her dungarees at the knee. Edie used the line she had been practicing on the way home.

"Did religion make him look like that? I'm heading for the church right now. But no, I suspect it was you."

She watched her mother's eyes liven as though they were connected to her chuckle.

"Oh, he's a decent enough man," said Mrs. Reddle. "I'm just trying to cover up his stupidity by dressing it as enthusiasm."

"Is he dumb?" asked Edie. She bent to peer into the intense face on the canvas.

"I hope you can't tell from my painting. But just look at these." Mrs. Reddle spread glossy photographs and snapshots on the base of the easel. Edie stared.

"You mean how close together his eyes are? And how small?"

Mrs. Reddle pointed with the tip of the brush.

"That's sometimes a clue, but it can go with a low kind of shrewdness too. I've added some distance there and enlarged them a hair. But look how low his ears are set on his head. This is the dead giveaway. The top of each ear is a half inch below the level of his eye. And look at all that flab under his chin. That's not fat, that's just gaping room. He lets his jaw hang in private and has to think about jutting it out when he's in public."

Edie giggled and examined the painting. Mrs. Reddle watched the freckled skin pucker across her daughter's round face, the hunch of the plump shoulders, and the spread of the stubby white hands next to her own long, strong ones. The girl turned to her, brown eyes smiling.

"Is he taking this to Africa with him to impress the natives?"

"He's presenting it to his fan club, the ladies of the Overseas Mission Group. According to him all he's taking is his New Standard Bible and a million cc's of antibiotics. The ladies will send him care packages — homemade jam and silk undies."

They laughed as they set the table. Mrs. Reddle made the salad and Edie stood at the sink peeling potatoes.

"And while the highway patrol and local police forces are continuing their investigations of the rash of sightings, this reporter asked Dr. A. R. Ziegler, professor of astrophysics at......' What can I say? Anything is possible......'" said the radio.

The door slammed and Edie's younger brother jostled her for room to wash his hands at the sink.

"Shove over, Fats."

Edie felt a sudden weight of hatred for his skinny, golden arms and the black grease that he sluiced and dripped over the coils of potato peel. Her mother's quick step behind her tightened the muscles of her neck but the punishing hand clipped the boy's head instead of hers.

"How many times, young man, have I told you to come home from school and change your clothes before you go over to that grease pit? Your father doesn't care. He doesn't have to wash your filthy clothes, nor his own either. There'll come a day...."

The voice soaring higher, losing control. The boy's face wrinkling in mute resentment near Edie's shoulder. He flipped water drops off his fingers at Edie and marched out of the room. Edie's ears strained to read the note of her mother's heels on the linoleum.

"Have you been listening to all the UFO reports, Mama? Everybody's talking about it at school." Edie's fingers turned the potato under her knife. She waited for the distraction to take effect.

"I have my own idea about them," said Mrs. Reddle. "I think they're looking for someone."

Edie turned to look at her. Mrs. Reddle shook back the stripe of stiff gray hair that sprang from her temples and nodded firmly at her daughter.

"Who?"

"Someone they can talk to."

Edie felt her mouth skewing in slow, embarrassed sarcasm, nearly giving her away before she turned back to the sink, her voice rattling ironically as she cut the potatoes into a pan.

"I got a talking-to today. Mr. Dolbeer stopped me in the hall."

"He's the algebra teacher?" Mrs. Reddle asked the cucumbers.

"He asked if it was my mother who'd painted the portrait of the President for the auditorium. When I said yes he kind of shook his head and said, 'How did she ever end up in this hole?' It made me mad. I said you hadn't ended up yet by a long way. And he apologized. He said he just meant that a talent like yours should be more widely recognized." Edie nonchalantly dumped peelings into the garbage can.

"What a nice man!" Mrs. Reddle's hands rested among the lettuce leaves and cucumber slices.

"He's not a nice man. He's critical of everything. The only people he likes in this world are Bach and Euclid. Everybody else is 'Vulgar' or 'In Poor Taste.'"

Edie could feel the glow of her mother's pleasure filling the room. The soft laugh and the lighter touch of Mrs. Reddle's knife sliding on the cutting board.

"Well, you get good grades in his class. He must like you, too."

"He probably likes me better now that he knows who my mother is."

"Can you tell the listeners exactly what happened, Mr. Tindall?" said the radio. "I'm a salesman, see? I was coming back from San Antonio about 10 P.M. I'd got this hitchhiker, said he was going as far as Little Ross. He'll tell you this is true, what I'm saying."

The potatoes boiled wildly. Edie's plump hand lifted the lid slightly askew so the steam could escape. Mrs. Reddle stood in the open refrigerator door and stared at the small dark face of the radio.

"I'd think you were bats if you told me this... But there it was. Right in the middle of the road with a ramp leading up inside. Size of Wichita City Hall. What was I supposed to do?"

"Let's eat!" said Mr. Reddle coming through the door with a smile. Mrs. Reddle took the milk from the refrigerator and shut the door.

"Five minutes, I think. Have a wash."

"By God, Irma, I just sold four hundred dollars worth of tires and got twenty recaps for nothing! What do you call that?"

"I'd probably call it fraud if I knew how you did it."

"Business, dear lady. Good business."

There was a hunk of yellow soap in a plastic dish near the sink. It was reserved for Mr. Reddle's use. His were the only hands it wouldn't scorch. A steady scent of unrefined petroleum followed him. Edie finished the table while Mrs. Reddle took the meat from the oven. Mr. Reddle grinned over his shoulder at the alcove as he scrubbed.

"You sure have been pecking away at the Reverend Arn. You know that asshole drives all the way across town rather than buy his gas from me? I was figuring today there's not a person who goes to that church that *does* trade with me. Is that a coincidence? I don't know why in hell you're painting that for him. And what's he going to pay you? A hundred bucks! Shit. You've been fiddling with the thing for weeks."

Edie's fingers dug into the spoon handle.

"That's right, Mama," she hurried. "It's ridiculous to charge so little for your work. Any of your pictures would sell at five times the price."

Mrs. Reddle cocked a sarcastic eyebrow at her husband's splashing.

"I'm not a salesman like your father. Call your brother."

Dinner. The food passed. Talk of old farts in Ford Cortinas and the character with the four plumbers' vans who'd been buying tires that day.

Edie's brother gave her a nudge under the table,

"Pass the spuds, Pudge."

"Don't call her that!" screamed Mrs. Reddle, slamming her fork onto the table and lunging up over her plate. The boy dropped down in his chair, arms guarding his head, squealing, "No, Ma! No, Ma! No, Ma!"

"Oh for Christ's sake, Irma," protested Mr. Reddle. "It was just a joke. That kid's teasing doesn't bother Edie. She's too smart to let a little ragging get to her."

Mrs. Reddle's arm still tensed, her body poised above the table, her eyes squinting rage at the boy. Her mouth folded tight till the full lips were completely invisible. She sank slowly into her chair. The boy sat up and turned a sullen face to his plate.

After dinner Mr. Reddle went back across to the station and took his son with him. The old man who helped him at mealtimes didn't know how to close up.

Dishes done, Mrs. Reddle wiped the kitchen counters while Edie arranged her homework on the table.

"Oh, I found this book in the school library. It's mostly landscapes but it has some nice color plates of Velásquez portraits. The color reproduction is supposed to be a new thing, much more accurate."

Mrs. Reddle looked over Edie's shoulder at the vivid pages and then sat at the table, taking the book in her own hands. The radio sang and sold toothpaste softly.

The night came down tight. Only the red blink of the neon from the gas station appeared in the black windows. Mrs. Reddle bent over the picture book.

Edie's eyes flicked sideways from her work and took in the soft curve of her mother's cheek, the pale down that was becoming more pronounced as she grew older. The sculpted muscles of her mother's arms were graceful, beautiful to Edie. Her own thick arms grew heavier on the table.

"Is the Halloween dance fancy dress?" Mrs. Reddle's voice shook Edie from her blank stare to instant wariness.

"I think so."

The book lay open on dancers, their limbs thoughtful extensions of the lines of their bodies, skirts in clouds. Mrs. Reddle tapped the page.

"You'd look lovely in something like that. I'll get paid as soon as I deliver the portrait next week. I'll bet I can find real tulle even in this town."

Edie's face and neck oozed thin, cold sweat.

"I'm not going to that dance, Mama."

"Oh, you should! You don't go out enough at all. Hasn't that Jerry asked you?" Mrs. Reddle's face in anxious lines, her brows tilting her whole forehead up in a little wrinkled tent beneath her hair.

"He asked me all right." Edie picked the corner of a page, pinched it between her thumb and finger until the pain made her stop. "But I said no. He's been skipping classes lately. And hanging out with some filthy people."

Edie's head sinking deeper into her shoulders, the hump of flesh on her shoulders riding up into the folds at the back of her neck.

"And I wouldn't want to go with anyone else. I'll just wait until he straightens out."

"Oh, my dear," Mrs. Reddle reaching tenderly for her daughter's hand. "When you're older you'll know the best way to make that boy take a look at himself is to give him some competition."

Edie pulled her hand away and bit viciously on the flat of her thumbnail.

"I'm not going, Mama. I don't want to."

Mrs. Reddle looked down at the girls in their white dresses caught dancing before a mirror. She turned the page.

"The latest on the rash of UFO sightings across the nation on the news at 8:30...." said the radio.

"This UFO business goes on practically every year around now, doesn't it? Halloween madness?" Edie grinned, her voice harsh with humor. Mrs. Reddle looked at her gently, lingering on the round flat face and the wispy hair lifting around it.

"I think it's real," said Mrs. Reddle. "Not all of it. Some of it is a joke, or people making themselves important for a minute or two."

Leaning toward her daughter, Mrs. Reddle poured urgency into her eyes, grave intensity into her voice. "But I think there are beings from ... somewhere else ... trying to contact us. Don't you see how careful they'd have to be? If they landed in a major city they'd be attacked immediately. There would be total panic and nobody capable of communicating with them reasonably. The political leaders, if they didn't panic themselves, would be under enormous pressure from the populace to do something military. No, they couldn't do that. They have to take it this way, looking for a few individuals who can think without fear, who have minds open enough to accept what they see and yet are intelligent enough to understand whatever message it is that they have for us."

Mrs. Reddle's eyes fixed on Edie, her hands resting flat on the open pages of the book. Her voice was sure and eager as it always was when she was swept by an Idea.

Edie sternly prevented her left eyebrow and that whole side of her face from quirking or lifting in irony.

"Well, nobody knows what's out there, I guess. And I can't think of one good reason there couldn't be a civilization more advanced than ours...."

Edie shoveled the heavy words out slowly, and watched what she thought of as "The Idiot Glint" thrust the lids of her mother's eyes open, watched the protrusion of the eye increase until a thin, precise line of white showed above and below her mother's iris. She nearly flinched when her mother's hand touched her own and closed over it.

"I have good reason to believe it. And I'll tell you now. You're old enough to understand. You are exactly what they're looking for."

The chill struck Edie's neck. A roar of air followed a truck past the house. She felt her own eyes spreading.

"Mama..."

"You must not be afraid, child." The sudden pity in her mothers voice spread a blankness over her thoughts, bundled her skeptic's logic up and hid it away.

"There's nothing to be afraid of. I've always known. Since you were born. I knew when I saw how your eyes would turn to watch things you shouldn't have been able to see. And I've watched it grow in you, this awareness, consciousness. You know it yourself. You sense your own uniqueness without being able to pinpoint it. But you must not doubt that it is for a purpose and that you will be called upon to use it." Mrs. Reddle's eyes filled with water, ran over, dripping as they held Edie's eyes.

"To use it for the good of us all. The wide earth. So you must not be afraid if they come for you, if they need you. Do you understand, dear?"

Mrs. Reddle held Edie's hands in her own and her tears fell on them. Edie's throat was closed tight. Her own eyes seeping, burning. She nodded convulsively.

"There, dear. It's all right. As long as you understand," said her mother. "Here come the men."

Feet hit the porch and the women flicked quick hands at their tears and set their faces. The door opened. Edie bent over her book.

Her brother chirped, "Hey, there's a great movie on TV in about ten seconds."

"I've finished the bills if you want to mail them out tomorrow, Irma," said her father.

"I'm going to bed, folks. Good night," said Edie.

❊ ❊ ❊

She paced the dark bedroom in flannel pajamas, rolling her bare feet carefully on the floor so no thump or shudder would be noticeable in the rooms below her.

"Uniquely ugly," she muttered.

A coward, a flatterer, a liar, she called herself, counting the night's crop of soft phrases spewed to control her mother's moods and fears. The imaginary conversation with Mr. Dolbeer. The shame of that long-standing invention, "The Boy Friend," the mythical Jerry who had *almost* taken her to a dozen dances. That lie was the heaviest.

"Why won't she let me be ugly? Why does she blind herself and cripple me?" The streetlights threw bright gray across her as she passed the window. She saw herself in the mirror. "No. You're not a cute little girl," Edie mocked her wide reflection. "You're on your way to becoming a *beautiful* woman." She propped her hands on her waist and saw her own bulk shivering above and below them. "A very feminine figure, my dear," minced Edie. "A lovely little bosom," she hissed. "Mama," she whispered, "the boys moo at me in the halls. Mama," she muttered, "Mama, you're crazy and I'm a sucker."

She sank down on the floor near the window and leaned her hot face against the cold glass. The white and red lights of the cars and the black night cooled her. "Space aliens," she whispered. "I should probably pack a bag and keep it by the window, just in case." She stifled a giggle. "Ah, Mama, you're slipping away from us."

But still, before morning she dreamed that the great ship came, whirring softly, shaped like a child's top. It hovered outside her window and the light of it filled her room. In the dream a silent door opened in the side and a ramp came out to her window. She stepped out onto it and walked lightly, gracefully, with her pajamas flowing around her, toward the opening where the silver beings reached toward her saying, "You must help us. We've looked for you so long."

❧ Cleaning Up

MARY GORDON

WHEN THE FIRST MAN walked on the moon, Loretta's mother, as the town said, "snapped." And it was almost like that, as if you could hear a sound and then see something fly up into the air, not like a bird but like a rubber strap that had broken from too much strain.

"Her life was just too hard for her," Martine Lavin said to Loretta, sympathetically, without a hint of judgment. Loretta understood that Martine was being kind and that she ought to be grateful. So many people avoided talking to her, so they gave her meals and washed her clothes and tried to find a place for her in their homes beside their own children. She wasn't uncared for, the parish saw to that. But as they packed her bologna sandwiches, identical to their own children's, as they poured milk or juice, careful to distribute identical amounts, they rigorously avoided mentioning her mother or what had happened in St. Rita's church on the day of the moon walk.

Martine Lavin never went so far as to bring that up, but she did at least refer to Loretta's mother, didn't erase her from the pages of life, not as if she'd been dead but as if she'd never lived. And Loretta was grateful to her, but only partly, because what she could see in everyone's eyes was how much they loved themselves for doing what they did, how much they loved themselves for their knowledge of their own humility, "Well, I didn't do much. I did what anyone would do."

If one of them, just one, had been without that shadow of self-love, so visible to Loretta, perhaps she would have felt free to relinquish the hard stone she carried beneath the flesh of the palms of her hands. The thin flesh, the pointed stone that had penetrated beneath the skin, causing a new skin to grow up around her hate. She hated Martine Lavin most of all because of her belief that she was different from the others. And she wasn't different, or only in ways that carried the kind of tiny risk that allowed her to think of herself as an adventurer, when really, she had never been in any danger and would never be. She was only different enough to be a problem, because she created the temptation in Loretta to let down her guard. And that was dangerous.

Loretta knew about danger. It was the element her mother lived in and carried with her. The women in the altar society (Martine was one of them) had seen it, and they wanted to turn their eyes away from it, but they couldn't entirely, because Loretta was a child, thirteen years old.

Her mother had smashed through the barriers of decency that day in church. Why had she chosen a time when the Altar Society was there? The decent women of the parish, polishing, arranging flowers, genuflecting with dustcloths in their hands each time they passed the tabernacle.

Loretta had seen it all, she had to, she had to follow her mother out into the street. Her mother was raving, tearing at her clothes, shouting out words of the most unbelievable filth, some unrecognizable to Loretta, some recognizable to her as the names of body parts she associated with the bathroom.

"Mama, please, mama come home, be quiet, you're disturbing people, Mama come home with me, we'll eat something, you can lie down, we can lie down together, we can take a nap."

But she didn't listen and Loretta knew she couldn't, knew, really, that her mother couldn't hear her, no matter how loudly she spoke. But she couldn't speak too loudly. She was trying to encourage her mother to be quiet so she tried to keep as quiet as she could herself. It didn't matter. Whatever she said the words were wrong. Her mother's words didn't make sense to her, either. They were speaking to each other in languages the other didn't understand. Loretta recognized the foreignness although up to that time she had never heard a foreign language spoken, except the Latin of the Mass and that she knew there was no need to understand.

She had hoped that her mother would be calmed and silenced by being in the church, but she wasn't. Being in the church made her wilder. Or maybe that wasn't it, maybe she was acting the same way she had on the street and it just seemed worse in church.

Loretta's mother took her blouse off at the church door. She began raving about the men walking on the moon and saying it was an abomination, an abomination of desolation because the moon was desolate and the astronauts were abominable. She said that God should not allow it and she was here to punish God for his abomination and filthy, filthy, filthy shit and filthy piss and filthy filthy she was going to punish God.

The Altar Society ladies got scared, thinking she meant to do something to the Host. One of them went next door to the rectory to get Father Rafferty. He was watching the television, watching like everyone else, the sight of the men walking on the moon.

Father Rafferty came in with his red face and red dome of a bald head and said, "Now Margaret, now Margaret," and all she said was filthy filthy and that he was as filthy as the rest of them, particularly the astronauts, they were the filthiest of all, the moon had always been a clean place, she'd relied on that, but now they were going to make it filthy just like they were and how could the Blessed Mother look on and let it be, she was going to tear the Blessed Mother's eyes out to punish her, no not to punish her just so that she couldn't see. She was walking toward Our Lady's altar, she was starting to climb onto it, when Father Rafferty came behind her and pinned back her arms. And then the police came and took her away, and Father Rafferty told the Altar Society ladies not to say anything of what they'd seen and he told Martine Lavin to take Loretta home with her and her family for the night.

She had never before that night slept in a strange bed, since she and her mother didn't know anybody. Certainly not well enough to sleep in one of their guest beds. In all her life Loretta had never slept in any bed but her own. She and her mother had never taken a vacation, and so she had never so much as brushed her teeth in a sink other than the one where she saw her face each morning in front of the accustomed mirror, really the door to the medicine chest. She felt at a complete loss as to how to behave in the Lavins' house. Martine Lavin had driven her home and tried to straighten up the devastated kitchen. Her mother had pulled everything off the shelves, emptied bags of sugar and flour into the sink, saying they were filthy, she knew they had bugs in them, but the stuff didn't go down the drain, it stuck in an igloo shape in the sink, solidifying, to a texture like cement.

Her mother had left the water on and run to the church. Of course

Loretta had followed her, horrified at her mother's exposure. Going outside, she went beyond her rights. Loretta felt that whatever her mother did or said in their house was her right, really, she had paid for the house. "My hard-earned money," were the words she always used when Loretta failed to turn the light off in the bathroom or filled the bath too full. She earned her money as a saleswoman in a children's clothing store on Madison Avenue. Her job fed her bitterness. She hated her customers and their children, hated the effort she had to make at tailored suits and coiffure and manicure to be acceptable to them, hated their money and their carelessness and the easiness of their lives.

Loretta confused the term "hard-earned" with "hard labor," words that she'd heard in a movie that had frightened her. It was on the Late Show one Saturday night and her mother had fallen asleep watching it, not noticing Loretta, rapt and horrified, looking through the banister rails. The movie was called *I Was a Fugitive from a Chain Gang*, and it made visible one of her greatest fears, that someone could be punished, punished terribly, for something he hadn't done. But she understood why people thought he had, why they wanted to punish him. He had that look, that dark look around his eyes that made people feel in themselves the wish to punish. "That hangdog look," her mother said about her, ordering her out of the room sometimes just for having it. And she understood why her mother did it, why her mother said, "You make me feel hunted with that look." She saw the look in the mirror, saw it again in the Lavins' mirror, a mirror not surrounded by chrome but by white-painted wood with a light on the top that was softer than the one in her own bathroom, but not soft enough to hide the look that she knew would always make people, as it had her mother, want to be in a place away from her.

"Your father was always sickly," her mother would say resentfully whenever Loretta would get a cold or the flu. Only once she was nicer, when Loretta got the croup. Her mother seemed to like the flight from the steamy bathroom to the cold outside, she sang as she ran through the house, her coat open, holding Loretta as she ran, as if the shock of the cold was a delight to her, a particularly pleasant and imaginative game they were playing, not a desperate effort to restore a child's breath.

Cleaning Up

❈ ❈ ❈

Loretta couldn't sleep in the spare room in Martine Lavin's house. She lay much of the night wakeful on the cot beside the headless figure that Loretta supposed represented Martine's body. What was it called? A form? As the hours passed, Loretta grew more and more anxious about not sleeping, not about the wakefulness itself but about her fatigue the next morning. Because however tired she was she would have to go to school and school was in the world and the world required alertness. Particularly now when she knew all the children knew about her mother. They had heard it from their mothers, who had either seen it for themselves or heard it from their own friends. She had to keep alert to clarify the smudgy look around her eyes so that she would seem not like one of their potential victims, but a potential danger to them.

In the mornings, wakened by her own alarm clock, she would try to lie alert in her bed until Martine's husband Richard had gotten out of the bathroom. And then Martine would use it herself; she'd stay in there until she heard the baby cry. Then she would leave it and only then Loretta knew it was all right for her to use the bathroom.

The house where she'd lived with her mother hadn't had a shower, only a tub, she'd never taken a shower. She knew, somehow, that the Lavins would have thought it strange if they'd heard her taking a bath in the morning. Or even a bath at night. Their children took baths; it was a playful, time-consuming ritual, only in a minor way having to do with cleansing. Loretta felt that, in taking a bath, she was putting herself in the camp of the Lavins' children, suggesting she required the same brand or quality of care as they, suggesting she thought herself entitled to it.

But she didn't know how to use the shower. She didn't understand what was to be done with the curtain, whether it was to be put inside the tub or outside. And she knew she couldn't ask. She couldn't say the words, "How do you take a shower?" They sounded too pathetic, too deprived, simply, too odd. And she knew it was crucial for her not to sound any of those ways. So in the six weeks she lived with the Lavins, she washed only at the sink. She didn't know what they thought of that. But she could be sure that they had not assumed she was claiming any kind of false position as a child of the house.

Martine wanted Loretta to share her joy in her young children. Four of them, four sons, four blond boys, four perfect angels. John was five, Matthew four, Mark three, and Luke, the baby, seven months. Richard said maybe they'd quit when they'd gone through all the books of the Bible. "Of course Hebbukah might feel a little badly done by." "Or who knows, darling," Martine said, with a reminder, sunny, irrepressible, that all those babies had to do with something bodily between her husband and herself, "we might, one day, between us, actually produce a girl."

Loretta did not like children. She wished she could have been in a house without them, or at least without ones so near babyhood, so full of incessant hungers and incessantly expressed demands.

Of all of them she preferred John, because he was the oldest and the most self-sufficient. Martine remarked over and over what an independent child he was, but Loretta was so disgusted by the endless circle of need and response to need that made up the relations between Martine and her children that she couldn't muster anything like admiration for John's behavior. It seemed the only slightly less reprehensible behavior of someone who understood he had only to express the slightest wish to have it granted by his mother. A wish having nothing to do with whether or not he was capable of accomplishing what he wanted for himself. She judged those children for their weakness, and Martine for fostering this quality, which, she was sure, would serve them badly later on. She was sure that her mother was right in what she said, in what became, later, one of the few things Loretta could remember her saying, "You've got to look out for yourself in this world, there's no one looking out for you."

No one making you another beautiful breakfast if you didn't like your scrambled eggs, no one making you a placemat out of one of your laminated drawings, no one finding you a wooden napkin ring in the shape of your favorite animal, no one taking you on their lap to hear your side of the story when clearly your behavior had been abominable, no one singing you songs in Spanish or in French or teaching you the words of Mass in Latin, which no one used any more but which you would know because you were special children, and you must remember that, it must be marked.

❈ ❈ ❈

The Lavin family life made her feel choked and suffocated and disoriented, as if she were in a tepid whirlpool where distasteful objects were constantly being thrown up against her, in her way, then out of her grasp: placemats, napkin rings, foreign picture books. In the vortex she attached herself to one thing which of all the unbearable things seemed least unbearable to her: the five-year-old John.

For she knew she was expected to attach herself to something. People did. Or at least, they had to appear to be doing so. She understood perfectly well the currency of the transaction in which she was involved. She paid her board by seeming to be aware of the superiority of her new situation to her native one, by suggesting tender yearning and a poignant sense of loss, and always always, everything backlit by a constant sense of gratitude. It sickened her, but she had no choice. She had to have a place to live. Her house was empty. She was a child; she could not live in an empty house.

So she did a few things, as few, she calculated, as she could do and still pay her rent. She made clay animals with John. She rather enjoyed it. Not very much, but she didn't enjoy anything very much, and at least, shaping the clay with John she could be silent, or nearly. She enjoyed silence. And she almost allowed herself to admire the little boy's ability to be silent for quite a long time. Much more than most people. More than most adults. She almost liked him for it, but she saw the trap of that. She was an employee, a tenant, and it was another thing her mother had taught her: the boss is the boss and whatever he says, at the end of the day he gives you your money or he doesn't, whatever he likes, it's up to him. Loretta kept in her mind that she was a wage earner. And, like her mother, she considered herself overworked.

Martine could be said, Loretta knew, to work very hard. Yet there was nothing in her that conveyed the strained burdened sense that had been so much a part of Loretta's mother's posture. Martine sang while she worked; she played the record player while she cooked; she told Loretta it was a way of keeping up with the music. She'd majored in music in college, had played the piano, although she knew that because of the children these were not her years for "the instrument." At Christmastime, or teaching the children, yes. "But those days," she told Loretta, "of hours upon hours of practice, hours lost in, given up to music, those are in my past. Maybe in my future. My family is my present tense," she said, with a smile that Loretta turned against, feeling herself excluded from what the smile suggested, and glad to be.

After six weeks with the Lavins, Loretta was sent to her uncle and his wife in Hartford. They didn't want her and they made it clear that they had money and would send her to boarding school at the Madames of the Sacred Heart when she graduated from eighth grade the next year. She could spend her holidays with them. Christmas and Easter. Other arrangements would be made for summers, as their summers were for traveling. Loretta's uncle was eighteen years older than her mother; he'd just retired from Hartford Accident and Indemnity; they'd had no children, they'd saved for years for their new freedom, and they weren't going to let Loretta get in their way. Brother and sister had not been close; Loretta hardly knew her uncle, and she understood his position.

Her years in the Convent of the Sacred Heart were better than any that had gone before. She excelled in foreign languages, particularly Latin. The Latin teacher, Mother Perpetua, arranged for her to attend summer programs at the Sacred Heart Convent in Rome the first three years of high school. The last year, she was sent to a summer program at Harvard to learn Greek. "My smattering's not good enough for you," Mother Perpetua said. "You can do better than me."

She liked Mother Perpetua, although the other girls were afraid of her. She liked her white hands, and the unhealthy pallor of her face beneath her wimple, liked the fact that she didn't change out of her old habit when the younger sisters modified or discarded theirs. She admired Mother Perpetua's deliberate and unwavering impersonality. Unlike the other nuns, she didn't lapse into jokes or slip in some details of mothers, sisters, mischievous younger brothers, schoolgirl episodes, lovable teenage pranks. Loretta and Mother Perpetua met only in the high, unfinished rooms of a language which, being spoken by none of the living, being not at all part of the mess of daily life, was high and calm and beautifully inhuman.

Mother Perpetua sent her to Bryn Mawr for college. She graduated with highest honors in classics. From there she went to Berkeley where her thesis on Horatian odes was given highest honors as well. Jobs in Latin were scarce, the young had little interest in this language of the imperial-minded dead, so she was lucky, very lucky to be hired at

Peabody College, so near Boston, so near New York, arguably the most prestigious small college in America, where the tradition of the classics was honored even if the classes were nearly empty.

She had had no training in what might be called personal life, and so friendships with her colleagues were difficult for her. Friendship didn't tempt her; she mistrusted most people, and they bored her. She was fond of Mother Perpetua and she knew it would have pleased the nun if she'd joined the order. Loretta guessed that Mother Perpetua's thinking of her being part of the community was the one fantasy, the one indulgence she'd allowed herself in a life made up of strict self-discipline. But Loretta knew the convent, living in a circle of women, even, as the life was constituted now, living in apartments in university towns or in the poorer parts of cities, was impossible for her.

She learned that there was one connection that was possible. She craved the bodies of men. Not their love or even their attention, or not the kind of attention that could go on over time. What she wanted was an unclean place she had to travel to, treasured, a place of truth, the other side of the light high truthfulness of the Latin language, of the surgical precision of the Horatian line. This low dark place pleased her, made her smile, secretly, because it itself was secret and a home to her in a way no home had ever been. It pleased her because it was such a transgression to invest in this place the word "home." She knew what she thought of when she thought of the word "home," and she compared it with what came to other people's minds: dining tables covered with rich foods, soft furniture, a predictable cast of characters — mom, pop, brother, sis, grandma, gramps. Her idea of home was silent and anonymous, populated only by furtive creatures taken up only with their own drives, frozen in the postures of their striving toward each other, toward satiation and the oblivion to which it would inevitably lead.

The darkness that she knew was in and around her eyes, the darkness that her mother saw and hated, that made her mother drive her from the room, was the sign of her true homeland, and the sign by which she could be recognized by other inhabitants. She was small and dressed, as befit the academic fashion beginning with the mid-seventies, almost entirely in black: close-fitting but unrevealing knits, overlarge shoes or boots that made a joke, a parody of her smallness.

In the déclassé bars where she liked to go, no one had college degrees and Horace was the name of somebody's cracked uncle. They played Kenny Loggins and Kenny Rogers on the jukebox, and she stood out among the women because of her short hair and boyish clothing. She gave the signal to these men, who at first could not understand her, that she might be easily approached. She might have been in danger, but she had known danger once, with her mother, and she knew its smell. Nothing bad had ever happened to her at the hands of one of these men, or in their beds, the motel beds where they met for what it was they both knew they wanted, leaving an hour, two hours later, not meeting again. Thirty years earlier this kind of behavior might, if it were found out, cause a kind of nontenurable scandal, but by the 80s such activities were commonplace in the academy, the ordinary fare of faculty dining-table talk, and she risked nothing. Most of the people who would judge her fitness to be among them were men, and although she was careful not to approach them physically or allow herself to be approached, she knew that she suggested to them an allure far from their comfortable wives, women of large amber beads and madrigal groups and Birkenstock sandals. And so, craving what they only guessed at, they would want to keep her close to them. So that, if ever, or in case... Meanwhile she attended their dinner parties, and gave a couple a year of her own, and produced work that earned their respect, that they couldn't ignore (for fear of lawsuit). She had, she believed, everything she wanted. She had chosen what she wanted in a life.

She had seen his name first on the roster. It had jumped out at her "John Lavin." An intrusion, an eruption, a penetration into the matte backdrop of her life, of the thunderous, and violent, unmanageable past. In three days, the days between the first sight of his name on the roster and the first meeting of the class, she allowed the form of the intrusion, the propulsion, to recede. John Lavin was, after all, not an uncommon name, it was unlikely that it would be he.

She knew everything when she saw him seated at the seminar table — one of only six students in a course on Horace in the original Latin — the only stranger in class, the rest having been brought to this rare level of proficiency by Loretta herself. It was not his face she saw but a boyish version of Martine, the same thin, light gold curls, the skin, milky white with an undertone of bluing, transformed only a little by a residual, not yet manly beard. When she saw the slope of his shoulders as he bent over his notebook, the combination he had learned from his mother of uprightness yet devotion to a task, the shoulders of a supplicant who would never fully abandon himself to his petition, when she saw the shape of his hands, the thumbnail, more recessive than the ordinary, heard the hesitation when she asked them for a sight translation and he paused after what she understood was a false semblance of puzzlement or frustration, when he put his hands on his head, a girlish gesture, that she had seen his mother perform, especially if she knew herself to be in the range of her husband's appreciation — she knew there was no doubt.

For a brief while she wondered if he knew her connection to his life. But her name — Moran — was no more unusual than his. And she had disappeared entirely from the life, not only of his family, but of the parish. Martine had for several years sent copies of a Christmas letter to her at her uncle's address. "John has made us all proud playing Bach solos at his school recital. Mark, our athlete, continues to astound us all as the perfect shortstop. Luke began by playing with his Daddy's movie camera and did what we think of as the Lavin version of *A Child's Christmas in Wales* — it had us all in stitches. Matt loves to garden, and seems able to make anything grow."

But she had last seen them thirteen years ago, and after many years of nonresponsiveness, Martine had stopped writing. Loretta wondered if Martine had ever talked to the children about her time with them. Which would have meant, of course, that she had talked to them about Loretta's mother, the "scandal," the "performance." It was then that her bitter protective heart contracted to a point under the thin bones of her chest. "How dare they?" were the only words that came into her mind. "How dare they speak of her?" Her mother had made a performance of it, insisted on an audience, insisted upon being watched, and, then, of course, spoken of. It was then that she was steeped in her dark pool of unforgiveness that spilled over onto everyone. Her mother should have kept herself hidden. And she, herself, Loretta, thirteen years old, what should she have done? The torrent of her mother's madness was too strong for her, a hurricane of disorder and discreet force. And yet, in the thousand times when she replayed the scene, focusing on her non-silence, then her timid, pitiful, half whimpers of suggestions, "Mama, go in the house, mama lie down, mama don't go outside," it was herself she hated, for her weakness, and her failure to think boldly or at all.

She began to realize that he didn't know that she had a connection to his past. And with that understanding grew the struggle in her mind. Should she deal with him justly, a gifted first-year student with a passion for the Latin language, and attend to him as his gifts deserved, as she would any other gifted young man in his place. Or should she reveal their connection and say that she was unable to work with him, he should find someone else. But there was nothing to justify that; the connection would seem too weak, too tentative, too far in the past, and then she would have to bring her mother and her mother's fate to light. Her mother, whom she went months without thinking of, still in the hospital in Central Islip where she'd been brought fifteen years before, whom she had not seen after that, not even once, her mother whom the doctors agreed was too far gone, even, for de-institutionalization. And that had been a blessing, if not for her mother, Loretta knew, then for herself; it allowed her to think she was right not to think of seeing her mother again. There was no real mercy for her mother but the mercy of death.

She tried to behave justly or at least professionally, but the darkness underneath the thin bones of her breast sharpened, then hardened to a solid point. John Lavin would be punished. She would punish him. She would punish him in his place as representative of the people of the parish. And in her mother's name.

He made it easy for her, he made it easy by being completely himself, blond, quiet, with a series of identical Bic pens clipped to the pocket of his short-sleeved shirt, always some variety of blue (to match his eyes?), some plain, some with a white stripe, or a yellow. His translations were always on time and always nearly perfect, yet not so perfect as to render them unlovable: there were one or two words crossed out, never an infelicity, but occasionally a slight swerving away from the most desirable nuance, the word's best, truest sense.

And he helped by the way he looked at her, adoring, and yet with a calmness none of the others, particularly the young men, could muster. It was only the young men she gave her attention to; the young women, reminding her too sickeningly or too pathetically of herself, were never candidates for her full regard, with their implied dreams of palhood, confidences exchanged, cuddle-ups under quilts with the inevitable redolence of domestication.

Sometimes he came carrying an instrument in a small black case. She had heard a classmate ask which instrument it was and he said, simply, "oboe" with the confident person's lack of need for further explanation.

And yet, because, after all she was his teacher and possessed of a knowledge and accomplishment he clearly valued, because she was female and young and small of stature, with a hint of the fashionable in her close to the skull hair, the multiple silver studs in each of her ear-lobes, she knew she could, if she chose, exercise what all this had given her: the power to intrigue him, John Lavin, a young heterosexual man.

At first, she was undecided as to what her path might be. Would she keep him at arm's length, be hypercritical, hyper-demanding, and in the end order sex from him as her due, as a privilege he ought to think of himself as fortunate in having been asked to exercise? Or should she start this way and gradually soften, suggesting that everyone who had preceded him had been a disappointment and that he, only he, had fulfilled the promise which made her feel less futile, less alone.

She had no desire for him. He was all transparency, there was no place that was fecund or capable of the dense growth that was the only environment in which desire and then satisfaction could, for her, take root. His lightness was repulsive to her. But taking the place of a dark-ness emanating from him was the sense of stain she would impose from her own body onto his, his blondness, his fairness, his quiet sense of his own worth, his embodiment of the notion of right doing, of having got things straight once and for all and living that way, with no sense of any future need of emendation fueled her purpose. A pur-pose not sexual in its flavor but which, she knew, could only be worked out on the unused, pure body of this boy. She would approach him and leave him unfresh; his sweet skin would nevermore be lovable in quite the same way. The vessel of dreams would be, not only scratched and flawed, but its surface invaded with a growth.

She knew it would be easy, but circumstances made it easier still. He told her that the next year he was going to Rome, taking a year off to study with his oboe teacher, who had relocated there.

"Well, then," she said, handing him his final paper, on the shape of the Horatian line, which she had graded A+, "Your grade's in, I have no more power over you, I'd like you to join me for dinner, so I can wish you bon voyage, and congratulate you for your first-rate work."

John Lavin blushed. The boy is blushing, she said to herself, seeing his heart, the red tight muscle in the center of his chest, overflowing with blood from the presence of — what, she wondered — astonishment, embarrassment, desire, shamed desire, gratitude, the apprehension of a pleasure?

At dinner, in the town's best restaurant, which offered oversmall portions of pasta or fish, she insisted that he talk about his family. He was glad to, she could see the pleasure, greater than the one with which he approached his meal, at the prospect of opening up his family's life to her.

"I guess I'm proudest of my mother," he said. "She was trained as a musician, but she really gave it up for us. She went back and got a social work degree, she's working in the hospice movement. I mean, she does what I think of as the hardest thing in the world. She's with dying children and their families."

"My father works in insurance, but I don't think that's really where his heart is. But he had all of us to support, and he was great about it."

Loretta realized she never knew what Richard Lavin had done, she had never cared; he was hardly present, only as Martine's husband, or the children's father; for himself, he was nothing.

"His real love is woodworking, that's what makes him happy. He's set up an amazing workshop in the basement. And my mom's even got him to learn the recorder. I have three younger brothers, and we have a family recorder group. My mother really has to lean on the younger ones to practice. I'm the only one she didn't have to force, but everyone's glad she did it, because we always have our music. I'm the most grateful to her, she gave me my music, what an incredible gift. But we're really a happy family, I think it's because my mother's so incredible. All my brothers feel good about themselves. My brother Luke's into acting, Matt's a great organic gardener, I sometimes think Mark thinks of nothing but soccer, but my mother says I should get off his case. He's the least musical of us all.

"Sometimes I feel bad about my mother's music. She has a lot of talent as a pianist, but it's been so long since she's practiced. Sometimes I'd try to get her out of the kitchen to practice, but she'd just laugh at me, and say she'd made her choices, and she knew they were right."

❖ ❖ ❖

Loretta saw the kitchen. She would have liked to ask him if the kitchen had changed, but of course she knew she couldn't. She saw the shower that she was afraid to use, and the cot she slept in in the sewing room, and the form in the shape of Martine's body.

Then she saw her mother in the church, and what she imagined was the look on Martine's face, although she'd allowed herself to see nothing when her mother was doing what she did. But it was Martine who came over afterwards, when her mother was taken away, came to where she was standing near Our Lady's altar, which her mother had attempted to destroy. She leaned down towards Loretta, putting her arms around her shoulders. And, meeting Martine's eyes, Loretta didn't know what she needed to find there but she knew it had to be exactly the right thing.

What she saw was relief. She saw that Martine was relieved that it was Loretta's mother who had done this thing and not Martine and not anyone connected to her. And Loretta knew that Martine believed that because she'd seen it up close, but not so close that it had touched her, that she'd been spared.

But she had not been. Loretta would see to that now.

He accepted her invitation to come back to the apartment. She told him to sit on the couch while she made coffee.

In the kitchen, she put the coffee into the espresso pot and lit the flame. Then she walked into the living room. He was sitting with his eyes closed, his hands folded at the top of his head. She ran the top of her thumb around the outline of his lips. She allowed him to initiate the kiss, then she took over.

He was overwhelmed by his own ardor, and for a moment the simplicity of what he was so visibly experiencing made her want to send him home. But she thought of his mother's face, and of her mother's — wild, defeated — her mother whom she had not seen again after that day. Because of this she did not give in to her impulse to end the whole thing right there. She made herself go on.

She took his hand and led him, like a child into the bedroom. He seemed willing to leave everything up to her. She unbuckled his black belt and pulled his jeans down but did not take them off completely. She left his shoes on but kicked off her own. She took off her skirt and panty hose and underpants. She unhooked her bra but did not take it off and she kept her shirt on. She climbed on top of him. It was important to her that she felt she was doing something to him, that nothing was being done to her. It was she who was planting the seed, a seed which, without her might never have taken root in the pure soil that could have been his understanding of the world. He would know now that it was not a sure thing, not a guarantee that he would remain spared. That the darkness that invaded Loretta's mother and taken her over and made her do shameful things, a darkness stronger than anything that could be fought against, was not something to which he was impervious. And if he knew this was true of himself, he would know it was true of the people connected to him. Perhaps he might think there were people in the world who were impervious, who were safe. But he would understand that they were people very unlike himself, so unlike himself as to be unrecognizable.

As she expected, it was over quickly. So quickly that she ought not have been surprised at the speed and completeness of his transition from abandonment to shamed regret. She put on her skirt, leaving her panty hose in a coiled lump at the side of the bed. He didn't know what to do about covering himself.

"I haven't done this before," he said.

"Well, you have now," she said, stepping into her underpants.

She could smell the coffee, which had boiled over, she imagined the mess that had been made. She had stopped thinking of him. She was thinking of how angry it would make her to clean up the coffee which would have spattered all over the white surface of the stove, maybe onto the walls and floor, that the pot would be ruined, that the kitchen would be full of the dark, bitter, ruined smell of burnt coffee for days, perhaps.

"It's time you left," she said, and he obeyed her.

She was glad of his obedience. It made her feel that she had done her job and done it well.

As she wiped the brown spots from the stove, the walls, the floor, imagining all the time what he might be doing as she scrubbed, she knew that she was feeling something like what others might call happiness.

She thought it was unlikely that he would say anything of what had happened to his mother, and too bad she could say nothing to hers.

🌿 *La Lloradora*

LOIS GOULD

Excerpted from *La Presidenta*

The story is incredible, but it happened, and perhaps not once but many times, with different actors in different locales. It contains the perfect cipher of an unreal epoch; it is like the reflection of a dream or like that dream-within-the-drama we see in Hamlet. *The mourner was not Perón and the blond doll was not the woman Eva Duarte, but neither was Perón Perón, nor was Eva Eva. They were, rather, unknown individuals — or anonymous ones whose secret names and true faces we do not know — who acted out, for the credulous love of the lower middle classes, a crass mythology.*

El Simulacro
Jorge Luis Borges

IT WAS EARLY AFTERNOON in the village of Montaraz. The child María Rosa, eight years old, sat playing on the dirt floor with her new doll, a fine lady with soft black curls and a long red gauze skirt; a doll whose shiny black eyes snapped shut with a little click when she lay on her back. Rosa's brother Chepito lay watching her from his narrow cot; the two older girls napped fitfully, their limbs entangled on the straw mattress in the corner. Rosa was scolding the doll for dragging its dress in the dirt while strolling across the village square. Stupid Rósula the child said, frowning, I warned you not to parade before those boys! So they stare at you and make remarks; for this you spoil a beautiful dress — *puta!* — slut, fool, tramp. Chepito buried his head in his mattress stifling a laugh.

6 5

The children did not stir when they heard the voice of their father, José Andújar, calling their mother from the dirt path beyond the courtyard. Mama had said they must let him rest awhile after his long journey. Every week she said this, for every week José Andújar returned to them after the same long journey. Rosa whispered to Chepito, Do you think he has brought us chocolate?

Rosa was listening intently to the voices of her parents behind the brown curtain. She thought they might be arguing, though she knew their mama never scolded José Andújar the way other mothers in Montaraz scolded their husbands. The voice of Juana Ibáñez poured like sweet cream when she spoke to Papa, and she laughed often, even when he was not saying a joke, even when she was asking for something very important. Rosa always sat very still during Papa's visits; her eyes, big and dark in the thin little face, followed every gesture. It was María Rosa who knew the exact moment, just before Papa left in the morning, when he would put the money in the red clay jar above the stove. She could hear the crackling of the bills from her cot on the other side of the curtain.

José Andújar, sometimes called Pepe or Pepillo, thought of himself as a good man. He worked hard in the cement *factoría* of Don José Delgado; soon he would be made a foreman, and his wife and children in San Marcos would lack for nothing. As for his other little family in Montaraz, was he not as good to them as could be expected? Better, he often told himself, than most men he knew in similar circumstance. Had he not allowed Juana Ibáñez to use his name for the children's baptismal certificates, despite the trouble such an irregularity entailed, not to mention the additional contribution he had had to make to the church? Was he not, furthermore, entirely generous with money for these children, whose rope sandals were replaced almost as regularly as the leather ones of his own family? The good Lord knew it was not easy to satisfy most women; he had to admit that at least Juana Ibáñez did not complain much. In truth, he did not always begrudge her the money.

And she had borne him four healthy bastards. The older girls were growing round and soft like their mother; the boy Chepito was small for his age, with quick furtive eyes and a slight brown body that moved in spurts like a rabbit. José's hopes were not high for Chepito.

Even now he could tell that the best of the litter was Rosa, the youngest, his little field mouse. She had eyes like his own, fierce with life-hunger, and her small hard body, so unlike that of her mother and sisters, reminded him of the first girls of his youth, the ones who could run almost as fast as he, whose little pulses beat wildly in their delicate throats when they marched holding hands across the yard, their eyes searching the corners for boys watching them. He remembered one of these girls, a light-haired one with bright darting eyes; her name too had been Rosa. He had lusted for her in her short gray school uniform and her long white socks; he remembered still his restless dreams about her white legs, the imaginings of her blond pubic triangle, an impossibly beautiful thing that in his dreams he touched with wondering fingers and found silken like the belly of his dog. Now his daughter Rosa was growing up, she too would have such silken hair there; he often imagined it. Sometimes in San Marcos, lying in bed, José Andújar would rest his hand between the large moist thighs of his sleeping wife Elena and imagine the white buttocks of his youngest bastard daughter in Montaraz.

Early one Friday José came to visit his second family in Montaraz, and found Rosa kneeling beside the well in the dirt courtyard. Rusty streaks ran down her legs from the dust and the well water. She was perspiring, wisps of her hair pasted to her forehead and flushed cheeks, and she wore only a *camisa* of thin gauze, which lay flat against her body like a wet transparent veil. For a long moment he stood motionless, holding his breath, staring at her pale wet skin in the sunlight, at her slender waist, her thin legs too long for the small narrow torso, like a baby she-mule, a *burrita*. He crept up behind her and gathered her up into his arms, burying his head into her warm little chest, inhaling her. Papa! she shrieked, throwing her arms around him, laughing. Papa! He kissed her warm neck, her chest, her shoulders; he tossed her high into the air and caught her as she squealed with fright and pleasure. He tossed her again; again she squealed. Papa! Finally he wrapped her tight in his arms and carried her into the house, where he sank clumsily into a chair, still holding her tight. She began to wriggle against him then, crying now, Papa, let me go! But now he could not, would not let her go, pretending to tease her. I cannot, look, you are locked in, I have lost the key. Then he held her still with only one hand and with the other began to stroke her, saying, Sst, my little one

Rósula — my little Rosa — be still and I will tell you a fine story about when your Papa was a boy, playing so with a little girl named Rosa, a little white *burrita* like you —

Was she so smart? Rosa interjected. Did she have dolls?

Dolls, yes. José Andújar's hand went on stroking his daughter's back, gently squeezing her arms, her legs. Rósula, he murmured, burying his face in her neck, a little smart one just like you.

Don't, Papa, the child cried, you are hurting —

Sst, *niña*, he said, lie here softly in my arms.

But —

Sst. Then José Andújar lifted his daughter and carried her gently to Mama's bed, where he lay beside her, pressing against her with his whole body. Papa, don't, she whispered, and the pleasure in her voice was gone; only the fright was there. Sst! he commanded, harshly now, and slapped her hard across the mouth. She raised her hand to stop the shock of it; he caught the hand and kissed it, then gently stroked her arm, her chest, her small flat belly. Finally he turned her over, entering her hard and swift from behind, exclaiming Ah, ahh. She did not cry out again.

When he had finished he carried her back outside to the well and washed her gently with the harsh soap. Then he dressed her in clean underclothes and a white dress. Rósula, he said softly, Papa loves thee — *te quiero*. She said nothing. He slapped her again, not quite so hard this time, saying, Answer when your Papa talks to you. *Te quiero*, Papá, she answered.

María Rosa woke crying on the Saturday morning after this ordinary Friday, she would not say why. Perhaps it was only that she had forgotten to show Papa the new doll with the red gauze dress that Mama's new boarder, Señor Valdés, had bought for her in Corrientes. Next time you can show him, Juana Ibáñez said, studying her with a frown of puzzlement. Go back to sleep.

But the following Friday José Andújar did not come.

Señor López Figueroa was not the first of Mama's boarders to ask for a small kiss in appreciation for the fancy doll. María Rosa had never been so impolite as to refuse. She gave the kiss freely, and did not protest when they added a squeeze or pinch; nor did she pull away when they tumbled her into their laps. As a rule, Mama was in the room when these displays of affection occurred. She would wear a fixed faraway look, not quite approving, but surely not disapproving; the look of a well-trained accomplice who understands well the consequences of dissent. As it is said, one who sees much, yet says little, is one who knows which way the shadows move.

After a moment, Mama would ask with some impatience whether Rosa had forgotten to peel the potatoes for the stew, or to sweep and water the dirt courtyard. Rosa would say no or yes, Mama, gently extricating herself from the embrace of Señor García or Señor Valdés, and for his part the gentleman would have no reason to feel rebuffed.

But none of the boarders had ever forced his attentions on Rosa when her mother was not present. So the child was not especially concerned on this Sunday afternoon when Chepito went with his sisters to the social club dance, and Mama stopped at the church to visit the new baby of Señora Chavez, leaving Rosa alone in bed with a sour stomach from too much spice in last night's supper. Señor López Figueroa arrived earlier than usual. *Qué pobrecita!* he said solicitously, perching heavily on the edge of her narrow cot, and began to stroke her feverish forehead, asking if she were not too warm with such a thick blanket. She said nothing when he removed it and began to stroke her neck and shoulders with a cool soft cloth soaked in alcohol. Roll over, little one, so that I can bathe your back he said, and she obeyed. Soon he had her thin *camisa* rolled up to her shoulders, and was rubbing the cloth up and down her slender body; the cloth was cool and soothing, and made her feel drowsy, so that she barely heard him say, Now turn again; I must bathe the other side. When she did not respond, he turned her over himself. Then for a moment she felt nothing, which made her open her eyes. Señor López Figueroa was staring at her with a glazed expression, his mouth hung in a great O beneath the heavy black rope of a mustache; he held the dripping cloth now in one hand; with the other he was untying the belt of his trousers Something about his face frightened her, so that she tried to sit up crying, *Mama*, but he said in a sudden rough voice, pushing her back, be still, I have not hurt you. You must stop your mouth, do you hear? She whimpered and lay back. Look, he said, more gently, my cloth will make you feel nice all over, close your eyes. Rosa closed her eyes, squeezing tears. He rubbed her all over with the wet cloth, and then without it. He put the tip of himself between her legs and squeezed the tender nipples of her breasts with his rough fingers. She did not cry out again, although he hurt her very much. When it was over, he wet the cloth and bathed her again, pulling her *camisa* down like a curtain over her, and then the blanket on top as though to cover what he had done. Finally he kissed her forehead, whispering her name in a strange thick voice. She made no sound.

The following week Señor López Figueroa brought the doll with a black velvet dress and white ruffled petticoats, the most beautiful doll María Rosa had ever seen. He also brought a box of fine chocolates for Chepito, a red blouse each for Lola and Catuja, and for Mama a shawl of lace the color of a flamingo.

Rosa had said nothing to her mama about the incident, but Juana Ibáñez had wise eyes behind her round wire spectacles, and several days after the doll with the velvet dress and the other gifts, she suggested to Señor López Figueroa that he look for a larger room in a boarding house nearer the cement works. He replied that he was very satisfied with his present arrangement, and was prepared if necessary to pay a small increase in his rent. Later, Mama asked Rosa's opinion, a thing she had never done before, and Rosa looked solemnly into her mama's eyes and replied in a dreamy flat voice, Often I wish we could have a nice house near La Plata, a house with a real stone floor. Don't you agree, Mama?

For an instant Juana Ibáñez stared at her child, uncomprehending. Then she burst into tears.

The following afternoon Juana Ibáñez told Señor López Figueroa that she had been planning to move her family to a better house near La Plata, but that they would be willing to have him there as a boarder at double his present rent. Otherwise — She broke off abruptly with an apologetic shrug. Señor López Figueroa licked the bottom of his black mustache with a nervous tongue. Señora Ibáñez began again. My youngest daughter, she said, measuring the words carefully, has not been feeling well. We have the hope that her health will improve in a better house nearer the water, where the street is paved and there is not so much dust in the air.

Señor López Figueroa coughed. I am indeed sorry to hear this, Señora. Under the circumstances I will be happy to pay the increased rent. And if ... I can help in any way with the expenses of moving, please permit me to do so.

Juana Ibáñez gave a slight nod. We are grateful for your kindness, Señor, she said in an even tone.

One week later the family moved to a three-room house near La Plata. It had a real stone floor and thick walls between the rooms, reaching all the way to the ceiling. There was a fig tree in the courtyard, the roof was sound, and Juana Ibáñez sang the words of a tango as she pumped the rusty water from the cistern for her bath. The boarder Señor López Figueroa continued to come early Sunday afternoons, but he never again found Rosa at home alone. Often, however, he found Juana Ibáñez alone, and she always did her best to make him comfortable.

María Rosa entered the little chapel and knelt on the worn padded bar before the statue of La Lloradora, the *Virgen* who weeps. Rosa bowed her head quickly, not permitting herself to look just yet at the beauty of La Lloradora's face, or her gorgeous clothes. The statue stood in a circle of golden light, wearing her gown of white lace, with loops as thick as those on top of wedding cakes. Pinned to the gown were all her jewels that people who adored her had brought as gifts over the centuries: tiny candy-colored pins and medals set with real rubies and emeralds, stones that peered out from the holes in the lace like wise eyes winking in a face of sorrow. This lace, those very jewels, danced at night in the darkness of Rosa's dreams. Always in the dreams Rosa herself wore the gown, with La Lloradora's heavy gold cross on a long chain around her white neck, the medals and jewels scattered across her bosom, the gold letters spelling ESPERANZA on a scarlet sash at her waist. In the dreams she saw herself gazing at her own gold-and-scarlet image in a big mirror with a splendid frame. Last night La Lloradora had stood behind her in the dream, gazing in the same mirror. Rosa had stood very still with her eyes downcast, while La Lloradora leaned over whispering in her ear. Rosa looked up and saw La Lloradora holding out her great high crown with the long rays that shot out from its center like beams of the sun, ending in little stars like the points of magic wands. La Lloradora had taken the crown from her own head and held it out for Rosa to try on. *No!* Rosa had cried, horrified in the dream, knowing a terrible thing would happen. But La Lloradora kept nodding and smiling, *Sí.* Without her crown, she looked just like a fancy nun or a bride, with the lace mantilla covering all her hair, the lace curling down over her neck and shoulders like white smoke or the hair of an angel; and the silver tears that came out of the statue's eyes shone on her face in the dream, just like glass jewels attached to her skin, so they could never fall. The round tears dived in the corners of her beautiful black eyes and the long ones twinkled on her ivory cheeks like a magic rash, a condition that broke out from her everlasting grief, so that the rash could never go away.

Rosa was sure her dreams were serious sin, like evil thoughts; she would not confess them even to the statue itself, but would instead kneel before it trying to pray, saying a whole rosary and watching the tiny flames of other people's prayer candles, each one flickering in its little red glass like a devil's tongue whispering her dreams to God. There were not enough beads in the rosary, not enough *Salve Marías* to wash away a sin of dreaming that La Lloradora wore Hollywood lipstick, that under her mantilla streamed hair like that of a star of the cinema, hair that glowed and sparkled like the red-gold flames of votive candles, hair that burst above her gleaming naked shoulders while she danced in the gown of white lace. Oh, serious sin, to imagine La Lloradora taking off her crown of heaven and placing its shower of sunbeams and exploding gold stars on the sinful head of Rosa Andújar. It was bad enough when Catuja had said that Santa Ana, before she was pregnant with the *Madre de Dios*, was the image of Persuasión duPre, an *estrella* of the cinema; for did she not have exactly those big round sad foreign eyes and the dark swollen lips that looked like kisses? La Lloradora's lips were full and very dark too with shining paint, but of course it wasn't Hollywood lipstick; serious sin to picture La Lloradora looking in a compact mirror painting her beautiful holy virgin mouth with a stick of scarlet wax.

Rosa looked up only high enough to see La Lloradora's slender white hand holding its pearl rosary as though it were nothing but a fancy necklace, a strand of such gorgeous expensive pearls as the husband would give his rich spoiled wife in a movie where the bedroom was all white satin with flowers in a big glass bowl, and the husband was in love with somebody else. The wife would hold the necklace he gave her, just like that, dangling it between the thumb and finger as if she didn't care at all about such things unless he really loved only her.

Rosa now threaded her own rosary in that way, between her two fingers, and tried to practice La Lloradora's expression of divine sadness, without looking all the way up at the face of the statue. She wanted to make her eyes show perfect grief, which was not like feeling poor and sad, or wishing to live inside of a movie instead of here where everything was ugly gray except La Lloradora. Perfect grief was only two tiny lines between the eyebrows, not a real frown that would make the eyes turn down or the ends of the mouth, nothing in the eyes that shone with crystal tears except sadness for somebody else, not for yourself. In perfect grief, La Lloradora's eyes made you think that a little smile lived behind the tears. The smile was ESPE-RANZA. If La Lloradora cried for Rosa's sadness, then maybe the inside smile meant the dream was not serious sin after all. Maybe it meant something magic instead, a miracle like the tears that grew in her cheeks without falling. *Salve María*, Rosa whispered. Four more *Salve Marías* and then ten Lord's Prayers. I have a sin to confess, evil thoughts. La Lloradora's tear-filled eyes were shining, shining, and her lips so red. I have a sin....

· Naturally she did not hear the padre's quiet footsteps on the stone floor behind her; she never did. All the girls knew that he often came to stand outside the iron gate of La Lloradora's chapel when they knelt there; it was a thing they laughed about, it was a joke about whether he came because of their prayers, or because he too was in love with the statue, or because he liked to see the little girls kneeling down with their bare legs behind them on the padded bar, while they stole guilty wishing looks at La Lloradora's splendor. Father Padrón was old but still everyone in the town whispered about things he did to the girls who went to the nuns' school, not to the nuns themselves because they were too ugly, and their lips were so pale. But what happened when a girl was sent in to him for chastisement? Sometimes he hit her, but mostly he kissed her too, and touched her all over between hitting. Catuja didn't believe it but Lola who went to the nuns' school swore it was true. And Rosa knew such things, though she was the smallest.

Rosa, the padre whispered now. Rósula....

She turned a little. *Sí, mi padre.*

The fiesta of *purificación* is coming. Would you like to be *la reina* — queen of the fiesta? If you are a good *niñita* and do as I tell you. *If you want it enough —*

Rosa closed her eyes tight and saw La Lloradora standing on the platform in the center of the Plaza del 16 Enero, with the dancers and musicians in a whirl around her. The other statues bobbed up and down like excited children — a blur of saints and *monstruos*, of skeletons and animals, flowers and balloons of every color, white candles tall as men, and paper ribbons flying in the air like storms of bright rain. She sighed, a piteous sound filled with the broken ends of wishes. She tried to swallow. *La reina?* she whispered. Even if I have not yet twelve years?

Even so, whispered the padre, with a wink of sly mischief. You will march beside the statue with your white candle, so —

Rosa turned a little more, studying him.

Only if you do as I tell you, he whispered. *Niñita ... angelita....* Now she heard the heat in his voice; his breath came too fast; it was a sound she well knew. If you want it enough — *Te quiero, Rosa.*

The tears slid out of the sides of Rosa's eyes. Oh, it is not fair —

So? said the padre with a voice of righteous anger. Where is the sweet red smile of *la reina?* La Lloradorita — my little *Virgen* who weeps?

Hola, Señora Ibáñez. Father Padrón flashed his benevolent smile, even though she had interrupted him in his study. *Permiso!* She murmured her apology, making no move either forward or back. But you have not come to make confession again, since Saturday? He rose from his high-backed chair without beckoning her. No, padre. Señora Ibáñez lowered her eyes, though not so far that she could not watch his glance as it shifted. But ... I have come to you for help. My daughter Rosa —

The padre's eyes clouded at once, as though another person had drawn the confessional curtain between them. Rosa, he said uncertainly, testing the name upon his lips in the way one shows a great effort to remember. The youngest — ?

Juana Ibáñez did not reply; she would permit him the small evasion, but without comfort. At the same time she would not suggest that by now one knew how little trouble this padre with the face of a dry apple had in distinguishing the daughters of the village one from another.

I have come to you for help, she said again, simply, taking care that none of the words should bear more weight than was prudent. Her black eyes, without blinking, kept the boldness of her meaning well hidden. Then too she had worn the new spectacles with round silver frames, which her daughters said gave her the look of a serious plump *viscacha,* that most thoughtful small beast of the desert plain, whose secrets are as well guarded as its dangerous underground cave, into which a horse or a man may stumble at his peril. There were seldom tears in the wise *viscacha* eyes of Juana Ibáñez.

What troubles the child? asked the padre, his voice now tinged with the impatience of a busy man. He gestured with his glance at the papers on his big desk, at the clock on the wall, the fat black pen in his hand, the ink stain on his middle finger. A frown now made two dark creases between his heavy brows.

'Stá *enferma*, said Juana Ibáñez, slowly drawing her fingers with their swollen knuckles together upon her belly, joining them like the laces of a corset. The child is — There was a pause, a small one, to conserve the strength for what had to be spoken. Puffed up, she said at last. She looks . . . *encinta*. Like one who is pregnant. But I am certain she cannot be.

The priest's expression did not change, though his round pink head now shook like that of a foreigner struggling to understand a native dialect. She swells too quickly, the woman went on, hurrying now. And there is always blood —

You have taken her to the doctor?

No, said Juana Ibáñez, in a whisper of shame. If she should be *encinta* — my daughter —

If — ?

She has not even twelve years of age! the woman cried. Then she drew a breath, sharp as a sword. I have come, she said again with care, to you. *Mi padre.*

Father Padrón made a sudden gesture with his hands, as though to shoo the plump *viscacha* out of his sacred house, to make her disappear into the ground hole from where she had come. You must — he began, moving now from behind his desk, looming before her like a black cloud. If the condition — He broke off, staring at the woman. Not twelve years of age? he echoed, and fell silent.

Juana Ibáñez remained very still, allowing only the dark bulk of her presence in his whitewashed cell to disturb the peace of Father Padrón.

Then he was speaking again, now in another voice, the smooth familiar one that she heard on Sundays as it poured from the high stone *púlpito* of the little church. It was the voice with which he gave *esperanza* — a sweetness of hope to mix well with their bitterness and their fear of God the Father. You have heard, he was saying softly, the tale of Camila La Cruz, another girl of not twelve years ... do they speak of her trial still in this province?

Sí, padre, whispered Juana Ibáñez, crossing herself. She felt a fear stirring in her body like a fever chill; it made her hesitate, as though a string of knots were tied to her words. That Camila, she stammered, who was....

The priest nodded. *Sí,* that one. He spoke still in the soft voice. That one who was put to death, *encinta* — carrying her unborn child. As he spoke the last words, he turned abruptly in his chair, as though startled by a sound outside the door. Juana Ibáñez forced herself to murmur, The padre — ?

Sí, that Camila, the priest went on, pretending to search a dim memory. Was she not one who accused the padre of her village? Did she not swear it was he — ?

No hay de qué! exclaimed Juana Ibáñez. Do not speak of it! Her broad, placid face had turned white as a troubled moon. She seemed to shrink from him, swaying as though she might fall backward against the door. Father Padrón nodded again, and smiled the kind smile. Well, he breathed, a long time ago, such barbarities. But now your daughter. His crumpled face creased further with a look of concern. Your little Rosa....

In truth, my Rosa is *ill,* padre, protested Juana Ibáñez, struggling now to keep her voice from betraying her altogether. With a pain that slices so, like a knife within. The child screams when one touches her here — she gestured at a midpoint of her belly — and here — another point high on the side. The padre nodded again, without looking. And the blood, said the woman, is so dark. *Claro que no* — she is not, it cannot be —

Of course not, he said, soothing her. *Claro que no.* But we must pray —

— and that skin of hers, always so pale, but now the whiteness —

He nodded, moving slowly toward the woman; his arm settled about her shoulders; he walked firmly, propelling her closer to the door.

— even the swelling, so quick and big, it is not — not — ?

Claro que no, he murmured again. *Pobrecita.* Poor little one. It was wise that you came to tell me....

His words with their singsong cadence now fell like caresses upon her ears; despite herself she felt the fear recede like a wave, calmness flooding in its place. The padre's arm lay gently across her back like a soft shawl; behind the new spectacles, a mist of unfamiliar tears stung her eyes.

Take the child, he whispered, to the Señora Doctora Restell in San Luis. You have heard —

Juana Ibáñez' eyes widened in amazement. But —

Sí, said Father Padrón, with a brisk patting. *Sí.* You must go without fear, but with prayer and faith; this is a righteous act; as you say, the child is ill. In truth. Señora Restell, Calle Mendoza. Mention only that you bring Rosa from Montaraz, nothing more. She will do — what can be done. With the help of *el buen Dios. Claro?*

Juana Ibáñez searched the padre's face; there was nothing of himself to read. With his beautiful white hand he made the sign of the cross between them, then withdrew the hand quickly, hiding it within the folds of his cassock as though he feared she might steal it.

That night, Juana Ibáñez cried openly before her children, like a woman in a folk tale who has been promised evil magic. That the padre himself should speak so smoothly the name of an infamous woman. La Restell! That he should send us to such a one. Think of it.

Lola shrugged. Why does it surprise you, *Mamacita?* The padres, the *policía,* they all do what they must; have you not taught us this always? And what they must do ... must change from time to time. *Verdad?*

Juana Ibáñez sighed wearily at the sad wisdom of her child. But he knows that Rosa is not — that she will need —

What does it matter, said Chepito. Señora Restell is not a witch — only fools believe what is whispered by fools —

But neither is she —

She is a *doctor,* Mama, said Lola.

I do not trust such a *doctor* with the life of your sister.

Catuja stood in silence at the edge of the room, holding the pile of white cloths soiled with the dark blood of her sister's *enfermedad.*

I think she is worse tonight, she said. I think —

Ssst! Juana Ibáñez held a warning finger to her white lips.

❊ ❊ ❊

Rosa lay in her narrow cot staring up at the cracked ceiling, imagining a cinema in which *la Muerte* was a sad handsome man who fell in love with a young and beautiful girl, and once she loved him back it meant she must die to follow him. It was good to think of *la Muerte* in this way, Rosa had decided, not as an ugly big clown who danced his rude noisy dance in the procession of Holy Week. It was good because if *la Muerte* was so handsome in his formal evening clothes, with a white tie and dark gentle eyes full of pain, then when Rosa's own pain came like quick cuts of a swift blade, when she felt blood trickling inside as a slow river of life leaking away forever, it was easier to keep from crying out. She could close her hands into small tight fists and clutch the worn edges of the gray blanket in which she lay stiff as a doll; she could bite her lips and squeeze her eyes so that the tears would only slide in silence out of the corners; she could feel sadness for the girl in the *cine* instead of for herself, knowing La Lloradora was watching to see if she could. She thought La Lloradora must forgive her if she wept in this way, not crying out for her own *dolor*, her own pain, which she knew would be serious sin if she was having a bastard. That would be her fault no matter how it had come to be, and Father Padrón like a *cachadista*, one who plays sly tricks, would hear her confession without saying anything of how it was not her fault at all. If she wept in this way only for the beautiful girl in the *cine* who must die so young for the dark *Muerte* who loved her, then surely La Lloradora's painted heart would melt, and she would find a way to save the life of María Rosa Andújar and not let her have a bastard after all.

Only when the knife-pain struck so quick and deep that it took her breath — only then did she shriek *Aii! Aii!* with a cry so loud that Catuja and Mama had to come running, with their lips in a white line of fear. Then they would change the folded cloths that lay under her body to catch the dripping of blood. They would look at those dark spots, drops of poison from a wound that would not heal, and shake their heads at each other, thinking she did not see their eyes saying no, they could do nothing. How could they tell where such a wound had opened in her? Why could they not stop the blood that trickled so, as though from a rusty cup that had broken inside? Lloradora, she whispered softly, do not let me die. I am too little for so much pain.

And anyway why must *I* die as a *castigo*, a penitence for sin? Rosa knew, everyone knew, there were other girls who did not die even if they had bastards from letting boys walk in the woods with them. It was not fair, but she must not think of that. If La Lloradora was so angry, she must have her reasons. Maybe she was angry with Rosa for her dreams? Especially about the crown....

Well, La Lloradora would do what she wanted to do, Rosa had always accepted that. Still, she whispered to the ceiling, can you not at least let it be after Candlemas? After tomorrow? Don't you want me to stay alive for your own fiesta of *purificación? Claro que sí.* Why else would you have the padre choose me to be *la reina?* You did want me to march beside you in the procession! I know you did — in a white dress like yours. You want me beside you when they carry you from the church on the scarlet pillow. Beside you when the songs and dances start. You do love me best. I know it.

In the other room Catuja whispered, But if she is *encinta* with a bastard, how will they let her be *la reina?* It is a sin against —

Sst, said Lola fiercely. She is *enferma*, no one knows —

Well, but Mama will not let her go anyway, said Chepito. If she is bleeding, how can she march? Let alone —

Juana Ibáñez signaled them all to be still.

But *will* you let her? Lola persisted.

Claro que no! said Juana Ibáñez, sighing. I cannot.

Rosa sighed, a piteous sound filled with the broken ends of wishes. She tried to swallow. Did you not promise? The tears slid out of the sides of her eyes. Oh, it is not fair for the *Virgen* to break a promise!

Could La Lloradora be tormenting her as a trick? Could that be — ?

Rosa frowned, puzzling this. It was true that on Candlemas the *Virgen* must answer all the prayers she had left unanswered through the year. On her own day of honor, was she not powerful enough to grant everything, even without permission from God the Father? Then might she be afraid ... of Rosa's prayers?

Well, you need not worry, she whispered, stopping her tears. I will pray only for — And her eyes flew open again, to watch the picture of herself floating on the ceiling, a white angel floating through the film of her sinner's tears. Rosa on the ceiling could reach high enough to touch a star point of the statue's crown. Imagine: she might tear a

hole in the fragile cobweb of lace that floated around the statue's feet
... or catch the hem of that mantilla — and with a quick motion pull
it down, setting free La Lloradora's torrent of glorious hair that must
lie chastely pinned beneath, upon her perfect ivory scalp. If Rosa dared,
could she not untie the scarlet sash and pluck off the golden letters
that spelled ESPERANZA? Might she seize one of those tiny glowing
jewels that winked from within the lacy bosom like secret eyes —
And then Rosa gasped in horror, for the fingers of Rosa on the ceiling had darted out and snatched a tiny blood-red stone, only one, but
surely it must be worth fortunes of money — even though it belonged
to the dress of an old painted statue who would not even know, who
could not possibly care — *No!* she cried in sudden horror. *I did not
mean it!* Then she burst into real tears, of terror and guilt, of rage and
pity, not for the girl in the *cine* who gave herself to *la Muerte*, but for
herself. For Rosa; Rosa. She sobbed aloud, All right! *Bueno!* Then let
me die after Candlemas, if I am so horrid. She raised a defiant fist at
the statue she had just betrayed with her sinful thoughts. But you will
let me be *la reina* first, as you promised! You will let me kill the cock-
erel for you — who else has more need to kill the *gallo* of evil? Only
let me say the holy verse to get rid of it!

Solemnly she lowered the small angry fist and began to strike her
own breast in the ritual way. *Me confeso* ... I have sinned in my
thoughts....

Then she stopped and sat up, raising both arms to the ceiling, cock-
ing her head, smiling in the way she had to when the most important
thing of all was at stake. The way she had to smile at Father Padrón,
at Mama, at Señor López Figueroa and her brother Chepito, at her
Papa long ago after he hurt her.... She smiled so now, at the spot on the
cracked ceiling where La Lloradora had looked down and seen the terrible truth of Rosa's dreams. *Salve María*, she said contritely, with that
magic smile that could make others do things, sometimes. I am heartily
sorry for having offended thee. But you still love me best I know it. And
if I do everything just the way you want, you will forgive me. All right?
Bueno? There was no sign from the statue on the ceiling.

In the night Juana Ibáñez stood beside her daughter's bed and touched
her cool forehead. Rosa murmured, half-asleep, Do not worry, *Madre-
cita*. Tomorrow when I am *la reina* —

Sst, *niña*, whispered her mother, stroking the damp curls back from the child's pale face, rest now. There will be other fiestas —

Rosa sat up abruptly; in her round eyes the darkness shone like light. I will die if I do not go. I have promised. I am going, you will not dare to stop me.

Juana Ibáñez stood shaking her head; she had withstood many such tantrums, such attacks of rage, willfulness, defiance; in her mother's heart of stone she knew they always passed. Sleep now, she said in a soothing voice. Then she tiptoed away and lay wearily upon her bed, whispering a prayer of her own for the life of this child with a will so *fuerte*, too strong for either the body or the life that *Dios* had designed for her.

And in her sleep Rosa dreamed that the statue's tears of silver glass that could never fall began to rain down her painted face and splinter in the dirt of the Plaza del 16 Enero, and all the town stood watching in horror as they fell, and understood why. Rosa Andújar's shame was on their lips, behind their hands, for what other reason could it be that she was not there marching in the procession in her white communion dress, symbol of *purificación?* What other reason, after she had boasted to everyone of how the padre had promised she could be *la reina* even though she was not yet twelve. In her sleep the children of the town stood in circles and laughed, whispering her name, and the statue of La Lloradora had no more silver tears.

The morning came and Rosa lay in her bed so pale and still that Juana Ibáñez touched the child's brow in fear, thinking she would find it cold as death. *Dios*, she whispered, and Rosa stirred, opening her eyes with the dark shadows of pain like bruises underneath. I am better, Mama, she said, smiling. See — she gestured toward her belly — the swelling is less. The sleep of the night has cured me, and the blood — there is almost none.

Juana Ibáñez nodded and smiled. She had wakened her other children early, helping them dress in silence so that they could leave before their sister woke and cried again to go with them. If only one could have forbidden them all to march in that procession which meant so much more to this one than to any of the rest. But she had sighed and dressed them and let them go, quietly, to wait for her at the church. Now she must promise Rosa that she herself would not stay for the fiesta, not for the dancing or the killing of the cock, not for the fine dinner or the games. She would go only to the church, for the prayers and the chanting, and to light a candle for Rosa so that Lola might carry it for her in the children's march, high and proud for La Lloradora to see that Rosa had sent her prayers and her love.

In her bed Rosa nodded as her mother talked, and did not cry; instead she promised to rest and wait with patience until her mama came back; *gracias por todos*, she said several times — I thank you for everything. I am sorry for shouting and crying so last night. *Te quiero, Mamacita.*

And the moment Juana Ibáñez left the house Rosa got up from her bed and put on her white communion dress and ran barefoot through the woods, avoiding the streets of the town, though it was twice as far that way from their house to the church. At last she arrived, panting, to take her place among the others, making sure to stand far away from her sisters and brother so that they would not notice her until the march began. The procession was to last nearly an hour, with the children marching over a mile in the punishing sun; down one street and up another, round and round the Plaza del 16 Enero where the mayor waited for *la reina* to perform the ritual killing of the cock that must signify death to sin and evil, rebirth to virtue; a signal to the weeping *Virgen* that her purity must triumph in their hearts for all the long year to come.

After that the children would march again, back up the steep hill to the church, singing and chanting, tossing confetti and streamers, and at last deliver their bouquets of white flowers and their lighted candles to the altar before La Lloradora, who would be taken from her scarlet pillow and set in place again, far from reach, on her pedestal in the little chapel.

The procession began on a signal from Father Padrón; Rosa stepped into place at the head of the line, in front of Margarita Ordónez, who had been hastily selected to replace her. She began to march at the left side of the statue as it rode upon the shoulders of four husky, sweating boys from Chepito's class. Pale and unsteady, Rosa held her candle high, singing louder than all the others, weaving slightly like a *borrachón* after a night at the tavern. Rosa's brother and sisters looked at each other with alarm, not knowing whether to run out of the line to find their mama, to tell her that Rosa was out of bed marching crazily in the sun.

Rosa turned and smiled at them in a strange fierce way, and in between phrases of the holy song she whispered at them, *Do not dare stop me! Do not dare!*

How funny your little sister looks, she heard one of La Lloradora's bearers say to her brother Chepito. All fat and white like —

Sst, said Chepito, and kept his eyes down and his face straight in front.

Father Padrón, marching just ahead of them, swiveled his pink head around once or twice, to make sure the boys had not tipped over the precious statue, but he never turned far enough to look at Rosa; she could not tell if he knew who was marching there; perhaps he thought it was Margarita Ordónez. Never mind, she thought, if he does see me I will tell him the same: Do not dare stop me! *Salve María*, she murmured to the statue as she marched beside it. You hear me? See, I have come, sick as I am. Do not let me have a bastard, all right? Do not let me die, either. I love you, see what I am doing for you? *Por Dios*, give me a sign! *He!* Will you — if I give you half my life? Answer me!

An instant later she began to feel strangely lightheaded; there was a quick rush of blood inside her belly — as though some barrier had given way; and the sun seemed suddenly to press upon her shoulders like a heavy weight, pushing her down. Her knees trembled, and she looked up imploringly at the statue; were the silver tears still in place upon the ivory cheeks? *Gracias a Dios*, they had not come loose. Then as she gazed, the left hand of La Lloradora, the one that held the rosary of pearls so, between the thumb and first finger, began to blur before her as though it were moving by itself, not just from the swaying of the pillow or the bumpy forward motion of the sweating boys who carried it along the rough dirt path. *He!* The head too seemed to move, bowing a little toward Rosa as though to bend and whisper a secret; the red shiny lips seemed to part, and Rosa's ears heard a faint buzzing like the secret whisper of La Lloradora's voice in her dreams.

Sí, niña, said the voice, though the shiny scarlet lips did not seem to move at all. *Sí*, your prayer is heard.

Rosa shook her head and the buzzing stopped, but now the whorls of lace streaming down upon the statue's slender shoulders seemed to move and rustle too, a soft sighing sound like an echo in a cave. *Sí, Sí*, ESPERANZA. . . .

Now Rosa felt the ground rushing up toward her, but something held her and she did not slip all the way down; she stumbled on a stone, her head reeling and the pain now so sharp in her belly that she must bite her lip to keep from crying *Aii! Aii!* Do not let me fall now! she gasped. Not now! They had reached the Plaza del 16 Enero, though it blurred before her in a hundred colors. Now was the most important thing of all; now she must do what La Lloradora wanted her to do, as a *castigo*. She must wear the blindfold and turn and turn, then stand long enough in the white sun to recite the long verse about sin and punishment, evil and death. And at last she must lift up the big white sword of justice and bring it down on the head of a poor *gallo* buried up to its neck in the dirt at her feet. If she could do all she had to do, La Lloradora would forgive her. But if she failed, if she fainted or fell or forgot one single thing, then La Lloradora would send the worst *castigo* of all, she knew; for breaking her solemn oath, La Lloradora would strike her dead in the Plaza del 16 Enero, like the sinful *gallo* itself, in front of everyone.

Rosa could not remember one moment of how it went, but the others described it all to her later — how another girl helped fasten the blindfold, and two big boys buried the *gallo*, and turned her round and round; how she recited the whole long *copla*, telling in verse of all the serious sins the evil bird had committed in its short life — envy and greed, laziness and lies ... and how it must suffer and die at once, and that its last wish was only that all the treasures it had stolen — precious stones the color of blood, golden crowns with stars, pearls and medals — all these things must be dug up and given to the children of Montaraz who could stay as pure as the holy *Virgen* herself.

At last, they told Rosa, she lifted the broad white wooden sword high above her head, and brought it down hard on the head of that wicked bird; the *gallo* shrieked an awful cry when she killed it with one stroke, and at the same time she herself fell to the ground in a heap, which made her mama scream and her sisters and brother run to gather her up and carry her home.

The white communion dress, she could see, was all spattered with dirt and dark poison blood, but when Juana Ibáñez laid Rosa gently down upon her bed, she exclaimed *Mira!* For the swelling of the child's body had gone down a little, as if something had burst inside her like one of the red balloons of *carnaval*, and whatever it was that caused the *dolor* might now go away as mysteriously as it had come.

Juana Ibáñez had smoothed the child's blanket over her, and bathed her forehead with a cool white cloth, and knelt beside her with tears streaming down her face. She made the sign of the cross in silence, but even if there was a prayer for such a moment she could not have said it. Lola, Catuja, and Chepito stood white-faced at the door, clasping each other's hands. Colored streamers and bits of confetti clung to their heads and shoulders, and the shouts and music of the fiesta still rang in their ears from the streets outside.

Will she die now? Catuja whispered to Chepito.

Lola shook her head. No, she said aloud. She is too stubborn.

Then will she have a bastard? Chepito whispered.

Catuja made a funny face, like a twisted smile. If there is any bastard inside *la reina*, she said, do not dare come out. Hear me? Do not dare!

And in spite of herself Juana Ibáñez had lifted her face from her folded hands and burst out laughing.

It was not at all as one expected. Who would have thought the *abortista* inhabited such fine rooms filled with silken cushions and patterned rugs the color of rubies, such soft chairs, polished tables, and shining bowls of silver filled with yellow fruit? Upon the walls hung paintings of rose-colored ladies in ruffled gowns, and of unknown flowers on long slender stems. La Restell herself resembled such a flower, whose petals of pale orange hair, bright as coins in the sun, lay piled upon her head in a row of proud curls like a *cresta de gallo*. She walked like an actress, with her feet strapped so, in small leather harnesses like the heads of tiny horses, and under her white doctor's coat a dress of thin blue gauze brushed against her silken legs, making sounds like the sighing of leaves.

For the examination there was a small room all of white that shone with such cleanness as one would find in a hospital; everything in it new and smelling of strong soap; everything smooth and slippery to the touch, even the sheet stretched like skin across the narrow metal cot where Rosa must lie on her back, with her feet resting high on two silver stirrups, as though to be dragged by an invisible horse. In this room, behind a black curtain, a tall stand of silver metal stood like the skeleton of a tree, hung with fruits that were small lights, cords, and lenses; a microscope of a special kind, Señora Restell explained, to show on a screen small pictures made ten thousand times larger, so that one could see even a tiny infection, a wound no larger than the point of a pin. The picture she would show on the screen for Juana Ibáñez was of something she had cut away from the tender inner skin of the child's womb, a piece of tissue scraped with a delicate instrument; it was the size of a small coin, finer than gauze; she had pressed it within a thin wafer of wax, soaked it in colored dyes. Señora Restell had done these things in her laboratory, after giving Rosa an injection to make her sleep without pain. The picture she would make must show certain things that no one could see, not even with practiced eyes and skilled hands; certain things she could not learn from touching the child so, from making her sit up and lie down, and listening and touching everywhere, just as the *comadre*, the midwife, had done in Montaraz, to discover the source of her pain. While Rosa lay asleep with her feet high in the silver stirrups, on the clean bed that was hardly whiter than her skin, Señora Restell led Juana Ibáñez into the darkened corner on the other side of the black curtain. She snapped on the light of the shiny metal stand; upon the opposite wall the screen glowed pink like the edge of a sunset. Juana Ibáñez drew her breath sharply, but Señora Restell said nothing. She only adjusted a knob, and another, until the picture grew clearer. Still Juana Ibáñez saw only a fine mesh of pink lace, a cobweb of tiny lines crossing and recrossing like twisted strands from a broken web of spider's silk; here and there a tiny mote of brown, a ragged smear of blue appeared, as though a child had passed through the web dripping tears of paint from a handful of wet brushes. At the lower right corner of the screen a larger spot glowed darker blue, like a spreading stain, as though the child with his dripping brushes had grown more careless still, in his haste to escape from the web.

Qué significa? whispered Juana Ibáñez, when she could speak, What does it mean?

An extraordinary thing, said Señora Restell; one seldom sees —

What does it mean? the mother demanded; anger and fear fought each other in her voice.

The dark shape here — Señora Restell pointed like a *profesora* with a pale polished fingernail — means only that she appears to have been pregnant —

Parece? She appears — ?

Well, I see no sign of the *feto* — no tissues from the baby itself —

But nothing came out! I am sure. *Puf!* like a balloon the swelling went. No more of the poison blood. But nothing came out!

I know. Sometimes —

Then what can it mean? If the baby died inside…? Despite the darkness, Juana Ibáñez' round eyes now glowed with terror; her body began to tremble. It was the same fear that had made her come to the *abortista* whose name the padre had given her.

The doctor now laid a white hand gently upon the woman's dark sleeve. Sometimes, she said again in a soft voice, *y no sabemos por qué*, we do not understand, a thing will happen, a small accident of the womb, something tears the veil of tissue, the *amnios*, that must form for the baby.

But it did not come out! cried Juana Ibáñez. If there was a baby —

Señora Restell sighed, and her hands made a small helpless gesture, a turning of the palms. Señora, I cannot tell how it happened. But there must be an *operación* now, to remove the child's womb and examine —

No! cried Juana Ibáñez in a fierce whisper. Then she stared at this Señora Doctora, at her high, careful crown of curls, at her white coat and her slender fingers. *La abortista*, she thought. Yet she did not dislike her; this was a curious thing. What if, she said, what if one does nothing?

Señora Restell frowned. Nothing is a very dangerous thing to do in such a case. The cells —

Juana Ibáñez raised a hand, as though to ward off the power of the doctor's words. Señora Doctora, *en verdad*, what will happen to my child if one does not tear out her womb?

Señora Restell hesitated. It is possible, she said then, that she will heal.

Ah.

But it is more likely — The doctor spread her fingers apart, and then closed them.

She will not die. Juana Ibáñez made it not a question.

In the darkness the doctor's eyes now glowed as brightly as her own; like two cats they stared at each other unblinking in the light of the microscope screen.

Posible, Señora Restell said again, that she will heal. But if nothing is done, some of those cells may remain, embedded there — she gestured again toward the dark stain at the edge of the pink spider web — in the wall of the womb. They do not belong there.

But they will disappear when she grows — ?

Señora Restell shook her head firmly. One cannot know this. It is not a chance one takes. If they remain, it has happened that a few years later — She broke off; a silent shrug.

But if they disappear? Like the *feto?* She will be well, no? There will be no trace of this?

No, Señora. No matter what happens, there will be a trace of this. An important one —

Ya se ve, said Juana Ibáñez quickly. She will not conceive —

Señora Restell nodded. I am sorry.

Still, she will grow, she will be well? And . . . as a woman, normal? For a husband?

That too is a thing I cannot promise. She is very young; there was much damage. You must know she has been . . . badly hurt.

When, hurt? How?

Now the doctor made a sudden impatient gesture; her eyes moved away. I cannot tell with certainty. Did she not tell you — ?

No, said Juana Ibáñez. That one tells very little.

No importa, said the doctor. And Juana Ibáñez understood. Rosa's silence was the price for Señora Restell's services; and for the help of Father Padrón. *Ya se ve*, she thought. Now it is clear.

What matters, the doctor was saying, is that the child is not strong; she is fragile. That is why the *operación* —

Juana Ibáñez shook her head. That one is not fragile, she said. She had stopped trembling suddenly; there was heat now in her voice. You are wrong in this, Señora. Perhaps you are wrong in other things as well.

Puede ser. It may be so. There was a tight smile now on the pale smooth lips of the doctor. In such cases one must hope to be wrong. But of this I am sure: Without the *operación*, one risks the child's life.

Pero, Señora Doctora . . . with the *operación* one risks it too.

That is true.

And one marks the life that remains — a woman whose womb is torn out. . . .

Señora Restell sighed, with a shrug of despair. Or one who may have less than half a life to live.

Juana Ibáñez hesitated only an instant. *Bueno 'stá*, she said. Enough.

The doctor snapped off the light of the microscope and moved briskly to the other side of the black curtain. Lying still on the examining table, Rosa heard the sighing of blue leaves against silken legs and closed her eyes very tight, so that *La Señora Doctora* and Mama would not know what else she might have heard.

Juana Ibáñez stayed another moment in the darkness; she wanted to make the sign of the cross before the delicate metal microscope stand. *La Purificación de la Virgen*, she murmured, without bitterness. *Salve María*.

An Ordinary Woman

BETTE GREENE

I DIAL the number that for more than twenty years has been committed to memory and then begin counting the rings. One ... two ... three ... four ... five ... six — Christ! What's wrong with —

"Newton North High School. Good morning."

"Jeannette? Oh, good morning. This is Amanda Brooks. Look, I may be a few minutes late today. Something came up — no, dear, I'm fine, thanks for asking. It's just a ... a family matter that I must take care of. I shouldn't be more than ten to twenty minutes late for my first class, and I was wondering if you'd kindly ask one of my students, Dani Nikas, to start reading to the class from where we left off in *The Chocolate War*? ... Oh, that would help a lot. ... Thanks, Jeannette, thanks a lot."

Aimlessly I wander from bookcase to armchair to table and finally to the large French window that looks out upon my street. Like yesterday and so many yesterdays before, my neighbor's paneled station wagon is parked in the exact spot halfway up their blue asphalt driveway. And today, like yesterday, Roderick Street continues to be shaded by a combination of mature oaks and young Japanese maples.

How can everything look the same when nothing really feels the same? Good Lord, Mandy Brooks, how old are you going to have to be before you finally get it into your head that the world takes no interest in your losses?

The grandfather clock in the hall begins chiming out the hour of seven and suddenly fear gnaws at my stomach. What am I afraid of now? For one thing, all those minutes. At least thirty of them that I'll have to face alone, here, with just my thoughts.

Calm down now! It's only thirty minutes. Why, the last thing the locksmith said last night was that he'd be here first thing this morning. "Between seven-thirty and eight for sure!"

Anyway, nobody can make me think when I still have the kitchen counter to wipe and breakfast dishes to put into the dishwasher. Thinking hasn't come this hard since Steve's death on the eve of our eighteenth anniversary. That was major league pain all right, but so dear God is this. So is this....

No time for that now — no time! Tidying up the kitchen is the only thing that I want to think about. But upon entering the kitchen, I see that with the exception of a mug still half full of undrunk coffee, there is really nothing to do. I pour the now cold coffee into the sink before examining the mug with all those miniature red hearts revolving around the single word MOM.

It was a gift from Caren and not all that long ago either. Maybe a year, but certainly no more than a year ago. But even then I had had suspicions that something wasn't right. Maybe without Caren's loving gift coming at me out of the blue, I would have followed my instincts and checked things out. But frankly I doubt that. The thing is that I wanted — needed — to believe in my daughter.

And going through her drawers in search of I-knew-not-what offended me. It goes against my sense that everybody, even a seventeen-year-old, deserves privacy.

You make me sick, Mandy Brooks, you really do! Just when did you get to be such a defender of the constitutional rights of minors? Why don't you at least have the courage to come on out and tell the truth. Say that, at all costs, you had to protect yourself from the truth. The terrible truth that your daughter, your lovely daughter is a junkie!

Stop it! Stop it! I'm not listening to you anymore! And there's nothing you can do to make me! Steve ... Steve, oh my God, Steve, how I need you! There hasn't been a day, or even an hour, in all these twenty-two months since you left Caren and me that I haven't needed you. Don't believe those people who observe me from safe distances before patting my wrists and commenting on how strong I am. "How wonderfully you're carrying on alone."

Maybe I walk pretty much the same and talk pretty much the same, but, Steve, I don't feel the same. The moment I saw them close the coffin over you, Steve, I knew then what I know now. That the part of me that was most alive and loving got buried down there with you.

So you see, Steve, you've just got to find some way to help us because despite what people say, I'm not strong and I honestly don't know what to do. I look, but I can't find answers, only questions.

More and more questions demanding answers: Where did I go wrong with our daughter? Was I too strict? Or too lenient? Did I love her too little . . . or did I love her too much?

Outside a truck door slams. I look at my watch. Five minutes after seven. Could he be here already? I rush to the window to see a white panel truck with black lettering — NEWTON CENTRE LOCKSMITHS — at my curb. And a young man, not all that much older than my seniors, is walking briskly up the front walk.

As he takes the front steps, two at a time, I already have the door open. "I really appreciate your being so prompt. You're even earlier than you said you'd be."

"It wasn't me you spoke to. It was my dad, but when he said that a Mrs. Brooks had to have her locks changed first thing in the morning so she wouldn't be late for school, well, I just knew it had to be you."

"Good Lord, I remember you!" I say, grabbing his hand. "You were a student of mine!"

He nods and smiles as he holds tightly to my hand. "You were my favorite English teacher." Then his eyes drop as though he is taking in the intricate pattern of the hall rug. "I guess you were my all-time favorite teacher!"

"Oh, that's lovely of you to say, David — your name is David?"

He grins as though I have given him a present. "David, yes. David Robinson. Hey, you know that's something! You must have had a few hundred students since me. I graduated Newton North two years ago. . . . How do you remember all of your students?"

I hear myself laughing. Laughter, it feels strange, but nice. Very nice. "You give me too much credit, you really do. I'm afraid I can't remember all my students. There have been so many in twenty years. But I think I can probably remember all the students that I really liked."

He takes in the compliment silently as I ask, "Your dad said it wouldn't take long putting in a new cylinder?"

"Ten minutes, Mrs. Brooks. Fifteen at the outside. . . . How many sets of keys will you need?"

"Sets of keys?" I feel my composure begin to dissolve. Suddenly I'm not sure I can trust my voice, so like an early grade-school child, I hold out a finger. Only one finger.

As I quickly turn to start up the stairs, the acrid smell of yesterday's fire once again strikes my nostrils. Never mind that now! This isn't the time for thinking about what was ... and especially not the time for thinking about what could have been.

But even as I command myself to go nonstop into my bedroom for purse and checkbook and then quickly back down the stairs again, I see myself disobeying.

So I stand there at the threshold of Caren's room staring at the two things that had been burned by fire. Her canopy bed rests on only three legs and where the fourth leg once was there is a basketball-size burn in the thick lime colored rug. Her stereo, records, wall-to-wall posters of rock stars, like everything else in this room, are layered with soot.

I remember now that one of the firemen remarked last night that it was sure a lucky thing that the fire had been contained before it reached the mattress. "You just don't know," he said, "how lucky you are."

How lucky I am? Am I lucky? That's what they used to call me back when I was a high school cheerleader. It all started when Big Joe Famori looked up from the huddle and didn't see me on the sidelines so he bellowed out, "Where's lucky Mandy?"

But if I really was lucky twenty-five years ago for Big Joe and the Malden Eagles, then why can't I be just a little lucky for the ones I've really loved? 'Cause with a little luck, Steve's tumor could just as easily have been benign, but it wasn't. And with a little luck, Caren could have got her highs from life instead of from drugs. But she didn't.

Luck. Dumb, unpredictable luck. Maybe there's no such thing as luck. Or maybe I used up all my precious supply on Big Joe Famori and the Malden Eagles. Is that where I failed you, Caren? Not having any more luck to give you?

When you were a little thing, I knew exactly how to make your tears go away. A fresh diaper, a bottle of warm milk, or maybe a song or two while you slept in my arms. That was all the magic I owned, but in your eyes, all power rested in my hands. For you, my love, I lit the stars at night and every morning called forth the eastern sun.

Probably very early on, I should have warned you that your mother was a very ordinary woman with not a single extraordinary power to her name. But, honey, I don't think you would have believed me because I think you needed me to be a miracle mom every bit as much as I needed to be one.

The trouble, though, didn't start until you grew larger and your needs, too, grew in size. And the all-protecting arms that I once held out to you couldn't even begin to cover these new and larger dimensions. Because it wasn't wet diapers or empty stomachs that needed attending to. It was, instead, pride that was shaken and dreams that somehow got mislaid.

So I see now that what from the very beginning I was dedicated to doing, became, of course, impossible to do. And maybe, just maybe, somewhere in the most submerged recesses of our brains, way down there where light or reason rarely penetrates, neither of us could forgive my impotence.

"Mrs. Brooks," David calls from downstairs. "You're all set now."

"I'll be right down." And then without moving from the spot at the threshold, I speak softly to the empty room. Or, more to the point, to the girl who once lived and laughed and dreamed within these walls. "Caren, dear Caren, I don't know if you're in the next block or the next state. I don't know if I'll see you by nightfall or if I'll see you ever.

"But if you someday return to slip your key into a lock that it no longer fits, I hope you'll understand. Understand, at least, that I'm not barring you, but only what you have become.

"You should know too that if I actually possessed just a little of that magic that you once believed in, I wouldn't have a moment's trouble deciding how to spend it. I'd hold you to me until your crying stops and your need for drugs fades away."

David Robinson stands at the bottom of the hall stairs, waiting for me. "You know, you're a lucky lady, Mrs. Brooks," he says, dropping a single brass key into my hand. "You're not even going to be late for class."

Although the center hall has always been the darkest room in the house, I fumble through my purse for my sunglasses before answering. "Yes, David," I say, peering at him through smoke-gray glasses. "People have always said that about me."

🌿 *Girl*

JAMAICA KINCAID

WASH THE WHITE CLOTHES on Monday and put them on the stone heap; wash the color clothes on Tuesday and put them on the clothesline to dry; don't walk barehead in the hot sun; cook pumpkin fritters in very hot sweet oil; soak your little cloths right after you take them off; when buying cotton to make yourself a nice blouse, be sure that it doesn't have gum on it, because that way it won't hold up well after a wash; soak salt fish overnight before you cook it; is it true that you sing benna in Sunday school?; always eat your food in such a way that it won't turn someone else's stomach; on Sundays try to walk like a lady and not like the slut you are so bent on becoming; don't sing benna in Sunday school; you mustn't speak to wharf-rat boys, not even to give directions; don't eat fruits on the street — flies will follow you; *but I don't sing benna on Sundays at all and never in Sunday school*; this is how to sew on a button; this is how to make a buttonhole for the button you have just sewed on; this is how to hem a dress when you see the hem coming down and so to prevent yourself from looking like the slut I know you are so bent on becoming; this is how you iron your father's khaki shirt so that it doesn't have a crease; this is how you iron your father's khaki pants so that they don't have a crease; this is how you grow okra — far from the house, because okra tree harbors red ants; when you are growing dasheen, make sure it gets plenty of water or else it makes your throat itch when you are eating it; this is how you sweep a corner; this is how you sweep a whole house; this is how you sweep a yard; this is how you smile to someone you don't like too much; this is how you smile to someone you don't like at all; this is how you smile to someone you like completely; this is how you set a table for tea; this is how you set a table for dinner; this is how you set a table for dinner with an important guest; this is how you set a table for lunch; this is how you set a table for breakfast; this is how to behave in the presence of men who don't know you very well, and this way they won't recognize immediately the slut I have warned you against becoming; be sure to wash every day, even if it is with your own spit; don't squat down to play marbles — you are not a boy, you know; don't pick people's flowers — you might catch something; don't throw stones at blackbirds, because it might not be a blackbird at all; this is how to make a bread pudding; this is how to make doukona; this is how to make pepper pot; this is how to make a good medicine for a cold; this is how to make a good medicine to throw away a child before it even becomes a child; this is how to catch a fish; this is how to throw back a fish you don't like, and that way something bad won't fall on you; this is how to bully a man; this is how a man bullies you; this is how to love a man, and if this doesn't work there are other ways, and if they don't work don't feel too bad about giving up; this is how to spit up in the air if you feel like it, and this is how to move quick so that it doesn't fall on you; this is how to make ends meet; always squeeze bread to make sure it's fresh; *but what if the baker won't let me feel the bread?*; you mean to say that after all you are really going to be the kind of woman who the baker won't let near the bread?

 *Solitude*

URSULA K. LE GUIN

An addition to "POVERTY: The Second Report on Eleven-Soro"
by Mobile Entselenne'temharyonoterregewis Leaf,
by her daughter, Serenity.

MY MOTHER, a field ethnologist, took the difficulty of learning anything about the people of Eleven-Soro as a personal challenge. The
fact that she used her children to meet that challenge might be seen
as selfishness or as selflessness. Now that I have read her report I know
that she finally thought she had done wrong. Knowing what it cost
her, I wish she knew my gratitude to her for allowing me to grow up
as a person.

Shortly after a robot probe reported people of the Hainish Descent
on the eleventh planet of the Soro system, she joined the orbital crew
as backup for the three First Observers down onplanet. She had spent
four years in the tree-cities of nearby Huthu. My brother In Joy Born
was eight years old and I was five; she wanted a year or two of ship
duty so we could spend some time in a Hainish-style school. My
brother had enjoyed the rainforests of Huthu very much, but though
he could brachiate he could barely read, and we were all bright blue
with skin-fungus. While Borny learned to read and I learned to wear
clothes and we all had antifungus treatments, my mother became as
intrigued by Eleven-Soro as the Observers were frustrated by it.

All this is in her report, but I will say it as I learned it from her,
which helps me remember and understand. The language had been
recorded by the probe and the Observers had spent a year learning it.
The many dialectical variations excused their accents and errors, and
they reported that language was not a problem. Yet there was a communication problem. The two men found themselves isolated, faced

with suspicion or hostility, unable to form any connection with the native men, all of whom lived in solitary houses as hermits or in pairs. Finding communities of adolescent males, they tried to make contact with them, but when they entered the territory of such a group the boys either fled or rushed desperately at them trying to kill them. The women, who lived in what they called "dispersed villages," drove them away with volleys of stones as soon as they came anywhere near the houses. "I believe," one of them reported, "that the only community activity of the Sorovians is throwing rocks at men."

Neither of them succeeded in having a conversation of more than three exchanges with a man. One of them mated with a woman who came by his camp; he reported that though she made unmistakable and insistent advances, she seemed disturbed by his attempts to converse, refused to answer his questions, and left him, he said, "as soon as she got what she came for."

The woman Observer was allowed to settle in an unused house in a "village" (auntring) of seven houses. She made excellent observations of daily life, insofar as she could see any of it, and had several conversations with adult women and many with children; but she found that she was never asked into another woman's house, nor expected to help or ask for help in any work. Conversation concerning normal activities was unwelcome to the other women; the children, her only informants, called her Aunt Crazy-Jabber. Her aberrant behavior caused increasing distrust and dislike among the women, and they began to keep their children away from her. She left. "There's no way," she told my mother, "for an adult to learn anything. They don't ask questions, they don't answer questions. Whatever they learn, they learn when they're children."

Aha! said my mother to herself, looking at Borny and me. And she requested a family transfer to Eleven-Soro with Observer status. The Stabiles interviewed her extensively by ansible, and talked with Borny and even with me — I don't remember it, but she told me I told the Stabiles all about my new stockings — and agreed to her request. The ship was to stay in close orbit, with the previous Observers in the crew, and she was to keep radio contact with it, daily if possible.

I have a dim memory of the tree-city, and of playing with what must have been a kitten or a ghole-kit on the ship, but my first clear memories are of our house in the auntring. It is half underground, half above ground, with wattle-and-daub walls. Mother and I are standing outside it in the warm sunshine. Between us is a big mud-puddle, into which Borny pours water from a basket; then he runs off to the creek to get more water. I muddle the mud with my hands, deliciously, till it is thick and smooth. I pick up a big double handful and slap it onto the walls where the sticks show through. Mother says, "That's good! That's right!" in our new language, and I realize that this is work, and I am doing it. I am repairing the house. I am making it right, doing it right. I am a competent person.

I have never doubted that, so long as I lived there.

We are inside the house at night, and Borny is talking to the ship on the radio, because he misses talking the old language, and anyway he is supposed to tell them stuff. Mother is making a basket and swearing at the split reeds. I am singing a song to drown out Borny so nobody in the auntring hears him talking funny, and anyway I like singing. I learned this song this afternoon in Hyuru's house. I play every day with Hyuru. "Be aware, listen, listen, be aware," I sing. When Mother stops swearing she listens, and then she turns on the recorder. There is a little fire still left from cooking dinner, which was lovely pigi root, I never get tired of pigi. It is dark and warm and smells of pigi and of burning duhur, which is a strong, sacred smell to drive out magic and bad feelings, and as I sing "Listen, be aware," I get sleepier and sleepier and lean against Mother, who is dark and warm and smells like Mother, strong and sacred, full of good feelings.

Our daily life in the auntring was repetitive. On the ship, later, I learned that people who live in artificially complicated situations call such a life "simple." I never knew anybody, anywhere I have been, who found life simple. I think a life or a time looks simple when you leave out the details, the way a planet looks smooth, from orbit.

Certainly our life in the auntring was easy, in the sense that our needs came easily to hand. There was plenty of food to be gathered or grown and prepared and cooked, plenty of temas to pick and rett and spin and weave for clothes and bedding, plenty of reeds to make baskets and thatch with; we children had other children to play with, mothers to look after us, and a great deal to learn. None of this is simple, though it's all easy enough, when you know how to do it, when you are aware of the details.

It was not easy for my mother. It was hard for her, and complicated. She had to pretend she knew the details while she was learning them, and had to think how to report and explain this way of living to people in another place who didn't understand it. For Borny it was easy until it got hard because he was a boy. For me it was all easy. I learned the work and played with the children and listened to the mothers sing.

The First Observer had been quite right: there was no way for a grown woman to learn how to make her soul. Mother couldn't go listen to another mother sing, it would have been too strange. The aunts all knew she hadn't been brought up well, and some of them taught her a good deal without her realizing it. They had decided her mother must have been irresponsible and had gone on scouting instead of settling in an auntring, so that her daughter didn't get educated properly. That's why even the most aloof of the aunts always let me listen with their children, so that I could become an educated person. But of course they couldn't ask another adult into their houses. Borny and I had to tell her all the songs and stories we learned, and then she would tell them to the radio, or we told them to the radio while she listened to us. But she never got it right, not really. How could she, trying to learn it after she'd grown up, and after she'd always lived with magicians.

"Be aware!" she would imitate my solemn and probably irritating imitation of the aunts and the big girls. "Be aware! How many times a day do they say that? Be aware of what! They aren't aware of what the ruins are, their own history — they aren't aware of each other! They don't even talk to each other! Be aware, indeed!"

When I told her the stories of the Before Time that Aunt Sadne and Aunt Noyit told their daughters and me, she often heard the wrong things in them. I told her about the People, and she said, "Those are the ancestors of the people here now." When I said, "There aren't any people here now," she didn't understand. "There are persons here now," I said, but she still didn't understand.

Borny liked the story about the Man Who Lived with Women, how he kept some women in a pen, the way some persons keep rats in a pen for eating, and all of them got pregnant, and they each had a hundred babies, and the babies grew up as horrible monsters and ate the man and the mothers and each other. Mother explained to us that that was a parable of the human overpopulation of this planet thousands of years ago. "No, it's not," I said, "it's a moral story." — "Well, yes," Mother said. "The moral is, don't have too many babies." — "No, it's not," I said. "Who could have a hundred babies even if they wanted to? The man was a sorceror. He did magic. The women did it with him. So of course their children were monsters."

The key, of course, is the word "tekell," which translates so nicely into the Hainish word "magic," an art or power that violates natural law. It was hard for Mother to understand that some persons truly consider most human relationships unnatural; that marriage, for instance, or government, can be seen as an evil spell woven by sorcerors. It is hard for her people to believe magic.

The ship kept asking if we were all right, and every now and then a Stabile would hook up the ansible to our radio and grill Mother and us. She always convinced them that she wanted to stay, for despite her frustrations, she was doing the work the First Observers had not been able to do, and Borny and I were happy as mudfish, all those first years. I think Mother was happy too, once she got used to the slow pace and the indirect way she had to learn things. She was lonely, missing other grown-ups to talk to, and told us that she would have gone crazy without us. If she missed sex she never showed it. I think, though, that her Report is not very complete about sexual matters, perhaps because she was troubled by them. I know that when we first lived in the auntring, two of the aunts, Hedimi and Behyu, used to meet to make love, and Behyu courted my mother; but Mother didn't understand, because Behyu wouldn't talk the way Mother wanted to talk. She couldn't understand having sex with a person whose house you wouldn't enter.

Once when I was nine or so, and had been listening to some of the older girls, I asked her why didn't she go out scouting. "Aunt Sadne would look after us," I said, hopefully. I was tired of being the uneducated woman's daughter. I wanted to live in Aunt Sadne's house and be just like the other children.

"Mothers don't scout," she said, scornfully, like an aunt.

"Yes, they do, sometimes," I insisted. "They have to, or how could they have more than one baby?"

"They go to settled men near the auntring. Behyu went back to the Red Knob Hill Man when she wanted a second child. Sadne goes and sees Downriver Lame Man when she wants to have sex. They know the men around here. None of the mothers scout."

I realized that in this case she was right and I was wrong but I stuck to my point. "Well, why don't you go see Downriver Lame Man? Don't you ever want sex? Migi says she wants it all the time."

"Migi is seventeen," Mother said drily. "Mind your own nose." She sounded exactly like all the other mothers.

Men, during my childhood, were a kind of uninteresting mystery to me. They turned up a lot in the Before Time stories, and the singing-circle girls talked about them; but I seldom saw any of them. Sometimes I'd glimpse one when I was foraging but they never came near the auntring. In summer the Downriver Lame Man would get lonesome waiting for Aunt Sadne and would come lurking around, not very far from the auntring — not in the bush or down by the river, of course, where he might be mistaken for a rogue and stoned — but out in the open, on the hillsides, where we could all see who he was. Hyuru and Didsu, Aunt Sadne's daughters, said she had had sex with him when she went out scouting the first time, and always had sex with him and never tried any of the other men of the settlement.

She had told them, too, that the first child she bore was a boy, and she drowned it, because she didn't want to bring up a boy and send him away. They felt queer about that and so did I, but it wasn't an uncommon thing. One of the stories we learned was about a drowned boy who grew up underwater, and seized his mother when she came to bathe, and tried to hold her under till she too drowned; but she escaped.

At any rate, after the Downriver Lame Man had sat around for several days on the hillsides, singing long songs and braiding and un-braiding his hair which was long too, and shone black in the sun, Aunt Sadne always went off for a night or two with him, and came back looking cross and self-conscious.

Aunt Noyit explained to me that Downriver Lame Man's songs were magic; not the usual bad magic, but what she called the great good spells. Aunt Sadne never could resist his spells. "But he hasn't half the charm of some men I've known," said Aunt Noyit, smiling reminiscently.

Our diet, though excellent, was very low in fat, which Mother thought might explain the rather late onset of puberty; girls seldom menstruated before they were fifteen and boys often weren't mature till they were considerably older than that. But the women began looking askance at boys as soon as they showed any signs at all of adolescence. First Aunt Hedimi, who was always grim, then Aunt

Noyit, then even Aunt Sadne began to turn away from Borny, to leave him out, not answering when he spoke. "What are you doing playing with the children?" old aunt Dnemi asked him so fiercely that he came home in tears. He was not quite fourteen.

Sadne's younger daughter Hyuru was my soulmate, my best friend, you would say. Her elder sister Didsu, who was in the singing circle now, came and talked to me one day, looking serious. Borny is very handsome," she said. I agreed proudly.

"Very big, very strong," she said, "stronger than I am."

I agreed proudly again, and then I began to back away from her.

"I'm not doing magic, Ren," she said.

"Yes you are," I said. "I'll tell your mother!"

Didsu shook her head. "I'm trying to speak truly. If my fear causes your fear, I can't help it. It has to be so. We talked about it in the singing circle. I don't like it," she said, and I knew she meant it; she had a soft face, soft eyes, she had always been the gentlest of us children. "I wish he could be a child, " she said. "I wish I could. But we can't."

"Go be a stupid old woman, then," I said, and ran away from her. I went to my secret place down by the river and cried. I took the holies out of my soulbag and arranged them. One holy — it doesn't matter if I tell you — was a crystal that Borny had given me, clear at the top, cloudy purple at the base. I held it a long time and then I gave it back. I dug a hole under a boulder, and wrapped the holy in duhur leaves inside a square of cloth I tore out of my kilt, beautiful, fine cloth Hyuru had woven and sewn for me. I tore the square right from the front, where it would show. I gave the crystal back, and then sat a long time there near it. When I went home I said nothing of what Didsu had said. But Borny was very silent, and my mother had a worried look. "What have you done to your kilt, Ren?" she asked. I raised my head a little and did not answer; she started to speak again, and then did not. She had finally learned not to talk to a person who chose to be silent.

Borny didn't have a soulmate, but he had been playing more and more often with the two boys nearest his age, Ednede who was a year or two older, a slight, quiet boy, and Bit who was only eleven, but boisterous and reckless.

The three of them went off somewhere all the time. I hadn't paid much attention, partly because I was glad to be rid of Bit. Hyuru and

I had been practicing being aware, and it was tiresome to always have to be aware of Bit yelling and jumping around. He never could leave anyone quiet, as if their quietness took something from him. His mother, Hedimi had educated him, but she wasn't a good singer or storyteller like Sadne and Noyit, and Bit was too restless to listen even to them. Whenever he saw me and Hyuru trying to slow-walk or sitting being aware, he hung around making noise till we got mad and told him to go, and then he jeered, "Dumb girls!"

I asked Borny what he and Bit and Ednede did, and he said, "Boy stuff."

"Like what?"

"Practicing."

"Being aware?"

After a while he said, "No."

"Practicing what, then?"

"Wrestling. Getting strong. For the boygroup." He looked gloomy, but after a while he said, "Look," and showed me a knife he had hidden under his mattress. "Ednede says you have to have a knife, then nobody will challenge you. Isn't it a beauty?" It was metal, old metal from the People, shaped like a reed, pounded out and sharpened down both edges with a sharp point. A piece of polished flintshrub wood had been bored and fitted on the handle to protect the hand. "I found it in an empty man's-house," he said. "I made the wooden part." He brooded over it lovingly. Yet he did not keep it in his soulbag.

"What do you do with it?" I asked, wondering why both edges were sharp, so you'd cut your hand if you used it.

"Keep off attackers," he said.

"Where was the empty man's-house?"

"Way over across Rocky Top."

"Can I go with you if you go back?"

"No," he said, not unkindly, but absolutely.

"What happened to the man? Did he die?"

"There was a skull in the creek. We think he slipped and drowned."

He didn't sound quite like Borny. There was something in his voice like a grown-up; melancholy; reserved. I had gone to him for reassurance, but came away more deeply anxious. I went to Mother and asked her, "What do they do in the boygroups?"

"Perform natural selection," she said, not in my language but in hers, in a strained tone. I didn't always understand Hainish any more and had no idea what she meant, but the tone of her voice upset me; and to my horror I saw she had begun to cry silently. "We have to move, Serenity," she said — she was still talking Hainish without realizing it. "There isn't any reason why a family can't move, is there? Women just move in and move out as they please. Nobody cares what anybody does. Nothing is anybody's business. Except hounding the boys out of town!"

I understood most of what she said, but got her to say it in my language; and then I said, "But anywhere we went, Borny would be the same age, and size, and everything."

"Then we'll leave," she said fiercely. "Go back to the ship."

I drew away from her. I had never been afraid of her before: she had never used magic on me. A mother has great power, but there is nothing unnatural in it, unless it is used against the child's soul.

Borny had no fear of her. He had his own magic. When she told him she intended leaving, he persuaded her out of it. He wanted to go join the boygroup, he said, he'd been wanting to for a year now. He didn't belong in the auntring any more, all women and girls and little kids. He wanted to go live with other boys. Bit's older brother Yit was a member of the boygroup in the Four Rivers Territory, and would look after a boy from his auntring. And Ednede was getting ready to go. And Borny and Ednede and Bit had been talking to some men, recently. Men weren't all ignorant and crazy, the way Mother thought. They didn't talk much, but they knew a lot.

"What do they know?" Mother asked grimly.

"They know how to be men," Borny said. "It's what I'm going to be."

"Not that kind of man — not if I can help it! In Joy Born, you must remember the men on the ship, real men — nothing like these poor, filthy hermits. I can't let you grow up thinking that that's what you have to be!"

"They're not like that," Borny said. "You ought to go talk to some of them, Mother."

"Don't be naive," she said with an edgy laugh. "You know perfectly well that women don't go to men to *talk*."

I knew she was wrong; all the women in the auntring knew all the settled men for three days' walk around. They did talk with them, when they were out foraging. They only kept away from the ones they didn't trust, and usually those men disappeared before long. Noyit had told me, "Their magic turns on them." She meant the other men drove them away or killed them. But I didn't say any of this, and Borny said only, "Well, Cave Cliff Man is really nice. And he took us to the place where I found those People things" (some ancient artifacts that Mother had been excited about). "The men know things the women don't," Borny went on. "At least I could go to the boygroup for a while, maybe. I ought to. I could learn a lot! We don't have any solid information on them at all. All we know anything about is this auntring. I'll go and stay long enough to get material for our report. I can't ever come back to either the auntring or the boygroup once I leave them. I'll have to go to the ship, or else try to be a man. So let me have a real go at it, please, Mother?"

"I don't know why you think you have to learn how to be a man," she said after a while. "You know how already."

He really smiled then, and she put her arm around him.

What about me, I thought. I don't even know what the ship is. I want to be here, where my soul is. I want to go on learning to be in the world.

But I was afraid of Mother and Borny, who were both working magic, and so I said nothing and was still, as I had been taught.

Ednede and Borny went off together. Noyit, Ednede's mother, was as glad as Mother was about their keeping company, though she said nothing. The evening before they left, the two boys went to every house in the auntring. It took a long time. The houses were each just within sight or hearing of one or two of the others, with bush and gardens and irrigation ditches and paths in between. In each house the mother and the children were waiting to say goodbye, only they didn't say it; my language has no word for hello or goodbye. They asked the boys in and gave them something to eat, something they could take with them on the way to the Territory. When the boys went to the door everybody in the household came and touched their hand or cheek. I remembered when Yit had gone around the auntring that way. I had cried then, because even though I didn't much like Yit, it seemed so strange for somebody to leave forever, like they were dying. This time I didn't cry; but I kept waking and waking again, until I heard Borny get up before the first light and pick up his things and leave quietly. I know Mother was awake too, but we did as we should do, and lay still while he left, and for a long time after.

I have read her description of what she calls "An adolescent male leaves the Auntring a vestigial survival of ceremony."

She had wanted him to put a radio in his soulbag and get in touch with her at least occasionally. He had been unwilling. "I want to do it right, Mother. There's no use doing it if I don't do it right."

"I simply can't handle not hearing from you at all, Borny," she had said in Hainish.

"But if the radio got broken or taken or something, you'd worry a lot more, maybe with no reason at all."

She finally agreed to wait half a year, till the first rain; then she would go to a landmark, a huge ruin near the river that marked the southern end of the Territory, and he would try and come to her there. "But only wait ten days," he said. "If I can't come, I can't." She agreed. She was like a mother with a little baby, I thought, saying yes to everything. That seemed wrong to me; but I thought Borny was right. Nobody ever came back to their mother from boygroup.

But Borny did.

Summer was long, clear, beautiful. I was learning to starwatch; that is when you lie down outside on the open hills in the dry season at night, and find a certain star in the eastern sky, and watch it cross the sky till it sets. You can look away, of course, to rest your eyes, and doze, but you try to keep looking back at the star and the stars around it, until you feel the earth turning, until you become aware of how the stars and the world and the soul move together. After the certain star sets you sleep until dawn wakes you. Then as always you greet the sunrise with aware silence. I was very happy on the hills those warm great nights, those clear dawns. The first time or two Hyuru and I starwatched together, but after that we went alone, and it was better alone.

I was coming back from such a night, along the narrow valley between Rocky Top and Over Home Hill in the first sunlight, when a man came crashing through the bush down onto the path and stood in front of me. "Don't be afraid," he said, "Listen!" He was heavy-set, half naked; he stank.

I stood still as a stick. He had said "Listen!" just as the aunts did, and I listened. "Your brother and his friend are all right. Your mother shouldn't go there. Some of the boys are in a gang. They'd rape her. I and some others are killing the leaders. It takes a while. Your brother is with the other gang. He's all right. Tell her. Tell me what I said."

I repeated it word for word, as I had learned to do when I listened.

"Right. Good," he said, and took off up the steep slope on his short, powerful legs, and was gone.

Mother would have gone to the Territory right then, but I told the man's message to Noyit, too, and she came to the porch of our house to speak to Mother. I listened to her, because she was telling things I didn't know well and Mother didn't know at all. Noyit was a small, mild woman, very like her son Ednede; she liked teaching and singing, so the children were always around her place. She saw Mother was getting ready for a journey. She said, "House on the Skyline Man says the boys are all right." When she saw Mother wasn't listening, she went on; she pretended to be talking to me, because women don't teach women: "He says some of the men are breaking up the gang. They do that, when the boygroups get wicked. Sometimes there are magicians among them, leaders, older boys, even men who want to make a gang. The settled men will kill the magicians and make sure none of the boys gets hurt. When gangs come out of the Territories, nobody is safe. The settled men don't like that. They see to it that the auntring is safe. So your brother will be all right."

My mother went on packing pigi-roots into her net.

"A rape is a very, very bad thing for the settled men," said Noyit to me. "It means the women won't come to them. If the boys raped some woman, probably the men would kill *all* the boys."

My mother was finally listening.

She did not go to the rendezvous with Borny, but all through the rainy season she was utterly miserable. She got sick, and old Dnemi sent Didsu over to dose her with gagberry syrup. She made notes while she was sick, lying on her mattress, about illnesses and medicines and how the older girls had to look after sick women, since grown women did not enter one another's houses. She never stopped working and never stopped worrying about Borny.

Late in the rainy season, when the warm wind had come and the yellow honey-flowers were in bloom on all the hills, the Golden World time, Noyit came by while Mother was working in the garden. "House on the Skyline Man says things are all right in the boy-group," she said, and went on.

Mother began to realize then that although no adult ever entered another's house, and adults seldom spoke to one another, and men and women had only brief, often casual relationships, and men lived all their lives in real solitude, still there was a kind of community, a wide, thin, fine network of delicate and certain intention and restraint: a social order. Her reports to the ship were filled with this new understanding. But she still found Sorovian life impoverished, seeing these persons as mere survivors, poor fragments of the wreck of something great.

"My dear," she said — in Hainish; there is no way to say "my dear" in my language. She was speaking Hainish with me in the house so that I wouldn't forget it entirely. — "My dear, the explanation of an uncomprehended technology as magic *is* primitivism. It's not a criticism, merely a description."

"But technology isn't magic," I said.

"Yes, it is, in their minds; look at the story you just recorded. Before Time sorcerors who could fly in the air and undersea and underground in magic boxes!"

"In *metal* boxes," I corrected.

"In other words, airplanes, tunnels, submarines; a lost technology explained as supernatural."

"The *boxes* weren't magic," I said. "The *people* were. They were sorcerors. They used their power to get power over other persons. To live rightly a person has to keep away from magic."

"That's a cultural imperative, because a few thousand years ago uncontrolled technological expansion led to disaster. Exactly. There's a perfectly rational reason for the irrational taboo."

I did not know what "rational," and "irrational" meant in my language; I could not find words for them. "Taboo" was the same as "poisonous." I listened to my mother because a daughter must learn from her mother, and my mother knew many, many things no other person knew; but my education was very difficult, sometimes. If only there were more stories and songs in her teaching, and not so many words, words that slipped away from me like water through a net!

The Golden Time passed, and the beautiful summer; the Silver Time returned, when the mists lie in the valleys between the hills, before the rains begin; and the rains began, and fell long and slow and warm, day after day after day. We had heard nothing of Borny and Ednede for over a year. Then in the night the soft thrum of rain on the reed roof turned into a scratching at the door and a whisper, "Shh — it's all right — it's all right."

We wakened the fire and crouched at it in the dark to talk. Borny had got tall and very thin, like a skeleton with the skin dried on it. A cut across his upper lip had drawn it up into a kind of snarl that bared his teeth, and he could not say p, b, or m. His voice was a man's voice. He huddled at the fire trying to get warmth into his bones. His clothes were wet rags. The knife hung on a cord around his neck. "It was all right," he kept saying. "I don't want to go on there, though."

He would not tell us much about the year and a half in the boy-group, insisting that he would record a full description when he got to the ship. He did tell us what he would have to do if he stayed on Soro. He would have to go back to the Territory and hold his own among the older boys, by fear and sorcery, always proving his strength, until he was old enough to walk away — that is, to leave the Territory and wander alone till he found a place where the men would let him settle. Ednede and another boy had paired, and were going to walk away together when the rains stopped. It was easier for a pair, he said, if their bond was sexual; so long as they offered no competition for women, settled men wouldn't challenge them. But a new man in the region anywhere within three days' walk of an aunt-ring had to prove himself against the settled men there. "It would 'e three or four years of the same thing," he said, "challenging, fighting, always watching the others, on guard, showing how strong you are, staying alert all night, all day. To end up living alone your whole life. I can't do it." He looked at me. "I'ne not a 'erson," he said "I want to go ho'e."

"I'll radio the ship now," Mother said quietly, with infinite relief.

"No," I said.

Borny was watching Mother, and raised his hand when she turned to speak to me.

"I'll go," he said. "She doesn't have to. Why should she?" Like me, he had learned not to use names without some reason to.

Mother looked from him to me and finally gave a kind of laugh. "I can't leave her here, Borny!"

"Why should you go?"

"Because I want to," she said. "I've had enough. More than enough.

We've got a tremendous amount of material on the women, over seven years of it, and now you can fill the information gaps on the men's side. That's enough. It's time, past time, that we all got back to our own people. All of us."

"I have no people," I said. "I don't belong to people. I am trying to be a person. Why do you want to take me away from my soul? You want me to do magic! I won't. I won't do magic. I won't speak your language. I won't go with you!"

My mother was still not listening; she started to answer angrily. Borny put up his hand again, the way a woman does when she is going to sing, and she looked at him.

"We can talk later," he said. "We can decide. I need to sleep."

He hid in our house for two days while we decided what to do and how to do it. That was a miserable time. I stayed home as if I were sick so that I would not lie to the other persons, and Borny and Mother and I talked and talked. Borny asked Mother to stay with me; I asked her to leave me with Sadne or Noyit, either of whom would certainly take me into their household. She refused. She was the mother and I the child and her power was sacred. She radioed the ship and arranged for a lander to pick us up in a barren area two days' walk from the auntring. We left at night, sneaking away. I carried nothing but my soulbag. We walked all next day, slept a little when it stopped raining, walked on and came to the desert. The ground was all lumps and hollows and caves, Before-Time ruins; the soil was tiny bits of glass and hard grains and fragments, the way it is in the deserts. Nothing grew there. We waited there.

The sky broke open and a shining thing fell down and stood before us on the rocks, bigger than any house, though not as big as the ruins of the Before Time. My mother looked at me with a queer, vengeful smile. "Is it magic?" she said. And it was very hard for me not to think that it was. Yet I knew it was only a thing, and there is no magic in things, only in minds. I said nothing. I had not spoken since we left my home.

I had resolved never to speak to anybody until I got home again; but I was still a child, used to listen and obey. In the ship, that utterly strange new world, I held out only for a few hours, and then began to cry and ask to go home. Please, please, can I go home now.

Everyone on the ship was very kind to me.

Even then I thought about what Borny had been through and what I was going through, comparing our ordeals. The difference seemed total. He had been alone, without food, without shelter, a frightened boy trying to survive among equally frightened rivals against the brutality of older youths intent on having and keeping power, which they saw as manhood. I was cared for, clothed, fed so richly I got sick, kept so warm I felt feverish, guided, reasoned with, praised, befriended by citizens of a very great city, offered a share in their power, which they saw as humanity. He and I had both fallen among sorcerors. Both he and I could see the good in the people we were among, but neither he nor I could live with them.

Borny told me he had spent many desolate nights in the Territory crouched in a fireless shelter telling over the stories he had learned from the aunts, singing the songs in his head. I did the same thing every night on the ship. But I refused to tell the stories or sing to the people there. I would not speak my language, there. It was the only way I had to be silent.

My mother was enraged, and for a long time unforgiving. "You owe your knowledge to our people," she said. I did not answer, because all I had to say was that they were not my people, that I had no people. I was a person. I had a language that I did not speak. I had my silence. I had nothing else.

I went to school; there were children of different ages on the ship, like an auntring, and many of the adults taught us. I learned Ekumenical history and geography, mostly, and Mother gave me a report to learn about the history of Eleven-Soro, what my language calls the Before Time. I read that the cities of my world had been the greatest cities ever built on any world, covering two of the continents entirely, with small areas set aside for farming; there had been 120 billion people living in the cities, while the animals and the sea and the air and the dirt died, until the people began dying too. It was a hideous story. I was ashamed of it and wished nobody else on the ship or in the Ekumen knew about it. And yet, I thought, if they knew the stories I knew about the Before Time, they would understand how magic turns on itself, and that it must be so.

After less than a year, Mother told us we were going to Hain. The ship's doctor and his clever machines had repaired Borny's lip; he and

Mother had put all the information they had into the records; he was old enough to begin training for the Ekumenical Schools, as he wanted to do. I was not flourishing, and the doctor's machines were not able to repair me. I kept losing weight, I slept badly, I had terrible headaches. Almost as soon as we came aboard the ship, I had begun to menstruate; each time the cramps were agonizing. "This is no good, this ship life," she said. "You need to be outdoors. On a planet. On a civilized planet."

"If I went to Hain," I said, "when I came back, the persons I know would all be dead hundreds of years ago."

"Serenity," she said, "you must stop thinking in terms of Soro. We have left Soro. You must stop deluding and tormenting yourself, and look forward, not back. Your whole life is ahead of you. Hain is where you will learn to live it."

I summoned up my courage and spoke in my own language: "I am not a child now. You have no power over me. I will not go. Go without me. You have no power over me!"

Those are the words I had been taught to say to a magician, a sorceror. I don't know if my mother fully understood them, but she did understand that I was deathly afraid of her, and it struck her into silence.

After a long time she said in Hainish, "I agree. I have no power over you. But I have certain rights; the right of loyalty; of love."

"Nothing is right that puts me in your power," I said, still in my language.

She stared at me. "You are like one of them," she said. "You are one of them. You don't know what love is. You're closed into yourself like a rock. I should never have taken you there. People crouching in the ruins of a society — brutal, rigid, ignorant, superstitious — each one in a terrible solitude. And I let them make you into one of them!"

"You educated me," I said, and my voice began to tremble and my mouth to shake around the words, "and so does the school here, but my aunts educated me, and I want to finish my education." I was weeping, but I kept standing with my hands clenched. "I'm not a woman yet. I want to be a woman."

"But Ren, you will be! — ten times the woman you could ever be on Soro — you must try to understand, to believe me — "

"You have no power over me," I said, shutting my eyes and putting my hands over my ears. She came to me then and held me, but I stood stiff, enduring her touch, until she let me go.

The ship's crew had changed entirely while we were onplanet. The First Observers had gone on to other worlds; our backup was now a Gethenian archeologist named Arrem, a mild, watchful person, not young. Arrem had gone down onplanet only on the two desert continents, and welcomed the chance to talk with us, who had "lived with the living," as heshe said. I felt easy when I was with Arrem, who was so unlike anybody else. Arrem was not a man — I could not get used to having men around all the time — yet not woman; and so not exactly an adult, yet not a child: a person, alone, like me. Heshe did not know my language well, but always tried to talk it with me. When this crisis came, Arrem came to my mother and took counsel with her, suggesting that she let me go back down onplanet. Borny was in on some of these talks, and told me about them.

"Arrem says if you go to Hain you'll probably die," he said. "Your soul will. Heshe says some of what we learned is like what they learn on Gethen, in their religion. That kind of stopped Mother from ranting about primitive superstition.... And Arrem says you could be useful to the Ekumen, if you stay and finish your education on Soro. You'll be an invaluable resource." Borny sniggered, and after a minute I did too. "They'll mine you like an asteroid," he said. Then he said, "You know, if you stay and I go, we'll be dead."

That was how the young people of the ships said it, when one was going to cross the lightyears and the other was going to stay. Goodbye, we're dead. It was the truth.

"I know," I said. I felt my throat get tight, and was afraid. I had never seen an adult at home cry, except when Sut's baby died. Sut howled all night. Howled like a dog, Mother said, but I had never seen or heard a dog; I heard a woman terribly crying. I was afraid of sounding like that. "If I can go home, when I finish making my soul, who knows, I might come to Hain for a while," I said, in Hainish.

"Scouting?" Borny said in my language, and laughed, and made me laugh again.

Nobody gets to keep a brother. I knew that. But Borny had come back from being dead to me, so I might come back from being dead to him; at least I could pretend I might.

My mother came to a decision. She and I would stay on the ship for another year while Borny went to Hain. I would keep going to school: if at the end of the year I was still determined to go back onplanet, I could do so. With me or without me, she would go on to Hain then and join Borny. If I ever wanted to see them again, I could follow them. It was a compromise that satisfied no one, but it was the best we could do, and we all consented.

When he left, Borny gave me his knife.

After he left, I tried not to be sick. I worked hard at learning everything they taught me in the ship school, and I tried to teach Arrem how to be aware and how to avoid witchcraft. We did slow walking together in the ship's garden, and the first hour of the untrance movements from the Handdara of Karhide on Gethen. We agreed that they were alike.

The ship was staying in the Soro system not only because of my family, but because the crew was now mostly zoologists who had come to study a sea animal on Eleven-Soro, a kind of cephalopod that had mutated toward high intelligence, or maybe it already was highly intelligent; but there was a communication problem. "Almost as bad as with the local humans," said Steadiness, the zoologist who taught and teased us mercilessly. She took us down twice by lander to the uninhabited islands in the Northern Hemisphere where her station was. It was very strange to go down to my world and yet be a world away from my aunts and sisters and my soulmate; but I said nothing.

I saw the great, pale, shy creature come slowly up out of the deep waters with a running ripple of colors along its long coiling tentacles and a ringing shimmer of sound, all so quick it was over before you could follow the colors or hear the tune. The zoologist's machine produced a pink glow and a mechanically speeded up twitter, tinny and feeble in the immensity of the sea. The cephalopod patiently responded in its beautiful silvery shadowy language. "CP," Steadiness said to us, ironic — Communication Problem. "We don't know what we're talking about."

I said, "I learned something in my education here. In one of the songs, it says," and I hesitated, trying to translate it into Hainish, "it says, thinking is one way of doing, and words are one way of thinking."

Steadiness stared at me, in disapproval I thought, but probably

only because I had never said anything to her before except "Yes."
Finally she said, "Are you suggesting that it doesn't speak in words?"

"Maybe it's not speaking at all. Maybe it's thinking."

Steadiness stared at me some more and then said, "Thank you."
She looked as if she too might be thinking. I wished I could sink into
the water, the way the cephalopod was doing.

The other young people on the ship were friendly and mannerly.
Those are words that have no translation in my language. I was
unfriendly and unmannerly, and they let me be. I was grateful. But
there was no place to be alone on the ship. Of course we each had a
room; though small, the *Heyho* was a Hainish-built explorer, designed
to give its people room and privacy and comfort and variety and
beauty while they hung around in a solar system for years on end. But
it was designed. It was all human-made — everything was human. I
had much more privacy than I had ever had at home in our one-room
house; yet there I had been free and here I was in a trap. I felt the
pressure of people all around me, all the time. People around me,
people with me, people pressing on me, pressing me to be one of them,
to be one of them, one of the people. How could I make my soul? I
could barely cling to it. I was in terror that I would lose it altogether.

One of the rocks in my soulbag, a little ugly gray rock that I had
picked up on a certain day in a certain place in the hills above the
river in the Silver Time, a little piece of my world, that became my
world. Every night I took it out and held it in my hand while I lay
in bed waiting to sleep, thinking of the sunlight on the hills above
the river, listening to the soft hushing of the ship's systems, like a
mechanical sea.

The doctor hopefully fed me various tonics. Mother and I ate breakfast together every morning. She kept at work, making our notes
from all the years on Eleven-Soro into her report to the Ekumen, but
I knew the work did not go well. Her soul was in as much danger as
mine was.

"You will never give in, will you, Ren?" she said to me one morning out of the silence of our breakfast. I had not intended the silence
as a message. I had only rested in it.

"Mother, I want to go home and you want to go home," I said.
"Can't we?"

Her expression was strange for a moment, while she misunder-
stood me; then it cleared to grief, defeat, relief.

"Will we be dead?" she asked me, her mouth twisting.

"I don't know. I have to make my soul. Then I can know if I can come."

"You know I can't come back. It's up to you."

"I know. Go see Borny," I said. "Go home. Here we're both dying." Then noises began to come out of me, sobbing, howling. Mother was crying. She came to me and held me, and I could hold my mother, cling to her and cry with her, because her spell was broken.

From the lander approaching I saw the oceans of Eleven-Soro, and in the greatness of my joy I thought that when I was grown and went out alone I would go to the sea shore and watch the sea-beasts shimmering their colors and tunes till I knew what they were thinking. I would listen, I would learn, until my soul was as large as the shining world. The scarred barrens whirled beneath us, ruins as wide as the continent, endless desolations. We touched down. I had my soulbag, and Borny's knife around my neck on its string, a communicator implant behind my right earlobe, and a medicine kit Mother had made for me. "No use dying of an infected finger, after all," she had said. The people on the lander said good-bye, but I forgot to. I set off out of the desert, home.

It was summer; the night was short and warm; I walked most of it. I got to the auntring about the middle of the second day. I went to my house cautiously, in case somebody had moved in while I was gone; but it was just as we had left it. The mattresses were moldy, and I put them and the bedding out in the sun and started going over the garden to see what had kept growing by itself. The pigi had got small and seedy, but there were some good roots. A little boy came by and stared; he had to be Migi's baby. After a while Hyuru came by. She squatted down near me in the garden in the sunshine. I smiled when I saw her, and she smiled, but it took us a while to find something to say.

"Your mother didn't come back," she said.

"She's dead," I said.

"I'm sorry," Hyuru said.

She watched me dig up another root.

"Will you come to the singing circle?" she asked.

I nodded.

She smiled again. With her rose brown skin and wide-set eyes, Hyuru had become very beautiful, but her smile was exactly the same

as when we were little girls. "Hi, ya!" she sighed in deep content-
ment, lying down on the dirt with her chin on her arms. "This is
good!"

I went on blissfully digging.

That year and the next two, I was in the singing circle with Hyuru
and two other girls. Didsu still came to it often, and Han, a woman
who settled in our auntring to have her first baby, joined it too. In the
singing circle the older girls pass around the stories, songs, knowledge they learned from their own mother, and young women who
have lived in other auntrings teach what they learned there; so
women make each other's souls, learning how to make their children's souls.

Han lived in the house where old Dnemi had died. Nobody in the
auntring except Sut's baby had died while my family lived there. My
mother had complained that she didn't have any data on death and
burial. Sut had gone away with her dead baby and never came back,
and nobody talked about it. I think that turned my mother against
the others more than anything else. She was angry and ashamed that
she could not go and try to comfort Sut and that nobody else did. "It
is not human," she said. "It is pure animal behavior. Nothing could
be clearer evidence that this is a broken culture — not a society, but
the remains of one. A terrible, an appalling poverty."

I don't know if Dnemi's death would have changed her mind.
Dnemi was dying for a long time, of kidney failure I think; she turned
a kind of dark orange color, jaundice. While she could get around,
nobody helped her. When she didn't come out of her house for a day
or two, the women would send the children in with water and a little
food and firewood. It went on so through the winter; then one morning little Rashi told his mother Aunt Dnemi was "staring." Several of
the women went to Dnemi's house, and entered it for the first and last
time. They sent for all the girls in the singing circle, so that we could
learn what to do. We took turns sitting by the body or in the porch of
the house, singing soft songs, child-songs, giving the soul a day and a
night to leave the body and the house; then the older women wrapped
the body in the bedding, strapped it on a kind of litter, and set off with
it toward the barren lands. There it would be given back, under a rock
cairn or inside one of the ruins of the ancient city. "Those are the
lands of the dead," Sadne said. "What dies stays there."

Han settled down in that house a year later. When her baby began to be born she asked Didsu to help her, and Hyuru and I stayed in the porch and watched, so that we could learn. It was a wonderful thing to see, and quite altered the course of my thinking, and Hyuru's too. Hyuru said, "I'd like to do that!" I said nothing, but thought, So do I, but not for a long time, because once you have a child you're never alone.

And though it is of the others, of relationships, that I write, the heart of my life has been my being alone.

I think there is no way to write about being alone. To write is to tell something to somebody, to communicate to others. CP, as Steadiness would say. Solitude is non-communication, the absence of others, the presence of a self sufficient to itself.

A woman's solitude in the auntring is, of course, based firmly on the presence of others at a little distance. It is a contingent, and therefore human, solitude. The settled men are connected as stringently to the women, though not to one another; the settlement is an integral though distant element of the auntring. Even a scouting woman is part of the society — a moving part, connecting the settled parts. Only the isolation of a woman or man who chooses to live outside the settlements is absolute. They are outside the network altogether. There are worlds where such persons are called saints, holy people. Since isolation is a sure way to prevent magic, on my world the assumption is that they are sorcerors, outcast by others or by their own will, their conscience.

I knew I was strong with magic, how could I help it? and I began to long to get away. It would be so much easier and safer to be alone. But at the same time, and increasingly, I wanted to know something about the great harmless magic, the spells cast between men and women.

I preferred foraging to gardening, and was out on the hills a good deal; and these days, instead of keeping away from the man's-houses, I wandered by them, and looked at them, and looked at the men if they were outside. The men looked back. Downriver Lame Man's long, shining hair was getting a little white in it now, but when he sat singing his long, long songs I found myself sitting down and listening, as if my legs had lost their bones. He was very handsome. So was the man I remembered as a boy named Tret in the auntring, when I was little, Behyu's son. He had come back from the boygroup and from wandering, and had built a house and made a fine garden in the valley of Red Stone Creek. He had a big nose and big eyes, long arms and legs, long hands; he moved very quietly, almost like Arrem doing the untrance. I went often to pick lowberries in Red Stone Creek valley.

He came along the path and spoke. "You were Borny's sister," he said. He had a low voice, quiet.

"He's dead," I said.

Red Stone Man nodded. "That's his knife."

In my world, I had never talked with a man. I felt extremely strange. I kept picking berries.

"You're picking green ones," Red Stone Man said.

His soft, smiling voice made my legs lose their bones again.

"I think nobody's touched you," he said. "I'd touch you gently. I think about it, about you, ever since you came by here early in the summer. Look, here's a bush full of ripe ones. Those are green. Come over here."

I came closer to him, to the bush of ripe berries.

When I was on the ship, Arrem told me that many languages have a single word for sexual desire and the bond between mother and child and the bond between soulmates and the feeling for one's home and worship of the sacred; they are all called love. There is no word that great in my language. Maybe my mother is right, and human greatness perished in my world with the people of the Before Time, leaving only small, poor, broken things and thoughts. In my language, love is many different words. I learned one of them with Red Stone Man. We sang it together to each other.

We made a brush house on a little cove of the creek, and neglected our gardens, but gathered many, many sweet berries.

Mother had put a lifetime's worth of nonconceptives in the little medicine kit. She had no faith in Sorovian herbals. I did, and they worked.

But when a year or so later, in the Golden Time I decided to go out scouting, I thought I might go places where the right herbs were scarce; and so I stuck the little noncon jewel on the back of my left earlobe. Then I wished I hadn't, because it seemed like witchcraft. Then I told myself I was being superstitious; the noncon wasn't any more witchcraft than the herbs were, it just worked longer. I had promised my mother in my soul that I would never be superstitious. The skin grew over the noncon, and I took my soulbag and Borny's knife and the medicine kit, and set off across the world.

I had told Hyuru and Red Stone Man I would be leaving. Hyuru and I sang and talked together all one night down by the river. Red Stone Man said in his soft voice, "Why do you want to go?" and I said, "To get away from your magic, sorceror," which was true in part. If I kept going to him I might always go to him. I wanted to give my soul and body a larger world to be in.

Now to tell of my scouting years is more difficult than ever. CP! A woman scouting is entirely alone, unless she chooses to ask a settled man for sex, or camps in an auntring for a while to sing and listen with the singing circle. If she goes anywhere near the territory of a boygroup, she is in danger; and if she comes on a rogue she is in danger; and if she hurts herself or gets into polluted country, she is in danger. She has no responsibility except to herself, and so much freedom is very dangerous.

In my right earlobe was the tiny communicator; every forty days, as I had promised, I sent a signal to the ship that meant "all well." If I wanted to leave, I would send another signal. I could have called for the lander to rescue me from a bad situation, but though I was in bad situations a couple of times I never thought of using it. My signal was the mere fulfilment of a promise to my mother and her people, the network I was no longer part of, a meaningless communication.

Life in the auntring, or for a settled man, is repetitive, as I said; and so it can be dull. Nothing new happens. The mind always wants new happenings. So for the young soul there is wandering and scouting, travel, danger, change. But of course travel and danger and change have their own dullness. It is finally always the same otherness over again; another hill, another river, another man, another day. The feet begin to turn in a long, long circle. The body begins to think of what it learned back home, when it learned to be still. To be aware. To be aware of the grain of dirt beneath the sole of the foot, and the skin of the sole of the foot, and the touch and scent of the air on the cheek, and the fall and motion of the light across the air, and the color of the grass on the high hill across the river, and the thoughts of the body, of the soul, the shimmer and ripple of colors and sounds in the clear

darkness of the depths, endlessly moving, endlessly changing, endlessly new.

So at last I came back home. I had been gone about four years.

Hyuru had moved into my old house when she left her mother's
house. She had not gone scouting, but had taken to going to Red Stone
Creek Valley; and she was pregnant. I was glad to see her living there.
The only house empty was an old half-ruined one too close to Hedimi's. I decided to make a new house. I dug out the circle as deep as
my chest; the digging took most of the summer. I cut the sticks, braced
and wove them, and then daubed the framework solidly with mud
inside and out. I remembered when I had done that with my mother
long, long ago, and how she had said, "That's right. That's good." I
left the roof open, and the hot sun of late summer baked the mud into
clay. Before the rains came, I thatched the house with reeds, a triple
thatching, for I'd had enough of being wet all winter.

My auntring was more a string than a ring, stretching along the
north bank of the river for about three kilos; my house lengthened
the string a good bit, upstream from all the others. I could just see the
smoke from Hyuru's fireplace. I dug it into a sunny slope with good
drainage. It is still a good house.

I settled down. Some of my time went to gathering and gardening
and mending and all the dull, repetitive actions of primitive life, and
some went to singing and thinking the songs and stories I had learned
here at home and while scouting, and the things I had learned on the
ship, also. Soon enough I found why women are glad to have children come to listen to them, for songs and stories are meant to be
heard, listened to. "Listen!" I would say to the children. The children
of the auntring came and went, like the little fish in the river, one or
two or five of them, little ones, big ones. When they came, I sang or
told stories to them. When they left, I went on in silence. Sometimes
I joined the singing circle to give what I had learned traveling to the
older girls. And that was all I did; except that I worked, always, to
be aware of all I did.

By solitude the soul escapes from doing or suffering magic; it escapes
from dullness, from boredom, by being aware. Nothing is boring if
you are aware of it. It may be irritating, but it is not boring. If it is
pleasant the pleasure will not fail so long as you are aware of it. Being
aware is the hardest work the soul can do, I think.

I helped Hyuru have her baby, a girl, and played with the baby. Then after a couple of years I took the noncon out of my left earlobe. Since it left a little hole, I made the hole go all the way through with a burnt needle, and when it healed I hung in it a tiny jewel I had found in a ruin when I was scouting. I had seen a man on the ship with a jewel hung in his ear that way. I wore it when I went out foraging. I kept clear of Red Stone Valley. The man there behaved as if he had a claim on me, a right to me. I liked him still, but I did not like that smell of magic about him, his imagination of power over me. I went up into the hills, northward.

A pair of young men had settled in old North House about the time I came home. Often boys got through boygroup by pairing, and often they stayed paired when they left the Territory. It helped their chances of survival. Some of them were sexually paired, others weren't; some stayed paired, others didn't. One of this pair had gone off with another man last summer. The one that stayed wasn't a handsome man, but I had noticed him. He had a kind of solidness I liked. His body and hands were short and strong. I had courted him a little, but he was very shy. This day, a day in the Silver Time when the mist lay on the river, he saw the jewel swinging in my ear, and his eyes widened.

"It's pretty, isn't it?" I said.

He nodded.

"I wore it to make you look at me," I said.

He was so shy that I finally said, "If you only like sex with men, you know, just tell me." I really was not sure.

"Oh, no," he said, "no. No." He stammered and then bolted back down the path. But he looked back; and I followed him slowly, still not certain whether he wanted me or wanted to be rid of me.

He waited for me in front of a little house in a grove of redroot, a lovely little bower, all leaves outside, so that you would walk within arm's length of it and not see it. Inside he had laid sweet grass, deep and dry and soft, smelling of summer. I went in, crawling because the door was very low, and sat in the summer-smelling grass. He stood outside. "Come in," I said, and he came in very slowly.

"I made it for you," he said.

"Now make a child for me," I said.

And we did that; maybe that day, maybe another.

Now I will tell you why after all these years I called the ship, not knowing even if it was still there in the space between the planets, asking for the lander to meet me in the barren land.

When my daughter was born, that was my heart's desire and the fulfilment of my soul. When my son was born, last year, I knew there is no fulfilment. He will grow toward manhood, and go, and fight and endure, and live or die as a man must. My daughter, whose name is Yedneke, Leaf, like my mother, will grow to womanhood and go or stay as she chooses. I will live alone. This is as it should be, and my desire. But I am of two worlds; I am a person of this world, and a woman of my mother's people. I owe my knowledge to the children of her people. So I asked the lander to come and spoke to the people on it. They gave me my mother's report to read, and have written my story in their machine, making a record for those who want to learn one of the ways to make a soul. To them, to the children I say: Listen! Avoid magic! Be aware!

How to Talk to Your Mother (Notes)

Lorrie Moore

1982. Without her, for years now, murmur at the defrosting refrigerator, "What?" "Huh?" "Shush now," as it creaks, aches, groans, until
the final ice block drops from the ceiling of the freezer like something
vanquished.

Dream, and in your dreams babies with the personalities of dachs-
hunds, fat as Macy balloons, float by the treetops.

The first permanent polyurethane heart is surgically implanted.

Someone upstairs is playing "You'll Never Walk Alone" on the
recorder. Now it's "Oklahoma!" They must have a Rodgers and
Hammerstein book.

1981. On public transportation, mothers with soft, soapy, corduroyed
seraphs glance at you, their faces dominoes of compassion. Their seraphs are small and quiet or else restlessly counting bus-seat colors:
"Blue-blue-blue, red-red-red, lullow-lullow-lullow." The mothers see
you eyeing their children. They smile sympathetically. They believe you
envy them. They believe you are childless. They believe they know why.
Look quickly away, out the smudge of the window.

1980. The hum, rush, clack of things in the kitchen. These are some
of the sounds that organize your life. The clink of the silverware inside
the drawer, piled like bones in a mass grave. Your similes grow grim,
grow tired.

Reagan is elected president, though you distributed donuts and
brochures for Carter.

Date an Italian. He rubs your stomach and says, "These are marks

125

of stretch, no? Marks of stretch?" and in your dizzy mind you think: Marks of Harpo, Ideas of Marx, Ides of March, Beware. He plants kisses on the sloping ramp of your neck, and you fall asleep against him, your underpants peeled and rolled around one thigh like a bride's garter.

1979. Once in a while take evening trips past the old unsold house you grew up in, that haunted rural crossroads two hours from where you now live. It is like Halloween: the raked, moonlit lawn, the mammoth, tumid trees, arms and fingers raised into the starless wipe of sky like burns, cracks, map rivers. Their black shadows rock against the side of the east porch. There are dream shadows, other lives here. Turn the corner slowly but continue to stare from the car window. This house is embedded in you deep, something still here you know, you think you know, a voice at the top of those stairs, perhaps, a figure on the porch, an odd apron caught high in the twigs, in the too-warm-for-a-fall-night breeze, something not right, that turret window you can still see from here, from outside, but which can't be reached from within. (The ghostly brag of your childhood: "We have a mystery room. The window shows from the front, but you can't go in, there's no door. A doctor lived there years ago and gave secret operations, and now it's blocked off.") The window sits like a dead eye in the turret.

You see a ghost, something like a spinning statue by a shrub.

1978. Bury her in the cold south sideyard of that Halloweenish house. Your brother and his kids are there. Hug. The minister in a tweed sportscoat, the neighborless fields, the crossroads, are all like some stark Kansas. There is praying, then someone shoveling. People walk toward the cars and hug again. Get inside your car with your niece. Wait. Look up through the windshield. In the November sky a wedge of wrens moves south, the lines of their formation, the very sides and vertices mysteriously choreographed, shifting, flowing, crossing like a skater's legs. "They'll descend instinctively upon a tree somewhere," you say, "but not for miles yet." You marvel, watch, until, amoeba-slow, they are dark, faraway stitches in the horizon. You do not start the car. The quiet niece next to you finally speaks: "Aunt Ginnie, are we going to the restaurant with the others?" Look at her. Recognize her: nine in a pile parka. Smile and start the car.

1977. She ages, rocks in your rocker, noiseless as wind. The front strands of her white hair dangle yellow at her eyes from too many cigarettes. She smokes even now, her voice husky with phlegm. Sometimes at dinner in your tiny kitchen she will simply stare, rheumy-eyed, at you, then burst into a fit of coughing that racks her small old man's body like a storm.

Stop eating your baked potato. Ask if she is all right.

She will croak: "Do you remember, Ginnie, your father used to say that one day, with these cigarettes, I was going to have to 'face the mucus'?" At this she chuckles, chokes, gasps again.

Make her stand up.

Lean her against you.

Slap her lightly on the curved mound of her back.

Ask her for chrissakes to stop smoking.

She will smile and say: "For chrissakes? Is that any way to talk to your mother?"

At night go in and check on her. She lies there awake, her lips apart, open and drying. Bring her some juice. She murmurs, "Thank you, honey." Her mouth smells, swells like a grave.

1976. The Bicentennial. In the laundromat, you wait for the time on your coins to run out. Through the porthole of the dryer, you watch your bedeviled towels and sheets leap and fall. The radio station piped in from the ceiling plays slow, sad Motown; it encircles you with the desperate hopefulness of a boy at a dance, and it makes you cry. When you get back to your apartment, dump everything on your bed. Your mother is knitting crookedly: red, white, and blue. Kiss her hello. Say: "Sure was warm in that place." She will seem not to hear you.

1975. Attend poetry readings alone at the local library. Find you don't really listen well. Stare at your crossed thighs. Think about your mother. Sometimes you confuse her with the first man you ever loved, who ever loved you, who buried his head in the pills of your sweater and said magnificent things like "Oh god, oh god," who loved you unconditionally, terrifically, like a mother.

The poet loses his nerve for a second, a red flush through his neck and ears, but he regains his composure. When he is finished, people clap. There is wine and cheese.

Leave alone, walk home alone. The downtown streets are corridors of light holding you, holding you, past the church, past the community center. March, like Stella Dallas, spine straight, through the melodrama of street lamps, phone posts, toward the green house past Borealis Avenue, toward the rear apartment with the tilt and the squash on the stove.

Your horoscope says: Be kind, be brief.

You are pregnant again. Decide what you must do.

1974. She will have bouts with a mad sort of senility. She calls you at work. "There's no food here! Help me! I'm starving!" although you just bought forty dollars' worth of groceries yesterday. "Mom, there is too food there!"

When you get home the refrigerator is mostly empty. "Mom, where did you put all the milk and cheese and stuff?" Your mother stares at you from where she is sitting in front of the TV set. She has tears leaking out of her eyes. "There's no food here, Ginnie."

There is a rustling, scratching noise in the dishwasher. You open it up, and the eyes of a small rodent glint back at you. It scrambles out, off to the baseboards behind the refrigerator. Your mother, apparently, has put all the groceries inside the dishwasher. The milk is spilled, a white pool against blue, and things like cheese and bologna and apples have been nibbled at.

1973. At a party when a woman tells you where she bought some wonderful pair of shoes, say that you believe shopping for clothes is like masturbation — everyone does it, but it isn't very interesting and therefore should be done alone, in an embarrassed fashion, and never be the topic of party conversation. The woman will tighten her lips and eyebrows and say, "Oh, I suppose you have something more fascinating to talk about." Grow clumsy and uneasy. Say, "No," and head for the ginger ale. Tell the person next to you that your insides feel sort of sinking and vinyl like a Claes Oldenburg toilet. They will say, "Oh?" and point out that the print on your dress is one of paisleys impregnating paisleys. Pour yourself more ginger ale.

1972. Nixon wins by a landslide.

Sometimes your mother calls you by her sister's name. Say, "No, Mom, it's me. Virginia." Learn to repeat things. Learn that you have a way of knowing each other which somehow slips out and beyond the ways you have of not knowing each other at all.

Make apple crisp for the first time.

1971. Go for long walks to get away from her. Walk through wooded areas; there is a life there you have forgotten. The smells and sounds seem sudden, unchanged, exact, the papery crunch of the leaves, the mouldering sachet of the mud. The trees are crooked as backs, the fence posts splintered, trusting and precarious in their solid grasp of arms, the asters spindly, dry, white, havishammed (Havishammed!) by frost. Find a beautiful reddish stone and bring it home for your mother. Kiss her. Say: "This is for you." She grasps it and smiles. "You were always such a sensitive child," she says.

Say: "Yeah, I know."

1970. You are pregnant again. Try to decide what you should do.

Get your hair chopped, short as a boy's.

1969. Mankind leaps upon the moon.

Disposable diapers are first sold in supermarkets.

Have occasional affairs with absurd, silly men who tell you to grow your hair to your waist and who, when you are sad, tickle your ribs to cheer you up. Moonlight through the blinds stripes you like zebras. You laugh. You never marry.

1968. Do not resent her. Think about the situation, for instance, when you take the last trash bag from its box: you must throw out the box by putting it in that very trash bag. What was once contained, now must contain. The container, then, becomes the contained, the enveloped, the held. Find more and more that you like to muse over things like this.

1967. Your mother is sick and comes to live with you. There is no place else for her to go. You feel many different emptinesses.

The first successful heart transplant is performed in South Africa.

1966. You confuse lovers, mix up who had what scar, what car, what mother.

1965. Smoke marijuana. Try to figure out what has made your life go wrong. It is like trying to figure out what is stinking up the refrigerator. It could be anything. The lid off the mayonnaise, Uncle Ron's honey wine four years in the left corner. Broccoli yellowing, flowering fast. They are all metaphors. They are all problems. Your horoscope says: Speak gently to a loved one.

1964. Your mother calls long distance and asks whether you are coming home for Thanksgiving, your brother and the baby will be there. Make excuses.

"As a mother gets older," your mother says, "these sorts of holidays become increasingly important."

Say: "I'm sorry, Mom."

1963. Wake up one morning with a man you had thought you'd spend your life with, and realize, a rock in your gut, that you don't even like him. Spend a weepy afternoon in his bathroom, not coming out when he knocks. You can no longer trust your affections. People and places you think you love may be people and places you hate.

Kennedy is shot.

Someone invents a temporary artificial heart, for use during operations.

1962. Eat Chinese food for the first time, with a lawyer from California. He will show you how to hold the chopsticks. He will pat your leg. Attack his profession. Ask him whether he feels the law makes large spokes out of the short stakes of men.

1961. Grandma Moses dies.

You are a zoo of insecurities. You take to putting brandy in your morning coffee and to falling in love too easily. You have an abortion.

1960. There is money from your father's will and his life insurance. You buy a car and a green velvet dress you don't need. You drive two hours to meet your mother for lunch on Saturdays. She suggests things for you to write about, things she's heard on the radio: a woman with telepathic twins, a woman with no feet.

1959. At the funeral she says: "He had his problems, but he was a generous man," though you know he was tight as a scout knot, couldn't listen to anyone, the only time you remember loving him being that once when he got the punchline of one of your jokes before your mom did and looked up from his science journal and guffawed loud as a giant, the two of you, for one split moment, communing like angels in the middle of that room, in that warm, shared light of mind.

Say: "He was okay."

"You shouldn't be bitter," your mother snaps. "He financed you and your brother's college educations." She buttons her coat. "He was also the first man to isolate a particular isotope of helium, I forget the name, but he should have won the Nobel Prize." She dabs at her nose.

Say: "Yeah, Mom."

1958. At your brother's wedding, your father is taken away in an ambulance. A tiny cousin whispers loudly to her mother, "Did Uncle Will have a hard attack?" For seven straight days say things to your mother like: "I'm sure it'll be okay," and "I'll stay here, why don't you go home and get some sleep."

1957. Dance the calypso with boys from a different college. Get looped on New York State burgundy, lose your virginity, and buy one of the first portable electric typewriters.

1956. Tell your mother about all the books you are reading at college. This will please her.

1955. Do a paint-by-numbers of Elvis Presley. Tell your mother you are in love with him. She will shake her head.

1954. Shoplift a cashmere sweater.

1953. Smoke a cigarette with Hillary Swedelson. Tell each other your crushes. Become blood sisters.

1952. When your mother asks you if there are any nice boys in junior high, ask her how on earth would you ever know, having to come in at nine! every night. Her eyebrows will lift like theater curtains. "You poor, abused thing," she will say.

Say, "Don't I know it," and slam the door.

1951. Your mother tells you about menstruation. The following day you promptly menstruate, your body only waiting for permission, for a signal. You wake up in the morning and feel embarrassed.

1949. You learn how to blow gum bubbles and to add negative numbers.

1947. The Dead Sea Scrolls are discovered.
   You have seen too many Hollywood musicals. You have seen too many people singing in public places and you assume you can do it, too. Practice. Your teacher asks you a question. You warble back: "The answer to number two is twelve." Most of the class laughs at you, though some stare, eyes jewel-still, fascinated. At home your mother asks you to dust your dresser. Work up a vibrato you could drive a truck through. Sing: "Why do I have to do it now?" and tap your way through the dining room. Your mother requests that you calm down and go take a nap. Shout: "You don't care about me! You don't care about me at all!"

1946. Your brother plays "Shoofly Pie" all day long on the Victrola.
   Ask your mother if you can go to Ellen's for supper. She will say, "Go ask your father," and you, pulling at your fingers, walk out to the living room and whimper by his chair. He is reading. Tap his arm. "Dad? Daddy? Dad?" He continues reading his science journal. Pull harder on your fingers and run back to the kitchen to tell your mother, who storms into the living room, saying, "Why don't you ever listen to your children when they try to talk to you?" You hear them arguing. Press your face into a kitchen towel, ashamed, the hum of the refrigerator motor, the drip in the sink scaring you.

1945. Your father comes home from his war work. He gives you a piggyback ride around the broad yellow thatch of your yard, the dead window in the turret, dark as a wound, watching you. He gives you wordless pushes on the swing.
   Your brother has new friends, acts older and distant, even while you wait for the school bus together.
   You spend too much time alone. You tell your mother that when you grow up you will bring your babies to Australia to see the kangaroos.
   Forty thousand people are killed in Nagasaki.

1944. Dress and cuddle a tiny babydoll you have named "the Sue." Bring her everywhere. Get lost in the Wilson Creek fruit market, and call softly, "Mom, where are you?" Watch other children picking grapes, but never dare yourself. Your eyes are small, dark throats, your hand clutches the Sue.

1943. Ask your mother about babies. Have her read to you only the stories about babies. Ask her if she is going to have a baby. Ask her about the baby that died. Cry into her arm.

1940. Clutch her hair in your fist. Rub it against your cheek.

1939. As through a helix, as through an ear, it is here you are nearer the dream flashes, the other lives.

There is a tent of legs, a sundering of selves, as you both gasp blindly for breath. Across the bright and cold, she knows it when you try to talk to her, though this is something you never really manage to understand.

Germany invades Poland.

The year's big song is "Three Little Fishies" and someone somewhere, is playing it.

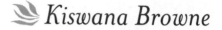 *Kiswana Browne*

GLORIA NAYLOR

FROM THE WINDOW of her sixth-floor studio apartment, Kiswana could see over the wall at the end of the street to the busy avenue that lay just north of Brewster Place. The late afternoon shoppers looked like brightly clad marionettes as they moved between the congested traffic, clutching their packages against their bodies to guard them from sudden bursts of the cold autumn wind. A portly mailman had abandoned his cart and was bumping into indignant window shoppers as he puffed behind the cap that the wind had snatched from his head. Kiswana leaned over to see if he was going to be successful, but the edge of the building cut him off from her view.

A pigeon swept across her window, and she marveled at its liquid movements in the air waves. She placed her dreams on the back of the bird and fantasized that it would glide forever in transparent silver circles until it ascended to the center of the universe and was swallowed up. But the wind died down, and she watched with a sigh as the bird beat its wings in awkward, frantic movements to land on the corroded top of a fire escape on the opposite building. This brought her back to earth.

Humph, it's probably sitting over there crapping on those folks' fire escape, she thought. Now, that's a safety hazard.... And her mind was busy again, creating flames and smoke and frustrated tenants whose escape was being hindered because they were slipping and sliding in pigeon shit. She watched their cussing, haphazard descent on the fire escapes until they had all reached the bottom. They were milling around, oblivious to their burning apartments, angrily planning to march on the mayor's office about the pigeons. She materialized placards and banners for them, and they had just reached the corner, boldly sidestepping fire hoses and broken glass, when they all vanished.

A tall copper-skinned woman had met this phantom parade at the corner, and they had dissolved in front of her long confident strides. She plowed through the remains of their faded mists, unconscious of the lingering wisps of their presence on her leather bag and black fur-trimmed coat. It took a few seconds for this transfer from one realm to another to reach Kiswana, but then suddenly she recognized the woman.

"Oh, God, it's Mama!" She looked down guiltily at the forgotten newspaper in her lap and hurriedly circled random job advertisements.

By this time Mrs. Browne had reached the front of Kiswana's building and was checking the house number against a piece of paper in her hand. Before she went into the building she stood at the bottom of the stoop and carefully inspected the condition of the street and the adjoining property. Kiswana watched this meticulous inventory with growing annoyance, but she involuntarily followed her mother's slowly rotating head, forcing herself to see her new neighborhood through the older woman's eyes. The brightness of the unclouded sky seemed to join forces with her mother as it highlighted every broken stoop railing and missing brick. The afternoon sun glittered and cascaded across even the tiniest fragments of broken bottle, and at that very moment the wind chose to rise up again, sending unswept grime flying into the air, as a stray tin can left by careless garbage collectors went rolling noisily down the center of the street.

Kiswana noticed with relief that at least Ben wasn't sitting in his usual place on the old garbage can pushed against the far wall. He was just a harmless old wino, but Kiswana knew her mother only needed one wino or one teenager with a reefer within a twenty-block radius to decide that her daughter was living in a building seething with dope factories and hangouts for derelicts. If she had seen Ben, nothing would have made her believe that practically every apartment contained a family, a Bible, and a dream that one day enough could be scraped from those meager Friday night paychecks to make Brewster Place a distant memory.

As she watched her mother's head disappear into the building, Kiswana gave silent thanks that the elevator was broken. That would give her at least five minutes' grace to straighten up the apartment. She rushed to the sofa bed and hastily closed it without smoothing the rumpled sheets and blanket or removing her nightgown. She felt that somehow the tangled bedcovers would give away the fact that she had not slept alone last night. She silently apologized to Abshu's memory as she heartlessly crushed his spirit between the steel springs of the couch. Lord, that man was sweet. Her toes curled involuntarily at the passing thought of his full lips moving slowly over her instep. Abshu was a foot man, and he always started his lovemaking from the bottom up. For that reason Kiswana changed the color of the polish on her toenails every week. During the course of their relationship she had gone from shades of red to brown and was now into the purples. I'm gonna have to start mixing them soon, she thought aloud as she turned from the couch and raced into the bathroom to remove any traces of Abshu from there. She took up his shaving cream and razor and threw them into the bottom drawer of her dresser beside her diaphragm. Mama wouldn't dare pry into my drawers right in front of me, she thought as she slammed the drawer shut. Well, at least not the bottom drawer. She may come up with some sham excuse for opening the top drawer, but never the *bottom* one.

When she heard the first two short raps on the door, her eyes took a final flight over the small apartment, desperately seeking out any slight misdemeanor that might have to be defended. Well, there was nothing she could do about the crack in the wall over that table. She had been after the landlord to fix it for two months now. And there had been no time to sweep the rug, and everyone knew that off-gray always looked dirtier than it really was. And it was just too damn bad about the kitchen. How was she expected to be out job hunting every day and still have time to keep a kitchen that looked like her mother's, who didn't even work and still had someone come in twice a month for general cleaning. And besides...

Her imaginary argument was abruptly interrupted by a second series of knocks, accompanied by a penetrating, "Melanie, Melanie, are you there?"

Kiswana strode toward the door. She's starting before she even gets in here. She knows that's not my name anymore.

She swung the door open to face her slightly flushed mother. "Oh, hi, Mama. You know, I thought I heard a knock, but I figured it was for the people next door, since no one hardly ever calls me Melanie." Score one for me, she thought.

"Well, it's awfully strange you can forget a name you answered to for twenty-three years," Mrs. Browne said, as she moved past Kiswana into the apartment. "My, that was a long climb. How long has your elevator been out? Honey, how do you manage with your laundry and groceries up all those steps? But I guess you're young, and it wouldn't bother you as much as it does me." This long string of questions told Kiswana that her mother had no intentions of beginning her visit with another argument about her new African name.

"You know I would have called before I came, but you don't have a phone yet. I didn't want you to feel that I was snooping. As a matter of fact, I didn't expect to find you home at all. I thought you'd be out looking for a job." Mrs. Browne had mentally covered the entire apartment while she was talking and taking off her coat.

"Well, I got up late this morning. I thought I'd buy the afternoon paper and start early tomorrow."

"That sounds like a good idea." Her mother moved toward the window and picked up the discarded paper and glanced over the hurriedly circled ads. "Since when do you have experience as a forklift operator?"

Kiswana caught her breath and silently cursed herself for her stupidity. "Oh, my hand slipped — I meant to circle file clerk." She quickly took the paper before her mother could see that she had also marked cutlery salesman and chauffeur.

"You're sure you weren't sitting here moping and daydreaming again?" Amber specks of laughter flashed in the corner of Mrs. Browne's eyes.

Kiswana threw her shoulders back and unsuccessfully tried to disguise her embarrassment with indignation.

"Oh, God, Mama! I haven't done that in years — it's for kids. When are you going to realize that I'm a woman now?" She sought desperately for some womanly thing to do and settled for throwing herself on the couch and crossing her legs in what she hoped looked like a nonchalant arc.

"Please, have a seat," she said, attempting the same tones and gestures she'd seen Bette Davis use on the late movies.

Mrs. Browne, lowering her eyes to hide her amusement, accepted the invitation and sat at the window, also crossing her legs. Kiswana saw immediately how it should have been done. Her celluloid poise clashed loudly against her mother's quiet dignity, and she quickly uncrossed her legs. Mrs. Browne turned her head toward the window and pretended not to notice.

"At least you have a halfway decent view from here. I was wondering what lay beyond that dreadful wall — it's the boulevard. Honey, did you know that you can see the trees in Linden Hills from here?"

Kiswana knew that very well, because there were many lonely days that she would sit in her gray apartment and stare at those trees and think of home, but she would rather have choked than admit that to her mother.

"Oh, really, I never noticed. So how is Daddy and things at home?"

"Just fine. We're thinking of redoing one of the extra bedrooms since you children have moved out, but Wilson insists that he can manage all that work alone. I told him that he doesn't really have the proper time or energy for all that. As it is, when he gets home from the office, he's so tired he can hardly move. But you know you can't tell your father anything. Whenever he starts complaining about how stubborn you are, I tell him the child came by it honestly. Oh, and your brother was by yesterday," she added, as if it had just occurred to her.

So that's it, thought Kiswana. That's why she's here.

Kiswana's brother, Wilson, had been to visit her two days ago, and she had borrowed twenty dollars from him to get her winter coat out of layaway. That son-of-a-bitch probably ran straight to Mama — and after he swore he wouldn't say anything. I should have known, he was always a snotty-nosed sneak, she thought.

"Was he?" she said aloud. "He came by to see me, too, earlier this week. And I borrowed some money from him because my unemployment checks hadn't cleared in the bank, but now they have and everything's just fine." There, I'll beat you to that one.

"Oh, I didn't know that," Mrs. Browne lied. "He never mentioned you. He had just heard that Beverly was expecting again, and he rushed over to tell us."

Damn. Kiswana could have strangled herself.

"So she's knocked up again, huh?" she said irritably.

Her mother started. "Why do you always have to be so crude?"

"Personally, I don't see how she can sleep with Willie. He's such a dishrag."

Kiswana still resented the stance her brother had taken in college.

When everyone at school was discovering their blackness and protesting on campus, Wilson never took part; he had even refused to wear an Afro. This had outraged Kiswana because, unlike her, he was dark skinned and had the type of hair that was thick and kinky enough for a good "Fro." Kiswana had still insisted on cutting her own hair, but it was so thin and fine textured, it refused to thicken even after she washed it. So she had to brush it up and spray it with lacquer to keep it from lying flat. She never forgave Wilson for telling her that she didn't look African, she looked like an electrocuted chicken.

"Now that's some way to talk. I don't know why you have an attitude against your brother. He never gave me a restless night's sleep, and now he's settled with a family and a good job."

"He's an assistant to an assistant junior partner in a law firm. What's the big deal about that?"

"The job has a future, Melanie. And at least he finished school and went on for his law degree."

"In other words, not like me, huh?"

"Don't put words into my mouth, young lady. I'm perfectly capable of saying what I mean."

Amen, thought Kiswana.

"And I don't know why you've been trying to start up with me from the moment I walked in. I didn't come here to fight with you. This is your first place away from home, and I just wanted to see how you were living and if you're doing all right. And I must say, you've fixed this apartment up very nicely."

"Really, Mama?" She found herself softening in the light of her mother's approval.

"Well, considering what you had to work with." This time she scanned the apartment openly.

"Look, I know it's not Linden Hills, but a lot can be done with it. As soon as they come and paint, I'm going to hang my Ashanti print over the couch. And I thought a big Boston Fern would go well in that corner, what do you think?"

"That would be fine, baby. You always had a good eye for balance."

Kiswana was beginning to relax. There was little she did that attracted her mother's approval. It was like a rare bird, and she had to tread carefully around it lest it fly away.

"Are you going to leave that statue out like that?"

"Why, what's wrong with it? Would it look better somewhere else?"

There was a small wooden reproduction of a Yoruba goddess with large protruding breasts on the coffee table.

"Well," Mrs. Browne was beginning to blush, "it's just that it's a bit suggestive, don't you think? Since you live alone now, and I know you'll be having male friends stop by, you wouldn't want to be giving them any ideas. I mean, uh, you know, there's no point in putting yourself in any unpleasant situations because they may get the wrong impressions and uh, you know, I mean, well. . ." Mrs. Browne stammered on miserably.

Kiswana loved it when her mother tried to talk about sex. It was the only time she was at a loss for words.

"Don't worry, Mama." Kiswana smiled. "That wouldn't bother the type of men I date. Now maybe if it had big feet..." And she got hysterical, thinking of Abshu.

Her mother looked at her sharply. "What sort of gibberish is that about feet? I'm being serious, Melanie."

"I'm sorry, Mama." She sobered up. "I'll put it away in the closet," she said, knowing that she wouldn't.

"Good," Mrs. Browne said, knowing that she wouldn't either. "I guess you think I'm too picky, but we worry about you over here. And you refuse to put in a phone so we can call and see about you."

"I haven't refused, Mama. They want seventy-five dollars for a deposit, and I can't swing that right now."

"Melanie, I can give you the money."

"I don't want you to be giving me money — I've told you that before. Please, let me make it by myself."

"Well, let me lend it to you, then."

"No!"

"Oh, so you can borrow money from your brother, but not from me."

Kiswana turned her head from the hurt in her mother's eyes. "Mama, when I borrow from Willie, he makes me pay him back. You never let me pay you back," she said into her hands.

"I don't care. I still think it's downright selfish of you to be sitting over here with no phone, and sometimes we don't hear from you in two weeks — anything could happen — especially living among these people."

Kiswana snapped her head up. "What do you mean, these people. They're my people and yours, too, Mama — we're all black. But maybe you've forgotten that over in Linden Hills."

"That's not what I'm talking about, and you know it. These streets — this building — it's so shabby and rundown. Honey, you don't have to live like this."

"Well, this is how poor people live."

"Melanie, you're not poor."

"No, Mama, *you're* not poor. And what you have and I have are two totally different things. I don't have a husband in real estate with a five-figure income and a home in Linden Hills — *you* do. What I have is a weekly unemployment check and an overdrawn checking account at United Federal. So this studio on Brewster is all I can afford."

"Well, you could afford a lot better," Mrs. Browne snapped, "if you hadn't dropped out of college and had to resort to these dead-end clerical jobs."

"Uh-huh, I knew you'd get around to that before long." Kiswana could feel the rings of anger begin to tighten around her lower backbone, and they sent her forward onto the couch. "You'll never understand, will you? Those bourgie schools were counterrevolutionary. My place was in the streets with my people, fighting for equality and a better community."

"Counterrevolutionary!" Mrs. Browne was raising her voice. "Where's your revolution now, Melanie? Where are all those black revolutionaries who were shouting and demonstrating and kicking up a lot of dust with you on that campus? Huh? They're sitting in wood-paneled offices with their degrees in mahogany frames, and they won't even drive their cars past this street because the city doesn't fix potholes in this part of town."

"Mama," she said, shaking her head slowly in disbelief "how can you — a black woman — sit there and tell me that what we fought for during the Movement wasn't important just because some people sold out?"

"Melanie, I'm not saying it wasn't important. It was damned important to stand up and say that you were proud of what you were and to get the vote and other social opportunities for every person in this country who had it due. But you kids thought you were going to turn the world upside down, and it just wasn't so. When all the smoke had cleared you found yourself with a fistful of new federal laws and a country still full of obstacles for black people to fight their way over — just because they're black. There was no revolution, Melanie, and there will be no revolution."

"So what am I supposed to do, huh? Just throw up my hands and not care about what happens to my people? I'm not supposed to keep fighting to make things better?"

"Of course, you can. But you're going to have to fight within the system, because it and these so-called 'bourgie' schools are going to be here for a long time. And that means that you get smart like a lot of your old friends and get an important job where you can have some influence. You don't have to sell out, as you say, and work for some corporation, but you could become an assemblywoman or a civil liberties lawyer or open a freedom school in this very neighborhood. That way you could really help the community. But what help are you going to be to these people on Brewster while you're living hand-to-mouth on file-clerk jobs waiting for a revolution? You're wasting your talents, child."

"Well, I don't think they're being wasted. At least I'm here in day-to-day contact with the problems of my people. What good would I be after four or five years of a lot of white brainwashing in some phony, prestige institution, huh? I'd be like you and Daddy and those other educated blacks sitting over there in Linden Hills with a terminal case of middle-class amnesia."

"You don't have to live in a slum to be concerned about social conditions, Melanie. Your father and I have been charter members of the NAACP for the last twenty-five years."

"Oh, God!" Kiswana threw her head back in exaggerated disgust. "That's being concerned? That middle-of-the-road, Uncle Tom dumping ground for black Republicans!"

"You can sneer all you want, young lady, but that organization has been working for black people since the turn of the century, and it's still working for them. Where are all those radical groups of yours that were going to put a Cadillac in every garage and Dick Gregory in the White House? I'll tell you where."

I knew you would, Kiswana thought angrily.

"They burned themselves out because they wanted too much too fast. Their goals weren't grounded in reality. And that's always been your problem."

"What do you mean, my problem? I know exactly what I'm about."

"No, you don't. You constantly live in a fantasy world — always going to extremes — turning butterflies into eagles, and life isn't about that. It's accepting what is and working from that. Lord, I remember how worried you had me, putting all that lacquered hair spray on your head. I thought you were going to get lung cancer — trying to be what you're not."

Kiswana jumped up from the couch. "Oh, God, I can't take this anymore. Trying to be something I'm not — trying to be something I'm not, Mama! Trying to be proud of my heritage and the fact that I was of African descent. If that's being what I'm not, then I say fine. But I'd rather be dead than be like you — a white man's nigger who's ashamed of being black!"

Kiswana saw streaks of gold and ebony light follow her mother's flying body out of the chair. She was swung around by the shoulders and made to face the deadly stillness in the angry woman's eyes. She was too stunned to cry out from the pain of the long fingernails that dug into her shoulders and she was brought so close to her mother's face that she saw her reflection, distorted and wavering, in the tears that stood in the older woman's eyes. And she listened in that stillness to a story she had heard from a child.

"My grandmother," Mrs. Browne began slowly in a whisper, "was a full-blooded Iroquois, and my grandfather a free black from a long line of journeymen who had lived in Connecticut since the establishment of the colonies. And my father was a Bajan who came to this country as a cabin boy on a merchant mariner."

"I know all that," Kiswana said, trying to keep her lips from trembling.

"Then, know this." And the nails dug deeper into her flesh. "I am alive because of the blood of proud people who never scraped or begged or apologized for what they were. They lived asking only one thing of this world — to be allowed to be. And I learned through the blood of these people that black isn't beautiful and it isn't ugly — black is! It's not kinky hair and it's not straight hair — it just is.

"It broke my heart when you changed your name. I gave you my grandmother's name, a woman who bore nine children and educated them all, who held off six white men with a shotgun when they tried to drag one of her sons to jail for 'not knowing his place.' Yet you needed to reach into an African dictionary to find a name to make you proud.

"When I brought my babies home from the hospital, my ebony son and my golden daughter, I swore before whatever gods would listen — those of my mother's people or those of my father's people — that I would use everything I had and could ever get to see that my children were prepared to meet this world on its own terms, so that no one could sell them short and make them ashamed of what they were or how they looked — whatever they were or however they looked. And Melanie, that's not being white or red or black — that's being a mother."

Kiswana followed her reflection in the two single tears that moved down her mother's cheeks until it blended with them into the woman's copper skin. There was nothing and then so much that she wanted to say, but her throat kept closing up every time she tried to speak. She kept her head down and her eyes closed, and thought, Oh, God, just let me die. How can I face her now?

Mrs. Browne lifted Kiswana's chin gently. "And the one lesson I wanted you to learn is not to be afraid to face anyone, not even a crafty old lady like me who can outtalk you." And she smiled and winked.

"Oh, Mama, I..." and she hugged the woman tightly.

"Yeah, baby." Mrs. Browne patted her back. "I know."

She kissed Kiswana on the forehead and cleared her throat. "Well, now, I better be moving on. It's getting late, there's dinner to be made, and I have to get off my feet — these new shoes are killing me."

Kiswana looked down at the beige leather pumps. "Those are really classy. They're English, aren't they?"

"Yes, but, Lord, do they cut me right across the instep." She removed the shoe and sat on the couch to massage her foot.

Bright red nail polish glared at Kiswana through the stockings. "Since when do you polish your toenails?" she gasped. "You never did that before."

"Well..." Mrs. Browne shrugged her shoulders, "your father sort of talked me into it, and, uh, you know, he likes it and all, so I thought, uh, you know, why not, so..." And she gave Kiswana an embarrassed smile.

I'll be damned, the young woman thought, feeling her whole face tingle. Daddy's into feet! And she looked at the blushing woman on her couch and suddenly realized that her mother had trod through the same universe that she herself was now traveling. Kiswana was breaking no new trails and would eventually end up just two feet away on that couch. She stared at the woman she had been and was to become.

"But I'll never be a Republican," she caught herself saying aloud.

"What are you mumbling about, Melanie?" Mrs. Browne slipped on her shoe and got up from the couch.

She went to get her mother's coat. "Nothing, Mama. It's really nice of you to come by. You should do it more often."

"Well, since it's not Sunday, I guess you're allowed at least one lie."

They both laughed.

After Kiswana had closed the door and turned around, she spotted an envelope sticking between the cushions of her couch. She went over and opened it up; there was seventy-five dollars in it.

"Oh, Mama, darn it!" She rushed to the window and started to call to the woman, who had just emerged from the building, but she suddenly changed her mind and sat down in the chair with a long sigh that caught in the upward draft of the autumn wind and disappeared over the top of the building.

A Rose in the Heart of New York

Edna O'Brien

DECEMBER NIGHT. Jack Frost in scales along the outside of the windows giving to the various rooms a white filtered light. The ice like bits of mirror beveling the puddles of the potholes. The rooms were cold inside, and for the most part identically furnished. The room with no furniture at all — save for the apples gathered in the autumn — was called the Vacant Room. The apples were all over the place. Their smell was heady, many of them having begun to rot. Rooms into which no one had stepped for days, and yet these rooms and their belongings would become part of the remembered story. A solemn house, set in its own grounds, away from the lazy bustle of the village. A lonesome house, it would prove to be, and with a strange life-likeness, as if it were not a house at all but a person observing and breathing, a presence amid a cluster of trees and sturdy windshorn hedges.

The overweight midwife hurried up the drive, her serge cape blowing behind her. She was puffing. She carried her barrel-shaped leather bag in which were disinfectant, gauze, forceps, instruments, and a small bottle of holy water lest the new child should prove to be in danger of death. More infants died around Christmastime than in any other month of the year. When she passed the little sycamore tree that was halfway up, she began to hear the roaring and beseeching to God. Poor mother, she thought, poor poor mother. She was not too early, had come more or less at the correct time, even though she was summoned hours before by Donal, the serving boy who worked on the farm. She had brought most of the children of that parish into the world, yet had neither kith nor kin of her own. Coming in the back door, she took off her bonnet and then attached it to the knob by means of its elastic string.

❈ ❈ ❈

It was a blue room — walls of dark wet morose blue, furniture made of walnut, including the bed on which the event was taking place. Fronting the fireplace was a huge lid of a chocolate box with the representation of a saucy-looking lady. The tassel of the blind kept bobbing against the frosted windowpane. There was a washstand, a basin and ewer of off-white, with big roses splashed throughout the china itself, and a huge lumbering beast of a wardrobe. The midwife recalled once going to a house up the mountain and finding that the child had been smothered by the time she arrived; the fatherless child had been stuffed in a drawer. The moans filled that room and went beyond the distempered walls out into the cold hall outside, where the black felt doggie with the amber eyes stood sentinel on a tall varnished whatnot. At intervals the woman apologized to the midwife for the untoward commotion, said sorry in a gasping whisper, and then was seized again by a pain that at different times she described as being a knife, a dagger, a hell on earth. It was her fourth labor. The previous child had died two days after being born. An earlier child, also a daughter, had died of whooping cough. Her womb was sick unto death. Why be a woman? Oh, cruel life; oh, merciless fate; oh, heartless man, she sobbed. Gripping the coverlet and remembering that between those selfsame, much-patched sheets, she had been prized apart, again and again, with not a word to her, not a little endearment, only rammed through and told to open up. When she married she had escaped the life of a serving girl, the possible experience of living in some grim institution, but as time went on and the bottom drawer was emptied of its gifts, she saw that she was made to serve in an altogether other way. When she wasn't screaming she was grinding her head into the pillow and praying for it to be all over. She dreaded the eventual bloodshed long before they saw any. The midwife made her ease up as she put an old sheet under her and over that a bit of oilcloth. The midwife said it was no joke and repeated the hypothesis that if men had to give birth there would not be a child born in the whole wide world. The husband was downstairs getting paralytic. Earlier when his wife had announced that she would have to go upstairs because of her labor, he said, looking for the slightest pretext for a celebration, that if there was any homemade wine or altar wine stacked away, to get it out, to produce it, and also the cut glasses. She said there was none and well he knew it, since they could hardly afford tea and sugar. He started to root and to rummage, to empty cupboards of their contents of rags, garments, and provisions, even to put his hand inside the bolster case, to delve into pillows; on he went, rampaging until he found a bottle in the wardrobe, in the very room into which she delivered her moans and exhortations. She begged of him not to, but all he did was to wield the amber-colored bottle in her direction, and then put it to his head so that the spirit started to go glug-glug. It was intoxicating stuff. By a wicked coincidence a crony of his had come to sell them another stove, most likely another crock, a thing that would have to be coaxed alight with constant attention and puffing to create a draft. The other child was with a neighbor, the dead ones in a graveyard six or seven miles away, among strangers and distant relatives, without their names being carved on the crooked rain-soaked tomb.

"O Jesus," she cried out as he came back to ask for a knitting needle to skewer out the bit of broken cork.

"Blazes," he said to her as she coiled into a knot and felt the big urgent ball — that would be the head — as it pressed on the base of her bowels and battered at her insides.

Curses and prayers combined to issue out of her mouth, and as time went on, they became most pitiful and were interrupted with screams. The midwife put a facecloth on her forehead and told her to push, in the name of the Lord to push. She said she had no strength left, but the midwife went on enjoining her and simulating a hefty breath. It took more than an hour. The little head showing its tonsure would recoil, would reshow itself, each time a fraction more, although, in between, it was seeming to shrink from the world that it was hurtling toward. She said to the nurse that she was being burst apart, and that she no longer cared if she died, or if they drank themselves to death. In the kitchen they were sparring over who had the best greyhound, who had the successor to Mick the Miller. The crucifix that had been in her hand had fallen out, and her hands themselves felt bony and skinned because of the way they wrenched one another.

"In the name of God, push, missus."

She would have pushed everything out of herself, her guts, her womb, her craw, her lights, and her liver, but the center of her body was holding on and this center seemed to be the governor of her. She wished to be nothing, a shell, devoid of everything and everyone, and she was announcing that, and roaring and raving, when the child came hurtling out, slowly at first, as if its neck could not wring its way through, then the shoulder — that was the worst bit — carving a straight course, then the hideous turnabout, and a scream other than her own, and an urgent presage of things, as the great gouts of blood and lymph followed upon the mewling creature itself. Her last bit of easiness was then torn from her, and she was without hope. It had come into the world lopsided, and the first announcement from the midwife was a fatality, was that it had clubbed feet. Its little feet, she ventured to say, were like two stumps adhering to one another, and the blasted cord was bound around its neck. The result was a mewling piece of screwed-up, inert, dark-purple misery. The men subsided a little when the announcement was shouted down and they came to say congrats. The father waved a strip of pink flesh on a fork that he was carrying and remarked on its being unappetizing. They were cooking a goose downstairs and he said in future he would insist on turkey, as goose was only for gobs and goms. The mother felt green and disgusted, asked them to leave her alone. The salesman said was it a boy or a child, although he had just been told that it was a daughter. The mother could feel the blood gushing out of her, like water at a weir. The midwife told them to go down and behave like gentlemen.

Then she got three back numbers of the weekly paper, and a shoe box with a lid, and into it she stuffed the mess and the unnecessaries. She hummed as she prepared to do the stitching down the line of torn flesh that was gaping and coated with blood. The mother roared again and said this indeed was her vinegar and gall. She bit into the crucifix and dented it further. She could feel her mouth and her eyelids being stitched, too; she was no longer a lovely body, she was a vehicle for pain and for insult. The child was so quiet it scarcely breathed. The afterbirth was placed on the stove, where the dog, Shep, sniffed at it through its layers of paper and for his curiosity got a kick in the tail. The stove had been quenched, and the midwife said to the men that it was a crying shame to leave a good goose like that, neither cooked nor uncooked. The men had torn off bits of the breast so that the goose looked wounded, like the woman upstairs, who was then tightening her heart and soul, tightening inside the array of catgut stitches, and regarding her whole life as a vast disappointment. The midwife carried the big bundle to the cellar, put an oil rag to it, set a match to it, and knew that she would have to be off soon to do the same task elsewhere. She would have liked to stay and swaddle the infant, and comfort the woman, and drink hot sweet tea, but there was not enough time. There was never enough time, and she hadn't even cleaned out the ashes or the cinders in her grate that morning.

The child was in a corner of the room in a brown cot with slats that rattled because of the racket they had received from the previous children. The mother was not proud, far from it. She fed the child its first bottle, looked down at its wizened face, and thought, Where have you come from and why? She had no choice of a name. In fact, she said to her first visitor, a lieutenant from the army, not to tell her a pack of lies, because this child had the ugliest face that had ever seen the light of day. That Christmas the drinking and sparring went on, the odd neighbor called, the mother got up on the third day and staggered down to do something about the unruly kitchen. Each evening at nightfall she got a bit of a candle to have handy and re-oiled the Sacred Heart lamp for when the child cried. They both contracted bronchitis and the child was impounded in masses of flannel and flannelette.

Things changed. The mother came to idolize the child, because it was so quiet, never bawling, never asking for anything, just weirdly still in its pram, the dog watching over it, its eyes staring out at whatever happened to loom in. Its very ugliness disappeared. It seemed to drink them in with its huge, contemplating, slightly hazed-over navy eyes. They shone at whatever they saw. The mother would look in the direction of the pram and say a little prayer for it, or smile, and often at night she held the candle shielded by her hand to see the face, to say pet or tush, to say nonsense to it. It ate whatever it was given, but as time went on, it knew what it liked and had a sweet tooth. The food was what united them, eating off the same plate, using the same spoon, watching one another's chews, feeling the food as it went down the other's neck. The child was slow to crawl and slower still to walk, but it knew everything, it perceived everything. When it ate blancmange or junket, it was eating part of the lovely substance of its mother.

They were together, always together. If its mother went to the post office, the child stood in the middle of the drive praying until its mother returned safely. The child cut the ridges of four fingers along the edge of a razor blade that had been wedged upright in the wood of the dresser, and seeing these four deep, horizontal identical slits the mother took the poor fingers into her own mouth and sucked them, to lessen the pain, and licked them to abolish the blood, and kept saying soft things until the child was stilled again.

Her mother's knuckles were her knuckles, her mother's veins were her veins, her mother's lap was a second heaven, her mother's forehead a copybook onto which she traced A B C D, her mother's body was a recess that she would wander inside forever and ever, a sepulcher growing deeper and deeper. When she saw other people, especially her pretty sister, she would simply wave from that safe place, she would not budge, would not be lured out. Her father took a hatchet to her mother and threatened that he would split open the head of her. The child watched through the kitchen window, because this debacle took place outdoors on a hillock under the three beech trees where the clothesline stretched, then sagged. The mother had been hanging out the four sheets washed that morning, two off each bed. The child was engaged in twisting her hair, looping it around bits of white rag, to form ringlets, decking herself in the kitchen mirror, and then every other minute running across to the window to reconnoiter, wondering what she ought to do, jumping up and down as if she had a pain, not knowing what to do, running back to the mirror, hoping that the terrible scene would pass, that the ground would open up and swallow her father, that the hatchet would turn into a magic wand, that her mother would come through the kitchen door and say "Fear not," that travail would all be over. Later she heard a verbatim account of what had happened. Her father demanded money, her mother refused same on the grounds that she had none, but added that if she had it she would hang sooner than give it to him. That did it. It was then he really got bucking, gritted his teeth and his muscles, said that he would split the head of her, and the mother said that if he did so there was a place for him. That place was the lunatic asylum. It was twenty or thirty miles away, a big gray edifice, men and women lumped in together, some in straitjackets, some in padded cells, some blindfolded because of having sacks thrown over their heads, some strapped across the chest to quell and impede them. Those who did not want to go there were dragged by relatives, or by means of rope, some being tied on to the end of a plow or a harrow and brought in on all fours, like beasts of the earth. Then when they were not so mad, not so rampaging, they were let home again, where they were very peculiar and given to smiling and to chattering to themselves, and in no time they were ripe to go off again or to be dragged off. March was the worst month, when everything went askew, even the wind, even the March hares. Her father did not go there. He went off on a batter and then went to a monastery, and then was brought home and shook in the bed chair for five days, eating bread and milk and asking who would convey him over the fields, until he saw his yearlings, and when no one volunteered to, it fell to her because she was the youngest. Over in the fields he patted the yearlings and said soppy things that he'd never say indoors, or to a human, and he cried and said he'd never touch a drop again, and there was a dribble on his pewter-brown mustache that was the remains of the mush he had been eating, and the yearling herself became fidgety and fretful as if she might bolt or stamp the ground to smithereens.

The girl and her mother took walks on Sundays — strolls, picked blackberries, consulted them for worms, made preserve, and slept side by side, entwined like twigs of trees or the ends of the sugar tongs. When she wakened and found that her mother had got up and was already mixing meals for the hens or stirabout for the young pigs, she hurried down, carrying her clothes under her arm, and dressed in whatever spot she could feast on the sight of her mother most. Always an egg for breakfast. An egg a day and she would grow strong. Her mother never ate an egg but topped the girl's egg and fed her it off the tarnished eggy spoon and gave her little sups of tea with which to wash it down. She had her own mug, red enamel and with not a chip. The girl kept looking back as she went down the drive for school, and as time went on, she mastered the knack of walking backward to be able to look all the longer, look at the aproned figure waving or holding up a potato pounder or a colander, or whatever happened to be in her hand.

The girl came home once and the mother was missing. Her mother had actually fulfilled her promise of going away one day and going to a spot where she would not be found. That threatened spot was the bottom of the lake. But in fact her mottler had gone back to her own family, because the father had taken a shotgun to her and had shot her but was not a good aim like William Tell, had missed, had instead made a hole in the Blue Room wall. What were they doing upstairs in the middle of the day, an ascent they never made except the mother alone to dress the two beds? She could guess. She slept in a neighbor's house, slept in a bed with two old people who reeked of eucalyptus. She kept most of her clothes on and shriveled into herself, not wanting to touch or be touched by these two old people buried in their various layers of skin and hair and winceyette. Outside the window was a climbing rose with three or four red flowers along the bow of it, and looking at the flowers and thinking of the wormy clay, she would try to shut out what these two old people were saying, in order that she could remember the mother whom she despaired of ever seeing again. Not far away was their own house, with the back door wide open so that any stranger or tinker could come in or out. The dog was probably lonely and bloodied from hunting rabbits, the hens were forgotten about and were probably in their coops, hysterical, picking at one another's feathers because of their nerves. Eggs would rot. If she stood on the low whitewashed wall that fronted the cottage, she could see over the high limestone wall that boundaried their fields and then look to the driveway that led to the abandoned house itself. To her it was like a kind of castle where strange things had happened and would go on happening. She loved it and she feared it. The sky behind and above gave it mystery, sometimes made it broody, and gave it a kind of splendor when the red streaks in the heavens were like torches that betokened the performance of a gory play. All of a sudden, standing there, with a bit of grass between her front teeth, looking at her home and imagining this future drama, she heard the nearby lych-gate open and then shut with a clang, and saw her father appear, and jumped so clumsily she thought she had broken everything, particularly her ribs. She felt she was in pieces. She would be like Humpty-Dumpty and all the king's horses and all the king's men would not be able to put her together again. Dismemberment did happen, a long time before, the time when her neck swelled out into a big fleshed balloon. She could only move her neck on one side, because the other side was like a ball and full of fluid and made gluggles when she touched it with her fingers. They were going to lance it. They placed her on a kitchen chair. Her mother boiled a saucepan of water. Her mother stood on another chair and reached far into the rear of a cupboard and hauled out a new towel. Everything was in that cupboard, sugar and tea and round biscuits and white flour and linen and must and mice. First one man, then another, then another man, then a last man who was mending the chimney, and then last of all her father each took hold of her — an arm, another arm, a shoulder, a waist, and her two flying legs that were doing everything possible not to be there. The lady doctor said nice things and cut into the big football of her neck, and it was like a pig's bladder bursting all over, the waters flowing out, and then it was not like that at all; it was like a sword on the bone of her neck saw-ing, cutting into the flesh, deeper and deeper, the men pressing upon her with all their might, saying that she was a demon, and the knife went into her swallow or where she thought of forever more as her swallow, and the lady doctor said, "Drat it," because she had done the wrong thing — had cut too deep and had to start scraping now, and her older sister danced a jig out on the flagstones so that neighbors going down the road would not get the impression that someone was being murdered. Long afterward she came back to the world of voices, muffled voices, and their reassurances, and a little something sweet to help her get over it all, and the lady doctor putting on her brown fur coat and hurrying to her next important work of mercy.

When she slept with the neighbors the old man asked the old woman were they ever going to be rid of her, were they going to have this dunce off their hands, were they saddled with her for the rest of their blooming lives. She declined the milk they gave her because it was goat's milk and too yellow and there was dust in it. She would answer them in single syllables, just yes or no, mostly no. She was learning to frown, so that she, too, would have A B C's. Her mother's forehead and hers would meet in heaven, salute, and all their lines would coincide. She refused food. She pined. In all, it was about a week.

The day her mother returned home — it was still January — the water pipes had burst, and when she got to the neighbors' and was told she could go on up home, she ran with all her might and resolu-tion, so that her windpipe ached and then stopped aching when she found her mother down on her knees dealing with pools of water that had gushed from the red pipes. The brown rag was wet every other second and had to be wrung out and squeezed in the big chipped basin, the one she was first bathed in. The lodges of water were every-where, lapping back and forth, threatening to expand, to discolor the tiles, and it was of this hazard they talked and fretted over rather than the mother's disappearance, or the dire cause of it, or the reason for her return. They went indoors and got the ingredients and the utensils and the sieve so as to make an orange cake with orange filling and orange icing. She never tasted anything so wonderful in all her life. She ate three big hunks, and her mother put her hand around her and said if she ate any more she would have a little corporation.

The father came home from the hospital, cried again, said that sure he wouldn't hurt a fly, and predicted that he would never break his pledge or go outside the gate again, only to Mass, never leave his own sweet acres. As before, the girl slept with her mother, recited the Rosary with her, and shared the small cubes of dark raisin-filled chocolate, then trembled while her mother went along to her father's bedroom for a tick, to stop him bucking. The consequences of those visits were deterred by the bits of tissue paper, a protection between herself and any emission. No other child got conceived, and there was no further use for the baggy napkins, the bottle, and the dark-brown mottled teat. The cot itself was sawn up and used to back two chairs, and they constituted something of the furniture in the big upstairs landing, where the felt dog still lorded over it but now had an eye missing because a visiting child had poked wire at it. The chairs were painted oxblood red and had the sharp end of a nail dragged along the varnish to give a wavering effect. Also on the landing was a bowl with a bit of wire inside to hold a profusion of artificial tea roses. These tea roses were a two-toned color, were red and yellow plastic, and the point of each petal was seared like the point of a thorn. Cloth flowers were softer. She had seen some once, very pale pink and purple, made of voile, in another house, in a big jug, tumbling over a lady's bureau. In the landing at home, too, was the speared head of Christ, which looked down on all the proceedings with endless patience, endless commiseration. Underneath Christ was a pussycat of black papier-mâché that originally had sweets stuffed into its middle, sweets the exact image of strawberries and even with a lime leaf at the base, a leaf made of green-glazed angelica. They liked the same things — applesauce and beetroot and tomato sausages and angelica. They cleaned the windows, one the inside, the other the outside, they sang ducts, they put newspapers over the newly washed dark-red tiles so as to keep them safe from the muck and trampalations of the men. About everything they agreed, or almost everything.

In the dark nights the wind used to sweep through the window and out on the landing and into the other rooms, and into the Blue Room, by now uninhabited. The wardrobe door would open of its own accord, or the ewer would rattle, or the lovely buxom Our Lady of Limerick picture would fall onto the marble washstand and there was a rumpus followed by prognostications of bad luck for seven years. When the other child came back from boarding school, the girl was at first excited, prepared lovingly for her, made cakes, and, soon after, was plunged into a state of wretchedness. Her mother was being taken away from her, or, worse, was gladly giving her speech, her attention, her hands, and all of her gaze to this intruder. Her mother and her older sister would go upstairs, where her mother would have some little treat for her, a hanky or a hanky sachet, and once a remnant that had been got at the mill at reduced price, due to a fire there. Beautiful, a flecked salmon pink.

Downstairs *she* had to stack dishes onto the tray. She banged the cups, she put a butter knife into the two-pound pot of blackcurrant jam and hauled out a big helping, then stuck the greasy plates one on top of the other, whereas normally she would have put a fork in between to protect the undersides. She dreamed that her mother and her rival sister were going for a walk and she asked to go too, but they sneaked off. She followed on a bicycle, but once outside the main gate could not decide whether to go to the left or the right, and then, having decided, made the wrong choice and stumbled on a herd of bullocks, all butting one another and endeavoring to act up into one another's backside. She turned back, and there they were strolling up the drive, like two sedate ladies linking and laughing, and the salmonflecked remnant was already a garment, a beautiful swagger coat that her sister wore with a dash.

"I wanted to be with you," she said, and one said to the other, "She wanted to be with us," and then no matter what she said, no matter what the appeal, they repeated it as if she weren't there. In the end she knew that she would have to turn away from them, because she was not wanted, she was in their way. As a result of that dream, or rather the commotion that she made in her sleep, it was decided that she had worms, and the following morning they gave her a dose of turpentine and castor oil, the same as they gave the horses.

When her sister went back to the city, happiness was restored again. Her mother consulted her about the design on a leather bag that she was making. Her mother wanted a very old design, something concerning the history of their country. She said there would have to be battles and then peace and wonderful scenes from nature. Her mother said that there must be a lot of back history to a land and that education was a very fine thing. Preferable to the bog, her mother said. The girl said when she grew up that she would get a very good job and bring her mother to America. Her mother mentioned the street in Brooklyn where she had lodged and said that it had adjoined a park. They would go there one day. Her mother said maybe.

The growing girl began to say the word "backside" to herself and knew that her mother would be appalled. The girl laughed at bullocks and the sport they had. Then she went one further and jumped up and down and said "Jumping Jack," as if some devil were inside her, touching and tickling the lining of her. It was creepy. It was done outdoors, far from the house, out in the fields, in a grove or under a canopy of rhododendrons. The buds of the rhododendrons were sticky and oozed with life, and everything along with herself was soaking wet, and she was given to wandering flushes and then fits of untoward laughter, so that she had to scold herself into some state of normality and this she did by slapping both cheeks vehemently. As a dire punishment she took cups of Glauber's salts three times a day, choosing to drink it when it was lukewarm and at its most nauseating. She would be told by her father to get out, to stop hatching, to get out from under her mother's apron strings, and he would send her for a spin on the woeful brakeless bicycle. She would go to the chapel, finding it empty of all but herself and the lady sacristan, who spent her life in there polishing and rearranging the artificial flowers; or she would go down into a bog and make certain unattainable wishes, but always at the end of every day, and at the end of every thought, and at the beginning of sleep and the precise moment of wakening, it was of her mother and for her mother she existed, and her prayers and her good deeds and her ringlets and the ire on her legs — created by the serge of her gym frock — were for her mother's intention, and on and on. Only death could part them, and not even that, because she resolved that she would take her own life if some disease or some calamity snatched her mother away. Her mother's three-quarter-length jacket she would don, sink her hands into the deep pockets, and say the name "Delia," her mother's, say it in different tones of voice, over and over again, always in a whisper and with a note of conspiracy.

A lovely thing happened. Her mother and father went on a journey, by hire car to do a transaction whereby they could get some credit on his lands, and her father did not get drunk but ordered a nice pot of tea, and then sat back gripping his braces and gave her mother a few bob, with which her mother procured a most beautiful lipstick in a ridged gold case. It was like fresh fruit, so moist was it, and coral red. Her mother and she tried it on over and over again, were comical with it, trying it on, then wiping it off, trying it on again, making cupids so that her mother expostulated and said what scatterbrains they were, and even the father joined in the hilarity and daubed down the mother's cheek and said Fanny Anny, and the mother said that was enough, as the lipstick was liable to get broken. With her thumbnail she pressed on the little catch, pushing the lipstick down into its case, into its bed. As the years went on, it dried out and developed a peculiar shape, and they read somewhere that a lady's character could be told by that particular shape, and they wished that they could discover whether the mother was the extrovert or the shy violet.

The girl had no friends, she didn't need any. Her cup was full. Her mother was the cup, the cupboard, the sideboard with all the things in it, the tabernacle with God in it, the lake with the legends in it, the bog with the wishing well in it, the sea with the oysters and the corpses in it, her mother a gigantic sponge, a habitation in which she longed to sink and disappear forever and ever. Yet she was afraid to sink, caught in that hideous trap between fear of sinking and fear of swimming; she moved like a flounderer through this and that — through school, through inoculation, through a man who put his white handkerchief between naked her and naked him, and against a galvanized outhouse door came, gruntling and disgruntling like a tethered beast upon her; through a best friend, a girl friend who tried to clip the hairs of her vagina with a shears. The hairs of her vagina were mahogany-colored, and her best friend said that that denoted mortal sin. She agonized over it. Then came a dreadful blow. Two nuns called and her mother and her father said that she was to stay outside in the kitchen and see that the kettle boiled and then lift it off so that water would not boil over. She went on tiptoe through the hall and listened at the door of the room. She got it in snatches. She was being discussed. She was being sent away to school. A fee was being discussed and her mother was asking if they could make a reduction. She ran out of the house in a dreadful state. She ran to the chicken run and went inside to cry and to go berserk. The floor was full of damp and gray-green mottled droppings. The nests were full of sour sops of hay. She thought she was going out of her mind. When they found her later, her father said to cut out the "bull," but her mother tried to comfort her by saying they had a prospectus and that she would have to get a whole lot of new clothes in navy blue. But where would the money come from?

In the convent to which they sent her she eventually found solace. A nun became her new idol. A nun with a dreadfully pale face and a master's degree in science. This nun and she worked out codes with the eyelids, and the flutter of the lashes, so they always knew each other's moods and feelings, so that the slightest hurt imposed by one was spotted by the other and responded to with a glance. The nun gave another girl more marks at the mid-term examination, and did it solely to hurt her, to wound her pride; the nun addressed her briskly in front of the whole class, said her full name and asked her a theological conundrum that was impossible to answer. In turn, she let one of the nun's holy pictures fall on the chapel floor, where of course it was found by the cleaning nun, who gave it back to the nun, who gave it to her with a "This seems to have got mislaid." They exchanged Christmas presents and notes that contained blissful innuendos. She had given chocolates with a kingfisher on the cover, and she had received a prayer book with gilt edging and it was as tiny as her little finger. She could not read the print but she held it to herself like a talisman, like a secret scroll in which love was mentioned.

Home on holiday it was a different story. Now *she* did the avoiding, the shunning. All the little treats and the carregeen soufflé that her mother had prepared were not gloated over. Then the pink crêpe-de-Chine apron that her mother had made from an old dance dress did not receive the acclamation that the mother expected. It was fitted on and at once taken off and flung over the back of a chair with no praise except to remark on the braiding, which was cleverly done.

"These things are not to be sniffed at," her mother said, passing the plate of scones for the third or fourth time. The love of the nun dominated all her thoughts, and the nun's pale face got between her and the visible world that she was supposed to be seeing. At times she could taste it. It interfered with her studies, her other friendships, it got known about. She was called to see the reverend Mother. The nun and she never had a tête-à-tête again and never swapped holy pictures. The day she was leaving forever they made an illicit date to meet in the summerhouse, out in the grounds, but neither of them turned up. They each sent a message with an apology, and it was, in fact, the messengers who met, a junior girl and a postulant carrying the same sentence on separate lips — "So-and-so is sorry — she wishes to say she can't..." They might have broken down or done anything, they might have kissed.

Out of school, away from the spell of nuns and gods and flower gardens and acts of contrition, away from the chapel with its incense and its brimstone sermons, away from surveillance, she met a bakery man who was also a notable hurley player and they started up that kind of courtship common to their sort — a date at Nelson's pillar two evenings a week, then to a café to have coffee and cream cakes, to hold hands under the table, to take a bus to her digs, to kiss against a railing and devour each other's face, as earlier they had devoured the mock cream and the sugar-dusted sponge cakes. But these orgies only increased her hunger, made it into something that could not be appeased. She would recall her mother from the very long ago, in the three-quarter-length jacket of salmon tweed, the brooch on the lapel, the smell of face powder, the lipstick hurriedly put on so that a little of it always smudged on the upper or the lower lip and appeared like some kind of birthmark. Recall that they even had the same mole on the back of the left hand, a mole that did not alter winter or summer and was made to seem paler when the fist was clenched. But she was recalling someone whom she wanted to banish. The bakery man got fed up, wanted more than a cuddle, hopped it. Then there was no one, just a long stretch, doing novenas, working in the library, and her mother's letters arriving, saying the usual things, how life was hard, how inclement the weather, how she'd send a cake that day or the next day, as soon as there were enough eggs to make it with. The parcels arrived once a fortnight, bound in layers of newspaper, and then a strong outer layer of brown paper, all held with hideous assortments of twines — binding twine, very white twine, and colored plastic string from the stools that she had taken to making; then great spatters of sealing wax adorning it. Always a registered parcel, always a cake, a pound of butter, and a chicken that had to be cooked at once, because of its being nearly putrid from the four-day journey. It was not difficult to imagine the kitchen table, the bucket full of feathers, the moled hand picking away at the pinfeathers, the other hand plunging in and drawing out all the undesirables, tremulous, making sure not to break a certain little pouch, since its tobacco-colored fluid could ruin the taste of the bird. Phew. Always the same implications in each letter, the same cry —

"Who knows what life brings. Your father is not hard-boiled despite his failings. It makes me sad to think of the little things that I used to be able to do for you." She hated those parcels, despite the fact that they were most welcome.

She married. Married in haste. Her mother said from the outset that he was as odd as two left shoes. He worked on an encyclopedia and was a mine of information on certain subjects. His specialty was vegetation in pond life. They lived to themselves. She learned to do chores, to bottle and preserve, to comply, to be a wife, to undress neatly at night, to fold her clothes, to put them on a cane chair, making sure to put her corset and her underthings respectfully under her dress or her skirt. It was like being at school again. The mother did not visit, being at odds with the censuring husband. Mother and daughter would meet in a market town midway between each of their rural homes, and when they met they sat in some hotel lounge, ordered tea, and discussed things that can easily be discussed — recipes, patterns for knitting, her sister, items of furniture that they envisaged buying. Her mother was getting older, had developed a slight stoop, and held up her hands to show the rheumatism in her joints. Then all of a sudden, as if she had just remembered it, she spoke about the cataracts, and her journey to the specialist, and how the specialist had asked her if she remembered anything about her eyes and how she had to tell him that she had lost her sight for five or six minutes one morning and that then it came back. He had told her how lucky it was, because in some instances it does not come back at all. She said yes, the shades of life were closing in on her. The daughter knew that her marriage would not last, but she dared not say so. Things were happening such as that they had separate meals, that he did not speak for weeks on end, and yet she defended him, talked of the open pine dresser he had made, and her mother rued the fact that she never had a handyman to do odd things for her. She said the window had broken in a storm and that there was still a bit of cardboard in it. She said she had her heart on two armchairs, armchairs with damask covers. The daughter longed to give them to her and thought that she might steal from her husband when he was asleep, steal the deposit, that is, and pay for them on hire purchase. But they said none of the things that they should have said.

"You didn't get any new style," the mother said, restating her particular dislike for a sheepskin coat.

"I don't want it," the girl said tersely.

"You were always a softie," the mother said, and inherent in this was disapproval for a man who allowed his wife to be dowdy. Perhaps she thought that her daughter's marriage might have amended for her own.

When her marriage did end, the girl wrote and said that it was all over, and the mother wrote posthaste, exacting two dire promises — the girl must write back on her oath and promise her that she would never touch an alcoholic drink as long as she lived and she would never again have to do with any man in body or soul. High commands. At the time the girl was walking the streets in a daze and stopping strangers to tell of her plight. One day in a park she met a man who was very sympathetic, a sort of tramp. She told him her story, and then all of a sudden he told her this terrible dream. He had wakened up and he was swimming in water and the water kept changing color, it was blue and red and green, and these changing colors terrified him. She saw that he was not all there and invented an excuse to go somewhere. In time she sold her bicycle and pawned a gold bracelet and a gold watch and chain. She fled to England. She wanted to go somewhere where she knew no one. She was trying to start afresh, to wipe out the previous life. She was staggered by the assaults of memory — a bowl with her mother's menstrual cloth soaking in it and her sacrilegious idea that if lit it could resemble the heart of Christ, the conical wick of the Aladdin lamp being lit too high and disappearing into a jet of black; the roses, the five freakish winter roses that were in bloom when the pipes burst; the mice that came out of the shoes, then out of the shoe closet itself, onto the floor where the newspapers had been laid to prevent the muck and manure of the trampling men; the little box of rouge that almost asked to be licked, so dry and rosy was it; the black range whose temperature could be tested by just spitting on it and watching the immediate jig and trepidation of the spit; the pancakes on Shrove Tuesday (if there wasn't a row); the flitches of bacon hanging to smoke; the forgotten jam jars with inevitably the bit of moldy jam in the bottom; and always, like an overseeing spirit, the figure of the mother, who was responsible for each and every one of these facets, and always the pending doom in which the mother would perhaps be struck with the rim of a bucket, or a sledgehammer, or some improvised weapon; struck by the near-crazed father. It would be something as slight as that the mother had a splinter under her nail and the girl felt her own nail being lifted up, felt hurt to the quick, or felt her mother's sputum, could taste it like a dish. She was possessed by these thoughts in the library where she worked day in and day out, filing and cataloguing and handing over books. They were more than thoughts, they were the presence of this woman whom she resolved to kill. Yes, she would have to kill. She would have to take up arms and commit a murder. She thought of choking or drowning. Certainly the method had to do with suffocation, and she foresaw herself holding big suffocating pillows or a bolster, in the secrecy of the Blue Room, where it had all begun. Her mother turned into the bursting red pipes, into the brown dishcloths, into swamps of black brown blooded water. Her mother turned into a streetwalker and paraded. Her mother was taking down her knickers in public, squatting to do awful things, left little piddles, small as puppies' piddles, her mother was drifting down a well in a big bucket, crying for help, but no help was forthcoming. The oddest dream came along. Her mother was on her deathbed, having just given birth to her — the little tonsured head jutted above the sheet — and had a neck rash, and was busy trying to catch a little insect, trying to cup it in the palms of her hands, and was saying that in the end "all there is, is yourself and this little insect that you're trying to kill." The word "kill" was everywhere, on the hoardings, in the evening air, on the tip of her thoughts. But life goes on. She bought a yellow two-piece worsted, and wrote home and said, "I must be getting cheerful, I wear less black." Her mother wrote, "I have only one wish now and it is that we will be buried together." The more she tried to kill, the more clinging the advances became. Her mother was taking out all the old souvenirs, the brown scapulars salvaged from the hurtful night in December, a mug, with their similar initial on it, a tablecloth that the girl had sent from her first earnings when she qualified as a librarian. The mother's letters began to show signs of wandering. They broke off in midsentence; one was written on blotting paper and almost indecipherable; they contained snatches of information such as "So-and-so died, there was a big turnout at the funeral," "I could do with a copper bracelet for rheumatism," "You know life gets lonelier."

She dreaded the summer holidays, but still she went. The geese and the gander would be trailing by the riverbank, the cows would gape at her as if an alien had entered their terrain. It was only the horses she avoided — always on the nervy side, as if ready to bolt. The fields themselves as beguiling as ever, fields full of herbage and meadow-sweet, fields adorned with spangles of gold as the buttercups caught the shafts of intermittent sunshine. If only she could pick them up and carry them away. They sat indoors. A dog had a deep cut in his paw and it was thought that a fox did it, that the dog and the fox had tussled one night. As a result of this, he was admitted to the house. The mother and the dog spoke, although not a word passed between them. The father asked pointed questions, such as would it rain or was it teatime. For a pastime they then discussed all the dogs that they had had. The mother especially remembered Monkey and said that he was a queer one, that he'd know what you were thinking of. The father and daughter remembered further back to Shep, the big collie, who guarded the child's pram and drove thoroughbred horses off the drive, causing risk to his own person. Then there were the several pairs of dogs, all of whom sparred and quarreled throughout their lives, yet all of whom died within a week of one another, the surviving dog dying of grief for his pal. No matter how they avoided it, death crept into the conversation. The mother said unconvincingly how lucky they were never to have been crippled, to have enjoyed good health and enough to eat. The curtains behind her chair were a warm red velveteen and gave a glow to her face. A glow that was reminiscent of her lost beauty.

She decided on a celebration. She owed it to her mother. They would meet somewhere else, away from that house, and its skeletons and its old cunning tug at the heartstrings. She planned it a year in advance, a holiday in a hotel, set in beautiful woodland surroundings on the verge of the Atlantic Ocean. Their first hours were happily and most joyfully passed as they looked at the rooms, the view, the various tapestries, found where things were located, looked at the games room and then at the display cabinets, where there were cut glass and marble souvenirs on sale. The mother said that everything was "poison, dear." They took a walk by the seashore and remarked one to the other on the different stripes of color on the water, how definite they were, each color claiming its surface of sea, just like oats or grass or a plowed land. The brown plaits of seaweed slapped and slathered over rocks, long-legged birds let out their lonesome shrieks, and the mountains that loomed beyond seemed to hold the specter of continents inside them so vast were they, so old. They dined early. Afterward there was a singsong and the mother whispered that money wasn't everything; to look at the hard-boiled faces. Something snapped inside her, and forgetting that this was her errand of mercy, she thought instead how this mother had a whole series of grudges, bitter grudges concerning love, happiness, and her hard impecunious fate. The angora jumpers, the court shoes, the brown and the fawn garments, the milk complexion, the auburn tresses, the little breathlessnesses, the hands worn by toil, the sore feet, these were but the trimmings, behind them lay the real person, who demanded her pound of flesh from life. They sat on a sofa. The mother sipped tea and she her whiskey. They said, "Cheers." The girl tried to get the conversation back to before she was born, or before other children were born, to the dances and the annual race day and the courtship that preempted the marriage. The mother refused to speak, balked, had no story to tell, said that even if she had a story she would not tell it. Said she hated raking up the past. The girl tweezed it out of her in scraps. The mother said yes, that as a young girl she was bold and obstinate and she did have fancy dreams but soon learned to toe the line. Then she burst out laughing and said she climbed up a ladder once into the chapel, and into the confessional, so as to be the first person there to have her confession heard by the missioner. The missioner nearly lost his life because he didn't know how anyone could possibly have got in, since the door was bolted and he had simply come to sit in the confessional to compose himself, when there she was, spouting sins. What sins?

The mother said, "Oh, I forget, love. I forget everything now."

The girl said, "No, you don't."

They said night-night and arranged to meet in the dining room the following morning.

The mother didn't sleep a wink, complained that her eyes and her nose were itchy, and she feared she was catching a cold. She drank tea noisily, slugged it down. They walked by the sea, which was now the color of gunmetal, and the mountains were no longer a talking point. They visited a ruined monastery where the nettles, the sorrel, the clover, and the seedy dock grew high in a rectangle. Powder shed from walls that were built of solid stone. The mother said that probably it was a chapel, or a chancery, a seat of sanctity down through the centuries, and she genuflected. To the girl it was just a ruin, unhallowed, full of weeds and buzzing with wasps and insects. Outside, there was a flock of noisy starlings. She could feel the trouble brewing. She said that there was a lovely smell, that it was most likely some wild herb, and she got down on her knees to locate it. Peering with eyes and fingers among the low grass, she came upon a nest of ants that were crawling over a tiny bit of ground with an amazing amount of energy and will. She felt barely in control.

They trailed back in time for coffee. The mother said hotel life was demoralizing as she bit into an iced biscuit. The porter fetched the paper. Two strange little puppies lapped at the mother's feet, and the porter said they would have to be drowned if they were not claimed before dusk. The mother said what a shame and recalled her own little pups, who didn't eat clothes on the line during the day but when night came got down to work on them.

"You'd be fit to kill them, but of course you couldn't," she said lamely. She was speaking of puppies from ten or fifteen years back.

He asked if she was enjoying it, and the mother said, "I quote the saying 'See Naples and die,' the same applies to this."

The daughter knew that the mother wanted to go home there and then, but they had booked for four days and it would be an admission of failure to cut it short. She asked the porter to arrange a boat trip to the island inhabited by seabirds, then a car drive to the Lakes of Killarney and another to see the home of the liberator Daniel O'Connell, the man who had asked to have his dead heart sent to Rome, to the Holy See. The porter said certainly and made a great to-do about accepting the tip she gave him. It was he who told them where Daniel O'Connell's heart lay, and the mother said it was the most rending thing she had ever heard, and the most devout. Then she said yes, that a holiday was an uplift, but that it came too late, as she wasn't used to the spoiling. The girl did not like that. To change the conversation the girl produced a postcard that she used as a bookmark. It was a photograph of a gouged torso and she told the porter that was how she felt, that was the state of her mind. The mother said later she didn't think the girl should have said such a thing and wasn't it a bit extreme. Then the mother wrote a six-page letter to her friend Molly and the girl conspired to be the one to post it so that she could read it and find some clue to the chasm that stretched between them. As it happened, she could not bring herself to read it, because the mother gave it to her unsealed, as if she had guessed those thoughts, and the girl bit her lower lip and said, "How's Molly doing?"

The mother became very sentimental and said, "Poor creature, blind as a bat," but added that people were kind and how when they saw her with the white cane, they knew. The letter would be read to her by a daughter who was married and overweight and who suffered with her nerves. The girl recalled an autograph book, the mother's, with its confectionery-colored pages and its likewise rhymes and ditties. The mother recalled ice creams that she had eaten in Brooklyn long before. The mother remembered the embroidery she had done, making the statement in stitches that there was a rose in the heart of New York. The girl said stitches played such an important role in life and said, "A stitch in time saves nine." They tittered. They were getting nearer. The girl delicately inquired into the name and occupation of the mother's previous lover, in short, the father's rival. The mother would not divulge, except to say that he loved his mother, loved his sister, was most thoughtful, and that was that. Another long silence. Then the mother stirred in her chair, coughed, confided, said that in fact she and this thoughtful man, fearing, somehow sensing, that they would not be man and wife, had made each other a solemn pact one Sunday afternoon in Coney Island over an ice. They swore that they would get in touch with each other toward the end of their days. Lo and behold, after fifty-five years the mother wrote that letter! The girl's heart quickened, and her blood danced to the news of this tryst, this long-sustained clandestine passion. She felt that something momentous was about to get uttered. They could be true at last, they need not hide from one another's gaze. Her mother would own up. Her own life would not be one of curtained shame. She thought of the married man who was waiting for her in London, the one who took her for delicious weekends, and she shivered. The mother said that her letter had been returned; probably his sister had returned it, always being jealous. The girl begged to know the contents of the letter. The mother said it was harmless. The girl said go on. She tried to revive the spark, but the mother's mind was made up. The mother said that there was no such thing as love between the sexes and that it was all bull. She reaffirmed that there was only one kind of love and that was a mother's love for her child. There passed between them then such a moment, not a moment of sweetness, not a moment of reaffirmation, but a moment dense with hate — one hating and the other receiving it like rays, and then it was glossed over by the mother's remark about the grandeur of the ceiling. The girl gritted her teeth and resolved that they would not be buried in the same grave, and vehemently lit a cigarette, although they had hardly tasted the first course.

"I think you're very unsettled," her mother said.

"I didn't get that from the ground," the daughter said.

The mother bridled, stood up to leave, but was impeded by a waiter who was carrying a big chafing dish, over which a bright blue flame riotously spread. She sat down as if pushed down and said that that remark was the essence of cruelty. The girl said sorry. The mother said she had done all she could and that without maid or car or checkbook or any of life's luxuries. Life's dainties had not dropped on her path, she had to knit her own sweaters, cut and sew her own skirts, be her own hairdresser. The girl said for God's sake to let them enjoy it. The mother said that at seventy-eight one had time to think.

"And at thirty-eight," the girl said.

She wished then that her mother's life had been happier and had not exacted so much from her, and she felt she was being milked emotionally. With all her heart she pitied this woman, pitied her for having her dreams pulped and for betrothing herself to a life of suffering. But also she blamed her. They were both wild with emotion. They were speaking out of turn and eating carelessly; the very food seemed to taunt them. The mother wished that one of those white-coated waiters would tactfully take her plate of dinner away and replace it with a nice warm pot of tea, or better still, that she could be home in her own house by her own fireside, and furthermore she wished that her daughter had never grown into the cruel feelingless hussy that she was.

"What else could I have done?" the mother said.

"A lot," the girl said, and gulped at once.

The mother excused herself.

"When I pass on, I won't be sorry," she said.

Up in the room she locked and bolted the door, and lay curled up on the bed, knotted as a fetus, with a clump of paper handkerchiefs in front of her mouth. Downstairs she left behind her a grown girl, remembering a woman she most bottomlessly loved, then unloved, and cut off from herself in the middle of a large dining room while confronting a plate of undercooked lamb strewn with mint.

Death in its way comes just as much of a surprise as birth. We know we will die, just as the mother knows that she is primed to deliver around such and such a time, yet there is a fierce inner exclamation from her at the first onset of labor, and when the water breaks she is already a shocked woman. So it was. The reconciliation that she had hoped for, and indeed intended to instigate, never came. She was abroad at a conference when her mother died, and when she arrived through her own front door, the phone was ringing with the news of her mother's death. The message though clear to her ears was incredible to her. How had her mother died and why? In a hospital in Dublin as a result of a heart attack. Her mother had gone there to do shopping and was taken ill in the street. How fearful that must have been. Straightaway she set back for the airport, hoping to get a seat on a late-night flight.

Her sister would not be going, as she lived now in Australia, lived on a big farm miles from anywhere. Her letters were always pleas for news, for gossip, for books, for magazines. She had mellowed with the years, had grown fat, and was no longer the daffodil beauty. To her it was like seeing pages of life slip away, and she did not bend down to pick them up. They were carried away in the stream of life itself. And yet something tugged. The last plane had gone, but she decided to sit there until dawn and thought to herself that she might be sitting up at her mother's wake. The tube lighting drained the color from all the other waiting faces, and though she could not cry, she longed to tell someone that something incalculable had happened to her. They seemed as tired and as inert as she did. Coffee, bread, whiskey, all tasted the same, tasted of nothing or at best of blotting paper. There was no man in her life at the moment, no one to ring up and tell the news to. Even if there was, she thought that lovers never know the full story of one another, only know the bit they meet, never know the iceberg of hurts that have gone before, and therefore are always strangers, or semi-strangers, even in the folds of love. She could not cry. She asked herself if perhaps her heart had turned to lead. Yet she dreaded that on impulse she might break down and that an attendant might have to lead her away.

When she arrived at the hospital next day, the remains had been removed and were now on their way through the center of Ireland. Through Joyce's Ireland, as she always called it, and thought of the great central plain open to the elements, the teeming rain, the drifting snow, the winds that gave chapped faces to farmers and cattle dealers and croup to the young calves. She passed the big towns and the lesser towns, recited snatches of recitation that she remembered, and hoped that no one could consider her disrespectful because the hire car was a bright ketchup red. When she got to her own part of the world, the sight of the mountains moved her, as they had always done — solemn, beautiful, unchanging except for different ranges of color. Solid and timeless. She tried to speak to her mother, but found the words artificial. She had bought a sandwich at the airport and now removed the glacé paper with her teeth and bit into it. The two days ahead would be awful. There would be her father's wild grief, there would be her aunt's grief, there would be cousins and friends, and strays and workmen; there would be a grave wide open and as they walked to it they would walk over other graves, under hawthorn, stamping the nettles as they went. She knew the graveyard very well, since childhood. She knew the tombs, the headstones, and the hidden vaults. She used to play there alone and both challenge and cower from ghosts. The inside of the grave was always a rich broody brown, and the gravedigger would probably lace it with a trellis of ivy or convolvulus leaf.

At that very moment she found that she had just caught up with the funeral cortege, but she could hardly believe that it would be her mother's. Too much of a coincidence. They drove at a great pace and without too much respect for the dead. She kept up with them. The light was fading, the bushes were like blurs, the air bat-black; the birds had ceased, and the mountains were dark bulks. If the file of cars took a right from the main road toward the lake town, then it must certainly be her mother's. It did. The thought of catching up with it was what made her cry. She cried with such delight, cried like a child who has done something good and is being praised for it and yet cannot bear the weight of emotion. She cried the whole way through the lakeside town and sobbed as they crossed the old bridge toward the lovely dark leafy country road that led toward home. She cried like a homing bird. She was therefore seen as a daughter deeply distressed when she walked past the file of mourners outside the chapel gate, and when she shook the hands or touched the sleeves of those who had come forward to meet her. Earlier a friend had left flowers at the car-hire desk and she carried them as if she had specially chosen them. She thought, They think it is grief, but it is not the grief they think it is. It is emptiness more than grief. It is a grief at not being able to be wholehearted again. It is not a false grief, but it is unyielding, it is blood from a stone.

Inside the chapel she found her father howling, and in the first rows closest to the altar and to the coffin the chief mourners, both men and women, were sobbing, or, having just sobbed, were drying their eyes. As she shook hands with each one of them, she heard the same condolence — "Sorry for your trouble, sorry for your trouble, sorry for your trouble."

That night in her father's house people supped and ate and reminisced. As if in mourning a huge bough of a nearby tree had fallen down. Its roots were like a hand stuck up in the air. The house already reeked of neglect. She kept seeing her mother's figure coming through the door with a large tray, laden down with things. The undertaker called her out. He said since she had not seen the remains he would bring her to the chapel and unscrew the lid. She shrank from it, but she went, because to say no would have brought her disgrace. The chapel was cold, the wood creaked, and even the flowers at night seemed to have departed from themselves, like ghost flowers. Just as he lifted the lid he asked her to please step away, and she thought, Something fateful has happened, the skin has turned black or a finger moves or, the worst, she is not dead, she has merely visited the other world. Then he called her and she walked solemnly over and she almost screamed. The mouth was trying to speak. She was sure of it. One eyelid was not fully shut. It was unfinished. She kissed the face and felt a terrible pity. "O soul," she said, "where are you, on your voyaging, and O soul, are you immortal?"

Suddenly she was afraid of her mother's fate and afraid for the fact that one day she, too, would have to make it. She longed to hold the face and utter consolations to it, but she was unable. She thought of the holiday that had been such a fiasco and the love that she had first so cravenly and so rampantly given and the love that she had so callously and so pointedly taken back. She thought why did she have to withdraw, why do people have to withdraw, why?

After the funeral she went around the house tidying and searching, as if for some secret. In the Blue Room damp had seeped through the walls, and there were little burrs of fungus that clung like bobbins on a hat veiling. In drawers she found bits of her mother's life. Emblems. Wishes. Dreams contained in such things as an exotic gauze rose of the darkest drenchingest red. Perfume bottles, dance shoes, boxes of handkerchiefs, and the returned letter. It was to the man called Vincent, the man her mother had intended to marry but whom she had forsaken when she left New York and came back to Ireland, back to her destiny. For the most part it was a practical letter outlining the size of her farm, the crops they grew, asking about mutual friends, his circumstances, and so forth. It seems he worked in a meat factory. There was only one little leak — "I think of you, you would not believe how often." In an instinctive gesture she crumpled the letter up as if it had been her own. The envelope had marked on the outside — *Return to sender.* The words seemed brazen, as if he himself had written them. There were so many hats, with flowers and veiling, all of light color, hats for summer outings, for rainless climes. Ah, the garden parties she must have conceived. Never having had the money for real style, her mother had invested in imitation things — an imitation crocodile handbag and an imitation fur bolero. It felt light, as if made of hair, there were, too, pink embroidered corsets, long bloomers, and three unworn cardigans.

For some reason she put her hand above the mantelpiece to the place where they hid shillings when she was young. There wrapped in cobweb was an envelope addressed to her in her mother's hand writing. It sent shivers through her, and she prayed that it did not bristle with accusations. Inside, there were some trinkets, a gold sovereign, and some money. The notes were dirty, crumpled, and folded many times. How long had the envelope lain there? How had her mother managed to save? There was no letter, yet in her mind she concocted little tendernesses that her mother might have written —

such as "Buy yourself a jacket," or "Have a night out," or "Don't spend this on Masses." She wanted something, some communiqué. But there was no such thing.

A new wall had arisen, stronger and sturdier than before. Their life together and all those exchanges were like so many spilt feelings, and she looked to see some sign or hear some murmur. Instead, a silence filled the room, and there was a vaster silence beyond, as if the house itself had died or had been carefully put down to sleep.

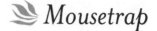 *Mousetrap*

JANE SHAPIRO

WHEN I VISITED, Mom asked me questions. "What is love?" she wanted to know. "Do you believe that hearts can truly break?"

In the year since Stu's death, she'd never stopped asking. Mom was sixty-three now, tiny, deeply stylish. She had new MTV hair, so short it was fuzzy, dark with a whitish glaze on it. This time I was visiting for her neck lift — a surgery to fine-tune her already startlingly youthful appearance and complement the wonderful-looking baby wolf's hair. As I traveled toward Boston, the train always seemed to rise; I'd ascend into the North, finally stepping out into sheets of wintry air. Mom lived these days on a square like one in London, in the interesting, changing South End. As usual, Mom was on some kind of cutting edge. All around her, the neighborhood was shifting economically — some areas drastically gentrifying, others falling into neglect.

Back in New Jersey, I was trying to grow up. On Union Square, in the foyer, pleasure would drop over me; being a child again, in my mother's house, just gathered me up and carried me away. Faint music was always playing in the background at Mom's. Before I got my jacket off, she'd be asking, "Could you put a baby up for adoption?"

My mother's old friend Hilary from Newton took me aside. Hilary was a large imposing woman, a former actress, disorientingly flashy, a wearer of cloaks and scarves. On her right index finger, she had a tiny jewel screwed into the point of her polished nail. She followed me into the pantry, pressed me against the cabinet, and told me about Mom: "I'd say *aren't you cute to visit*, but it's so much more. How crucial you and Rhoda are to Mother! Stuart was irreplaceable! Who does Mother have?"

Hilary and Mom, one big, one little, were, in some way, about as glamorous as you get. Hilary was Mom's surgery mentor; she'd had her entire face tightened and polished twice, back in her glittering other life. Several times a week, Hilary drove in from Newton and sat on the velvet couch until Mom was ready to go out. Today, after the pantry, she took her place on the middle cushion, while I worried about her question.

Well, my mother had Florence, her labrador, and Baby Blue, her Burmese. She also had Raymond, a sort of boyfriend, eighty years old, whom she claimed to hate, in the brownstone across the square. Their windows lined up precisely. Several times a day, Mom looked carefully out the living-room windows, from her house into his, to be sure he hadn't fallen unconscious.

Hilary said, "Ray and Mother are like Beauvoir and Sartre."

"Snooze on," Mom said. She left the room and immediately returned — this was an old habit of hers, departing the conversation for a moment; if you waited a couple of beats, she'd come back. Today she was wearing a cashmere dress, carrying a crystal atomizer, spraying about her throat. She said, "Raymond — it takes a lot of applause to keep *that* Tinkerbell in the air."

Hilary shrieked and fell on her side into the pillows. "She is so adorable! She is a cute adorable little minx, your mother! What a troublemaker!"

Mom's face got pink. She said, "If you think this codger is a boyfriend of mine, Hilary, you are losing it. *You are lost in the wild.*"

Mom and Hilary tried to decide where to eat. "Hilary wants it cheap," Mom told me privately. And to Hilary: "I won't go to the Italian place. Last week the lettuce tasted like a rubber raft."

In the Palestinian restaurant, a fly was on its back in the Arabian salad, kicking its little legs. "Oh stop the fuss, Hil," my mother said, and flicked it onto the floor.

When I got back from the ladies' room, they were talking about medical matters, and Mom was curled over the table, impersonating a friend with a back problem. Under her miniature Chanel suit, she had got her spine bent like a twig. The friend needed surgery on a disk and had consulted two doctors, one empathic, the other brusque.

"It sounds like a good cop/bad cop routine," Hilary said.

"It's not that he's such a good cop!" my mother cried, sitting up and shoving at the pita basket. "But he's *sentient*. Unlike this Thanksgiving turkey she's employed to be her surgeon!"

Inevitably, over the honeyed pastry, we talked about Raymond —

talking about him, Mom pointed out, was an index of our exaggerated collective longing for men: "Are we so desperate that the dis-
cussion has to be continuous?" I told her she was right — it does,
because we are. Actually, for some months I had been seeing Steven,
a handsome, consistently pleasant lawyer, who mainly acted as if, out
of deep reserves of goodwill toward humankind, he were letting me
date him. The kids didn't like Steven and they couldn't say why. They
disliked him the way a dog might.

"I envy you, Lolly," said Hilary. "You know I am no groupie for
Ray. You're right he's a sob sister. But face it, dear, at times he can be
a nice surprise: perceptive and acute."

Mom said sweetly, "Doddering, and arch, and blind."

"Blind?"

"Literally, no. Figuratively, almost completely," she told us. She
waved wildly at the restaurateurs, who were clustered in the back on
the phone to the West Bank, and one of them rushed forward, looking at her with what appeared to be love. When Raymond died, as he
certainly would before Mom, she would say that he was the sharpest,
warmest, most intelligent old man she had ever known. She would
lay his silk hankie in her underwear drawer, folded like a little flag.

Earlier today, before we had come out to lunch, Ray had said, "I
would just wonder what your mother — all you girls — think about
this fellow Jackson."

Mom looked suspicious. "Why do you use the term 'fellow'?" She
flushed and her eyes grew bright with unshed tears of rage about
racism.

"Oh Lolly," Hilary said. "Go right on, Ray. And please continue to
call me a girl whenever you see fit."

Raymond said genially, "Lolly, you're full of soup." My mother spun
around and looked at me and crossed her eyes as if being garroted.

My sister, Rhoda, and her husband were also in Boston, for the year,
trying it out — Rhody was teaching drawing and printmaking. Hilary
was sitting in the club chair looking interested, wearing a silk jump-
suit and silk dancing pumps. Tom was telling Mother Stories. His
mother had once taken him to a rodeo, claimed her dress faded, and
dragged him home by the leg, screaming *I'll never take you to an out-
door event again!*

We moaned and laughed. Mom went to the kitchen and came right back.

Tom said, "My mother equated inconvenience with death."

Rhody grinned at Mom, who cut her dead.

Tom said, "While I was at school, she gave my dog away. This was during Korea. She said, 'Our president came on the radio and asked us to contribute to the war effort, so I gave Captain to the Defense Department.' I remember thinking, 'Well, maybe he'll be an asset. After all, he's a biter.'"

Hilary and I got hysterical. Mom said, "Oh poo. It's always the mother."

"Not always," Tom said, smiling. "Frequently."

Mom stood up, looked at us, and walked out. When I found her in the bathroom, she said, "Please make an excuse to your sister. But get that lightweight out of my house."

Tom was Rhoda's second husband. After they left, Hilary said, "Tommy is charming. Not constantly spaced out, like Number One."

Mom regarded her with elaborate interest, then walked out again. When I found her in the bathroom, she said, "Get Hilary rolling."

Sleeping in the television room, in the middle of the night I rolled over on the clicker and the TV turned on. A younger Telly Savalas came into view, tough and disgusted, reflectively sucking his lollipop. I had to sleep again, fast: late-night loneliness was starting to crash over me like a wave breaking. From three rooms away, I could hear my mother's music playing, in the walls.

In the morning, when I came out, everything was cool and quiet and the Burmese had thrown up furry puddles. On the polished floor, the wet spots sat like tiny islands crossing a luminous calm dark sea. Baby Blue lay staring in the cat opium den, upon a square of Bokhara where he habitually did his catnip.

Mom came out, looked at the puddles, and peered at Florence, her Labrador, then identified the culprit. She cried, "Don't you try that!" as if the cat were still in the act of vomiting. She crept along in her satin pajamas and scrubbed at the floor. She glared at Baby Blue under the armoire: "Doesn't he see what a burden he is?"

In the dining room, surrounded by hammered silver bowls and crystal goblets behind glass doors, we ate cinnamon toast together. We said what we'd been saying all year:

"How's it going?"

Mom: "Sucks."

"Oh, Ma."

"Well, please correct me and then I'll be quiet: does it suck to have nobody, to have no friends — "

"You do have friends. You know a hundred people — the phone rings constantly." This was true, but a wrong tack.

"What would you say if I said that to you?" she cried. "'Not helpful!' And you'd be right!"

"Maybe it doesn't help very much. I know it's hard without Stu. I'm just saying you do have a lot of nice friends."

"Acquaintances. Not always such nice ones either."

"What about Eliot, who we ran into on Appleton Street? He was wonderful."

She snorted. "A lonely man with Scotty dogs."

"Mom, you do not have no friends."

"I have a limited circle. You don't realize. Yes, Hilary I have. A Nobel laureate she's not. I'm not criticizing her, but one friend coming over to wait for me to ferry her out to a restaurant hardly constitutes a broad social network. Raymond, as you know, is hopeless. His idea of a hot time is sitting in the Barcalounger nodding off while in the act of dialing the weather."

I laughed. Mom looked pleased.

"So, see?" I said. I was as stubborn as Mom. "You have some friends."

My point, though not precisely relevant, was supported by evidence. In fact Mom had given a New Year's Day party only a month before, where eighty people had embraced her until her hair was mashed and her face was smudged. Two young men had grabbed her by the head and, together, pressed her to their shirtfronts, crying, "Promnight noogie!" A beautiful young Swedish woman in a velvet hat had said Mom was her best friend. The caterer, passing a tray, had said Mom was *his* best friend. Nobody was smoking, everybody looked serene and healthy, the room smelled like a garden. There were three hairdressers (the youngest, who appeared to be a boy of twelve, had created Mom's new look), several painters and printmakers, two psychiatrists, two gallery owners, a woman filmmaker named Sluggo, a genial and sneaky looking Harvard Medical School student, Mom's yoga teacher,

Mom's accountant, Mom's lawyer, Mom's dentist, Mom's dogwalker and catsitter, Mom's women's group, and a superior court judge. The mean age of the guests, even factoring in Raymond and Hilary, was about thirty-six.

When reminded of her huge social world, Mom liked to say, "My life is *colorful*. That's all it is." Now, she said instead that she'd forgotten how to feel like getting up in the morning — it was like a skill she'd just lost.

"Oh Ma. Do you feel that bad?"

"What can I do?" she asked, quite seriously.

Talking too loud, I recited a list of things she could do — take or teach a painting class, study at Harvard Extension, volunteer at the Gardner, help feed the homeless, read to the blind: a boilerplate version of the sincere advice I'd labored over as a child. When I was young, in the year after my father died, while we tried together to figure out the shape our life might assume, the moment she would become happy was always just ahead. I was trying just as hard now — the time ahead was short.

I said that Stu hadn't been gone very long, that this was probably still the hardest part.

She pinched at her sprigs of hair. "Did I tell about the mousetrap?"

They had had a mouse. Ida, who comes to clean, had gone to buy a trap, and they sold her a little glueboard: the mouse gets stuck by its feet. When Mom came into the kitchen late at night, the mouse was attached and struggling.

"I thought, 'I can't face it.' I went to bed. In the morning he had dragged it all the way to the sink and ripped his front feet off, but his back foot was still stuck. He was getting exhausted. He could still move, but he was permanently bogged down. I'll never set a trap like that again. It was horrible for him. I thought: 'Little rat, you're acting out the story of my life.'"

"*Oh Ma.*"

Mom, grimly chewing: "Yes. 'Oh Ma.'"

I touched my mother's hand.

She looked at my hand on hers. My mother said, "I never say this. But I am deadended here. I am sixty-three years old. I am behind a wall. And I cannot break through."

Two days before the surgery, on a morning of sudden spring weather popping into February, we visited with Rhoda in Cambridge. In Harvard Square, where everybody on the street had a crazed look of penetrating intelligence, we walked around, Rhody and Mom and I, passing Rhoda's baby back and forth. We sat at a tiny table and drank coffee, and Mom dabbed a bit of cappuccino foam on the baby's lip. "Oh, I recall you both as babies," she said. "Can you imagine, you're this big and you were *this* big?"

Rhoda, gazing at Nicholas in his little seat: "It sounds like we just now attained our full growth."

"You were *this* big. Are you saying it isn't amazing?"

Of course it was. I remembered her leaving for the hospital when Rhoda was to be born — not what Mom looked like herself, but the hem of her skirt as she climbed into the car. Now I thought, like a child: I don't want her to go to a hospital again. That morning Mom had stood looking into the bathroom mirror with her palms flat against her temples, tightening the skin of her small, already beautiful face.

In the ladies' room, Rhody said, "Is this whole thing fucking nuts?"

In the mirror I pulled at my neck from the sides and stared myself down. I said, "I'm thirty-six. Soon I'll look older than Ma."

She laughed. "You already do."

"I might do it myself," I said.

"*Pardon?*"

"I think I'll have some kind of lift myself when I'm fifty or sixty." She looked at me until I felt shy, then closed the stall door.

"Are you sorry she's doing it?" I called to her.

"Oh no," she said. "Not at all. This is a fragile old lady getting shot up with anesthesia in order to smooth out three lines in her neck area. It's not fucked up in the least. It's valorous and adorable." A minute later, coming out of the stall: "Have you been getting letters from Ma?"

"This year? Sure," I said, surprised. Did she think she was Mom's only daughter? I actually had been in that position, and could almost remember it: strolling on green lawn, a cloud of scented air, my mother's hand in its kid glove.

On the way back to the table, Rhoda told me she sometimes waited to read Mom's letter, because she felt anxiety shimmering off the envelope. Also because it was a chore to get it open. "There's so much Scotch Tape sealing them up, you have to practically break in with a crowbar," she said, sliding into her chair, snatching the baby out of Mom's cradling arms.

Mom looked at us. "What's so funny?"

Nothing, we said. I was laughing, Rhoda was chewing the baby's arm. Our mother was already on her feet. "I am exiting, you people," she said.

Ma, sit down! Sit down! we cried. We pushed her back into the chair — I was amazed that it was so easy to sit her down genuinely against her will. She struggled and grabbed for her coat, but she was lighter than ever: each contributing one hand, Rhody and I could easily keep her seated. "Stop it!" she cried. "I am not going to be ganged up on!" She ripped twenties out of her bag, threw them on the table. Her eyes were bright. But as we kept our hands on her shoulders, she stopped being frantic and became merely restive, then subdued, then calm. She sipped coffee. She waved at the baby, into the baby's eyes.

My sister's hand on Mom's cashmere shoulder had been slightly blue. Rhoda's hands were always faintly stained with pastels, the nails edged in fading color. My mother was still painting too, but erratically now — her dreamy landscapes had recently given way to huge canvases thickly covered with oil paint. All year as she'd become noticeably sadder, the paintings had grown more lavish — the most recent were giant abstractions painted in flamboyant, despairing strokes.

Mom talked about colors as if they were people, or animals — their special natures, the way each typically behaved, what it was like to enter a room where one of them was dominating the scene. This year she'd stopped getting excited about finding new ones. "Do other people get starved for colors the way I do?" she occasionally asked, staring out the window like a child forbidden to go out into the bright street.

That night, two nights before the hospital, Mom and Hilary had a fight. Hilary wept, took me into the pantry. "Mother doesn't realize how she treats me. I am sensitive about being talked to roughly, and Mother doesn't see how she hurts my feelings. Just because I don't say what she *wants*."

Fierce and pale, my mother held her palm an inch from her face and stared into it: "This is how Hilary sees."

She wouldn't call Hilary and she wouldn't talk about it. We stayed up and intently watched Henry Kissinger converse with Ted Koppel. Mom and Koppel looked alike: somber, quietly angry. Mom, through clamped teeth: "Mr. Koppel, siss iss a comblete lie. . . . But I know this lie eggsists. It follows me everywhere, ass I dravel siss verld."

The next morning, her face was puffed up and she went back and stayed in her room. Her eyes swelled. She came out and walked back and forth in the dining room, the glasses in the breakfront tinkling. She walked, talked for hours, grew hoarse.

I think she's depressed, I told her — she's bereaved; maybe we could talk about it, maybe she could consult a shrink, somebody who could actually help, give her some perspective. I talked on like that for quite a while.

She looked away.

She said, "I am not going to tolerate being condescended to. I am still a piece of the person I was."

The next night, when the kids called, Nora wanted to know how to help Zack press his shirt for his eighth-grade dance. "He's freaked," she told Mom, and Mom sang, "He won't be all freaked when we get him pressed!" She stood in the kitchen on the phone for a long time, running an imaginary steam iron over the sleeves, then the back, then the front, then the placket, of Zack's imaginary dance shirt, talking Nora through it. "Now hold it up!" she cried, and she mimed holding it up, and stood back. "Doesn't it look flash?"

For the calm hopeful minutes Mom was on the phone, she looked familiar: as I remembered her from some earlier time.

Finally the surgery was over. Mom and I were staying together while she recuperated for two nights, in a hotel attached to the hospital, where, painstakingly patting at their lips, the guests sipped meals brought on trays. The necklift surgeon was an old friend of my mother's, "Uncle" Daniel, a man I found I resented, as if he were the culprit, the person who had — done what? Taken Stu away. Dealt my mother the gratuitous blow from which she must now hope to recover. He stood in the doorway, hale and effervescent, teasing Mom while I subtly snubbed him. I now recalled that as I rode up on the train, I'd imagined the surgery might change her horribly. But she looked like a cartoon character — a cunning little rabbit with a toothache.

Later, she took a Valium, shredded her napkin. "Should I have not done this? Was this crazy? Did I make another mistake?"

"Not at all, Ma," I said. "You haven't really been making mistakes, have you? Isn't it just a bad year?" Together we were casting our doubts in the appropriate interrogative form: How best to live?

Mom asked: "Do you believe that people can ever truly heal?"

"In most cases, absolutely. Don't you?"

"And in other cases?"

"I want to think they can."

"*But do you?*"

I said, "I'm sorry. I'm not sure."

Mom said, "I knew it!"

After dinner, I finally made us laugh. I was telling about a bat mitzvah, how the Resnik boys — now two melancholy grown men wearing crumpled suits — kept coming up and asking about our family, crying, "What ever happened to Rhody?" Finally I'd said to one of them, "Bruce. Please. Nothing happened to Rhody. You just haven't seen her. Just because you haven't personally seen somebody doesn't mean they died." My mother started shrieking, "My stomach hurts! I'm wetting my pants!" and jumped up and crossed her legs. As she staggered toward the bathroom, her pajama cuffs dropped over her pretty little feet.

While she was in the bathroom, there was a knock on the door, and while I was letting Rhoda in we heard a thud. Then silence.

Ma, Ma!

Mom had fainted deftly — not cracked her head against any porcelain, just folded onto the bathmat and the floor. She was lying on her back with her eyes open. She was looking at the ceiling, which had a gilded wallpaper describing outer space as a sort of supper club — festive planets and opalescent moons, comets trailing silver dust.

"Don't pick me up yet," she said. She batted our hands away, as if we were trying to knock her down. Then while we made some further assisting gestures, she sort of gently smacked at us, until finally we gave up and stood still. Mom had a point: Rhody and I were young and robust and Mom was old and lying on the floor — there was nothing she'd let us do to obscure those facts.

The planets twirled above us. Mom kept looking up, blinking fiercely, as if the stars could rain down and fall into her eyes.

After a while Rhody said, "Wow, you fell beautifully."

"You didn't hit your head," I said. "Your fall was actually perfect."

Rhody and I were out of moves. Mom was out of questions. "Oh poo," Mom said. "What a picture. The gang of two. There you are just standing there, upside down in space, saying the things I knew you would say before you were even born."

Up Above Diamond City

MARTHA SOUKUP

"KEEP UP," she says without looking back.

Her legs are twice as long as mine and her heels smack tap tap along the concrete, tap tap tap tap in the time she can say Keep up. I don't say "Okay" and I don't say anything because she'd have to turn around to listen instead of tap tap tap. I pump my legs fast, tennis shoes and no tapping, quiet. Really I like how it feels in my legs, in my muscles, to pull them back and forth so fast.

In the clothing store she buys a blouse and a dress and a sweater from the marked-down rack. She holds a pink dress with lace and a red sale tag up against my chest. It might look nice on a six-year-old. "No thank you," I say, and hope she won't buy it anyway. I'm lucky and she puts it back.

We go out to the car and put the bag in the trunk, then tap tap tap tap tap back to the shoe store, where I hope she won't get me the tennis shoes with flowers all over them. She makes me try them on. I say they pinch my toes. We leave the store with the flower shoes, but too big, half a size larger.

Tap tapping with the cart back to the car, behind me because she's putting her wallet back in her purse with the shopping bag under her arm, she sees me stop to look at the gum machines. I start to go on, but she pulls out her wallet slowly and deliberately and gives me a quarter, which is a lot of money. I watch her to make sure it's okay, then put it in the machine full of compasses.

A compass comes out: about as wide around as a quarter, with plastic over the markings and the needle, and sitting snug inside a little black tire, made out of rubber and with treads and everything. I twist the plastic egg it's in and take it out. The compass is small, but the tire-nest fills the palm of my hand, making a dark rubber smell.

The needle points north, which is toward the pet store in the mall. I wish I could go in and get Joker a dog toy.

"Don't say I never gave you anything," she says, which means now I can't say she never gave me anything, and she doesn't expect an answer because she's pushing the cart out to the car and I have to hop to catch up.

It's three blocks north through the campus to Diamond City, when you check it with the compass needle. I never thought about whether it was north before, just that it was across the college campus on the way to grade school before you turn right. I read in a book once that moss grows on the north side of trees, and with my compass I find out that's right. The trees on the way to Diamond City all have dark mossy green sides away from my house.

If I'm playing outside I'm supposed to stay on my block. I look very carefully when I cross each street, because if a car hit me I would be in trouble for leaving the block.

Along the way I find two pieces of broken clear glass, and a tiny piece of red glass, and a big piece from the bottom of a green bottle, maybe 7-Up, with rings pressed into it like Robin Hood's target. I have the compass in my right hand and I hold all the glass in my left hand, except the green which is too big so I put it in my shorts pocket. It's sharp through my pocket against my leg.

Diamond City is best in the winter, but it wouldn't be fair to ignore it in the summer, just because I don't walk to school past it. It's my responsibility.

I reach the corner and squat down at the curb. A big brick building is on the other end of the lawn that comes down to the corner. It's a college building, but I don't know which one. I only know the chapel, because it has a cross on top. In the summer there aren't college students coming in and out.

I put the two pieces of clear glass and the little piece of red glass on the curb by the grate. I pull the big piece of green glass out of my pocket.

Looking both ways there's no grown-up or kid in sight. I lean over the grate in the street and look way down to Diamond City.

In the winter, steam floats up through the chill air from the narrow river that runs down the middle of the city. It's a magic river and never freezes, and even when there is snow all around the curb by the grate, the people in the city are warm because they build their roads and their houses and their libraries and their schools right along the river.

I put the compass on the curb next to the pieces of glass, and I tip the big green bottle bottom edgewise and slip it down the grate. Maybe it will break when it lands. There's a chunk sound with a little music in it and a little rattle after.

The people in the city run out of their houses to see what they have. I didn't hear it break, so what they find is a giant green circle of emerald, real dazzling emerald, hard and brilliant, what it turned into as it fell toward the river and the city. I know what they'll do with it, because they're smart: they will take all their strongest people and maybe some horses — but even the horses are so much smaller than the giant emerald disk — and they will move it to a park by a bend in the river. In the summer everyone will sweat working so hard. But then they will have a skating rink, a round skating rink with round lanes molded in, and when they polish down the sharp edges and they polish out the numbers pressed into the emerald when it was a glass bottle, it will be perfect, and it will glow night and day.

Everything in Diamond City glows night and day because everything is made from diamonds and emeralds and rubies and sometimes sapphires.

The people in Diamond City give thanks for the giant emerald. They don't know where the jewels they use to build their city come from, but they think whoever drops them from the sky (the dark sky with slits of blue in its darkness) is powerful and very kind. They need jewels to build their city.

I think about the children in Diamond City skating on the emerald rink, around in circles in the grooves, so they can't even make a mistake.

I wait a while to let them be excited. Then I drop down the tiny red piece of glass. As it reaches the place where the river would mist if it was winter it becomes a perfect ruby. Maybe they will carve dishes and goblets from it. River water in them would look like wine and taste like cherry Kool-Aid.

Then I drop the white glass, which is the most boring kind outside of Diamond City, but in Diamond City becomes the most dazzling and prized building material of all. All the streets are paved with diamonds, and the buildings can't have windows without diamonds.

The gratitude of the citizens embarrasses me but it's very important to help them make their beautiful city more beautiful. I can't see it, except for the river, from high up where I am. Nobody can see, so nobody else knows.

I wait until I know they've finished celebrating and start to take their magical presents off to do practical things with them. Then I pick up my compass, stand up, and walk home away from the red North needle.

My bedroom closet is long and narrow. The door is on one end, so when you line the other end with blankets and pillows you can snuggle into it like a caterpillar reading in its cocoon.

Tap tap tap tap. She can't see me just when she opens the bedroom door. I can hear her. The book, which is actually a comic book, which isn't allowed, goes under the blankets and I'm on my feet. Tap tap tap and I'm up on my feet messing with hangers.

"You're putting your clothes away?"

I nod.

She looks at me with her lips thin. Finally she nods one sharp nod and says "Good. Come downstairs and set the table." I nod again and refold a sweater, staring up at the high shelf to get it even with the other sweaters. She waits a while, then tap tap tap tap tap, then the creaks of the stairs.

The cover of the comic book is bent back. I tried to be careful. I don't cry. I go downstairs.

The thing I always think about at dinner is not knocking my milk over, but it happens anyway.

Yesterday she dropped a carton of milk the milkman left, and milk squirted out of it onto the cupboard doors under the sink. It was Sunday and Dad was home. "No use crying over spilt milk," she said then, and laughed, and slapped herself on the wrist and said "Bad!" and laughed again.

Now she grabs my wrist. Her fingers go all the way around and against her white-tight thumb. "You are to pay attention and not waste milk," she says, slapping my hand, not laughing. Dad smiled yesterday, but tonight he's at the office, doing accounting, which takes a long time this time of year and most times of year.

I sit as she goes to the kitchen for paper towels to mop up the milk. My wrist is milk-white starting to red. I eat lima beans and feel Joker's whiskery black nose on my knee. I am the only person in the world who really likes lima beans, but I slip a couple of beans under the table and put them on my knee. It tickles when Joker eats them. She gets back from the kitchen and talks about what kind of life she could have had while she wipes up milk, and doesn't notice Joker under the table, so I am lucky.

After dinner she wants to play cards. We Go Fish. She wins twice, I win once. She laughs because the last two games both, it's the jacks that win, and she makes a joke about how we should just play jacks instead. I laugh too, but then she's had enough of Fish. She shows me how to lay out a solitaire game that takes both decks that she plays all the time.

"Don't say I never taught you anything," she says.

I play the solitaire game for a while. She keeps telling me about a red queen that goes on a black king or a black four that goes on a red five. I'm not playing cleverly enough. After three hands I can go to bed.

I sit in the back of my closet reading until it's safe. When I've waited long enough, I creep out the bedroom door to the top landing of the stairs and slap my hand lightly against my pajama'd thigh in five short bursts.

Joker sneaks around the railing from the hall side, glances once at the living room, and tears up the stairs. It sounds loud from the top of the stairs but she doesn't hear over the television, or she doesn't come out. I shut the door behind Joker and he snuggles between my ankles, and we go to sleep.

She pushes the grocery cart up aisles and around corners. I remember sitting in the seat with my feet sticking out, but I wouldn't fit now and I wouldn't want to. Sometimes when she's in a good mood I can push the cart while she shops, putting a tennis shoe up on the bar between the back wheels and kicking along with the other foot. Most carts don't go straight very far, so you can't ride them all the way down the aisle even if it's clear and you're allowed to.

Today she goes tap tap tap on the grocery linoleum and I just keep up behind. At the cereal she stops and lets me pick one. The first one I pick is too expensive so we get the second one, which is on sale.

At home she lets me go outside. I take the compass and walk around the block once, watching the needle point four different directions on each side. Then I put the compass in my shorts pocket and walk around the block again with my eyes closed. The church chapel chimes after I start and chimes again before I finish. I only open my eyes twice when I think I've gone wrong. Once I was about to turn up someone's front sidewalk, which would have been hard to explain, and once I was right, I'd reached the corner. It would be hard to be blind. I think I could do it in less than fifteen minutes if I tried again.

I go home. I clip Joker's collar to his leash and walk around the block again. I try closing my eyes but he wants to go up everyone's driveway, and when we see another dog he forgets about sidewalks. I wonder why dogs stay on sidewalks the rest of the time. How do people explain to them that's what sidewalks are for?

I let Joker loose in the kitchen and she nods at me shortly. Walking Joker is a duty. Giving Joker lima beans or letting him upstairs is trouble.

The compass points north to Diamond City. I walk looking at the curb all the way and only find one long sliver of green. I crouch at the grate and let it drop, looking at the magic river and wondering which people come out. One of my days is many days for them. I haven't figured out how many. I'm big so time goes slower for me. In Diamond City children have grown up and taught their children about the jewels from the sky since I started helping them. They are tiny, though they don't know it, and time goes fast and fast and fast. They can only tell stories about winter, when huge snowflakes melt as they float down toward the steaming river. Their grandmothers told them the stories. Winter is warm down there, and in their stories they say nothing about cold.

The green sliver chunks faintly at the bottom. There is a lot of emerald lately, the city is getting greener. I think it fell in the river. Now divers will have to come out, diving into the warm water and touching the warming sides of the long emerald gift, careful not to cut themselves. One by one they'll pull down ropes and tie them around the emerald, and then dozens of people on shore will haul on the ropes until it comes sparkling out of the water, and the children clap and the dogs bark.

"Where have you been?" she says when I come in the back door. A line goes down between her eyebrows and her lips are tight. I go set the table, two places, little forks outside and long forks inside. I hurry, and she doesn't make me give the answer.

Dad is on a business trip. She sits by the kitchen door and my place is set right around the table corner next to her. I don't like dinner. The corn is canned and the meat is dry. There are three cherry tomatoes on my plate. I swallow the first one whole before she can say anything and wash it down with milk.

"Young lady, chew your food," she says sharply. I chew the next tomato once down the middle. Tomato juice squirts in my mouth. I glance sideways. She's looking intently at me. I chew again in the same place my teeth cut the tomato, and again. I glance sideways after the third chew. She nods shortly. I swallow and grab my milk fast.

Then I do the same with the last tomato.

I don't spill the milk.

I ask to be excused. I go to the bathroom and rinse my mouth under the faucet.

Before bed she squeezes the place by my nose she thinks will be a pimple. Health class said some of us would start getting pimples in a year or two, and never to squeeze them. I don't say anything.

It's been raining. The city people need more diamonds to make the roof shingles for the sun to shine through and rain to run off. They'll get wet. They only use diamonds for shingles, so the people don't all look red and green in the daylight. At night the diamonds glow for light.

She won't let me play outside. She lets me walk Joker around the block. I don't find anything in the wet grass. Water gets in the rubbers on my tennis shoes. Joker doesn't mind. Rain runs off his springy black fur. The wind smells like rain and dog.

In Diamond City people dance in the rain in their bare feet. It's always warm because of the magic river, so they don't catch cold. The raindrops are giant but soft, and everyone laughs. When it rains for an hour up here, it rains for days and days down there, but it's warm and it's okay.

You can't hide with diamond walls, but no one cares. Emerald and ruby rooms are dark for sleeping, and the rest of the time people do what they want, and work together when it makes things better. They've been building a beautiful shining blue library with the rare sapphire gems, but I don't know if they have the roof on yet. It's rained for days and they've had no new gems for I don't know how long. Years. Maybe they think something's wrong. Maybe they're peering up between the raindrops trying to figure out if they've been abandoned.

I have to leave Joker on the enclosed back porch until he's mostly dry. I take off my wet rubbers and my wet shoes and my wet socks and tiptoe up the stairs to my room. She calls for me to come to the living room. I'm already in my room so I couldn't hear. She might want me to dust the living room, or make cookies with her, or Go Fish. If she calls again I'll go.

It's dry in the cocoon of my closet. The blankets are fuzzy and warm on my damp bare feet and legs. I use the flashlight instead of turning on the closet light. With the dark clouds and the rain it feels like night. Maybe there will be thunder.

I read an Oz book inside a nest of comic books I'm saving to reread, tucked all around. Dorothy is trying to figure which makes more sense, the people whose houses are beautiful on the outside and slobby on the inside, or the people whose houses are pretty on the inside and ugly on the outside. In Diamond City, everything is gorgeous inside and out, because it can't help but be, with the jewels their benefactor gives them to make everything with. I hope the sun comes out soon.

The closet door bursts open. "What are you doing here!" she screams. "I have called you and called you! What are you doing in your closet?" She is in her stocking feet. No tap tap.

I'm standing and trying to scuff the comic books behind me with my toes.

"I am so *tired* of your disobedience and your bad attitude," she says. "What are these!" She has picked up two of the comic books, Green Lantern and Superman with Bizarro Superman. "What have I told you about reading this trash?"

I stand there.

"What have I told you about reading this trash!"

I'm not supposed to, I try to say. Nothing comes out.

She grabs my wrist. She squeezes hard. This time she uses her sharp red nails. They stab my skin. It feels like they could stab through the veins.

"What have I told you!" she says, but if I open my mouth I might cry. "Do you ever listen!" she says.

I look at her instead of my wrist.

"Do you know what I've given up for you? I could have been a lawyer! I could have taken over your grandfather's business! You self-ish ingrate, you'll never understand what I've sacrificed, will you.

Will you! You're not stupid! What's wrong with you? Do you do this on purpose?"

She lets go of the wrist. I let it drop to my side. I don't clutch it. It throbs. Four angry fingernail moons glower on the white skin. Next to the whiter moons from last week.

"What is this damn trash!" She rips Superman apart from Bizarro Superman. She rips up Green Lantern. "With all the advantages I've given you!"

She picks up the Oz book.

"This was mine. If you're going to treat it like this with no respect, you can't have it," she says, and she rips the hard cover from the pages with a loud sound and throws it against the closet wall behind me. "There is no excuse for your behavior," she says.

My feet run around her leg, brushing me against her red tanned knee. She grabs for a hold on my left hand. I keep going. She leaves tracks in the skin inside my forearm from her nails. I see them as my arms pump down the stairs. Little shreds of skin stick up from the lines, but I don't think it's bleeding.

I turn corners best. The dishwasher is full of clean milk glasses. I grab one of the paper grocery bags she keeps folded between the dishwasher and the counter and throw two glasses into it. There's a fancy blue glass I'm not supposed to use in the dishwasher, too. I hear her tearing down the stairs. The blue glass is heavier than the milk glasses and something breaks in the bag. I fold the top over and press the bag against my chest with my left arm so I can open doors with my right hand.

She's coming in the kitchen and I'm going out the back door. Joker wants to jump up on me and play. "Go!" I shout. I open the porch door to the back yard. He understands. He runs out so fast I can't see where in the rain. I run right after him. I hear her shouting about the mess in the kitchen.

It's a short cut to the other side of the block, north, if I run to the right through Mrs. Weaver's yard and past the garage, where I can circle around and go through the gap in the fence behind the garage. The ground is wet and sharp things poke my feet. I come through the gap to the back yard of the blue house on the other side of the block. They have a sidewalk that goes from the back yard along the side of the house. My bare feet slap loud on the wet pavement. Something sharp is stuck in my heel.

I don't need to look at the compass. I keep running until I'm at Diamond City. Joker has gone somewhere else.

I squat at the grate. I have the soggy grocery bag clutched in my arms.

"I didn't forget," I say. I put the grocery bag on the curb.

It tears open easily when I pull on the paper. Inside are the glasses.

I use the heavy blue glass like a hammer to smash the other glasses, making diamonds. I have to smash the blue glass on the curb. My hands sting and throb. I drop the blue glass for sapphires down first. They'll finish the library.

Then, fast as I can, I pick pieces of clear glass up from where they lie on the soggy grocery bag. I make sure no wet smelly brown paper is stuck to each piece.

One after another diamonds rain into Diamond City. The people are happy and then amazed and then dumbstruck. There are no stories about this many diamonds at once.

"Make them last," I say. They can't hear me. I hope they'll know.

I wad up the empty paper. Rain presses my hair in strings on my forehead and sticks my shirt to my shorts. I start to go, then I stop and pull the compass out of my soaked shorts pocket.

"Here."

On the way down to the magic river, it transforms into something better. By the time it lands it is a huge town-square clock, in an ebony frame. When they put it on the library's highest tower, the one they build with the new sapphire, they will see it from a mile away. They'll see it and know where they are.

I keep walking north. I know where north is. The sharp thing in my heel is probably glass, but I don't turn to give it to Diamond City. Diamond City must never be found by anyone who doesn't understand. She'll find me soon.

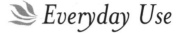 Everyday Use

ALICE WALKER

for your grandmama

I WILL WAIT for her in the yard that Maggie and I made so clean and wavy yesterday afternoon. A yard like this is more comfortable than most people know. It is not just a yard. It is like an extended living room. When the hard clay is swept clean as a floor and the fine sand around the edges lined with tiny, irregular grooves, anyone can come and sit and look up into the elm tree and wait for the breezes that never come inside the house.

Maggie will be nervous until after her sister goes: she will stand hopelessly in corners, homely and ashamed of the burn scars down her arms and legs, eying her sister with a mixture of envy and awe. She thinks her sister has held life always in the palm of one hand, that "no" is a word the world never learned to say to her.

You've no doubt seen those TV shows where the child who has "made it" is confronted, as a surprise, by her own mother and father, tottering in weakly from backstage. (A pleasant surprise, of course: What would they do if parent and child came on the show only to curse out and insult each other?) On TV mother and child embrace and smile into each other's faces. Sometimes the mother and father weep, the child wraps them in her arms and leans across the table to tell how she would not have made it without their help. I have seen these programs.

Sometimes I dream a dream in which Dee and I are suddenly brought together on a TV program of this sort. Out of a dark and soft-seated limousine I am ushered into a bright room filled with many people. There I meet a smiling, gray, sporty man like Johnny Carson who shakes my hand and tells me what a fine girl I have. Then we are on the stage and Dee is embracing me with tears in her eyes. She pins on my dress a large orchid, even though she has told me once that she thinks orchids are tacky flowers.

In real life I am a large, big-boned woman with rough, man-working hands. In the winter I wear flannel nightgowns to bed and overalls during the day. I can kill and clean a hog as mercilessly as a man. My fat keeps me hot in zero weather. I can work outside all day, breaking ice to get water for washing; I can eat pork liver cooked over the open fire minutes after it comes steaming from the hog. One winter I knocked a bull calf straight in the brain between the eyes with a sledge hammer and had the meat hung up to chill before nightfall. But of course all this does not show on television. I am the way my daughter would want me to be: a hundred pounds lighter, my skin like an uncooked barley pancake. My hair glistens in the hot bright lights. Johnny Carson has much to do to keep up with my quick and witty tongue.

But that is a mistake. I know even before I wake up. Who ever knew a Johnson with a quick tongue? Who can even imagine me looking a strange white man in the eye? It seems to me I have talked to them always with one foot raised in flight, with my head turned in whichever way is farthest from them. Dee, though. She would always look anyone in the eye. Hesitation was no part of her nature.

"How do I look, Mama?" Maggie says, showing just enough of her thin body enveloped in pink skirt and red blouse for me to know she's there, almost hidden by the door.

"Come out into the yard," I say.

Have you ever seen a lame animal, perhaps a dog run over by some careless person rich enough to own a car, sidle up to someone who is ignorant enough to be kind to him? That is the way my Maggie walks. She has been like this, chin on chest, eyes on ground, feet in shuffle, ever since the fire that burned the other house to the ground.

Dee is lighter than Maggie, with nicer hair and a fuller figure. She's a woman now, though sometimes I forget. How long ago was it that the other house burned? Ten, twelve years? Sometimes I can still hear the flames and feel Maggie's arms sticking to me, her hair smoking and her dress falling off her in little black papery flakes. Her eyes seemed stretched open, blazed open by the flames reflected in them.

And Dee. I see her standing off under the sweet gum tree she used to dig gum out of; a look of concentration on her face as she watched the last dingy gray board of the house fall in toward the red-hot brick chimney. Why don't you do a dance around the ashes? I'd wanted to ask her. She had hated the house that much.

I used to think she hated Maggie, too. But that was before we raised the money, the church and me, to send her to Augusta to school. She used to read to us without pity; forcing words, lies, other folks' habits, whole lives upon us two, sitting trapped and ignorant underneath her voice. She washed us in a river of make-believe, burned us with a lot of knowledge we didn't necessarily need to know. Pressed us to her with the serious way she read, to shove us away at just the moment, like dimwits, we seemed about to understand.

Dee wanted nice things. A yellow organdy dress to wear to her graduation from high school; black pumps to match a green suit she'd made from an old suit somebody gave me. She was determined to stare down any disaster in her efforts. Her eyelids would not flicker for minutes at a time. Often I fought off the temptation to shake her. At sixteen she had a style of her own: and knew what style was.

I never had an education myself. After second grade the school was closed down. Don't ask me why: in 1927 colored asked fewer questions than they do now. Sometimes Maggie reads to me. She stumbles along good-naturedly but can't see well. She knows she is not bright. Like good looks and money, quickness passed her by. She will marry John Thomas (who has mossy teeth in an earnest face) and then I'll be free to sit here and I guess just sing church songs to myself. Although I never was a good singer. Never could carry a tune. I was always better at a man's job. I used to love to milk till I was hooked in the side in '49. Cows are soothing and slow and don't bother you, unless you try to milk them the wrong way.

I have deliberately turned my back on the house. It is three rooms, just like the one that burned, except the roof is tin; they don't make shingle roofs any more. There are no real windows, just some holes cut in the sides, like the portholes in a ship, but not round and not square, with rawhide holding the shutters up on the outside. This house is in a pasture, too, like the other one. No doubt when Dee sees it she will want to tear it down. She wrote me once that no matter where we "choose" to live, she will manage to come see us. But she will never bring her friends. Maggie and I thought about this and Maggie asked me, "Mama, when did Dee ever *have* any friends?"

She had a few. Furtive boys in pink shirts hanging about on wash-day after school. Nervous girls who never laughed. Impressed with her they worshiped the well-turned phrase, the cute shape, the scalding humor that erupted like bubbles in lye. She read to them.

When she was courting Jimmy T she didn't have much time to pay to us, but turned all her faultfinding power on him. He *flew* to marry a cheap city girl from a family of ignorant flashy people. She hardly had time to recompose herself.

When she comes I will meet — but there they are!

Maggie attempts to make a dash for the house, in her shuffling way, but I stay her with my hand. "Come back here," I say. And she stops and tries to dig a well in the sand with her toe.

It is hard to see them clearly through the strong sun. But even the first glimpse of leg out of the car tells me it is Dee. Her feet were always neat-looking, as if God himself had shaped them with a certain style. From the other side of the car comes a short, stocky man. Hair is all over his head a foot long and hanging from his chin like a kinky mule tail. I hear Maggie suck in her breath. "Uhnnnh," is what it sounds like. Like when you see the wriggling end of a snake just in front of your foot on the road. "Uhnnnh."

Dee next. A dress down to the ground, in this hot weather. A dress so loud it hurts my eyes. There are yellows and oranges enough to throw back the light of the sun. I feel my whole face warming from the heat waves it throws out. Earrings gold, too, and hanging down to her shoulders. Bracelets dangling and making noises when she moves her arm up to shake the folds of the dress out of her armpits. The dress is loose and flows, and as she walks closer, I like it. I hear Maggie go "Uhnnnh" again. It is her sister's hair. It stands straight up like the wool on a sheep. It is black as night and around the edges are two long pigtails that rope about like small lizards disappearing behind her ears.

"Wa-su-zo-Tean-o!" she says, coming on in that gliding way the dress makes her move. The short stocky fellow with the hair to his navel is all grinning and he follows up with "Asalamalakim, my mother and sister!" He moves to hug Maggie but she falls back, right up against the back of my chair. I feel her trembling there and when I look up I see the perspiration falling off her chin.

"Don't get up," says Dee. Since I am stout it takes something of a push. You can see me trying to move a second or two before I make it. She turns, showing white heels through her sandals, and goes back to the car. Out she peeks next with a Polaroid. She stoops down quickly and lines up picture after picture of me sitting there in front of the house with Maggie cowering behind me. She never takes a shot without making sure the house is included. When a cow comes nibbling around the edge of the yard she snaps it and me and Maggie *and* the house. Then she puts the Polaroid in the back seat of the car, and comes up and kisses me on the forehead.

Meanwhile Asalamalakim is going through motions with Maggie's hand. Maggie's hand is as limp as a fish, and probably as cold, despite the sweat, and she keeps trying to pull it back. It looks like Asalamalakim wants to shake hands but wants to do it fancy. Or maybe he don't know how people shake hands. Anyhow, he soon gives up on Maggie.

"Well," I say. "Dee."

"No, Mama," she says. "Not 'Dee,' Wangero Leewanika Kemanjo!"

"What happened to 'Dee'?" I wanted to know.

"She's dead," Wangero said. "I couldn't bear it any longer, being named after the people who oppress me."

"You know as well as me you was named after your aunt Dicie," I said. Dicie is my sister. She named Dee. We called her "Big Dee" after Dee was born.

"But who was *she* named after?" asked Wangero.

"I guess after Grandma Dee," I said.

"And who was she named after?" asked Wangero.

"Her mother," I said, and saw Wangero was getting tired. "That's about as far back as I can trace it," I said. Though, in fact, I probably could have carried it back beyond the Civil War through the branches.

"Well," said Asalamalakim, "there you are."

"Uhnnnh," I heard Maggie say.

"There I was not," I said, "before 'Dicie' cropped up in our family, so why should I try to trace it that far back?"

He just stood there grinning, looking down on me like somebody

ALICE WALKER

inspecting a Model A car. Every once in a while he and Wangero sent eye signals over my head.

"How do you pronounce this name?" I asked.

"You don't have to call me by it if you don't want to," said Wangero.

"Why shouldn't I?" I asked. "If that's what you want us to call you, we'll call you."

"I know it might sound awkward at first," said Wangero.

"I'll get used to it," I said. "Ream it out again."

Well, soon we got the name out of the way. Asalamalakim had a name twice as long and three times as hard. After I tripped over it two or three times he told me to just call him Hakim-a-barber. I wanted to ask him was he a barber, but I didn't really think he was, so I didn't ask.

"You must belong to those beef-cattle peoples down the road," I said. They said "Asalamalakim" when they met you, too, but they didn't shake hands. Always too busy: feeding the cattle, fixing the fences, putting up salt-lick shelters, throwing down hay. When the white folks poisoned some of the herd the men stayed up all night with rifles in their hands. I walked a mile and a half just to see the sight.

Hakim-a-barber said, "I accept some of their doctrines, but farming and raising cattle is not my style." (They didn't tell me, and I didn't ask, whether Wangero (Dee) had really gone and married him.)

We sat down to eat and right away he said he didn't eat collards and pork was unclean. Wangero, though, went on through the chitlins and corn bread, the greens and everything else. She talked a blue streak over the sweet potatoes. Everything delighted her. Even the fact that we still used the benches her daddy made for the table when we couldn't afford to buy chairs.

"Oh, Mama!" she cried. Then turned to Hakim-a-barber. "I never knew how lovely these benches are. You can feel the rump prints," she said, running her hands underneath her and along the bench. Then she gave a sigh and her hand closed over Grandma Dee's butter dish. "That's it!" she said. "I knew there was something I wanted to ask you if I could have." She jumped up from the table and went over in the corner where the churn stood, the milk in it clabber by now. She looked at the churn and looked at it.

"This churn top is what I need," she said. "Didn't Uncle Buddy whittle it out of a tree you all used to have?"

"Yes," I said.

"Uh huh," she said happily. "And I want the dasher, too."

"Uncle Buddy whittle that, too?" asked the barber.

Dee (Wangero) looked up at me.

"Aunt Dee's first husband whittled the dash," said Maggie so low you almost couldn't hear her. "His name was Henry, but they called him Stash."

"Maggie's brain is like an elephant's," Wangero said laughing. "I can use the churn top as a centerpiece for the alcove table," she said sliding a plate over the churn, "and I'll think of something artistic to do with the dasher."

When she finished wrapping the dasher the handle stuck out. I took it for a moment in my hands. You didn't even have to look close to see where hands pushing the dasher up and down to make butter had left a kind of sink in the wood. In fact, there were a lot of small sinks; you could see where thumbs and fingers had sunk into the wood. It was beautiful light yellow wood, from a tree that grew in the yard where Big Dee and Stash had lived.

After dinner Dee (Wangero) went to the trunk at the foot of my bed and started rifling through it. Maggie hung back in the kitchen over the dishpan. Out came Wangero with two quilts. They had been pieced by Grandma Dee and then Big Dee and me had hung them on the quilt frames on the front porch and quilted them. One was in the Lone Star pattern. The other was Walk Around the Mountain. In both of them were scraps of dresses Grandma Dee had worn fifty and more years ago. Bits and pieces of Grandpa Jarrell's paisley shirts. And one teeny faded blue piece, about the size of a penny matchbox, that was from Great Grandpa Ezra's uniform that he wore in the Civil War.

"Mama," Wangero said sweet as a bird. "Can I have these old quilts?"

I heard something fall in the kitchen and a minute later the kitchen door slammed.

"Why don't you take one or two of the others?" I asked. "These old things was just done by me and Big Dee from some tops your grandma pieced before she died."

"No" said Wangero. "I don't want those. They are stitched around the borders by machine."

"That'll make them last better," I said.

"That's not the point," said Wangero. "These are all pieces of dresses Grandma used to wear. She did all this stitching by hand. Imagine!" She held the quilts securely in her arms, stroking them.

"Some of the pieces, like those lavender ones, come from old clothes her mother handed down to her," I said moving up to touch the quilts. Dee (Wangero) moved back just enough so that I couldn't reach the quilts. They already belonged to her.

"Imagine!" she breathed again, clutching them closely to her bosom.

"The truth is," I said, "I promised to give them quilts to Maggie for when she marries John Thomas."

She gasped like a bee had stung her.

"Maggie can't appreciate these quilts!" she said. "She'll probably be backward enough to put them to everyday use."

"I reckon she would," I said. "God knows I been saving 'em for long enough with nobody using 'em. I hope she will!" I didn't want to bring up how I had offered Dee (Wangero) a quilt when she went away to college. Then she had told me they were old-fashioned, out of style.

"But they're *priceless*!" she was saying now furiously; for she has a temper. "Maggie would put them on the bed and in five years they'd be in rags. Less than that!"

"She can always make some more," I said. "Maggie knows how to quilt."

Dee (Wangero) looked at me with hatred. "You just will not understand. The point is these quilts, *these* quilts!"

"Well," I said, stumped. "What would *you* do with them ?"

"Hang them," she said. As if that was the only thing you *could* do with quilts.

Maggie by now was standing in the door. I could almost hear the sound her feet made as they scraped over each other.

"She can have them, Mama," she said, like somebody used to never winning anything, or having anything reserved for her. "I can 'member Grandma Dee without the quilts."

I looked at her hard. She had filled her bottom lip with checkerberry snuff and it gave her face a kind of dopey, hangdog look. It was Grandma Dee and Big Dee who taught her how to quilt herself. She stood there with her scarred hands hidden in the folds of her skirt. She looked at her sister with something like fear but she wasn't mad at her. This was Maggie's portion. This was the way she knew God to work.

When I looked at her like that something hit me in the top of my head and ran down to the soles of my feet. Just like when I'm in church and the spirit of God touches me and I get happy and shout. I did something I never had done before: hugged Maggie to me, then dragged her on into the room, snatched the quilts out of Miss Wangero's hands and dumped them into Maggie's lap. Maggie just sat there on my bed with her mouth open.

"Take one or two of the others," I said to Dee.

But she turned without a word and went out to Hakim-a-barber.

"You just don't understand," she said, as Maggie and I came out to the car.

"What don't I understand?" I wanted to know.

"Your heritage," she said. And then she turned to Maggie, kissed her, and said, "You ought to try to make something of yourself, too, Maggie. Its really a new day for us. But from the way you and Mama still live you'd never know it."

She put on some sunglasses that hid everything above the tip of her nose and her chin.

Maggie smiled; maybe at the sunglasses. But a real smile, not scared. After we watched the car dust settle I asked Maggie to bring me a dip of snuff. And then the two of us sat there just enjoying, until it was time to go in the house and go to bed.

🌿 Death Mother

JOYCE CAROL OATES

*Driving the car fast, then faster. Then braking. Then releasing the
brake. And again her foot hard on the gas pedal and the car leapt forward and I wasn't crying, the side of my head striking the door handle but I wasn't crying.* It's right for you to die with your mother *she
was saying.* I'm your mother, I'm your mother, I'm your mother.
*Drinking from the thermos clasped tight between her knees. Radio
turned up high. So she'd sing. Talk to herself, and to me, break off
singing and begin to laugh, and to sob.* You love me, too, don't you,
you're my baby girl, they can't take you from me. I'm your mother
*and the car began to shudder, the gas pedal pressed to the floor and
my head struck the window and everything went flamey bright and
went out. I was nine years old, it was November 1949.*

She saw, on the opposite bank, across the gorge, perhaps fifty feet
away, an absolutely still, unmoving figure — a woman? in white? —
and came to a halt, staring. Her mind was struck blank. She had no
thoughts at all. Someone brushed past her pushing a bicycle, a young
man who seemed to know her name, addressed her familiarly, but she
didn't hear him, didn't reply. It was all happening swiftly yet with
dreamlike slowness yet still she couldn't quite comprehend except to
think *But I would sense it: I would know. If she comes back. If that's
possible.*

It was 6:50 A.M. The thermometer on the front porch of Jeannette's
residence had read −5° F. but here on the open pedestrian bridge, in
knifelike gusts of wind, it was even colder. Vapor rose in patches out of
the gorge where thirty feet below water spilled noisily from conduits,
flowing and steaming in a saw-toothed passage through ice. So Jeannette's view of the figure on the other side of the gorge was obscured.

She was in motion again, crossing the bridge, at about the halfway point now, *no turning back*. It was a familiar route, she took it every day, twice a day, over the deep gorge that wound through the wooded campus, the trick she'd learned at the very start was not to look down, still less to stare down, to slow to a dreamy halt and lean against the railing, stare down at rocks, trickling water. It was hypnotic but not if you didn't look. The footbridge sometimes swayed in the wind, and sometimes it swayed in no discernible wind at all. There were tales of student suicides from this bridge, rumors of other, not quite successful attempts, before Jeannette's time she believed, the tragedies of strangers. She was not thinking of that now, nor of the eerie-humming vibration of the bridge. She was all right. And not alone, she was just one of a number of students on the footbridge, not likely to be singled out. Others passed her with quick fearless strides, making the bridge sway even harder. The delicious manic-energy of dawn: you woke abruptly from sleep already excited, breath shortened, eager — for what? *Not possible. Don't be ridiculous. You know better.* Yet there the woman stood, unmistakably.

In one stiffening arm Jeannette carried her canvas satchel crammed with books and purse, with her free hand she groped for the railing, to steady herself. Below, where she dared not look, were jagged hunks of ice, icicles six feet long, gigantic glittering teeth, thin rapid hissing trickle of water, stunted shrubs growing weirdly sideways, even downward out of rock. Winter had been long, the gorge was filled with snow, unevenly, a look of caprice, the consequence of sudden small avalanches. Above, a gunmetal sky, lightening by slow degrees without warming. *You know better.*

She knew. She'd left home, she'd come to Nautauga College, she was a striking and lively and much admired young woman here, she was not a person readily identified by those she'd left behind. If the woman on the opposite bank was in fact watching Jeannette she'd be confused, thrown off the scent, seeing how in a clumsy down khaki parka with a hood, in dark wool slacks tucked neatly into boots to conserve body warmth, hauling her satchel, she resembled any student at the college, or nearly.

Somehow, how? — this person I've become.

It was March 1959. She was on her way to Reed Hall, where she worked in the cafeteria. It was an ordinary morning. It would be an ordinary day. If she could force herself to cross the footbridge: to ignore the woman waiting for her. *Not for me. Impossible.*

Yet now — now she'd lost her nerve, that happened sometimes. It was something physical, you felt it in the pit of the belly. Anxiously recalling she'd left her desk lamp on, had she? — in her room. Had she left it on? Getting up so early, before dawn, winter mornings pitch-black as night, yet her pulse already racing, all sleep banished with icy water splashed on her face, in her eyes. Though she'd be late at the cafeteria she couldn't bear the possibility of her lamp burning for hours in the empty room. And maybe she hadn't made up her bed, she couldn't remember. It tore at her nerves like ripped silk to think of such small imperfections. So there was no choice but for her to head back. Already turning, hurrying. Against the flow of others, thickly bundled in winter clothes, breaths steaming, all of them known to Jeannette as she was known to them, their eyes caught curiously at her, they were mildly surprised at the look on her face, but she had no time for them, scarcely heard them, desperate to get off the foot-bridge, her head lowered, tears on her cheeks like flame swiftly turn-ing to rivulets of frost she brushed at irritably, blindly with her mittened hand.

The last time, seven years ago? — when I was twelve. In the locked ward of the State Psychiatric Hospital at Port Oriskany. A three-year sentence to the women's prison at Red Bank ran concurrently with psychiatric treatment, so-called. Mother? — it's Jeannette. Don't you know me? Mother? *She'd been so drugged, her eyes so puffy, the pupils retracted to pinpricks, I couldn't tell whether she recognized me, or even saw me.*

But then it hadn't ever been clear — whether she'd known me, or my sister Mary. Loving, hugging, kissing us. Pummeling, punching, kicking, yanking at our hair that was wheat-colored, fine, a wan curl in it like hers. Trying to set me afire — an "accident" with a space heater. Trying to kill us all in the car. And Mary, what she'd done to Mary. Never clear whether she saw us, recognized us, at all: her daughters. Not herself.

The second time, no mistaking her.

Late morning, descending the steep granite steps of the Hall of Lan-guages, Jeannette was talking animatedly with friends, talking and laughing when suddenly she saw the figure, the woman: *her.* Not twenty feet away. So calmly, obviously waiting for Jeannette, her daughter. Fixed and unmoving as a stone figure amid a diverging stream of students who scarcely glanced at her, and of whom she was oblivious. An eccentrically dressed woman of no immediately evident age except not young.

One of Jeannette's friends was asking was something wrong, Jeannette who was Jeannie to them, pretty Jeannie Harth, so suddenly still, frightened, staring. But recovering enough to assure them no nothing, nothing wrong, please go on without her.

Moving quickly away before anyone could question her. And calmly too making her way to the woman, the woman who waited for her. Thinking, *She was never so tall before!*

"Mother? — is it you?"

Of course, Mrs. Harth — simply standing there, waiting. How like her if you knew her, or if you didn't. The pale pebble-colored lips drawn back from stained, uneven teeth, a sudden fierce smile — and her eyes deep-set and shadowed and the eyelids puffy, red-rimmed, faded brown eyes how like Jeannette's own, and Mary's. *We don't laugh, and we don't cry. Nobody knows our secrets.* Jeannette was clutching her mother's hand, Mrs. Harth was clutching Jeannette's, not taking her eyes from Jeannette's face.

For a long moment neither spoke. Then, awkwardly, both at once — "My God, Mother, it *is* you!" and "I — was afraid you wouldn't know me, Jeannette."

So strange, amid the boisterous commotion of young people, in the bright-dazzling sun of noon; on this ordinary weekday, with no warning. Always, Jeannette had thought she'd be notified beforehand, her father at least would have called her, some warning if only a dream, a nightmare of her own. She was saying, trying to speak evenly, "Where have you come from, Mother? Are you — ?"

Mrs. Harth continued to stare at her, hungrily. "Am I 'out'? Yes, Jeannette. I'm 'out.'"

She spoke with that air of almost girlish, flirtatious irony, an irony that invited you to laugh though of course you must not laugh, that Jeannette remembered with sudden, sick clarity.

Now we should hug one another, should kiss but Jeannette stood awkward and unmoving, still clutching her mother's hand; as her mother clutched hers, her fingers surprisingly strong. But then she'd always been a strong woman, don't be deceived.

How odd, how eccentric, Mrs. Harth's appearance: on this freezing winter day in upstate New York she wore a cream colored, somewhat soiled and wrinkled cloth coat in a bygone feminine style, a sash tied and drooping at her waist, like a negligee; her gloves were beige lace; about her head, only partly covering her thin, graying-yellow hair, was a gauzy pink-translucent scarf of the kind a romantic-minded woman might wear on a cool summer evening. An odor of dried leaves, like camphor, lifted from her. Mrs. Harth's eyes were slyly quick–darting and alert as if she was aware of others watching yet would not acknowledge these others. Her papery-pale, puckered skin was tightly creased across her forehead, a maze of wrinkles, though she was only — how old? — not old! — forty-two, forty-three? And that face once so beautiful, was it possible?

Jeannette said quickly, fighting the urge to cry, "Let's go somewhere warm, Mother — you must be freezing."

"Me? *I* don't mind the cold, I'm used to it."

A quick comeback reply, like TV. And the ironic smile, the anxious eyes.

And there suddenly Jeannette was leading her mother, arm linked firmly through her mother's arm, in the direction of Nautauga's Main Street, away from the college. She knew of a tea room patronized by local women shoppers, where students rarely went. Friends called out to her, *Hi Jeannie!* like chattering birds she did not hear. A young man, a tenor in the college choir, who'd taken Jeannette out several times, passed within inches speaking to her and Jeannette may have murmured a response but did not look up, staring in confusion at the trampled snow underfoot. Mrs. Harth said brightly, "There's a friend of yours," as if she expected to be introduced, or was teasing Jeannette with this possibility, and quickly Jeannette murmured, "I don't know him well, really," and Mrs. Harth said, "But you have many friends here, Jeannette? Don't you?" her voice low and even and not at all accusing, and Jeannette said, laughing nervously, "Not many! A few," and Mrs. Harth said, emphatically, "You were always selective about your friends. Like me."

They walked on. It could not be happening yet, how simply, it was. Mother and daughter, daughter and mother. Jeannette Harth's mother Mrs. Harth, come to visit. Why was it so unusual, why should it seem to upset Jeannette quite so much? Mrs. Harth was saying, giving Jeannette's arm a little tug, "No one can betray you like a friend — or a 'loved one.' You know the expression 'loved one'? Eh?"

"I ... don't know."

"It isn't strangers who break our hearts!"

This was uttered with such smiling vehemence, such a steaming breath and a coquettish toss of the pink-gauzy head, Jeannette stared at her mother, uncomprehending.

Why. Why here. Why now. What do you want of me.

Making their way across the icy quadrangle, through a gauntlet of sorts, Jeannette hearing, not hearing her name called out that pretty lyric melodic name that so suited her, in this place: *Jeannie! Jeannie Harth!* Girls from her cottage, girls from the dining hall, a young man from her philosophy class. Jeannette dared not look at them, with Mrs. Harth gripping her arm. Dared not reply beyond a vague mumble of recognition, acknowledgment. For of course Mrs. Harth was staring at them critically. For of course she would judge them, her daughter's friends, what few friends she had. *Eh! God! Is that the best you can do! I call that pitiful.*

Yet how fair-minded how pleasant saying, "It seems very nice here. 'Nautauga College.' Not like Port Oriskany, not like Erie Street, at all. Or your old school, eh? You fit right in here, Jeannette, I can see!" Clearing her throat, a gravely-grating sound, and Jeannette flinched thinking *she will spit, she will spit it out* but no she did not, must have swallowed it, all the while smiling and glancing about lurching a little, slipping on the sidewalk so that Jeannette had to steady her, practically support her. What ridiculous shoes Mrs. Harth was wearing, Jeannette stared in disbelief: cheaply shiny black patent-leather pumps with painfully pinched toes and a thin, near-stiletto heel. A ladder-run in one of her beige nylon stockings.

They were standing on the curb waiting for the light to change. Flashing red, warning DON'T WALK DON'T WALK. Jeannette was saying what a surprise, how wonderful to see her mother, hesitantly asking how long would she be visiting, did she think? and Mrs. Harth said "That depends."

"Depends — ?"

The light changed to green WALK WALK WALK. Hand in hand, Jeannette and Mrs. Harth crossed Main Street. "Upon circumstances," Mrs. Harth said, clearing her throat. "Upon *you*."

Jeannette's breath was gone, she could not reply. Mrs. Harth squeezed her hand in girlish excitement, like one sharing a secret just a bit prematurely. She said, "I have all my earthly possessions with me in my car. Did you know I have a car? Did you know I have my license? I'm parked there." Pointing beyond Main Street, matter-of-factly. "There is nowhere else I have to be now that I'm here, Jeannette. With you."

She was driving the car fast, then faster. Then she braked. Then released the brake. And again her foot hard on the gas pedal and the car leapt forward and I wasn't crying, the side of my head hit against the door handle but I wasn't crying. I couldn't see where we were going only the tops of trees rushing past. It's right for you to die with your mother *she was saying.* I'm your mother, I'm your mother, I'm your mother. *That smell of her when she hadn't bathed, hadn't washed her hair. The animal-smell. Her hair snarled and matted. But she was pretty — Mother. Even with the smeared Noxema on her face, where she'd been picking at herself. Sometimes a trickle of bright blood through the greasy white face cream. From a scab on her face she'd picked. And her fingers, her nails, the nails bright red. The cuticles bloody.* Just you and me, nobody will know where we are, it's right for us to be together. I'm your mother forever and always. Forever and always! *Drinking from the thermos held tight between her knees. Drinking then wiping her mouth on the back of her hand. The radio turned up high. So she'd sing. She'd talk to herself, and to me, as she'd sing, and she'd break off singing and begin to laugh, and to sob. Speeding through a red light pressing the palm of her hand against the car horn. The sound of it filled the car, so loud. And her laughing, angry sobbing.* You love me don't you, you're my baby girl, they can't take you away from me. I'm your mother, I'm your mother *as she hit the brakes and the car jumped and skidded and swerved and there was the sound of another car's horn and Mother yelled out the window sobbing and jammed her foot on the gas pedal again and the car leapt forward throwing up gravel where we'd drifted onto the gravel shoulder of the highway. I wasn't crying, my face was wet and my breath coming choked but I wasn't crying, I knew there was no way out,* Mother was saying You love me, I'm your mother and I love you, you're my little girl, it's right for us to die together *and there was a siren coming up fast behind us and the car swerved and shuddered, the red speedometer needle at eighty-five miles an hour, the car wouldn't go any faster and Mother was sobbing and I was thrown against the door, my head hit the window and everything went flamey-bright and then out. I was nine years old. That was November 1949. I hadn't known about Mary. What had happened to Mary. Where Mother had taken her, and left her.*

"I don't know what your father has told you about me, Jeannette. Or any of them. It's in their interests to lie about me."

In the cozy interior of The Village Tea Room, amid a clatter of dishware, cutlery, women's raised voices, amid lavender-floral wallpaper and hanging pots of ivy, Mrs. Harth had reluctantly removed her gauzy scarf, her soiled cream-colored coat that was draped over the back of her chair. Yet she'd kept her beige lace gloves on. Her hands shook just slightly as she poured tea for Jeannette and for herself. Her eyes were sunken but bright, alert. Watchful. Her mouth twitched and smiled. *You love me, I'm your mother. I'm mother, mother.* As Mrs. Harth spoke in her low, intense, earnest voice she repeatedly touched Jeannette's arm; and Jeannette shivered at the strangeness of it, the wonder, not simply that after seven years her mother had returned to her, in fact it had been much longer, many times Mrs. Harth had disappeared from the house and returned and disappeared and returned again, the times confused, bleeding into one another like loose snapshots in an album, and the child Jeannette had once been was not a child she knew or could recall or wished to recall. Not simply that strangeness, but the strangeness too of touch: another living being touching you: flesh and bone, another's secret heartbeat, warm-coursing blood, another's vision of you, knowledge of you, desire. For there were men who had touched Jeannette too, or had wanted to touch her, in desire. And always that immediate response, that panicked shuddering sensation *Don't touch me! Don't hurt me!* yet again *Please touch me, please hold me, I'm so lonely, I love you.*

"Jeannette?" Mrs. Harth's lips pursed, hurt. Creases like bloodless knife cuts bracketed her mouth. "Aren't you listening?"

Jeannette said quickly, "Yes. But I don't remember."

"What don't you remember?"

Jeannette ducked her head, smiled. For the question was really a riddle, wasn't it. *What don't you remember?*

Jeannette said, childlike in earnest, staring at her mother's hand gripping a delicate china cup, the tattered fingertips of the beige lace gloves, " — I don't remember very much about what Dad told me, it was a long time ago and we never talk about it any longer." She paused, still smiling. *We never talk about you any longer. I would not ask, and he would not tell if I did ask.* "And I don't remember much about — what happened."

Mrs. Harth's lips twitched in a smile. Her eyes were steely, resolute. "What happened — when?"

When Mary died. When they took you away.

Carefully, Jeannette said, "When Mary died."

There was a silence. Mrs. Harth touched her hair with beige-lace fingers; her hair that was stiff-looking, thin, the hue of stained ivory. Groped for her tea cup. At the sound of Mary's name, so soft as to be almost inaudible, Mrs. Harth's subtly ravaged face became impassive, almost peaceful.

Her mother was wearing an oyster-white dress, or was it layers of filmy pale cloth like curtains? — there seemed to be no collar to the costume, no visible buttons. The gauzy material was draped loose across Mrs. Harth's bosom in rumpled layers. Since they'd been seated in the tea room a sharp, acrid smell as of something brackish wafted against Jeannette's nostrils amid the warm yeasty smell of baked goods. Her mother's body. Her mother's hair, clothes. Recalling the odor of her mother's body in the days of her mother's sickness which she had believed, as a young child, to be the odor of the very air, very life itself. The rank tallow-like smell of the hair that was so fascinating, the briny stench of the champagne-colored negligee Mrs. Harth wore inside the house, and wore, and wore as if it were a loose second skin. The soiled undergarments on the bathroom floor, kicked about, blood-stained panties, Jeannette and Mary crouched staring in fascinated horror, reaching out daringly to touch. *Dirty girls! Both of you! Aren't you ashamed!*

What is there to do with *shame*, where exactly do you hide *shame*, you pretty girl, and "popular," too!

Every morning no matter how freezing the fourth-floor bathroom of the residence, showering, shampooing her hair, vigorously, harshly. The body can't distinguish between *cleansing* and *punishing* for the body is ignorant, and mute besides.

In high school, back in Port Oriskany: she'd been a different girl, then. Where they know you, you're known. Where you're known, you're *you.* Shrinking in the restrooms dreading what she might overhear, you don't want to eavesdrop, not ever. And after gym class having to strip naked amid the squealing giggles of the other girls so easily naked, pale and slippery as fish, darting through the stinging needles of water, the hot shower first, then warm then cold then the foot rinse, in a paroxysm of shame so her body prickled and her eyes rolled in their sockets. *Don't look! don't look! I'm a freak, I'm not one of you!*

Mrs. Harth was watching her closely, it was possible that Mrs. Harth knew exactly what she was thinking. Saying, "So! You're happy here, Jeannette? So far from home?" Inside the woman's level, uninflected voice, doubt sounded sly as a hinge that needs oiling.

Jeannette said quickly, "I — love it here."

"Eh?"Mrs. Harth cupped a hand to her ear.

"I love it here."

There was a pause: a moment for contemplating such a claim.

Mrs. Harth sipped her tea in thin, savorless swallows, like a duty. She did not mean to sound suspicious of course, but — "How did you happen to come *here*, Jeannette? Of all places?"

"I have a scholarship. A work-scholarship. It pays my full tuition and — "

Mrs. Harth interrupted, "*Only* here? You didn't win any other scholarships, anywhere in the state?"

Jeannette's gaze plummeted to the table top. Lavender tablecloth, so attractive, feminine. Just-visible stains, rings from the teapot. Scattered crumbs from the cinnamon toast Mrs. Harth had broken into small pieces, most of which lay on her plate uneaten. *Don't you know I can read your mind. Don't you know I'm your mother, your mother, your mother.*

Jeannette said quietly, stubbornly, "I did. But I wanted to come here, to study music."

"Music! That's new."

"Music education. So that I can teach."

"Teach."

Mrs. Harth took a small sip of tea, swallowed with an expression of disdain. After a pause she said, as if they'd been speaking of this all along, "Your father is a bitter man — I don't wonder, Jeannette, you've come so far to escape him. And *her*."

Jeannette protested weakly, "But it wasn't for that reason at all, Mother. Really — "

"Yes," said Mrs. Harth, grimly, laying a beige–gloved hand on Jeannette's arm, both to comfort and to silence, " — I don't wonder."

※ ※ ※

It was past one o'clock when Jeannette and Mrs. Harth emerged from The Village Tea Room into the bright, cold, gusty March air, Jeannette had missed her one o'clock lecture not having wanted to hurry her mother, not wanting to be rude. The question in her mind was where would her mother spend the night.

Mr. Harth had remarried, soon after the divorce. The end of that, the beginning of something new. There was a second *Mrs. Harth* in Port Oriskany but the woman was not quite real to Jeannette, a nice woman, a kindly woman, generous and, yes, motherly. So many women of a certain age were motherly.

Never had Jeannette told her father's wife *Don't imagine that I need, or want, another mother: I don't.* But the woman seemed to know, just the same.

Jeannette had a class, her three o'clock music lecture, and somehow it happened that Mrs. Harth was coming with her. "Where else would I go, dear?" she said, smiling, sliding an arm through Jeannette's. "I'm all alone here except for *you*."

"You might not like the class, Mother. It's — "

"Oh, I'm sure I will! You know I like music."

"But this is — "

" — *love* music. You know I used to sing in the church choir when I was a girl."

No choice, then. Jeannette led the way.

"Introduction to Twentieth Century Music" was held in the amphitheater of the Music School, on the far edge of the quad. The lecturer was Professor Hans Reiter, a popular campus figure, burly and good-natured and explosive in his enthusiasms, a bearish darkbearded man with a boiled-looking skin, thick glinting glasses. He played records and tapes for the class at a deafening volume sometimes, and lectured over the music. Often, in the right mood, he played piano from a standing position as he spoke — rough, impassioned playing, the inner soul of music Jeannette supposed. She loved Professor Reiter and was shy of him. Usually she sat with her friends near the front of the room but this afternoon, Mrs. Harth's arm tight through hers, she avoided even glancing in that direction (were her friends looking for her? looking at her? at her and this woman so obviously her mother?) but sat with her mother at the very rear. The subject of today's lecture was Stravinsky and *The Rite of Spring*. Incantatory chords, breathless leaps of sound, that strident-erotic *beat beat beat* Jeannette tried to hear purely as music, not as pulsations in the blood. She hunched over her notebook taking notes rapidly, eyes downcast. Beside her Mrs. Harth sat stiff, arms folded across her chest. Now, in the amphitheater, she was cold. Would not remove her coat. Not at all charmed by the professor's lecture style, his bouncing-about at the front of the room, witty exegesis of the composer's "revolutionary genius" amid the "dense philistine ignorance" of the era. How forced, self-dramatizing, braying Reiter sounded, to Jeannette's ear! She was deeply embarrassed, after the class murmuring an apology to Mrs. Harth as they left the building, quickly as Jeannette could manage; Mrs. Harth laughed a dry mirthless laugh, arm tight through Jeannette's, saying, "So that's what a 'college lecture' is. A fat, loudmouth fool like that — 'professor.' And that ugly beard. And such silly music, like you'd hear on the radio. Imagine, a man gets *paid* for such nonsense!"

It was the very voice of Jeannette's childhood, raw envious spiteful Port Oriskany, glowering with satisfaction. Jeannette cast her eyes down to the trampled snow, and said nothing.

But Mrs. Harth, stimulated, was speaking animatedly. She was incensed, outraged, yet amused — you just had to laugh, didn't you? What a fancy college education is worth. So much fuss, people putting on airs, and what is it? *She'd* had to quit high school at the age of sixteen to work, to help support her family; oh yes, *she'd* hoped to be a teacher, too. "But nobody ever handed me a 'scholarship' on a silver platter." This was the first Jeannette had ever heard of any of this, but she did not question it; only murmuring she was sorry, and Mrs. Harth added, with bitter satisfaction, "*I* had to drop out of school to work, then to marry. Too young for any of it — but it had to be. And babies, too — had to be."

Had to be. Had to be. The words hung in the air like steaming exhaled breaths.

Jeannette heard herself asking, "Where — would you like to go now, Mother? I'm afraid I have library assignments, and I have to work the dinner shift at the cafeteria, and tonight I have a choir rehearsal — " Her voice trailed off weakly. *All I wanted was a life, a new life for myself that has nothing to do with who I am, or was. All I wanted was to be free.* Her body was chill and clammy inside her clothes and her heart beat so quickly, Mrs. Harth must sense it.

Mrs. Harth was squinting at her. That dry ironic smile playing about her lips. With the air of speaking to a small or dull child she said, "Jeannette, I'm all alone here in — 'Nautauga.' And anywhere in the world. Except for *you*, dear. How long I visit, where I go depends on *you*."

Laughing, that delicious cascading sound. And her eyes bright, her long nails fluttering the air like shiny crimson butterflies. Get in! Hurry get in, girls! Before it's too late! *That humid-hot August day, early evening; Mother had left us to live somewhere else and Dad would never speak of her but suddenly there Mother was — come home to pick Mary and me up at Grandma's in this car that was silver on top and aqua on the bottom — so pretty! — so shiny! Grandma was inside so didn't see, we were playing in the front yard and Mother came laughing to pull us away, her finger to her lips meaning* Quiet! quiet! *laughing driving us all the way to the beach to Lake Oriskany and she wasn't the way we remembered her but so pretty now, so happy! a sharp lemony smell in her hair, her hair not greasy but shiny, whipping in the wind like laughing and her mouth bright red like Ava Gardner's on a movie poster.* Hey: you know I love you, your mother's crazy about you, you're my baby girls aren't you! — *at a stoplight hugging and kissing us till it hurt, and another time pulling over at the side of the road so cars honked passing us, then at the beach Mother ran up and down the boardwalk pulling us by the hands buying us fizzing Cokes and orangesicles which were her favorite too, sharp-tasting orange ice and vanilla ice cream at the center so delicious! — and Mother's legs were pale and covered in pale brown hairs in the sun where she drew her dress up, past her knees, she was barefoot her toenails bright crimson and there was a man up on the boardwalk leaning on the railing watching us, watching her and he came down to the beach and he and Mother began talking, laughing, Mother said,* These are my little girls Jeannette and Mary, *saying,* Aren't they beautiful! *and the man squatted in the sand beside Mary and me smiling at us, said,* They sure are, yeah — they're beautiful *smiling up at Mother,* — just like you.

Mother and the man went away only for a few minutes Mother said kissing us I'll be right back: don't go away! don't go away or the police will come and arrest you! *but they didn't come back and didn't come back and we were crying and a woman asked us who we were, were we alone, two little girls like us? — she took us to the ladies' restroom up on the boardwalk and bought us Cokes and we took them back to the beach because Mother would be so angry if we were gone and after a while a policeman did come by, asked us where we lived and we were crying hard by now, we were afraid to tell him because if he took us away when Mother came back she would be so surprised so hurt so angry she would never take us away in her car again, she would never love us again so it was a long time before we told him, I think it must have been me who told, I was the older of the sisters, I was always the older I was Jeannette.*

That was why, she never wanted to be alone with another girl. Especially a girl she liked, trusted. One of the girls in Briarly Cottage where she roomed. You had to be careful. Might start talking, telling too much. Might start crying. Lose control, say too much, once it's out it can never be retracted. *The worst thing: to give yourself away in exchange for not enough love.*

"Tell me which way to turn, Jeannette! — I've never driven in this city before."

Mrs. Harth spoke gaily and coquettishly yet at the same time in reproach. Jeannette gave directions: left onto Main Street, three blocks to the bridge, left again on Portsmouth to South Street... Strange how, through the filmy windows of Mrs. Harth's lead-colored Dodge, the familiar streets, the redbrick "historic" buildings of Nautauga College, even the long sloping campus lawn were altered; how childish, self-absorbed, unattractive Jeannette's fellow students appeared, on the sidewalks, crossing against traffic. The car's windshield was coated with a fine grit that reflected sunshine in a way that made everything bleakly, flatly sepia-stained, as in a fading photograph.

Mrs. Harth's car was one Jeannette had never seen before, of course. A 1954 model Dodge, lead-colored, with rust-stippled fenders and bumpers; riding oddly high off the ground, so you had to step up to climb inside. The smell was brackish-sour. In the back, what appeared at first glance to be random debris was in fact Mrs. Harth's personal possessions: untidy piles of clothes, shoes, a pillow with a stained embroidered pillowcase, cardboard boxes, grocery bags stuffed with items. A soiled gray blanket, taped to the left rear window, had slipped partway. The car windows were rolled up tight and Jeannette's nostrils pinched against the smell her mother seemed not to notice.

Jeannette didn't want to think what such evidence suggested.

Crossing a two-lane bridge over the Nautauga River, which was a narrow but swift-flowing river, now covered in ice, Mrs. Harth overreacted at the approach of a truck, pressed down hard on the gas pedal and swerved toward the railing; Jeannette felt a moment's sick panic — *She will drive us off the bridge, that's her plan!* But Mrs. Harth regained control of the car, driving on.

Jeannette remembered those wild, wild rides, her mother at the wheel. To Lake Oriskany. But the return — back to Erie Street — was vague, undefined; like a dream of profound intensity that nonetheless fades immediately upon waking.

And now they were at Jeannette's residence, the quaintly called "Briarly Cottage" which was an ordinary woodframe dwelling of four floors with a shingled dormer roof like a heavy brow, on a half block of similar drab houses, once private and now partitioned into rooms for students who couldn't afford better housing, nearer campus. Mrs. Harth stared with a look of personal hurt, incredulity. "This is it? — your 'residence'"?

Jeannette murmured it was fine, fine for her, she'd made good friends here. There were eighteen girls, scholarship students —

"And you so proud of that, your 'scholarship,' eh!" Mrs. Harth said, removing the key from the ignition and throwing it, with an emphatic gesture, into her bag. "I wouldn't wonder this fancy college put you here on purpose, to insult you."

"Insult me? — why?"

The question hung in the air, unanswered.

With mincing steps, for of course the sidewalk hadn't been shovelled, Jeannette helped her mother ascend the walk to the house. The older woman's arm was tight through hers; their breaths steamed faintly, as if in anticipation. Beneath the dry camphor smell of Mrs. Harth's hair and clothes was a sharper lemony smell, all but indistinguishable. Her skin, maybe. That heat that used to rise from her skin. As Jeannette was about to open the front door, a Negro girl came out, one of Jeannette's friends, big smile, big eyes, a friendly and popular girl named Kitty, and in an instant Kitty glanced from Jeannette to

Mrs. Harth to Jeannette again, seeing whatever it was in Mrs. Harth's face, maybe noting how, with an involuntary intake of breath, Mrs. Harth's arm tightened on Jeannette's, and her smile dimmed discreetly, and she only murmured, "H'lo, Jeannie," in that way that signals no reply of any animation is expected.

Inside, Mrs. Harth said in a lowered voice, with grim satisfaction "*What* did I tell you? — there it is! Putting you in a place with one of *them*, that's the insult."

Jeannette protested, "But, Mother — "

"They give you tuition money, oh yes but they make you beg — *crawl* — for it. *I* would never."

"Mother, that's ridiculous. Nautauga College is — "

"'Ridiculous,' am I? Oh? For speaking the truth, miss? Which your father would never, eh? Which you're ashamed to hear." Mrs. Harth sighed, drawing her filmy glamor-scarf off her head, as if reluctantly; glancing about, her forehead creasing, nostrils pinching, into the cramped parlor off the front hall. Fortunately, none of Jeannette's housemates was in there. "*I* call this pitiful," Mrs. Harth said. "A daughter of *mine*."

"I'm happy here," Jeannette said, with childlike stubbornness. "This is my second year and I'm *happy here*."

"Of course, you'd tell yourself that," Mrs. Harth said simply. "That's what people do."

And there were the steep stairs, three flights to Jeannette's fourth-floor room. And there was the antiquated bathroom with its ineradicable odors, door ajar. When Jeannette opened the door to her room she winced at the sight, seeing it through Mrs. Harth's eyes: the ceiling that slanted beneath the eaves, the narrow cotlike bed covered with a cheap chenille spread, a college-issue pinewood chest of drawers, aluminum desk, ugly crook-necked lamp and shabby swivel chair. On the bare floorboards, a thin machine-woven rug Jeannette had bought for $9.98 at a local discount store, liking its rust-orange gaiety; on the walls cheap glossy prints of nature photographs and works of art — Van Gogh's "Starry Night," for one. Jeannette's hope had been to make the small room seem spacious by suggesting, as of windows opening out, other dimensions, other worlds. Instead, the reproductions, all of them slightly curling from the radiator heat, gave the room a cluttered, tacky look.

The single window in the room looked out over an expanse of

weatherworn roof and snow-smutty yards; in the distance, across the gorge, drained oddly of color and flattened like paper cutouts, the handsome spires and towers of the college.

Mrs. Harth was breathless from the stairs. But entered the room tall, incensed. "So! — *this*."

Jeannette closed the door behind them, trembling with dread.

"These hundreds of miles you've come — such pride in your 'scholarship' — imagining yourself so superior to your mother, eh? For *this*."

Jeannette protested, "Mother, I've never imagined myself — "

"Oh no? Don't lie: not to Mother. *I* can see into your heart."

Mrs. Harth paced about, untying the sash of her flared coat, sniffing and squinting and peering into corners. Here was her old energy, liquid-bright eyes and sharp elbows, that girlish air of conspiracy, angry elation. "It's good I came here! I knew I was wanted! To rescue you! Take you away, eh? I *knew*."

"Take me away, Mother? Where?"

Mrs. Harth put a forefinger to her lips, slyly. Then placed that same forefinger to Jeannette's lips, to seal them.

Yes it was an accident. I always believed so. She loved us, she held us and kissed us and slept sometimes in our bed with us or she would take us into her bed, hers and Dad's, during the day, for a nap. And she would bathe us. There was no difference between her and us. I always believed so. The accident was with Drano. You know what Drano is — liquid Drano. The sharp terrible fumes stinging your eyes, burning your nostrils. Sit! Damn you, sit! *she was screaming. Because we didn't want to, we were trying to get away. Because the enema bag, the tube, was known to us, and we hated it.* Sit! In this tub! You bad girls, you dirty girls, obey your mother! *But I squirmed out of the tub, out of her hands, naked and slippery as a fish.*

"Christus, der ist mein Leben, Sterben ist mein. Gewinn ... dem tu ich mich ergeben..."

Jeannette was singing as she'd never sung before, an edge of anxiety to her voice, eyes fixed urgently on the young choir master's face. Her soprano voice rising, pleading as if it were an impersonal cry through her throat, "...mit Freud fahr ich dahin." Bach's exquisite cantata, the music that coursed through her blood, filling her with an almost unbearable yearning; the tension of the long day, dread rising to panic yet to a strange sort of elation, now her mother had returned to her, now the waiting was over. She hadn't realized how long she'd been waiting.

There was a stop, phrases repeated. The choirmaster's name was McBride and he was demanding, sometimes impatient. Short-tempered. Jeannette imagined himself in love with him, he was so distant from her. Yet he'd chosen her to sing one of the solos in the upcoming Easter concert. Again, now, to the top of the page, and again: Jeannette sang until her lungs ached, her eyes welled with tears. Even if Mrs. Harth would be taking her from Nautauga, even if there would be no Easter concert. Did it matter what the German words meant? *Since Christ is all my Being, Dying is all my gain. To Him my soul is fleeing, Nought can her joy regain.*

Jeannette had left her mother back in her room, in her bed, sleeping. Mrs. Harth had been too exhausted even to have dinner. In the morning, she said, they would decide what course of action to take. What was best for Jeannette. What must be done, where they would go. She'd spoken softly, framing Jeannette's face with her cool dry hands. Jeannette had cried a little but Mrs. Harth had not cried for there was no need.

We don't laugh, and we don't cry. Nobody knows our secrets.

Mrs. Harth was not in the amphitheater yet midway in an ascending phrase *Mit Fried und Freud ich fahr dahin* Jeannette saw her figure there at the very rear, stiff with disapproval, arms folded across her chest, as she'd sat in that identical seat for Professor Reiter's lecture. Seeing, Jeannette lost the words of the cantata, faltered and broke. The other singers continued. Sopranos, altos, tenors, basses. It was as if a deer had fallen dead, shot by a hunter, as the herd ran on, oblivious. Jeannette hid her eyes and when she lowered her hands she saw at the shadowy rear of the banked rows of seats nothing more than carelessly slung-down coats, parkas.

Of course, Mrs. Harth wasn't there. What need, to follow Jeannette to choir rehearsal?

At this moment she was sleeping in Jeannette's bed in one of Jeannette's flannel nightgowns.

Later, McBride led Jeannette exactingly through her first recitativ which at the start of rehearsals she'd delivered self-consciously, as if distrusting her merely spoken, voice; tonight, the words seemed to burst from her throat. "Nun, falsche Welt! Nun hab ich weiter nichts mit dir zu tun. . ." McBride nodded: O.K. Then to Jeannette's chorale part, the rapturous evocation of a savior raised miraculously from the dead: "Valet will ich dir geben, du arge falsche Welt . . . Da wird Gott ewig lohnen dem, der ihm dient allhier." It was a spirited, demanding passage, and Jeannette was equal to it. Though her throat was beginning to ache and her eyes felt seared, burnt in their sockets from exhaustion.

McBride was smiling, he *was* impressed.

Rehearsal ended at 10:30 P.M. Jeannette edged away, grabbed her parka, hurried up the aisle to leave before anyone could speak to her; her problem was, at Nautauga, she had too many friends. Too many people who were attracted to her, or believed they were. *They don't know me but what they know, they like.* She was hurrying out of the semi-darkened building except at one of the front doors she paused leaning her forehead against the door, she felt her heart beating quickly yet calmly, what premeditation! what cunning! *It's a fantasy, you're being ridiculous. You know better.*

Still, she'd seen him looking at her, she'd been seeing, and not-seeing, for weeks. Since the start of rehearsals, though he'd never seemed explicitly to be favoring her.

Waiting for McBride, who, a few minutes later, as she'd known he would, came whistling by; McBride in his sheepskin jacket and fur hat, a swagger to him, the kind of man who controls by withholding praise until you're weak and ravenous with hunger. Others were with him but he waved them on, he was looking at Jeannette who'd turned her face toward him, baring it like a flame, mute and exposed.

McBride politely asked would Jeannette like a ride home and Jeannette said yes thank you, calling him, as all the undergraduates did, *Dr. McBride.*

They walked to McBride's Volkswagen parked in a nearby lot, their booted feet breaking icy crusts of snow. It was very cold now — $-10°$ F. But no wind, only a dry crackling air that burnt the nostrils and made the eyes well with tears of hurt and protest. Their breaths steamed like little private pockets of thought, or desire. When Jeannette slipped on a patch of ice, McBride murmured, "Hey!" and deftly caught her elbow, just enough to reposition her; his touch, his gloved fingers against the bulky fabric of the parka, made her feel giddy, faint. He was talking in his brisk animated way about the evening's rehearsal that had gone fairly well, considering the enormous difficulty of Bach's music and the choir's relatively untrained voices. There was a phrase of his he used often, wryly, yet with a kind of brotherly affection for his singers: "We're getting there, eh?"

A windless still night, palely illuminated by a three quarter's moon, a mad-eye moon, high overhead. Jeannette's eyes ached from just this moonlight as if she'd been crying, for hours, without knowing it.

Wait for you. Don't stay away long. Jeannette?

No, Mother. Where would I go?

This, then: they climbed into McBride's car laughing at their mutual awkwardness, their long legs, and McBride asked Jeannette where she lived for of course he had no idea and Jeannette told him and he asked was that the far side of the gorge and she said yes. He said she would have to direct him, then — he wasn't familiar with that side of campus. He lived on the east side, himself.

Driving then out of the lot and onto a side street and a few blocks to the very bridge, nearly deserted now, which eight hours before Mrs. Harth had driven them across in the lead-colored Dodge. Where they might have had an accident, swerving into the railing and through into the frozen river, but by chance had not. Jeannette's pulse raced now as then and she knew McBride sensed it.

Here too, as out of the gorge, thin drifting columns of mist rose dreamlike from the river; the effect was of something delicate as lace, or very breath itself, fading as you stared. McBride said casually, driving the Volkswagen as if it were a clever toy, "Jesus, it's beautiful here, isn't it? Upstate New York. It feels like the Arctic to me. I'm from Brooklyn, you know — this is all new to me."

It was the most Jeannette had ever heard the man utter, and the only personal revelation.

McBride followed Jeannette's soft-murmured directions, turning left, and again left, approaching hilly rutted South Street. At first he wasn't going to take note of Jeannette crying. For she cried that softly, unobtrusively; you could ignore it if you wished. For she was a well-mannered girl, discreet. She'd had no lovers, nor had ever been close to loving. This, McBride seemed to know, or to sense; he was eleven years her senior, a lifetime.

Finally he said, "Look, Jeannette, what's wrong? — has something happened to you?" and it was that plunge, a blind plunge like stepping through cracking ice, the irremediable shattering. It may happen but once in a lifetime, and that once will be enough. For Jeannette

heard herself cry, "I can't go back there! My room! Not yet! I can't
— " Already McBride had braked the car, jammed the brake down
with the heel of his boot; the car spun on the salt-strewn ice, but held.
They sat, side by side, at first motionless and not looking at each
other as Jeannette wept now freely, helplessly. "All right," McBride
said. "You don't have to. You can do something else."

McBride brought Jeannette Harth back to his apartment, where they
would spend the night.

And all this unpremeditated, the sheerest chance.

McBride who'd been married unwisely young, and divorced; who
knew better than to involve himself, or even to appear to involve
himself, with undergraduate women, many of whom openly adored
him — there he was, leading a terrified trembling girl into his darkened apartment, quiet as stealth; himself terrified as if he'd been
handed a musical composition he'd never before seen nor even heard
played and shoved out on stage before a vast audience and made to
perform, playing a musical instrument clumsy in his hands, exposed
to public ridicule. Yet: how excited, how happy he was, and how
Jeannette laughed, breathless, giddy, as he poured them each a glass
of red wine and his hand was perceived as shaking as much as hers,
or nearly. Jeannette meant to say, "I've never drunk this before!" but
the words came out, "I've never done this before!" Swallowing, she
tasted tartness as of overripe fruit; an inky pool spread immediately
in her panicked parched mouth, warming her throat, her chest, even,
uncomfortably, her belly. She could not have said if it was delicious,
or bitter, or both.

Bravely then Jeannette began to speak, as in a recitativ. She was in
love with him — Dr. McBride. She'd been in love with him for — a
long time. Her voice was so faint, McBride came to sit clumsily beside
her, stroking her hands which were chill and inert. "I know I should
be ashamed," Jeannette said miserably, "I know I shouldn't be telling
you this." McBride laughed, saying, "Who should you tell, then?"

Eventually they were in McBride's bedroom, and lying in an
anguished-delicious tangle on his bed. McBride may have sensed that
Jeannette was not telling him *why* exactly she was here, *why* tonight,
that there was something withheld; it was all happening too fast for
him. Though he was older, should have known better. But there was

Jeannette saying, "Please make love to me? You don't have to love me." So childlike in pleading, her voice slurred by wine. McBride kissed her eyelids and told her she was beautiful but did not make love to her precisely, nor would he. Jeannette said, "It's enough for me to love you, you don't have to love me, I promise!" McBride said, "Well, maybe." They were lying together perspiring and short of breath partly undressed on McBride's bed. How dizzy, and how happy! How strange to Jeannette that she should feel, in a stranger's arms, such extraordinary happiness, such buoyant happiness, she took to be love. And she might utter his full, remarkable name now: *Michael McBride.*

In this place unknown to her, a room darkened except where moonlight slyly entered an unshaded window.

When Jeannette awoke, wine-groggy, it was much later, yet still dark; by the faintly glimmering undersea-green numerals of a bedside clock she saw it was 6:15 A.M. Where was she, and what had she done! She eased herself from the part-undressed heavily sleeping man; crept silently into another room, where a single light still burned — there was her parka, there her mittens, her boots. On a coffee table cluttered with newspapers, magazines, books — two bottles of wine, one empty and one part-filled. *What have I done, what will happen now!*

In a bathroom mirror she examined her flushed, slightly swollen face, her vein-reddened eyes. She filled a basin and lowered her burning face to it, water cold as she could bear.

Leaving his apartment, by stealth leaving the red-brick apartment complex she'd known, in fact, was his, though had never before approached. How had she been so reckless! so shameless! *Weil du vom Tod erstanden bist, werd ich im Grab nicht bleiben* she was singing under her breath, there was McBride's habit of singing, whistling to himself, even if she never saw him again, never would she forget him, his kindness to her, and the intimacy between them — *Dein letztes Wort mein Auffahrt ist!*

And now she was approaching the gorge. Out of which vertical vapor-clouds were lifting, of the shape of icicles, dreamlike and silent. No one was in sight, it was just dawn. A somber dawn that more resembled dusk. Jeannette paused before stepping onto the foot-bridge — was there anyone on the other side, waiting? Through her life after this morning she would recall how, returning to the residence, to her mother, she had no idea of what she would say to the woman, nor even of how she would present herself: a daughter who had committed an unspeakable betrayal against her mother, a daughter who had simply done as she'd pleased, and not an ounce of guilt? She crossed the footbridge without daring to look down, and on the other side began to run, all the way up hill to South Street and to the gray-shingled woodframe house that was Briarly Cottage, where, with dream-logic, there stood Mrs. Harth in the street by the lead-colored Dodge, seemingly waiting for her. The car's motor was running, poisonous pale smoke billowed from the exhaust. And there, Mrs. Harth in her creamy flared cloth coat with the hastily tied sash, the gauzy scarf tied tight about her head. Waiting for Jeannette, for how long? She must have been sitting in the car, the motor running, and seeing Jeannette approach she'd climbed out, calling to her before she was well within earshot, "Get here! Get in this car! At once! We're leaving!"

Jeannette balked, stopping dead on the walk.

It was now dawn, faint bruised-red cloud strata in the eastern sky, by quick degrees lightening, though very cold. Jeannette saw her mother's mouth working angrily and her breath in steamy puffs that looked angry, too. "Jeannette, come here! Get in this car! How could you! Dirty, filthy girl! Get here, get *in*. I'm taking you *away*."

Jeannette shook her head. "Mother, no."

Mrs. Harth said contemptuously, "'No'? — how dare you! *I'm* your mother, I say get *in*."

Jeannette had approached, like a cautious child, or a dog, to about ten feet of the Dodge, whose chassis vibrated and shuddered as if in disbelief; she would come no closer, in terror that her mother might rush at her, grab her. How weakly she might yield, as she'd done long ago, if those talon-fingers seized her! Mrs. Harth's sunken eyes glared, her mouth worked. "Get *in*! I'm telling you — get *in*! I'm taking you away!"

Jeannette hid her eyes, banishing the sight. Yet: *I will see her, I will hear her, all my life.*

Had anyone heard her mother's cries, was anyone watching from the windows of the cottage, or from other houses on the block? would word of this, however *this* might be interpreted, be passed on, among Jeannette Harth's friends, and those who hardly knew her at all?

Would *he* hear, eventually? — or would she tell him herself, eventually? Jeannette stood mute and stubborn, shaking her head *no, no, no,* until finally, Mrs. Harth climbed into the car and slammed the door behind her and in a paroxysm of fury, tires spinning and sliding on the icy street, drove off: downhill on South Street, spewing exhaust, a right turn at the bottom of the hill, past a row of parked cars, within the space of twenty seconds, so quickly! — out of sight.

It was Friday morning she left. Sunday, my father called to tell me that Mother was dead. She'd driven her car off a bridge in the city of Derby, sixty miles east of Port Oriskany, into the Cassadaga River; the car had broken through ice, Mother had drowned. There were no witnesses to the "accident" and she'd left no message behind.

Everything Old Is New Again

JANET BERLINER

"THANK YOU for coming.

"Yes, brunch was a good idea, wasn't it? Thank you for coming.

"We'll get together soon."

"Thank you for — "

— Leaving. Thank you for leaving. Don't call me, I'll call you. Jenny shut the door, leaned against it, and stared at the label on the last of her birthday gifts, the one still wrapped, the one she'd steadfastly pushed to the end of the line, like the pumpkin people inevitably insisted upon piling onto her Thanksgiving dinner plate.

The parcel was from her mother. At eighty, her handwriting remained clean and firm. *Old Doll* it said next to Contents. Value: *Zero*.

Like me, Jenny thought. Value: Zero. Contents: Old.

"*Everything Old Is New Again,*" Peter Allen sang at her from her stereo set. She removed one fashionable black high-heeled shoe and hurled it at the CD player, uncaring of the damage she might do, though of course she'd care later. She always cared later.

"Everything old is *old* and getting older, you sonofabitch," she said. Old or dead. Like Peter Allen who was dead, who had written the song as a tribute to Judy Garland, who was dead, too. Her face lived on in reruns, her voice in recordings. But she was dead just the same.

"*Everything old is new again.*"

Jenny didn't sing along or think kindly of her friend Harlan whom she generally loved and who, seemingly a hundred years ago, had introduced her to the song. Instead, she drank the rest of her birthday champagne straight from the bottle, using it to swallow her last available dose of St. John's Wort, which was supposed to cure her depression but so far hadn't done a thing for her except make her itch. Then she curled up on the sofa with the leather bound special edition of *Anna Karenina* several of her friends had clubbed together to buy her because they knew it was her favorite book and because she was a writer. Or used to be.

One shoe off and one shoe on, she fell asleep. The phone woke her. She thought about letting it ring, but the residual hope that it might be her daughter changed her mind. It was the same hope that had sent her to the mailbox all week to retrieve cards from old friends with old lives, an ad for plastic surgery, a coupon for pizza, obligatory greetings from her doctor and her dentist.

Her hand hovered over the receiver. Maybe this year, this special year marked by her half century, her daughter would remember. Maybe, like a chrysalis, she had emerged from her Yuppie cocoon and become a caring, mature adult. Right. And maybe Jenny would fly to Vegas and win the Megabucks, or her publisher would offer her a million dollars to move to New York and become the darling of the Literati, scribbling away at the story of her miserable little life.

Which, she reminded herself, hadn't really been all that miserable. At least not all of the time.

She could probably even persuade herself that her present life was acceptable if they could only all forgive each other — her daughter for Jenny's treachery in insisting upon being a person, and she for her mother's — what? She'd hated her mother forever, and she couldn't remember why.

"Happy birthday, Mrs. Tobias. And how are you today?"

Disappointed, angered by a series of political calls, sales calls, "We're doing a quick survey" calls, Jenny Tobias felt less than generous toward this one. "If you're trying to sell me something, save your breath," she said.

"This is something you need, something everyone needs, but most especially you now that you've entered your golden years."

"My golden years? You must have the wrong Jennifer Tobias."

"You're fifty, Mrs. Tobias."

This was a new wrinkle, maybe not one that showed on her face, but a new wrinkle nonetheless.

"Here in California we care about our senior citizens. We can provide you with a plot..."

"There's something my editor would appreciate," Jenny said. She disconnected the voice and laughed at the state of her universe. She hadn't been able to write in a year and she'd finally been offered a plot. Only it was the wrong kind of plot. It was true what they said. Be careful about what you wish for and never fail to be specific.

On the other hand, maybe she had become a dinosaur. Maybe it was time to think about taking the big dirt nap?

She was a storyteller, born of the Diaspora into a long line of bards, but if she didn't find a plot soon — the writing kind — she might as well be dead.

She wasn't sure of much, but she did know that she did not love the new disposable society in which she lived; she did not love arthritis, or the fact that she was growing old. What she did love was Ibsen and Tolstoy, the look and feel of new yellow pads, the smell of newly sharpened pencils. Nor did she want much, just someone to give her back the wasted hours, for in regretting them, she had gained nothing and wasted more of the precious moments of her life.

She'd already lived for half a century and so what? She hadn't written the Great American Novel, she was neither rich nor famous. Jimmy Buffett had cashed in with *Pirate Looks At Fifty*; Jong had turned facing fifty into a raging success.

All she was doing was getting older. She needed rejuvenation, a young lover, adventure, perhaps a return trip to Jerusalem and another camel ride.

She'd pack a single suitcase and leave all material things behind. After a latté, a couple of cookies, and a quick trip to the drugstore for more Wort. After she'd called her daughter to say she'd forgiven her.

After she'd opened the parcel from her mother.

Which she might as well do now. Now was good. Now was fine. There'd never be another now, at least not exactly like this one.

She sat down and, balancing the gift on her lap, tore at the brown paper wrapping and lifted the lid of an old shoebox.

Happy birthday, Puppele, the note inside read.

Jenny flinched. She'd always hated being called Puppele, little doll, though why it distressed her so she had no idea.

I found this in an old suitcase and crocheted a new outfit for her, the note went on. *I would have sent it to a doll's hospital for repair, but there aren't any around anymore. Perhaps if I'd had it repaired for you years ago, right after I retrieved it, things might have been different between us. Truth is, I put it away and life intruded and I forgot that I had it. Now you are decades older than I was when it all happened. . . .*

The doll lay wrapped in a small, pink, satin-bound woolen blanket. Jenny removed it gently from its cardboard coffin. She opened the blanket and, operating through her fingertips like a blind person, caressed the porcelain. The doll's hands and feet were chipped. Cold. Frostbitten. A few tiny sprouts of hair grew around the fringes of a jagged hole which exposed an empty, hollow head.

The face was a Dorian Gray wreckage. Shattered. A baby's face, ravaged by layers of fine spider-web cracks

Crying, Jenny cradled the doll. Then she pillowed its head upon *Anna Karenina*. Seeing the juxtaposition, she picked up the brown paper wrapping and began to write. . .

Cape Town station. Winter cold and draughty on a June day in 1943. A child, her curly head lowered, her green eyes closed, sits on a bench marked "Whites Only." She is hugging a porcelain doll with short, curly brown hair. The doll is her best friend.

"Won't be long, *Puppele*," her mother calls out.

The child looks up. I am the child. "My name's Jenny," I whisper. I stare at the words on the bench, distracting myself by sounding them out. I'm a precocious child. At almost four, I can sound out the words, but I don't begin to comprehend their meaning any more than I understand what is happening on this strange day. My mother has abandoned the uniform of the South African reserves that she wears each day to her bookkeeping post at the Castle. She looks so pretty as she paces the platform, stopping every now and then to call me "Puppele" and hug me. Too hard. Too desperately. "He's been in North Africa fighting the Nazis," she says to me in German. "He's been up there making it with some *shiksa*," she will say later, when my eyes are closed and she thinks I'm asleep.

We are waiting for a stranger called Daddy. Waiting to take him home to a table laden with homemade *kuchen*. I am waiting to find out who he is. I've never seen him before but he must be important because Oma, Grandma, crocheted a new dress for me to wear, a pale blue dress with a string threaded through the waist. I roll the end of it around and around my finger until the tip is cold and white and has no feeling — like the rest of me.

I am supposed to be feeling something, aren't I?

Something.

"Can you hear it? It's coming. The train. Come over here. No, stay there."

Mutti is shouting, primping, crying, laughing.

The train pulls into the station. Leaning out of the window waving a doll as big as I — with long blonde hair and an organdy dress and bonnet — is a big man. Smiling, he climbs off the train.

I struggle to find the concrete that's there somewhere below my white button-down shoes. The man is with me before I reach the ground.

"You must be Jenny."

He crouches down, takes away my old doll, the one I love, and places the big new doll in my arms.

I start to cry. The new doll is a stranger, like he is. I want my old dolly back but I don't know how to tell him. The new doll is shiny and cold as my mother's face. The man speaks and she listens.

"How are you, Greta? Well, I hope."

He has not kissed me or my mother. He has not hugged us, touched us.

"No, I'm not coming home," he says. "Not now. Maybe not ever. I have an — arrangement. A nurse. We met in North Africa."

Jenny wanted to stop remembering. She got up, showered, made coffee to which she added a dash of brandy, but there was no escaping the story; it was like a physical presence, demanding her attention. Giving in to its urgency, she lit a candle against the waning day and sat down to watch the rest of it play out in her memory. United with the child she had long since buried, Jenny reexperienced her own pain. The pain that had caused her to hate her mother. The ache that had told her that her mother would have liked to throw *her* away so the stranger would stay and love her. . . .

"So it's out with the old and in with the new," her mother screamed. "You think you can do that? Abandon me? Or is it the responsibility of having a child. Do you want me to throw her away like an old doll? Like this?"

In a fury, she ripped Jenny's best friend from the man's arms and tossed it away. It flew through the air toward the train, which was slowly moving out of the station, smashed against it, disappeared.

If only she'd known that her mother had gone back to the station and retrieved the doll, Jenny thought. If only she'd been given the chance then to forgive her, to love her.

Crying softly over the lost years, Jenny picked up the doll. Cradling it in one arm, she picked up the phone and dialed her mother's number. "I love you, Mutti," she said.

"I love you, too, *Puppele*," her mother responded.

"I know you do," Jenny said. "I'll call you soon. I promise."

She replaced the receiver in its cradle and started to walk away. Darkness had settled on the world outside and the candle she'd lit was fluttering and almost burned out, but there was enough light to dial her daughter's phone number.

"Forgive me," she said, when her daughter picked up the phone.

"For what?" Her daughter's voice was tense with negative expectations.

"For whatever it is you think I've done," Jenny said lightly. "I do love you, you know."

"I love you, too." The voice was tentative, but it was a start. "Happy birthday, Mom. I have news for you. I'm going to have a baby. A boy."

"Congratulations," Jenny said. Ask his forgiveness early, she thought. But she didn't say a word except good-bye. Then she flooded the room with light, reset the CD player, and sang along with Peter Allen, because even if he was dead, she wasn't.

As a matter of fact, she was very much alive and everything old was new again. Maybe she wouldn't ride any more camels, but she wasn't ready for that big dirt nap yet, not while there was living and writing left undone.

Hell, if she played it right, she might even have time to inadvertently do more things for which she could ask forgiveness.

❧ Contributors' Notes

Chilean novelist and journalist ISABEL ALLENDE was one of the first female Latin American writers to win worldwide recognition and popularity. Her books include the novels *The House of the Spirits, Of Love and Shadows, Eva Luna, The Infinite Plan,* and *Paula* as well as the collections *Stories of Eva Luna* (short stories), and *Aphrodite* (recipes, stories, and other aphrodisiacs). Born in Peru where her ambassador father was stationed, Allende grew up a citizen of the world. In Chile, she was a journalist, a playwright, and also worked in television and films. She was exiled from Chile in 1972 after the military coup that unseated and killed her uncle, President Salvador Allende. Her exile was lifted in 1988 after democratic elections removed General Augusto Pinochet Ugarte who had led the coup against her uncle's government.

JULIA ALVAREZ spent her early childhood in the Dominican Republic, the homeland of both her parents. In 1960, when she was ten, her father's underground activities against the dictatorship were discovered, and her family fled to the United States.

Her first collection of poems, *Homecoming*, was published in 1984, and reissued with additional poems in 1996 as *Homecoming: New and Collected Poems.* Her second book of poems, *The Other Side/El Otro Lado*, was published in 1995. Her novels include *How The Garcia Girls Lost Their Accents, In the Time of the Butterflies,* and *Yo!* She has also published a book of essays, *Something to Declare,* and a children's story, *The Secret Footprints,* and has edited the anthologies *Yo Soy/I Am* and *Old Age Ain't for Sissies.* Since 1988, Alvarez has taught at Middlebury College where she is the writer-in-residence.

MARGARET ATWOOD is the author of nine novels, including the best-selling *The Handmaid's Tale*, fifteen collections of poetry, five collections of short fiction, four children's books, and four nonfiction works. She has also edited five anthologies, including *The Best American Short Stories 1989* (with Shannon Ravenel) and *The New Oxford Book of Canadian Short Fiction* (with Robert Weaver). *The Handmaid's Tale* was adapted for film by Harold Pinter and directed by Volker Schlorndorf.

Award-winning author JANET BERLINER was born in South Africa of parents who had escaped the Holocaust in Europe. Janet herself fled her homeland in 1961 under threat of imprisonment for her outspoken criticism of Apartheid. Her novel *Rite of the Dragon*, a political thriller set in South Africa, was banned there.

Her *Madagascar Manifesto* series, coauthored with George Guthridge, examined the premise of a Jewish homeland on Madagascar, created by Hitler to pen up its inmates' assets and abilities for his own ends. Combining rich history, Jewish mysticism, and African magic, the *Madagascar Manifesto* is a tour de force of magic realism. More recently, Janet and George Guthridge put together *Exotic Locals,* a collection of their coauthored short fiction released as a limited edition CD-ROM.

Janet has also edited the anthologies *Peter S. Beagle's Immortal Unicorn, David Copperfield's Tales of the Impossible, David Copperfield's Beyond Imagination,* and *Desire Burn: Women's Stories from the Dark Side of Passion.*

A member of the Council of the National Writers' Association, Janet also served as president of the Horror Writers Association in 1998. Her current projects include a stand-alone sequel to *Rite of the Dragon*, and a psychological thriller called *...And So Say All of Us.*

KATHERINE DUNN is the recipient of the Rockefeller Writing Fellowship, the Music Corporation of America Writing Grant, the Reed Summer Arts Fellowship, and multiple sportswriting and reporting awards. She has been active in radio and readings, nationally and internationally, since 1978. Her novels include *Attic, Truck,* and the highly acclaimed *Geek Love.* Her short story collections include *Why Do Men Have Nipples?* In 1990, she and sculptor Bill Will were commissioned by the city of Portland for a project called "Streetwise." Quotations, jokes, epigrams, and lone words were chosen by Katherine Dunn and carved into granite paving stones set into the sidewalk of Portland's Yamhill Street. She is at work on a new novel, *Cut-Man*.

MARY GORDON is the author of four best-selling novels: *Final Payments, The Company of Women, Men and Angels,* and *The Other Side*. She has also published a book of novellas, *The Rest of Life*; a collection of stories, *Temporary Shelter*; and a book of essays, *Good Boys and Dead Girls*. She is the recipient of a Lila Acheson Wallace Reader's Digest Writer's Award and a Guggenheim fellowship. Ms. Gordon lives in New York and is a professor of English at Barnard College.

In 1998, LOIS GOULD released *Mommy Dressing: A Love Story, After a Fashion*, a memoir of growing up as the child of her famous mother, the fashion designer Jo Copeland. Her novels include *No Brakes, Subject to Change, Final Analysis, La Presidenta, Medusa's Gift, Necessary Objects, Not Responsible for Personal Articles, A Sea Change, Such Good Friends,* and *X: A Fabulous Child's Story*.

BETTE GREENE'S autobiographical novel *Summer of My German Soldier* was a *New York Times* outstanding book of the year (1973) and was nominated for a National Book Award. The book, for which Greene also wrote a screenplay, won a Golden Kite Society children's book writer's award in 1974. *Philip Hall Likes Me, I Reckon Maybe* was a Newbery Honor Book in 1975 and also a *New York Times* outstanding book. She followed it with *Get on out Here, Philip Hall!* Greene also wrote *Morning Is a Long Time Coming, Them That Glitter and Them That Don't,* and *The Drowning of Stephan Jones*.

In her first three books — *At the Bottom of the River, Annie John,* and *A Small Place* — JAMAICA KINCAID focused on life in her birthplace, Antigua, West Indies, which she fled at the age of seventeen. She has also written the novels *Lucy* and *The Autobiography of My Mother* and the memoir *My Brother*. Kincaid was a regular contributor to *The New Yorker* from 1976 to 1995. Her work has been celebrated for its "highly poetic literary style" and its "rhythms, imagery, and characterization."

Ursula K. Le Guin, daughter of the anthropologist Alfred Kroeber and author Theodora (Ishi) Kroeber, has written poetry and fiction all her life. Her publications include more than one hundred short stories (collected in eight volumes), two collections of essays, ten books for children, four volumes of poetry, and sixteen novels. Among the honors she has received are a National Book Award, five Hugo and Five Nebula awards, the Kafka Award, a Pushcart Prize, and the Howard Vursell Award of the American Academy of Arts and Letters.

Her occupations, she says, are writing, reading, housework, and teaching. She is a feminist, a conservationist, and a Western American, passionately involved in West Coast literature, landscape, and life.

Lorrie Moore was the recipient of the National Endowment for the Arts award in 1989, the Rockefeller Foundation fellowship in 1989, and the Guggenheim fellowship in 1991. Her work frequently appears in *Fiction International, Ms., The New York Times Book Review, Paris Review, The New Yorker*, and others.

Her publications include *Self-Help, Anagrams, The Forgotten Helper, Like Life, Who Will Run the Frog Hospital?*, and *Birds of America*. She is also the editor of *I Know Some Things: Stories About Childhood by Contemporary Writers*.

Gloria Naylor won the National Book Award for first fiction in 1983 for *The Women of Brewster Place*. Her subsequent novels include *Linden Hills, Mama Day, Bailey's Café*, and *The Men of Brewster Place*. In addition to her novels, Naylor has written essays and screenplays as well as the stage adaptation of *Bailey's Café*. *The Women of Brewster Place* was made into a popular television miniseries starring and produced by Oprah Winfrey, who is an ardent fan of the novel and its writer.

A native New Yorker, Naylor is the recipient of Guggenheim and National Endowment for the Arts fellowships for her novels and the New York Foundation for the Arts Fellowship for screenwriting.

Twice nominated for the Nobel Prize in literature, Joyce Carol Oates is one of America's most versatile serious writers. She is the author of a number of distinguished books in several genres, all published within the last twenty-five years. In addition to numerous novels and short story collections, she has published several volumes of poetry, several books of plays, five books of literary criticism, and the book-length essay *On Boxing*.

Her writing has earned her much praise and many awards, including the PEN / Malamud Award for Excellence in short fiction, the Rosenthal Award from the American Academy-Institute of Arts and Letters, a Guggenheim fellowship, the O. Henry Prize for Continued Achievement in the Short Story. She was also nominated for the PEN / Faulkner Award, the National Book Circle Award, and the Pulitzer Prize.

Ms. Oates's latest novel, *Blonde* (about the life of Marilyn Monroe) was published earlier this year by HarperCollins. Her recent publications include the novel *Broke Heart Blues*, *My Heart Laid Bare* (a collection of short stories), and *Come Meet Muffin*, a children's book.

Born in upstate New York in 1938, Joyce Carol Oates received her B. A. from Syracuse University and her M. A. from the University of Wisconsin. She is the Roger S. Berlind Distinguished Professor of Humanities at Princeton University.

EDNA O'BRIEN was born in a rural Catholic village of about two hundred people in the west of Ireland and grew up on a farm. Her prolific output includes *Johnny I Hardly Knew You*, *The High Road*, *The Country Girls Trilogy* and *Epilogue*, *Time and Tide*, and most recently the novel *Down by the River*. Among her half-dozen collections of stories are *A Scandalous Woman*, *A Fanatic Heart*, and *Lantern Slides*.

She has also written stories for juveniles as well as stage, television and screen plays, and has been a contributor to magazines such as *The New Yorker*, *The Ladies' Home Journal*, and *Cosmopolitan*.

JANE SHAPIRO'S first novel, *After Moondog*, was a finalist for a *Los Angeles Times Book Prize*, a *New York Times* Notable Book, and among the *Village Voice's* Twenty-five Best Books of the Year. Her second novel is *The Dangerous Husband*. She has published short fiction and journalism in *The New Yorker*, *The New York Times*, *Harper's Bazaar*, *Mirabella*, and *Ms.*, among many other publications. She lives in Princeton, New Jersey.

MARTHA SOUKUP is a noted short story author whose works have been nominated for five Nebula awards, four Hugo awards, and one

World Fantasy award. She is the recipient of the Nebula award. Many of her stories have been collected in *The Stories So Far*, and she is working on a short series of fantasy books for middle-grade readers. Martha was born in suburban Chicago; played in the foresty back - yard of the imposing Baker house in which novelist Scott Baker was growing up; moved to Chicago for a decade and trod the boards in the semiprofessional comedy troupe, Moebius Theatre. She now lives in San Francisco and hosts the weekly Internet sf chat show Head Space.

ALICE WALKER is best known for her Pulitzer Prize-winning novel *The Color Purple*, which was made into a film produced by Quincy Jones and directed by Steven Spielberg. She is also the author of the novels *The Third Life of Grange Copeland, Meridian, Temple of My Familiar, Possessing the Secret of Joy*, and *By the Light of My Father's Smile*; the collections of poetry *Once, Revolutionary Petunias and Other Poems*, and *Her Blue Body Everything We Know* as well as books of short fiction (*In Love & Trouble: Stories of Black Women*, etc.) and essays (*In Search of Our Mother's Garden, Anything We Love Can Be Saved: A Writer's Activism*, etc.).

Ms. Walker has been an editor for *Ms.*, and continues to be a contributing editor. She is also active in many political causes, particularly the protection of indigenous peoples.

241